PRAISE FOR *THE*

The Beleaguered

Copyright 2019 by Lynne Golding

ISBN: 978-1-988279-83-1

All rights reserved

Editor: Allister Thompson

Published in Stratford, Canada, by Blue Moon Publishers.

The author greatly appreciates you taking the time to read this work. Please consider leaving a review wherever you bought the book, or telling your friends or blog readers about *The Beleaguered* to help spread the word. Thank you for your support.

Beneath the Alders

THE BELEAGUERED

LYNNE GOLDING

BlueMoon
PUBLISHERS

To Jessie Roberts Current,
a dear friend to so many

CONTENTS

Acknowledgements *7*

Prologue *11*

Chapter 1 – Declaration of Hostilities *16*

Chapter 2 – The First Contingent *34*

Chapter 3 – Snell's Lake *48*

Chapter 4 – The Knitting Club *63*

Chapter 5 – More Usual Than Usual *80*

Chapter 6 – The Hockey Game *98*

Chapter 7 – The Straussenhoffers *116*

Chapter 8 – Success *128*

Chapter 9 – Jim's Graduation *143*

Chapter 10 – Paulette *158*

Chapter 11 – The Cabal *173*

Chapter 12 – The Internees *202*

Chapter 13 – The Aeroplanist *222*

Chapter 14 – The Invalid *239*

Chapter 15 – The Farmettes *255*

Chapter 16 – Armistice *270*

A Preview of Book Three, *The Mending 300*

Author's Note *302*

About Lynne Golding *307*

Book Club Guide *308*

ACKNOWLEDGEMENTS

With thanks to my first readers, my mother-in-law Carol Clement and my late father-in-law John Clement, for their diligence and enthusiasm for every chapter dispensed; my good friend Candace Thompson for her marginal happy and sad faces letting me know that the parts intended to be humorous or sad hit their mark; my father, Douglas Golding, and his oldest friend, John McDermid, for their many helpful reflections about Brampton in years past.

With gratitude to the second-floor librarians at the Brampton Four Corners Library who helped me manage reels and reels of microfiche; to the thorough investigative work of Samantha Thompson and her team at the Peel Archives; to the fabulous team at Blue Moon Publishers: Heidi Sander, Talia Crockett, Jamie Arts, and Allister Thompson; to my amazingly talented website and graphic designer, Kevin Patterson; my dear friend and diligent researcher, Colleen Mahoney; and my dear friend Meghan Robertson for her encouragement and support, the provision of facts about certain Winnipeg connections and the supply of her lovely mother-in-law, Erica Rueter, for her knowledge of many things German and Austrian.

With heartfelt thanks to my husband, Tony Clement, who encouraged me year after year to continue the project and to my children Alex, Maxine, and Elexa, who endured countless retellings of "interesting" tidbits I came across in my research.

With thanks to my mother Barbara Golding, who taught me the importance of and the joy that comes from caring for those who came before us.

Finally, with special thanks to my many friends, whose love and support helped me complete this book this year. Space does not permit me to list all their names, but their names start with an: A, B, C, D, E, F, G, H, I, J, K, L, M, N, O, P, R, S, T, V, and W. You are angels!

— LG, February 2019

Stephens Family Tree

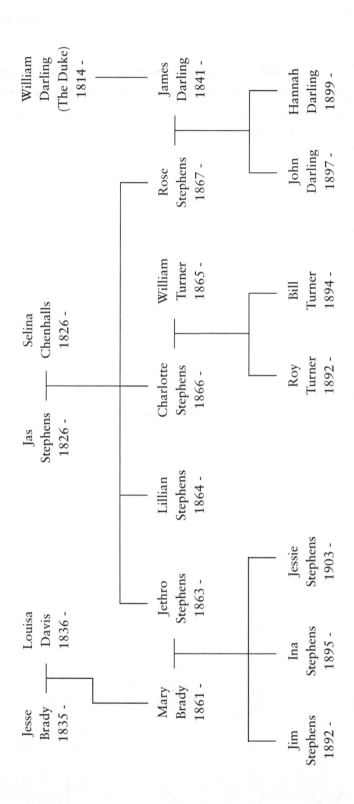

Straussenhoffer Family Tree

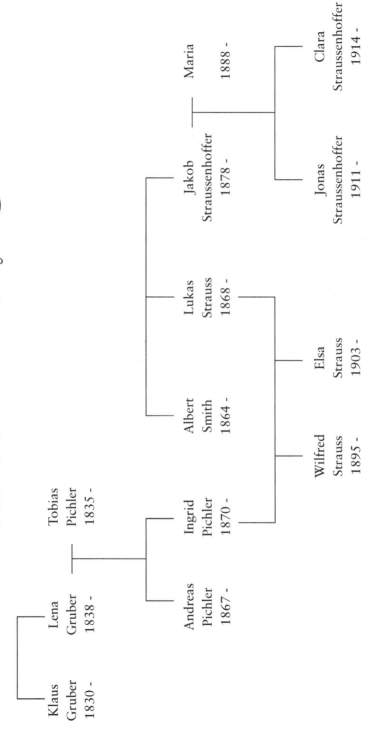

Klaus
Gruber
1830 -

Lena
Gruber
1838 -

Tobias
Pichler
1835 -

Andreas
Pichler
1867 -

Ingrid
Pichler
1870 -

Albert
Smith
1864 -

Lukas
Strauss
1868 -

Jakob
Straussenhoffer
1878 -

Maria
1888 -

Wilfred
Strauss
1895 -

Elsa
Strauss
1903 -

Jonas
Straussenhoffer
1911 -

Clara
Straussenhoffer
1914 -

...Christmas! The word comes with a new meaning in 1914. We have known peace so long that we can hardly comprehend war; we have dwelt so long beneath the flag of liberty that we know not what fetters mean but in our ease and our content we have perhaps grown selfish and indifferent to those less fortunate. Christmas of 1914 has torn away our selfish indolence. We know now that the brotherhood of man and the fatherhood of God have a deeper meaning than we have realized...

Editorial, *Conservator*, December 24, 1914

PROLOGUE

How fleeting is contentment? How transitory peace? How ephemeral joy? When these states leave us, must they take with them our innocence? In my case, in the case of my family, and in the case of my community, it seemed they must. They would be lost by prejudice; they would be lost by ignorance; they would be lost by fear; and they would be lost by patriotism. But that summer—my twelfth—I did not yet know it. It was July 1914. I had never been happier. My future, I thought, had never been so bright.

You might think this a rather grandiose statement to be uttered by an eleven-year-old—a mere child. But I had in the days and years before been beset by many disquieting trials, most of which were, finally, contentedly resolved. That day, sitting on a park lawn, I marvelled at the joy I felt within myself and those around me.

My brother Jim, a tall, reedy twenty-two-year-old, stood in a receiving line with his lacrosse teammates. The Brampton Excelsiors and their retinue had just returned from a month-long excursion to Vancouver. Although they came home without the coveted national Mann Cup, as the reigning Ontario lacrosse champions, the athletes received a hero's welcome. Hundreds of townspeople greeted the arriving train late that afternoon, participated in the homecoming parade that followed, and lustily cheered them that evening as they received the town's tributes. "A testament to the town," the mayor called them. The cleanest-living bunch of boys their professional coach had ever seen. Why, not a single one of them even smoked!

Not far away, near the temporary stage assembled for the tributes, stood my father, Jethro, or "Doc" as he was known to most people. As the president of the Brampton Excelsiors Lacrosse Club, he had raised the funds required to send the team west. Standing with him, wearing her signature full-length brown dress, was my sweet mother, Mary. My parents standing together in apparent equanimity with so many waiting to extend their approbation to my father was an amazing spectacle. It had been just over a year since his marital infidelity had been exposed. Our predominantly Christian town had demanded the penance, which might otherwise have been exacted by the Lord. Father's dental business had been boycotted and nearly destroyed; his positions on local boards threatened. Their marriage had been saved by my mother's grace; his reputation and his business by his efforts for the Excelsiors.

Near Jim was our sister Ina, eight years my senior. A round-faced, often dishevelled girl, she lived in a state of constant disappointment—a condition exacerbated by the rejection she experienced a year earlier from Eddie, Jim's friend and the boy she long but mistakenly believed shared a mutual affection with her. Her disappointment was compounded by the deferral at that time of her university studies, necessitated, in that case, by Father's compromised finances. Until recently, Ina had been one of the least happy people I knew. The source of the change in her demeanour was the person then standing next to her. Although she and Michael Lynch had been classmates for over twelve years, they seemed only to have noticed each other at their graduating class dance earlier that spring. Their affection was new and known only to a few of us. Michael took Ina's hand for just a second as the two moved toward Jim and the other team members.

On the far side of the park, away from the crowds, my grandfather, Jesse Brady, stood admiring the peony bushes. A builder of much of the town in his long working life, he was, at seventy-nine years of age, an avid gardener, curler, and lawn bowler and an active member of the International Order of Foresters, the Odd Fellows Club, and the church choir. He was fit and sturdy, with thick grey hair that adorned his head and formed his moustache and his square-cut beard. A widower, my grandfather came to live with my parents for a short while in 1905—two years after my birth—and still had not left.

Other members of my family were also present in the park that evening, scattered among the jubilant throngs. It was a rare day, in fact, since all three of my father's sisters were with us. My Aunt Rose, who lived down the street from us, was supervising the dispensation of cake. A widow for just over four years, she continued to own, though not operate, the local bakery that was once her husband's. Their children, John and Hannah, six and four years my senior, were present in the park. There as well was my Father's middle sister Charlotte Turner, her husband William, and their two children, Roy, who though the same age as my brother Jim, always seemed much younger, and Bill, two years younger yet. It had been seven years since William Turner resigned as mayor of our town and moved his family to Winnipeg. Since that time, we saw the Turners just one month a year, when they made their annual summer sojourn to Brampton.

Father's eldest sister, the red-headed Lillian, attired in her signature green, was also with us. A spinster, Aunt Lil lived in Toronto, where she ran a boarding house for male university students and taught history at the local high school. Among her many eccentricities was her disregard for society's customs—a characteristic that we children frequently used to our advantage, including when it came to bedtimes (there were none) and the proper order in which dessert should be consumed (there was none).

The park in which we were gathered that evening was located in the heart of our community, just down the street and across the bridge from my family's home. Along the park's eastern flank ran the Etobicoke Creek, a meandering watercourse that made its way through most of the downtown area, sometimes through underground caverns and other times in open streams. In the dry summer months, its small volume belied the need for the large bridge under which it flowed at the base of our street. But in the spring, the torrents produced by the melting ice and snow descending from the Caledon Hills to the north often proved the bridge just barely up to the task. Many lives had been sacrificed to those waters, including, two years earlier, that of my dear friend, Archie.

* * *

Gage Park was located in the town of Brampton in Peel County in the Province of Ontario, in the Dominion of Canada. In 1914, the town, comprised of four thousand people, had all the trappings of a county seat: a jail, a courthouse, a high school, churches of every Protestant denomination and even one Catholic, a hotel, a post office, and a library. The town had no taverns, its early forays in that area having been put asunder by the Primitive Methodists who first settled the area and its later forays having been extinguished by the Women's Christian Temperance Union, of which my mother was a dutiful, if not very enthusiastic member.

The town was dissected north-south by Hurontario Road, a former Indian trail that connected Lake Ontario to the south and Lake Huron to the north. As it ran through our town, it was called Main Street. In addition to pedestrians, horse carts, and coaches, the street was increasingly used by automobiles.

But the largest mover of the town's people and goods at that time was not the roadways but the railways, and Brampton was blessed with two. The main line, running generally on an east-west axis, was the Grand Trunk. North-south lay a spur of the Canadian Pacific Railway. In July 1914, Brampton had plenty of goods to be moved, including flowers from its many greenhouses and manufactured goods ranging from furnaces to shoes.

* * *

At 9:30 p.m., the music ended. The bandleader bid us a good evening, and the crowd began to disperse. The cake from my aunt's bakery had long been devoured, the tables from which they were served long since removed. My friends who had sat with me for the past hour rose to depart with their family members. Mine returned to me. Aunt Lil, whose bag I had been required to watch for a few minutes an hour and a quarter earlier, expressed surprised delight that it was where she had left it.

As the throngs began to leave the park, I was reminded of a similar exodus seven years earlier. At that time, the populace had gathered at another location for the sod turning ceremony of the future Carnegie Library. At its conclusion, those assembled were invited to the local Presbyterian Church to attend a short religious ceremony to consecrate the soon-to-be-built library. Everyone went—my friends, their parents, our neighbours, my aunts and uncles, my cousins—everyone except for me and my immediate family. I learned then that our family was not allowed to enter the Presbyterian Church. By posing dozens of near futile questions and through numerous prohibited eavesdroppings, I had in seven years learned that the edict preventing our entrance was Father's; that the genesis of the edict related to Grandpa; that Grandpa had been one of the builders of the church; that the edict had something to do with Grandpa being "self-made and others destroyed"; and that it was somehow related to a "Scottish fiasco." The mystery attached to this prohibition had plagued my early childhood years. Indeed, just earlier that evening, realizing how happy I was—how happy everyone in my family was—I had resolved to abandon my quest to solve it. Nothing was to be gained, I concluded, from a study of the past; it was only the future that mattered. That future, I concluded, was quite bright.

Chapter 1

DECLARATION OF HOSTILITIES

On the afternoon of August 4th, 1914, our family acknowledged what most Canadians knew to be true: Canada was at war. We acknowledged Canada to be at war, although our parliament had not yet proclaimed it. We acknowledged it, although Great Britain itself had not yet announced that it was at war; although the time provided for Germany to accede to Great Britain's ultimatum had not yet passed. We acknowledged it without knowing what the war would cost us in men or materials; without knowing where its battles would be fought or where our troops would be sent; without knowing the means by which mortal payloads would be delivered; without knowing the anxiety, uncertainty, and sacrifice that would be experienced by those at home; without knowing the innocence we would lose, the beleaguered state we would assume.

We did not know the vocabulary we would acquire; the songs we would sing; the names we would revere and the names we would revile. We did not know the foreign cities, towns, and villages that would become as familiar as our own; or the identities of those among us we would come to consider courageous or cowardly; patriotic or traitorous; leaders or followers. We did not know the alternative uses to which our buildings would be put; the way we would come to celebrate; the way we would come to mourn.

I was only eleven years of age when World War I commenced—the Great War, as we first came to know it. Just as I could remember where I was and what I was doing when I first sat in an automobile, when a room in our home was first illuminated by electricity, when I had my first telephone conversation, I remember where I was that day, August 4th, 1914, when we realized that hostilities with Germany were to commence.

It was a Tuesday, midafternoon. My mother and I were home alone, beating dust, food particles, and strands of hair from an enormous wool carpet. The rug, which ordinarily covered our dining room floor, was then off the ground, spread over the white wooden railing of our verandah and a number of wooden saw horses. A part of our semiannual ritual, we had earlier that afternoon exposed the dining room curtains to a similar vigorous walloping.

As was most often the case, my mother, then fifty-three years of age, wore a brown wool dress, a lighter-weight version of her winter attire. The colour complimented her warm brown eyes and her still-brown hair. The plain fabric covered her moderately plump form from the short neck below her sweet, round face to her delicate ankles, from her gently curved shoulders to her thin wrists. In case the garment she wore was not sufficiently modest—and Mother always dressed modestly—the brown dress itself was largely concealed by Mother's signature white apron, a shell she wore from dawn until dusk, removing it only when entertaining non-family members and during meals. The two-toned hand-tooled leather shoes that were the only extravagant aspect of her wardrobe were not visible below the many undulating folds of her long skirt.

I was wearing one of my two everyday summertime dresses, a light-weight navy and white gingham frock. Consistent with my age and the fact that the dress was then only two years old and so remotely within the dictates of the days' fashion, a two-inch expanse of skin could be seen between its hemline and the black socks that covered the remaining distance to my black buckled shoes. My hair, a mass of brown ringlets, was mostly pulled into a bow at the nape of my neck. I say "mostly" because its thick, unruly nature meant that it was rarely entirely captured within a ribbon, bow, or elastic. Ringlet tendrils poked out of the top and sides of the gathered mass.

As our arms and the brooms we batted released six months of accumulated grime, the lustrous violet, plum, lime, and gold threads of the rug were rerevealed. The bright colours complimented the large-patterned, similarly hued, Victorian paper that lined the walls of the room normally around it. Though the work was laborious, it was not unpleasant. Household chores were a constant part of my summer days. The day was bright, and our conversation was full and light.

The beating work was not continuous. In addition to breaks taken to rest our arms and to recover from fits of sneezes and coughs, not to mention the laughter that often followed such outbursts, we stopped occasionally to sip iced tea, and more often, to turn the carpet in order to expose our brooms to the portion of the carpet previously draped over the far side of the verandah's railing. It was while we were engaged in that turning exercise that an image appeared on the road before us. Pedalling up the hill from Main Street below, astride his bicycle, was Michael Lynch, a local telegram delivery boy.

"Mrs. Stephens! Mrs. Stephens! Did you hear the news? We are at war! Canada is at war!" Michael hollered without stopping. "Hurray! Canada is at war!" The basket of his bicycle appeared to be full of telegrams. We watched him continue on past our house.

"Do you think it's true?" I asked Mother with a combination of trepidation and incredulity. Proclamations of this nature were not in keeping with the manner in which telegrams were usually delivered. "I didn't think he was allowed to announce the contents of a telegram like that."

"He isn't permitted to disclose the contents of confidential telegrams," Mother replied. "He's been in that job for a long time. If he's making that kind of a statement, then it isn't a confidential matter." Mother looked at her timepiece, a small clock dangling within a pendant on a gold chain hanging from her neck. "It's only four o'clock," she said. We all knew that the Germans had until seven o'clock Eastern Standard Time to respond to the ultimatum of the British government, to respond or to find itself at war with Great Britain and her allies.

"Michael must know something. If we are at war—and I suspect we are—the Turners will cut short their trip to Toronto today. You'd better run down to your aunt's. The family should be together tonight."

"Here or there?" I asked, knowing the answer before I asked the question.

"There. It will take us a while to restore the dining room and," she confessed, "we are low on meat. Your aunt always has enough to serve us all." That was undoubtedly true, for although the dining room of my Aunt Rose, who lived just down the road from us, could accommodate the same number of people as our dining room, and although our pantries and kitchens were precisely the same size, my aunt's larder was always more full.

I was back on our verandah within five minutes, my Aunt Rose agreeing with Mother's suggestion. Over the next hour, Mother and I completed our beating of the rug. We half-dragged, half-carried the heavy carpet through our front foyer, parlour, and sitting room into the dining room, where we resettled it within the dark rectangular area of the elm floor that had escaped the sun's bleaching rays. We lifted the skeletal form of our dark walnut table onto the rug, setting its legs into the familiar wool divots, before reinserting six of the table's leaves. Finally, with ten of the fourteen petite point cushioned chairs tucked under the table, our work was complete. It was done in silence. The idle banter Mother and I shared earlier that afternoon in taking these steps in reverse was gone.

My Aunt Rose and her two children, John and Hannah Darling, lived in a house that was the mirror image to ours. Both located on Wellington Street, they were built by my grandfather, Jesse Brady, shortly after I was born. Each was clad in red brick and adorned with white trim. Tall windows topped with stained glass panes and surrounded by large green shutters graced two sides of each house. The first floor of each home had a grand front entrance or foyer, a parlour for entertaining visitors, a sitting room in which family gathered, a dining room, a kitchen, and a pantry. The second floor of each contained a bathroom and five bedrooms. The two floors were connected by two staircases: a wide, polished wood, carpet-lined staircase that wrapped around two walls of the foyer and which was the principal staircase used, and a small staircase entered from the pantry behind the kitchen. That staircase at the back of the house and the small second floor bedroom next to it were referred to by my aunt as the "back stairs" and the "back bedroom." In our house, the same set of stairs and the same bedroom were referred to as the "maid's stairs" and the "maid's bedroom." This was so, even though my family never once employed a maid, in contrast to my Aunt Rose, who often did.

The attic, which formed the third floor of each house, had two finely sculpted gabled windows. They sat below the house's dark green roofs, which rose at various levels. The most striking feature of each house was the cylinder-shaped three-story tower that stood where a corner would have otherwise, each topped with a graceful spherical dome and a small black spire. Grandpa's signature verandah formed another striking feature, in each case bordered by a white wooden railing wrapped around two sides of the house, including the tower. Grandpa believed that a verandah on a home was essential to the development of community; that families congregating there during their leisure hours in the four months of the year that the northern climate permitted it, while children played on the lawns and streets beyond, would foster a sense of true neighbourliness. In the seasons that our verandahs were not covered in snow, they were equipped as outdoor parlours, with wicker chairs, tables, stools, and swinging chaise lounges.

When my sister Ina and I were younger, our verandah had other uses too—an outdoor laboratory for Ina's scientifically minded endeavours and a make-believe ship for my less lofty pursuits. They took on these uses, that is until Father required the removal of the accompanying contrivances, a persistent occurrence that forestalled our recreational use of the verandah for at least a few weeks thereafter.

While these two houses had two separate owners, they were treated by all of us as though they were common property of not only our family, the Stephenses, and my aunt's family, the Darlings, but also of our Winnipeg cousins, the Turners, and my father's sister Lillian, who lived in Toronto. We all entered each house as though it was our own, never thinking of knocking before doing so, let alone waiting for an invitation to be extended. Meals among my extended family were frequently taken together, particularly when there was a special occasion (a holiday or a birthday) or when family was in from out of town.

Father agreed with Mother and Aunt Rose that our families should be together that night, August 4th, 1914. He had heard earlier that afternoon that the king had ordered the mobilization of the British army. It was that information, we concluded, that sent Michael, the telegraph delivery boy, on his premature town crier mission. But the announcement was, Father declared, likely only a few hours early. We would be at war at seven o'clock that night. It was a night to be spent with family.

The outbreak of the war did not come as a complete surprise. The imminent declaration had been predicted by many Canadians for months beforehand, although with each prediction not coming to pass, some were more surprised than others when the hostilities actually commenced. Over those months, at the various dining room tables of my family, I learned of the Triple Entente formed by France, Britain, and Russia the prior decade; the many acts of aggression of Germany in the interim; the assassination of the Archduke Franz Ferdinand of Serbia at the end of June; the creation of the German-Austrian pact at the beginning of July; the declaration of war by Serbia against Austria at the end of July; and the declaration of war by Germany against Serbia the next day. I learned that Germany had issued an ultimatum to the independent Belgium that German troops be granted access to its territories or Belgium would face German invasion. I learned that in response Britain had issued an ultimatum to Germany that Germany withdraw the demand made to Belgium or face British hostilities.

At those dining room tables, I also learned how my family members felt about that likely war, who was for it, and who was against it. Their positions, which had been evolving and eventually staked, were stated starkly that night at the Darlings' dining room table. Twelve of us were assembled there: my immediate family of five, the Darling family of three, and the four Turners, who had, as Mother suggested, returned from Toronto earlier than they had planned.

Of my parents, my aunts, and my uncle, nearly all of them considered a British concern to be a Canadian concern; a British cause to be a Canadian cause; a British war to be Canada's war. But their enthusiasm for the war, their confidence in the speed with which the battle could be won, and the resources required to attain that victory, varied between them.

At a time when most Canadians regardless of age, background, length of residency in Canada or language, wholeheartedly supported the British cause, my father's support was tepid at best. Father had a contrarian personality. It was in his nature to swim against the tide; to argue red when everyone else argued black. He took positions against ardent advocates; against seasoned specialists; against acknowledged experts. He would take his positions in a public meeting, perhaps at a meeting of the High School Board of which he was chairman, or of the Water Commission, of which he was also chairman. He would take his positions in our church, at which he was the choir leader. He even waged his arguments against his dental patients, including when (possibly preferably when) their mouths were pried open with his fingers and other devices, when their responses could only be an incomprehensible gurgle or a slap of their hand against their thigh or some other gesture.

There were three explanations for Father's contrary positions. One explanation had to do with politics. My father was an unrepentant Conservative. He took issue with almost anything said by a timid or fervent Liberal. Father's position on the war could not be explained on this basis, however, given the proposed formation of a union government between the ruling Conservatives and the opposition Liberals. On the subject of war, there was, at least in the early days, no dissonance between the positions of the two parties.

A second explanation for Father's contrarian nature, though it was not as obvious to me as a child, was my Father's conscious or subconscious need to take positions that varied from the consensus view of our town's "establishment." It was, I came to understand, his way of showing that he was not actually inferior to its rarefied members, something he was truly afraid of being; that he had a superior intellect, something he was not actually confident he had. This too did not account for Father's position on the war, for though he was not afraid of taking contrarian positions, this did not extend to being seen as treasonous or in any way unpatriotic.

The final reason for his often-contrary positions was his concern for our family economy. Though Father had for most of his career been a successful dentist, the method by which his patients paid for his services (sometimes with cash, often with goods or services in lieu, and sometimes not at all) meant that our family had to be careful with its funds. His significant loss of income for much of 1913 and early 1914 when his business was being boycotted meant that he had to be particularly careful. The amounts he and Mother had put aside for a rainy day were entirely depleted during that period that we ironically referred to as the "drought."

Thus, Father was unlikely to support any public policy that would require a larger outlay of funds on taxes. For that reason, he had years earlier opposed the purchase by the taxpayers of the local electricity supplier. It was for that reason that he still opposed plans to divert the Etobicoke Creek out of the downtown area, even though that watercourse, which ran along the main street of our town, caused at times hundreds of thousands of dollars in damage. It was his stated reason as well for opposing the war.

"It's going to cost us millions of dollars," Father said that night at Aunt Rose's dining room table, shortly after we began our end of day meal, something we then called "tea." After swallowing a large mouthful of mutton, he expounded on his view. "Millions! Colonel Sam said last Saturday that Canada is getting ready to ship twenty thousand men overseas—and that we will send five times that if required. Twenty thousand." Colonel Sam Hughes was Canada's Minister of the Militia and Defence. He was known affectionately by most Canadians as "Colonel Sam."

"Do you know how much it's going to cost to transport, shelter, feed, and equip those men?" Father asked. "That's before counting the amount we will have to pay them and their family members in benefits. And what if another twenty, thirty, or fifty thousand follow them? Our population is not even eight million. Can you imagine how much each taxpayer is going to have to pay to foot that bill? We can't afford it."

Mother, who sat kitty-corner to Father, nodded in agreement as he spoke. As was the case with most matters at this time, Mother's views on the war echoed Father's. Though Father liked to take contrarian views, he liked it best when others, having heard those views, came to share them, either because, in the case of his wife and children, they should, or in the case of all others, because he had persuaded them to do so. Father was rarely disappointed by Mother, who always agreed with him, or at least appeared to. When it came to his reticence about the war, Mother adopted a similar stance.

"I disagree," my Uncle William said, putting down his knife and fork. Father and Uncle William rarely agreed on anything political, my Uncle William being both a Liberal (he had previously sought election as a Liberal Member of Parliament for our area) and, though no longer a resident of Brampton, still a member of its establishment. Uncle William was a former mayor of our town, a position previously held by both of Father's brothers-in-law, but despite Father's ambitions, never a position held by him. Uncle William resigned as mayor of Brampton in 1907 in order to take an executive position with the Maple Leaf Milling Company in Winnipeg—an act that displayed so little confidence in the future of our town that Father never truly forgave him.

"We're already paying most of those costs," Uncle William said. "Colonel Sam is going to send men to England that we've already trained and equipped." Uncle William was referring to Canada's volunteer militia and our small standing army.

"You know that won't be enough," Father responded. "Colonel Sam has promised twenty thousand men. Our force is not that large. Even those that are equipped and trained will need more equipment and more training. They will need transportation and lodging, and we will have to pay them a wage. The British parliament approved $525 million today as an emergency fund for its war costs. Canada won't get away with spending less than $50 million. And we will spend even more if we increase the number of our troops beyond twenty thousand."

"Well, I doubt we will need more men than that," Uncle William replied. "Dublin has committed to sending a hundred thousand Irish soldiers. Add that to Britain's own and those from France, and that will be more than enough for a short war. This war is going to be over before Thanksgiving."

My Aunt Rose disagreed with both men. The youngest of Father's sisters, she was attractive, with thick light brown hair wound loosely at the top of her head. Never lacking in confidence or determination, she had acquired further measures of both in the four years that she had been a widow. She sat at the end of the table closest to the kitchen, opposite to Father. Though Aunt Rose never let her brother assume a role as head of her household, she had during her widowhood allowed him to sit in a location at the dining room table commensurate with that position.

"Jethro," she said, first addressing Father, "we can't escape our responsibilities to Britain. When it comes to foreign affairs, we *are* Great Britain. Once Parliament is recalled later this month and the new union government convenes, they will make that very clear. And the cost? Yes, it will cost us financially—not so much as you fear, Jethro, but more than you will allow,

William. Surely, no one is saying that this war will be over by Thanksgiving, William. Christmas. That is what they are saying. Christmas."

"It's true, William," said his wife, Charlotte. "Christmas is what they are saying." It was an amazingly short number of words to be uttered on a subject about which I knew she felt strongly. Over the past month, Aunt Charlotte had let it be known on a number of occasions that she firmly supported the position of Great Britain and that Canada should be prepared to support the mother country in its time of need, no matter the cost.

As for the young people at the table, we fell into two categories: those who enthusiastically supported the war and wanted to immediately enlist, and those who supported the war but had no intention of enlisting. The first group included my Turner cousins, Roy and Bill, and my other male cousin, John Darling.

"Father," Bill said, "please don't say that the war will be over by Thanksgiving or even Christmas, Aunt Rose. You know I can't enlist until next spring. Unless..." He turned to his Father "...unless you will allow me to seek a deferral of my law studies for a year?" Bill was then twenty years old. His tuition for the coming school year had already been paid. Aunt Charlotte and Uncle William repeated what was obviously a mantra, that Bill had to complete the first year of his studies before he could enlist.

"Uncle William," John said, "please don't say that the war will be over by Thanksgiving or even Christmas, Mother. You know I can't enlist for another year. Unless..." He turned to his Mother. "Unless you will allow me to enlist, though I am only seventeen?"

Aunt Rose laughed lovingly at her son. "John Darling, there are not too many things you can be sure of in this life, but there are two things I think we can be quite confident of: one, I will not be consenting to a minor child going to war; and two, the war will be over long before you turn eighteen next March." Of the three such cousins, he seemed the most resigned.

"Father," said Roy, then twenty-two and clearly agitated, "why did you insist I come to Brampton this summer? I told you that the war would be declared while we were here! I need to be home now. I need to be with my regiment. I have to leave tomorrow!" For two years, Roy had been a member of the Winnipeg militia. While completing his university education, he had been training for warfare in the evenings and on weekends.

"Roy," Uncle William said, clearly repeating another mantra, "the militia has not yet been called up. There is no point rushing to return to the west tomorrow. When the time comes, your commanding officer may prefer you to go directly to England from here. Let's wait and see." Roy was only slightly mollified. Ironically, in any other year, the Turners would have been home by August 4th. It was the threat of war that developed in the last week that required Uncle William to stay in Brampton. His firm sensed that his presence in Ontario at that time could be extremely helpful. "We'll leave next Sunday, per our current plans."

Roy was an adult. He could have left without his parents—but he knew that it would break his mother's heart if she was not at the train station when he entrained for England. His mother would not return west without his father.

Of the four remaining young people at the table, three were girls. Our strongest view was that no one we loved or cared about should get shot and killed.

"Like who?" Bill asked.

"Like....our fathers," I replied. I couldn't even bring myself to mention my brother and cousins.

"Don't worry," Roy said, "they are too old to enlist." Father, then fifty-one years of age, and Uncle William, two years younger, scowled at Roy, but neither objected.

"Like our brothers," Hannah said.

"Don't look at me," her brother John said. "Apparently I am too young to enlist."

"Don't look at me," her cousin Bill said. "Apparently I am too poor to forego my tuition." Uncle William scowled more.

"Don't look at me," Roy said. "At this rate the war will be over before I get back to my regiment. And if it isn't, well then, I will be just fine. I have plenty of training. I can take on one, two, or three Germans at a time! They won't know what hit them!" He ended his battle cry with a firm fist on the table. The cutlery around him leapt briefly above its station.

"Thank you, Roy," Aunt Rose said, patting his hand before rearranging her dessert cutlery. "We don't need quite that much enthusiasm at the table." Everyone turned to my brother Jim, also then twenty-two.

"Don't look at me," Jim said. "I have no intention of enlisting. I have important dental work to do, don't I, Father?" Jim was about to enter his last year of dental studies. Father nodded in agreement. "The war will be over before I graduate, I expect."

"Like our friends," Ina added, in response to the "like who" question. Her voice was timid, her tone melancholic, her gaze distant.

"Yes," Roy said, laughing, attempting to raise the mournful drift of the conversation. "Your friends may be worth worrying about!"

"It's true," Bill confirmed. "I know most of them. Many are unco-ordinated dullards! Hardly worthy of your friendship or mine!" He threw his napkin at Ina, laughing the entire time, expecting his action to lighten her mood. She instead used the napkin to wipe two tears falling down her cheeks.

This, then, summarizes the views of my entire extended family but for two of its members. The first, my grandfather, Jesse Brady, was not with us that night. He often spent time in Toronto while the Turners were visiting us, allowing a little more room for the accommodation of the four Winnipeg guests between our house and Aunt Rose's house. But Grandpa had made his views known over the preceding months. Though he was born and raised in England, and though he understood the legal niceties, Grandpa considered this war to be Britain's war and not Canada's war. In this way, his views at this time diverged from those of the Brampton establishment, though not for any of the reasons Father might advance. Grandpa, at seventy-eight years of age, held no property and thus paid no property taxes. The war would not materially affect his personal finances. He took no particular delight in taking views opposite to those of the town's establishment. England had not been unkind or unjust to him. He had arrived in Canada at the age of twenty-two, ten years before the country of Canada was formed. He came to forge a new life. He no longer felt any allegiance to the old one.

The other member of my extended family whose views on the war had not been presented that evening was my Aunt Lillian, Father's eldest sister.

It would have been impossible to state her position with certain knowledge, since she was as unpredictable as Father was contrarian. Her disdain for Brampton, the place of her birth, including her refusal to visit her home town more than twice a year, meant that we were all truly surprised when just before dessert was served and shortly after Bill was scolded by his father for throwing a napkin at his cousin, a persistent halloo issued from the front foyer.

"I think that's Lil," Aunt Rose said, rising from the table. She walked through the sitting room and the parlour before returning a few minutes later with the suspected guest. We naturally rose when she entered the room, but instead of rushing to embrace our favourite aunt as my siblings, my cousins and I would ordinarily have done, we froze in place.

"I'm sorry," Aunt Lil said in a halting voice as she entered the dining room. She was clearly distressed. Her long red hair, which when not captured in a large hat was always worn loosely down her back, was tied that night in a long braid. The green of her blouse and skirt (the only colour she ever wore) did not match. Her face was ashen and her eyes were bloodshot. She was shaking. What had happened to our favourite aunt, I wondered, the aunt whose zany ways and eccentricities always made her lively company? We loved her for that, for her disregard of convention (which made her a lenient chaperone), and for her inability to tell even a white lie (which made her a trusted source for the truth from which other adults often sought to shelter us).

"Lillian, what is it?" Charlotte asked as we sat back down. "What has brought you all this way? Why didn't you let us know you were coming? We'd have had someone meet you at the train station."

To our utter horror—at least to the horror of the younger generation of the family—our favourite aunt began to cry. None of us had ever seen our consummately steady aunt dissemble. We all rose to go to her before Father stopped us.

"Sit down, all of you!" he commanded. "None of you has been excused. Charlotte, Mary, will you please take Lillian away from the table and help her calm herself."

"No. No, Jethro," Aunt Lil said, putting her hand up in his direction. "I'm sorry. I will be fine. I don't want to be away from the children. They are the reason I came here tonight. It's the children. My boys." Jim pulled a spare chair from its resting spot next to the wall. After placing it beside Aunt Rose's chair, the two ladies sat down. We all turned to her.

"The children? The boys? What about them, Lil?" My father rarely had patience for what he considered to be the very odd ways of his eldest sister, who he sometimes referred to as "Lulu"—though never to her face. That night was no exception. "What the deuce is wrong with you?"

"With me?" she asked. "Not with me. Nothing is wrong with me. With the world. With your world," she said, confirming the other worldliness to which we children all knew she belonged. "Your world. Your way. Don't you know how many lives are going to be wasted on this war?"

"Wasted? What do you mean wasted? Lil, for once we are almost on the same side of an argument. I don't think we should have our boys over there, but I agree with what William said earlier." He then repeated it for her benefit. "If our troops do go, they'll be back quickly. With a minimal number of losses. Please, you must see this."

"I don't," she said. "I don't see that. Quick? It won't be quick. This is not South Africa—though that was not particularly quick either. Both sides have machine guns. And aeroplanes. There is no quick solution to this. And a minimal number of losses? You are thinking we will send twenty thousand men. We will send ten times that number. Or more. And they will not all come back. So many of them will not be back. My nephews, my boarders, my students, so many of them won't come back." She was crying, but she inhaled deeply before asking no one in particular, "And for what? What is the point of this war?"

No one had a reply. Eventually, Aunt Rose put an arm around her.

Finally, Roy stood up. "I'm coming back!" he said with all of the confidence of the unknowing.

"And I'm coming back!" Bill said, standing too. "If the war is not over before I can enlist."

"And I'm coming back!" said John, rising as well. "If I ever get over there."

"And I'm not going at all," said Jim from his seat. There being no suggestion that Ina, me, or our cousin Hannah would go to war, we too remained seated.

Aunt Lil, who had almost regained her composure, lost it again. "All right, you are all excused," Father said. "But Hannah, John, Jessie, none of you are to go out tonight. It's a night to be with family, those who are dear to you. It is not a night for frolicking." As he said that, we saw through the room's large picture window three young men walking down Wellington Street toward Gage Park, carrying a Union Jack, singing "Rule Britannia" at the top of their lungs.

* * *

"It's all that history," Father groused to Uncle William as I cleared the table. Mother and my three aunts were in the sitting room. "She spends too much time in the past," he continued. "She should know by now that she is knowledgeable about the past, not the future! She's a history teacher, not a prophesier! This is why I urge all of these young people to study sciences, not history. What can we learn from history?"

"Well, there are probably a few things we could learn from history," Uncle William conceded in defence of a course of study enjoyed by many members of our family.

"Yes. Some things. But not everything. Really, what does Lulu know about war?"

Uncle William had no answer to that. The two men rose to move to the verandah, where they could take in some fresh air and smoke their pipes. Those permitted to leave the house followed them out the door.

Jim was the first. He wanted to be with Millie Dale. Millie had been Jim's sweetheart for over two years. He had loved her for even longer. It was a night to be with those with whom you are close, Father said. He should go to her, of course, and he did.

Ina left for the McKechnies. They lived on Peel Avenue, just to the south of our house. Mrs. McKechnie had lost her husband four years earlier to a premature heart attack, and just two years later, her son, my friend Archie, died even more prematurely to a mishap in the Etobicoke Creek. Of the three female daughters, Katie was Ina's particular friend. Father agreed that it would be appropriate for Ina to call on the McKechnies that night. Father always approved of a nice turn in support of a family without a senior male member. Roy and Bill followed in close succession, each determined to visit old friends.

My young cousins and I, having been forbidden to engage in anything frivolous on that solemn night, looked for distractions. John eventually retreated to his room to work on the construction of a model train. Hannah and I moved through various rooms, listening to our elders. We quickly tired of watching the ladies try to calm Aunt Lil. We noticed that in reality, Aunt Rose and Mother were doing most of the calming. Aunt Charlotte, normally the one to take control of such situations, sat on her own, staring vacantly out the window into the darkness beyond.

Eventually, we found ourselves on the verandah, watching Father and Uncle William smoke their pipes and listening to their discussion about the war. Though as children we were generally prohibited from participating in such conversations, we were always welcome to listen to them. Father viewed our presence at such times as a means of educating us.

We sat on the Wellington Street side of the "L"-shaped verandah, the two men occupying the big wooden chairs facing the Wellington Street Bridge and the park beyond it. Hannah and I took the less comfortable chairs across from them, with mine closest to the street. From there I had a good view of our house and Chapel Street that crossed in front of it. Father and Uncle William were discussing whether Colonel Sam, who had earned his military credentials fighting in the Boer War, was likely to accompany the Canadian troops abroad.

"The current thinking is that he'll stay here in Canada," Uncle William said, turning his pipe over in the ashtray before refilling it.

"It would be better if he went over with the troops," Father said, his mouth full of smoke. "I can't say that I'm in favour of our men going to war, but if they do, they would be well served under his command."

"Apparently, not everyone thinks so," said Uncle William. "I hear he caused the British no end of aggravation during the Boer War."

As Father and Uncle William continued to discuss war leadership matters and whether one could be a cabinet minister being too far away to attend cabinet meetings, my mind began to wander. How was this war going to affect us? Roy said that Father was too old to enlist, but if Parliament decreed otherwise, would he have to go to war? Would Grandpa? Who would look after us if all the men left? Who would grow our food? Who would fill our furnaces with coal? Who would deliver our milk, our vegetables, or our meat? Who would teach us math and science? Who would lead our church services?

As I contemplated a manless reality, something caught my eye in the distance. It was Ina. She was walking toward our house along Chapel Street. Her visit with the McKechnies was apparently complete. I was about to announce her return when I saw her look furtively toward our verandah, then, presumably on ascertaining its vacant state, look equally furtively toward the Darlings' verandah. Seeing the backs of Father and Uncle William and apparently not noticing me looking her way, she ran quickly along Chapel Street, past our house and toward Queen Street beyond. It was clear she did not want to be seen.

Half an hour later, Mother and Aunt Charlotte joined us on the verandah. Aunt Lil's agitation had been quelled. She was now settled in Aunt Rose's back bedroom—the room then absent of any maids. We said goodnight to Hannah as my parents, the elder Turners, who were staying with us in Grandpa's vacated bedroom, and I left for our home just up the street.

Neither Ina nor Jim were there when we arrived, spent and tired. Minutes later, I lay in the double-sized bed that Ina and I shared, the drapes and sheers to the long window next to my side of the bed pulled open wide to allow as much cool night air as possible to enter the room. Though I was tired, I could not sleep. My mind was fixated on what Aunt Lil had said and how Father and Uncle William reacted to it. It was all about history. I knew some history. We had studied a number of battles in our history classes. I could think of a few: Culloden, Gettysburg, Waterloo, and Bosworth came to mind. We learned of the atrocities that men of one side inflicted on those of the other; we learned of crops and villages and government buildings burned to the ground; we learned of soldiers hacked to bits; of heads cut off and positioned on stakes; of women and children left to starve; of bridges and roads being destroyed. Was this to be our fate? Father had assured me that if Germany and Britain went to war, the battles would not be fought in Canada. But what if he was wrong? I thought about the courthouse, the registry office and the jail—all government buildings located just down the street from me; the Wellington Street Bridge beyond them; all the men I knew who could be called up for service. Eventually, I thought of their sweet heads.

Around eleven o'clock, I heard the front door open. A few minutes later, Ina opened the door to our room. "Where were you all this time?" I whispered after she had changed into her cotton nightgown and crawled into our bed. It was a sign of our maturing relationship that when she told me she had been with the McKechnies for the entire evening, I did not expose her. I knew who she had been with. I knew she should not have been with that person. But I was glad she was.

Chapter 2

THE FIRST CONTINGENT

The declaration of hostilities made on August 4th, 1914 epitomized the first days of the war. In Canada, at least, those days chiefly revolved around announcements, promises, and words. The prospect of a war had been known to the federal and provincial governments sufficiently long in advance to allow them following the declaration to make immediate promises, but not long enough it seemed, to allow them to take immediate actions.

The reality was that while the Canadian government had announced its intention to send twenty thousand troops to the aid of Britain, it had not yet determined the means by which to do so. Canada had a permanent army comprised of three thousand professional soldiers. It had a mobilization plan by which the best volunteers would be selected by such professionals. This, however, was not the plan of Colonel Sam, who did not trust the professional soldiers, or the "regulars," as they were called. He envisioned the volunteer militia, not the professional army, selecting the fit among the Canadians who volunteered to serve. It was not then known whose vision for the expeditionary force would prevail: that of the professional army or that of Colonel Sam.

The situation was no different with respect to pledges made of supplies. Within hours of the declaration of hostilities, the government of Canada and the governments of her nine provinces raced to make commitments of goods to Britain. Details regarding how these goods could be acquired and delivered had yet to be determined.

It was the promises of goods of three of those governments that kept the Turners in Brampton longer than their usual four weeks—a matter that brought pleasure to all of our family members but one. Every additional day spent in Brampton was an agony to Roy, who was fearful of not being in Winnipeg when his militia regiment was mustered.

* * *

I rose late the morning of August 5th, my fears of pending doom having led to a poor night's rest. Aunt Charlotte and Ina were in the dining room when I entered it, discussing the restored condition of Aunt Lil, who had just entrained for Toronto. Father had already left for his dental office. Jim was at the Dale Estate, the internationally known flower grower, where he worked in the summers. Uncle William was at a meeting with Richard Blain, our local Member of Parliament. Mother was upstairs making her bed.

I had nearly finished eating my cold toast when I heard Mother come down the maid's stairs and go out the back door. Minutes later, she joined us in the dining room. After wishing me a good morning, she turned to Ina. "I see that you rinsed your dress out this morning. Why did you leave it in the bathroom? There's a good breeze outside. I've put it on the line."

Ina thanked her, and then Mother went on. "My, you were out late last night, Ina. Were the McKechnies in that much need of your society?"

"The McKechnies were fine," Ina assured her. "We spoke about the war for a bit. They really don't know much more than we know. We played cards for a time, and then Katie and I went for a walk."

"A walk? Down to the park?" Mother asked.

"No. There were a lot of people down there cheering and singing, and I knew that Father did not want us to do anything very gay, so we walked to the flats." The "flats" were the flood plain areas that ran next to the Etobicoke Creek in certain parts of Brampton. They were undeveloped areas. "We stayed there for a while. I must have sat on some wet grass. I noticed the stain this morning."

"I see," Mother said as though it was normal for Ina to notice such things. For most of Ina's life, she had never cared or noticed how she looked. Of course, that had changed since her high school graduation dance a few months earlier.

"When were you there, Ina?" Aunt Charlotte asked. "I hope it wasn't dark at that time."

"It wasn't dark when we walked to the flats. I suppose it was dark when we returned." I said nothing as I watched her performance. All of the years of amateur theatrics had clearly stood her well.

"Ina, you and Katie can no longer carry on that way," Mother scolded. "You aren't fifteen anymore. You're nineteen. You are young ladies. In addition to your physical safety, you have your reputations to protect. I will hear no more of late night unchaperoned walks to secluded areas like the flats."

"Yes, Mother," Ina agreed demurely.

"I have a mind to speak with Mrs. McKechnie. Surely she must be concerned for Katie's safety and reputation too."

"Oh no, Mother, there's no need to do that." Ina was quite emphatic. "I'll make sure it doesn't happen again. With no men in the house, Mrs. McKechnie has so many other things to concern herself with."

"She certainly does," Mother agreed. "I'll thank you both to remember that."

Ina put down the knife she was using to peel an apple. She had lost her appetite for food requiring a steady hand. After glancing at her watch, she brought the conversation to an end, announcing her need to prepare for her shift at the telephone switch. She expected the day would be quite busy with calls, including those from people like Uncle William with wartime business to conduct. He would place most of his calls from Aunt Rose's bakery. Our family could not afford to own a telephone. While Aunt Rose likely could have, she did not see the point of having such an apparatus installed in both her house and the bakery. Like most local merchants, she had come to understand the necessity of having a telephone in her business.

* * *

In those first few hours of the war, governments in Canada pledged 1,300,000 bags of flour to Great Britain. Valued at nearly $4,000,000, they were made by the governments of Canada (1,000,000 bags), Ontario (250,000 bags), and Manitoba (50,000 bags). Uncle William's calls that week pertained to the fulfillment of those gifts. The three governments were not, of course, sitting on stockpiles of wheat or flour. It all had to be procured. Uncle William and others in the national grain industry were advising the governments on the means to grow the grain, to have it milled into flour, and to transport it both to the port in Montreal and ultimately to its delivery point in England.

"Why is this requiring so many meetings, Father?" Roy asked one night before trying again to convince his father to return to Winnipeg on an earlier train. "You deal with grain purchasing and milling every day. Why is this taking so much time?"

Uncle William would have been happy to answer that question if it had been posed by anyone else in the family. He thought his eldest son, who had been working as a part-time junior clerk at the Maple Leaf Milling Company for the two prior years, should have known better. "This involves enormous amounts of grain. You know how much wheat must first be purchased in order to create that much flour. And the milling of this wheat is in addition to the amounts that are being milled to satisfy existing customer orders. It will be difficult to meet the commitments made to Britain—particularly for Ontario. That province doesn't produce enough grain to support its own population, let alone the amount required to meet the commitment it just made to Britain." Ontario's days as Canada's wheat king had ended in the prior century.

"The Ontario government will urge its farmers to devote as much acreage as possible to fall wheat, but it's August. Decisions like this need to be made in the spring. Ontario will not be able to grow enough wheat to meet its commitment. It will have to purchase wheat from the west."

"Or from the States," Roy said, now applying more of his knowledge.

"Oh, no. Not from the United States. We've been working hard with the federal government on this. Canadian wheat! We are quite clear on this: the government orders must be filled with nothing but Canadian wheat."

"Unless it is more expensive than American wheat," Father said.

"*Even* if it is more expensive than American wheat," Uncle William replied firmly. By this, we knew that it was likely to be just that.

Then, showing his interest in Canadian families, Uncle William went on. "One million, three hundred thousand bags of flour—that much demand will certainly increase the price of wheat, flour, bread, and everything else made with flour and sold in our bakeries. That is to be expected. But if we don't procure this properly, there will be some real price-gouging. Farmers and mill owners will be seen to make unrealistic profits from these generous commitments. All Canadians will pay the price. We don't want that."

Fortunately for consumers, the other provinces pledged other gifts. Quebec pledged 4,000,000 pounds of cheese; New Brunswick, 100,000 bushels of potatoes; British Columbia, 1,200,000 cans of salmon; Prince Edward Island and Alberta, collectively, 150,000 bushels of oats; Nova Scotia, 500,000 tons of coal; and Saskatchewan, 1,500 horses. But all the gifts—the flour, potatoes, salmon, oats, coal, and horses—had to be transported. Uncle William was concerned about that as well.

"Trains and ships," Uncle William said in response to a question about the method of conveyance. "And of course, they will both be required for use at the same time we need to transport overseas twenty thousand men, all of their equipment, and thousands of horses—not just the fifteen hundred pledged by Saskatchewan. The federal government is preparing to commandeer a number of ships for its use during the war. That is one of the things we have been discussing with Dick Blain." Uncle William was again referring to our Member of Parliament. He went on, "But the ships—they raise another concern. They could be threatened by the German navy."

"Surely the Germans would have no ability to pirate our ships," Mother said.

"Don't be so sure of that, Mary," Uncle William replied. "It's for that reason we currently have over seven million bushels of wheat in our Montreal ports that we cannot ship east."

"Because you're afraid of the wheat being stolen?" I asked.

"Because we're afraid of the gold necessary to pay for the wheat being stolen. We fear an attack on the ships carrying the gold. It has affected trade between Canada and the United States with England—and others too. But a new scheme is being proposed. Our minister of finance is going to act as trustee for the Bank of England. It will no longer be necessary to ship gold.

The ships in our port should soon be able to depart."

"William, you seem to know a lot about the goings-on of our Conservative government," Father remarked in a not very complimentary way.

* * *

While Uncle William was using the telephone in Aunt Rose's bakery to conduct his communications. Roy was using the more traditional method—the telegram. In Brampton, telegrams were sent and received by our family friend and Brampton Excelsiors Lacrosse Club executive member, Thomas Thauburn. From his general store premises on Main Street, next to the jewellery store of Mr. Woods, the former telegraph master, Mr. Thauburn operated the local Canadian Pacific Railway ticket and telegraph office. Of the two businesses, Mr. Thauburn far preferred the telegraph business, for, being a caring man, he enjoyed knowing the details of the lives of his fellow townsmen. Of course, he regarded the confidentiality of all telegrams as a sacred trust. He would never divulge to others the content of a telegram, a feat that was not particularly difficult to observe when the telegrams pertained to such matters as the purchase and sale of livestock, birthday greetings, holiday reports, and other ordinary matters, which most telegrams did.

No matter the topic, each such missive, once received, was placed in a manila envelope, addressed to the recipient, sealed, and then handed to one of Mr. Thauburn's local bicycle-riding delivery boys, each of whom he called "Johnny," no matter the Christian name conferred on him by the boy's parents. If an illness or a family emergency prevented one of those boys from completing his delivery or if the destination was too far, Mr. Thauburn took charge of the sealed envelope and personally transported it by foot, horse, coach, or, later, by car.

Mr. Thauburn was acknowledged as being a fine telegraph master in large part due to two edicts by which he operated his business. The first edict was that no telegram was to be hidden. Mr. Thauburn, not wanting himself or any of his delivery boys to be accused of converting another person's property as his own, insisted that all telegrams be delivered in plain view—either in the carrier's hand or bicycle basket. They were never to be stored, even temporarily, in a pocket. The second edict was that all telegrams received during normal business hours were to be dispatched to the recipient promptly upon its receipt—ideally within ten minutes and certainly within thirty.

Being well aware of the efficiency of Mr. Thauburn's telegraph office and of his adherence to the second of those two requirements, a person expecting a telegram waited to receive it at his or her home or place of business. Only occasionally would a prospective telegram recipient have the temerity to enter Mr. Thauburn's premises and inquire as to whether a telegram had been sent to him. If the inquirer purported to be making the inquiry in an effort to save Mr. Thauburn the trouble of having it delivered, he or she would be politely thanked for the inquiry and provided with a reply. But that civil response applied only to a first inquiry. Mr. Thauburn viewed any subsequent inquiry not as a considerate gesture, but at best as an irritation and at worst as an aspersion on his service record.

"If I had a telegram for you, Mrs. Smith, would it not now be in the course of delivery to you?" This was as polite a response as one might receive for a first inquiry made without a suggestion of trying to save Mr. Thauburn the time of delivering it or as one might receive to any second inquiry. Few in Brampton knew his rejoinder to those who inquired more often than that. But on August 7th, 1914, three days after the hostilities commenced, my cousin Roy became one of them. It did not start that way.

For three successive days, Roy sent telegrams to his commanding officer in Winnipeg, seeking instructions as to how to proceed. Should he return to Winnipeg immediately? Should he instead proceed directly to Camp Petawawa? Should he wait and return home with his parents departing Toronto on August 16th? Roy's commanding officer responded to the first telegram sent August 4th with genuine appreciation for being consulted. "Acknowledging with thanks your telegram of yesterday's date. No orders have yet been received. Unless orders otherwise sent, suggest you return to Winnipeg with family Aug 16."

In response to a similar telegram sent by Roy on August 5th, his commanding officer replied in a less appreciative but still friendly manner.

"No orders received. Reiterate suggestion of yesterday."

The commanding officer's response to the third telegram, this one sent August 6th, was an order. "Pending further instructions, you are commanded to return to Winnipeg, departing Toronto Aug 16."

While the sending of such telegrams began to irritate Roy's commanding officer, they had no such deleterious effect on Mr. Thauburn, who never objected to sending telegrams. Nor was Mr. Thauburn bothered by the reply telegrams sent by Roy's commanding officer, since they were delivered to Roy in the ordinary manner at Aunt Rose's house.

Circumstances changed on August 7th. That was the day it became known that Colonel Sam's view of the recruitment of the expeditionary force had prevailed. Earlier that day, telegrams had been sent to the militia commanders across the country, advising them that they would be responsible for the recruitment of the volunteers that would form the Canadian Expeditionary Force. With that information and hanging on to those first few words of his commanding officer's missive, "pending further orders," Roy went to the telegraph office to ascertain whether a telegram with such further orders had been received.

"How many times did you go to the telegraph office today, Roy?" Bill asked him that night as the family gathered on the Darlings' verandah.

Roy hesitated before answering. "A few."

"A few?" Ina asked incredulously.

"A few plus a few," Roy confessed.

"Six times?" Uncle William asked, clearly startled. "I hope you are not bothering Mr. Thauburn."

To Roy's negative reply, Ina issued a small harrumph. We all looked at her.

"Do you know something about this, Ina?" Aunt Charlotte asked.

"No. No," Ina said, blushing slightly. "It's just that...well, I can imagine that it could be bothersome to have someone asking the same question of you six times in a day."

We couldn't really blame Roy for being anxious. Though the local armouries were not open for recruitment on August 4th, the day that hostilities were declared, reports abounded of the hundreds of men who encircled armouries across the country that day and the next. With no other way to disperse them, by the night of August 5th, the armouries began opening their doors to applicants. Roy was beside himself at the notion of new recruits being accepted in Winnipeg while he was still in Brampton. Colonel Sam said he would take any man who wished to serve. There were so many men who wished to serve, Roy was afraid that his captain might not need him.

Uncle William tried to calm him. "The armouries are taking the particulars of these men because they do not know what else to do with them. They are giving them application forms. That is all."

"Be patient, Roy," his mother said. "You'll hear soon if you should return to Winnipeg early or if you should go directly to Camp Petawawa." We all thought it would be a shame for Roy to travel twelve hundred miles west from Toronto to Winnipeg, only to take another train east from Winnipeg to Petawawa, a town two hundred and fifty miles northeast of Brampton.

"I'm not sure the troops will be gathering in Petawawa," Uncle William said to everyone's surprise.

"What?" Roy said. "Why wouldn't we gather there?" Petawawa was Canada's largest military camp.

"The talk is that Colonel Sam has other plans for this new Canadian volunteer force. Apparently, he doesn't want to use the grounds that have traditionally been used by the regulars. He wants a new training ground for the volunteers before they depart for England. Richard Blain told me about it while we were waiting to commence our meeting today with the local grain dealers."

"I continue to be impressed by how much time you spend with our Conservative Member of Parliament," Father said once again, in a way that made it clear he was really not impressed at all.

"Colonel Sam has his eye on a site northwest of Quebec City. Sal Cartier or something like that. I've never heard of it before." Far from providing a balm to Roy, the additional information his father imparted only stoked his anxiety.

"Do you think I should send another telegram?" he asked one and all.

"No!" we cried in unison. It would have been his fourth in as many days.

"No, Roy," his father repeated. "I do not. It will take time to get this Sal Cartier—or whatever it is called—to be prepared. The land has to be cleared. Latrines, plumbing, electricity, and telephone lines have to be installed. Buildings, parade grounds, and rifle ranges have to be constructed. I doubt any troops will be called up before September." That additional information seemed to appease Roy. He did not suggest sending another telegram or making an earlier departure for Winnipeg for a full twelve hours.

* * *

It was soon revealed that Uncle William's knowledge of the purchase and transport of wheat and flour exceeded his knowledge of military matters. The new military training grounds were being made ready in record time. Within ten days of the hostilities commencing, the local volunteer militias were preparing to be mustered.

Working an overnight shift at the telephone switch, Ina returned home the morning of Friday, August 14th, while my parents, Aunt Charlotte, Uncle William, and I were eating breakfast. She told us about one of the last calls she placed late the night before. It was from Captain Baldock, the regimental commander of the Peel 36th Regiment, to our Member of Parliament, Richard Blain.

"Ina, you know you're not supposed to listen to the calls you connect," Mother reprimanded. Ordinarily, it was Father who took Ina to task for this. I took pleasure in the scolding. There was a time when anything that brought Ina discomfort brought me an equal amount of pleasure. But that was less the case now. No, my pleasure on this occasion was derived from the knowledge that I was not the only member of our family who eavesdropped on other people's conversations. Further, I took delight in my higher moral ground. Unlike Ina, I generally did not disclose to others what I surreptitiously overheard.

"And if you accidentally overhear a conversation you are not to repeat it to others. How many times—"

"That's enough, Mother," Father interjected. Mother stopped to let Father assume his ordinary role as the dispenser of discipline.

"Will it affect the Brampton boys?" Father asked.

"Yes," she said. "They're all being called up."

All being called up. I was horrified. All of the Brampton boys. This was it. This was what I feared. I thought of Jim and his best friend, Eddie, and all the boys they worked with. I thought of Clarence Charters and Dutch Davis and all of the members of the Excelsior lacrosse team that went west earlier that very summer. I thought of the members of the Young Men's Debating Society, of which Jim was a member and all of the boys in his Sunday school. I thought of Ina's friend Michael and all the boys that had been at her high school graduation dance. Did the Brampton boys include those who were visiting Brampton at the time, like Bill and Roy? Not that either of them would mind if it did.

Father continued to question Ina, but I heard none of it. I was desolate at the thought of all these boys going to war. It had only been a month since I had concluded the future was so bright.

Eventually my tears turned into sobs and my sobs into wails. "Jessie, what is the matter?" Father demanded. "Why the deuce are you crying?"

Why was I crying? Why were the others *not* crying? "Jim," I said through what were now heaving sobs. "Jim."

"What about Jim?" Father asked.

"I don't want Jim going to war," I managed.

"No one wants Jim to go to war," Father snapped, "least of all Jim. Jim isn't going to war."

"But Ina said—" I stammered.

"Yes?"

"Ina said that the Brampton boys are being called up."

"Yes, the Brampton boys who are members of the militia. There are eighteen of them. They are all going. Not every Brampton boy. No one is being compelled to go." Mother and Aunt Charlotte looked at me with sympathy. Father and Ina shook their heads and continued their conversation.

"And where will the Brampton boys be taken to? Will they go directly to the new training grounds at this La Cartier, or whatever it's called?"

Ina did not hesitate to disclose the details, which were by that time all very public. "No, they are going to Ravina Rink in Toronto until La Cartier, or whatever it's called, is ready to receive them. But they do not think that will be very long."

"Ravina Rink is in the west end of Toronto," Uncle William offered. "I heard about it yesterday. There is no ice in it now, and it's a good-size piece of property. I heard Blain say that Jesse Smith, the owner, was going to donate its use to the 36th and a number of other regiments. It can serve as a temporary barracks and training ground until they go to Bal Cartier, or whatever it's called."

"There should be a group at the station when the boys leave. There should be speeches, hymns, and anthems," Father said. He was not particularly supportive of the war, but he wanted the Brampton boys to depart with at least the amount of ceremony accorded to the Excelsiors two months earlier when they left by train for Vancouver. "What train are they catching? Do you know?"

"The 9:30 a.m. from the CPR station," Ina replied. "But don't worry about ceremony. The bands have already been called. Mr. Blain is alerting the businesses. He's trying to encourage as many people as possible to accompany the boys to the station and to be there when they leave." It was already eight o'clock. Jim had left for work at the Dale Estate half an hour earlier.

We put down our napkins and stood to leave. We proposed to stop at Aunt Rose's house to retrieve the other members of the family. They were already on the verandah when we arrived, having been informed of the departure moments earlier by our neighbour, Mr. Hudson.

The eighteen Brampton boys did not leave Brampton quietly. They did not leave it without ceremony. Having gathered together at eight thirty that morning, dressed in their militia uniforms, they were paraded north along Main Street, the Citizens Band leading them and hundreds of citizens following them. At Queen Street, they were met by a similar throng of citizens walking south, in this case led by the workers of the Dale Estate under the furls of a massive Union Jack. Jim was near the front of the pack. Together the two groups proceeded west to the CPR station, where they were met by hundreds of others. All of the factories in the area had released their workers to provide the boys with a proper send-off. In the end, fifteen hundred people attended, including some who had fought in the 1885 Northwest Rebellion, the Fenian Raids that ended in 1871, and the Boer War that ended in 1902—some in their old, moth-damaged, now barely fitting uniforms.

After a number of solemn speeches and two heartfelt hymns, the Citizens Band led the assembled in the "Maple Leaf," "O Canada," and "Rule Britannia," all sung with the greatest solemnity. As we sang, I took stock of those there. Most of the eighteen boys were Jim's age, although none of them were his particular friends. The eighteen did not include any of his Excelsior teammates. They did not include any of his Sunday school classmates. Ten of the boys attended Christ Anglican Church. At least four were older than Jim—three quite a bit older. Two of them had fought in the Boer War, which had ended twelve years earlier. One of the older men was the only married man among the eighteen.

The boys returned to their families to say their final farewells. There was no cheering, no levity, no boasting, just a dignified adieu to those brave boys—those brave men—who volunteered to protect a nation—an empire—well before anyone knew such service would be required. With not a dry eye on the platform, the eighteen boys, the first from Brampton to flock to the colours, entrained for service to king and country.

After the train departed, I walked with Jim down Queen Street on its north side amid those jostling, ten or more abreast, as they returned to their homes and places of work. The pace was slow. At one point, Mr. Thauburn squeezed in between Jim and me.

"That was a wonderful send-off, wasn't it?" he asked. "I didn't think there could ever be a send-off better than the one they had for us when we went west in June." After Jim agreed, Mr. Thauburn asked him about his upcoming school year. Jim answered as we continued moving slowly along the street. We crossed George Street when Roy, pushing through the throng, joined us. He had been walking with a crowd on the other side of the road.

"Hello, Mr. Thauburn," Roy said enthusiastically. Mr. Thauburn returned the greeting with much less enthusiasm. "That was a wonderful send-off, don't you think?" Roy asked. But before Mr. Thauburn could reply, Michael Lynch, one of Mr. Thauburn's telegram delivery boys, tapped him on the shoulder. Mr. Thauburn fell back behind us.

Roy turned to us and shrugged. We knew he was trying to make amends for the annoyance he had caused. His frequent visits to Mr. Thauburn to inquire as to the arrival of telegrams had not stopped on August 7th. Roy could not understand why the 36th had been mustered but his regiment had not. "Don't worry, Roy. You'll be called up soon. I have no doubt about that," Jim said in response to an unspoken lament.

"I'd have asked Mr. Thauburn if he had a telegram for me, but Father has forbidden me to do so. Apparently, I am becoming a nuisance," he said.

"That you are," said Mr. Thauburn who, with Michael, was still just behind us.

"I apologize, Mr. Thauburn," Roy said. "Really I do. I won't bother you again. I will patiently wait and see if a telegram comes for me before we leave on Sunday."

"I rather doubt that you will," Mr. Thauburn replied dryly.

Before Roy could protest again, Mr. Thauburn reached into the inside pocket of his coat, extracted a manila envelope, and passed it to Roy. "Came in at eight o'clock this morning."

Michael looked at Mr. Thauburn in astonishment. It was now nine forty-five. Mr. Thauburn had breached his two cardinal rules. He had been in possession of the telegram for well over half an hour, and he had stored it in his pocket rather than holding it in plain view.

"Don't look at me that way, Johnny," Mr. Thauburn said to Michael. "I wasn't going to let you or anyone else miss sending those boys off right. Besides, who would have been home to accept this? I knew where I'd find young Roy."

Six days later, on August 20th, the 260 volunteers comprising the 36th Peel Regiment left their quarters at Ravina Rink in Toronto. Added to those first eighteen Brampton men were twenty-one others who had been members of the Brampton regiment in prior years, hailing from such places as Port Credit, Mono Mills, and Orangeville. Their destination: a new training ground for the first contingent of the Canadian Expeditionary Force, Canada's largest, in a place we all then knew was called Valcartier.

Chapter 3

SNELL'S LAKE

The telegram required Roy to report to his regiment five days later. He went into immediate action. After hours of pacing, investigation of train schedules, and consideration of other commitments, he finally concluded that the first train he could take to Winnipeg was the one for which he and the other members of his family had tickets: the Sunday train leaving two days hence. It would, his father calmly told him, arrive in Winnipeg well before his required reporting time.

With his travel plans settled, Roy resumed his anticipation of the leaving party. The leaving party, which occurred the day before the Turners left for their home in Winnipeg, was a much anticipated event. The get-together was not special for its list of attendees, since, with the exception of Aunt Lil, who sometimes joined us, it was attended by the same people who attended nearly every family gathering convened in the month of the Turners' attendance in Brampton. Unlike some other parties, it did not involve presents, or songs, or lengthy speeches, although Father could rarely resist the opportunity to publicly bestow some wishes on those gathered. It was sufficient, it seemed, for the three families to join at an event called a "leaving party" for the occasion to rise to the honorific of such a gathering; for it to transcend the ordinary picnic or dinner.

But this year—in August of 1914—there was a sense among us that the gathering truly was special. It had been a miracle, Mother said, that in the seven years since the Turners left Brampton, they had never once missed the return trip to the town from which they all hailed. We knew that the annual pilgrimage would one day come to an end; that the visits would ultimately become less regular; that they would eventually include fewer people. Even before the hostilities were declared, we recognized that Roy, a young man about to begin his career, and Bill, who would soon follow him, would not have the ability their father had to leave their places of employment for five weeks each summer. We planned this leaving party knowing that it might be the last such party for a time, not knowing when or where the remaining Darlings and Stephenses would next see the departing Turners, and not knowing, as it turned out, the full extent of those who would be departing for Winnipeg the next day.

Many locations had been proposed for the special occasion. Many had been rejected. The Forks of the Credit, a parkland in the Caledon Hills, where after enjoying a picnic lunch in the wild grasslands, the men fished, the women picked flowers, and the children ran and swam—was rejected as too commonplace. We had already been there twice that summer.

A day's excursion to Niagara Falls was rejected by John and Bill, who desired a location at which they could swim. "Swim and not drown," John clarified.

A drive to Mono Mills, proposed by Jim, was rejected by everyone as being too distant. Jim always suggested activities that involved cars. He was a fanatic about automobiles. He loved looking at them, touching them, and studying them. Jim also loved drawing cars. He drew them as they then were in their big carriage-like shape, and he drew them longer and sleeker as he envisaged they might be in the future. He drew their entire bodies and he drew their parts; just their tires; just their dashboards; any parts. To Mother's chagrin, he loved to tinker with a car's engine, to change its oil, to lift, push, prod, and replace various engine parts. He thought nothing of getting his hands and, consequently, his clothes covered in grease and oil. While Jim was at home in the summer or on weekends through the school year, a family member's car never sat dirty in a garage or a driveway. Each was cleaned and polished as soon as Jim noticed a streak of dust or a splash of slush marring its shiny exterior.

But mostly, Jim loved being in a car. Until recently, he could only make a suggestion that the family take a trip in a car during the month that the Turners were in residence, since Uncle William was the only member of our family to own an automobile. The recent acquisition of a Ford touring car by Aunt Rose enabled Jim to refer to outings involving cars in the plural. Father thought it absurd that his sister should make such an acquisition, but his feelings toward the automobile softened when Aunt Rose welcomed Jim to drive it whenever a car was required by our immediate family.

"How about a picnic at Snell's Lake?" I suggested. "We can drive there. It's not too far. And it has a place to swim." Snell's Lake was a naturally occurring lake located in the middle of a large parkland about six miles north of Brampton. Named for the original owner of the land on which it was situate, the body of water provided Brampton with water to service its industrial and other needs. It was surrounded by both treed and cleared lands, also making it ideal for summer picnics, games of hide-and-seek, swimming, boating, and other amusements. It was the place I learned to swim and canoe. In fact, the two went hand in hand. For three years, my method of water buoyancy involved lying stomach down across two ropes strung between two cedar logs. My desire to join my friend Frances in her new red canoe, something Father would only permit if I could swim independently for fifty yards, propelled me to abandon the flotation device. So determined was I to join Frances in her canoe, I learned to swim and paddle in one day.

It was the Sunday before the leaving party. The entire extended family was sitting on our verandah. Children from down the street were playing a game of catch. The ball had just rolled in front of our house. Roy ran down the verandah steps to throw it back to them.

"Snell's Lake. That's a great suggestion, Little One," Jim said. He gave one of my ringlets a pull. I never minded the nickname or the little tug, when applied by my beloved brother. I knew that they were both meant as acts of endearment. Everyone concurred, and we began to make further plans until Ina interrupted us.

"Wait a moment, did you mean this coming Saturday?" When this was confirmed, we continued our planning. Aunt Rose thought a white linen picnic was in order. She suggested a few dishes.

"I think we should pick another location," Ina said, interrupting the menu planning. "You know Aunt Lil will not travel in an automobile."

That was true. Among Aunt Lil's many peculiarities was her philosophical and practical opposition to cars. Claiming automobiles to be a danger to passengers, pedestrians, horses, and our way of life, Aunt Lil refused to enter one. In this she was not entirely alone. Other people were also opposed to the proliferation of the automobile—though she was the only one in our family among that group. Examples abounded to justify their view of the safety risk. We regularly heard about cars crashing or overturning as a result of missed turns or burst tires or cars being driven at excessive speeds, all of which claimed the lives of one or more passengers.

"It's not the fault of the car!" Jim would exclaim when these examples were raised by critics. "It's the fault of the drivers."

Nonetheless, we conceded Ina's point about Aunt Lil's aversion and began to consider closer locations. None offered the water recreation sought by John and Bill. Finally, Bill asked whether anyone thought Aunt Lil would actually attend the leaving party. It was a good question. One could never be sure about anything pertaining to Aunt Lil. The fact that she said she would attend the party was no guarantee whatsoever. Her record in attending Turner leaving parties was quickly established. Of the seven that had been held since the Turners left Brampton in 1907, she had attended five. Of those, she had said she would attend three. Of the two that she did not attend, she had told us to expect her at one.

"I know she felt badly about her appearance and demeanour on the night the hostilities were declared," Ina said. "So I think it is reasonably certain she will attend. We should look for another location. John and Bill can swim another day."

We continued thinking. It was somewhat ironic that we had to go to such lengths to find a picnic location near a watercourse when Brampton had running through it two creeks. Unfortunately, neither one of them served as a location for water pleasure, and one of them, the Etobicoke, which ran through the downtown area and frequently flooded, was often a cause of extreme displeasure. The flats that surrounded the creek did provide a recreational use, including a place to throw balls and climb trees, but swimming in the creek itself was out of the question. Strong currents made it dangerous when it was fast-moving; pollutants made it dangerous when it was slow-moving.

The neighbouring children had switched to playing tag. Three of them were running toward us, the "it" child gaining on the first two. Eventually, Mother spoke. "You know, the McKechnies go to Snell's Lake almost every Saturday in the summer. I expect that if we take a couple of the McKechnie girls in one of our cars, they will take Aunt Lil and one of our party in their carriage." The McKechnies still kept their horses. Our family was unique among our neighbours in having neither a car nor a horse.

Considering the matter settled, menu planning resumed among the women. Jim began a discussion among the boys about other activities to be undertaken at the party, including, he proposed, a game of baseball.

* * *

We were all delighted on the day of the leaving party, when two hours prior to our designated departure time, Aunt Lil arrived at our house, her carpet bag in hand. She looked far less deranged than the last time we had seen her, the green of her long-sleeved wool jacket complimenting her ankle-length green serge skirt. Her red hair, though quite visible, was loosely caught up in a tall felt hat.

She was delighted to be conveyed to Snell's Lake in the McKechnies' horse-drawn, low-down democrat. She flatly refused all suggestions that she change her attire into something cooler. It was nearly eighty degrees, and it was not yet noon. She declared her ensemble to constitute her picnic clothes. A suggestion that I carry her carpet bag upstairs into the room in which she would spend the night was similarly rebuffed. She would not put me to the trouble. I silently groaned. I could not help but think of the last time she had taken that bag to a social outing. While she and the rest of my family socialized with others, I was required to stay in one place and watch it.

Aunt Lil and I were the first of our party to arrive at the lake and its popular picnic area. Blankets of various colours dotted the ground before us. A large party was gathering just to the right of the entrance area. The signs posted indicated it was the summer picnic of St. Mary's Church. One of the signs listed the games to be played by the parishioners. In addition to the usual dashes (segregated by distance, age, and sex), wheelbarrow races, broad jump contests, and swimming races, there was a fat men's race, a married men's race, a needle threading contest, and a contest to catch a pig.

Aunt Lil and I found a spot we considered to be ideal. It was large enough to accommodate our party, close enough to the lake to view the swimming members of our family, and not too far from the parking area to carry the burgeoning picnic baskets once they arrived. Aunt Lil and I laid out the three blankets with which we had been entrusted and waited for the remaining members of our family.

The car driven by Uncle William was the next to arrive. Aunt Lil and I waved him, Roy, Bill, and Ina to the area we had reserved, excited about what we considered to be its ideal location. Ina, unfortunately, thought otherwise. It was too close to the blankets of other families. It did not have the right vantage point over the park. The ground below the blankets was too lumpy.

"Look at that stand of trees over there," she said, pointing to a spot quite some distance away. "Look how even the terrain appears there. We'll have some privacy. Father will be able to make a speech. You know how he likes to do that. The swimmers can easily walk back to the lake after we eat."

"Over there?" I exclaimed. "It's half a mile away. You can't expect the boys to carry the picnic baskets all the way over there."

This statement had all the markings of a challenge to Roy and Bill. They liked the look of the distant location. A baseball diamond could easily be created next to it. They committed to carry the heavy baskets. Ina pulled up the three blankets, and we walked to the more distant location, eventually being joined by the rest of our party.

With so much space around us, we were able to assemble the blankets in a long line before spreading a length of white linen across them and laying out the china and silver. As we ate cold duck slices with orange sauce, sausages wrapped in pastry, potato salad with watercress and bacon, a salad of carrots and raisins, another salad of green beans and pimento, and a selection of three cheeses, our conversation occurred much as it would have had we eaten at home.

"You'll never guess who I saw today," Uncle William said excitedly. We knew he had spent the morning with Richard Blain.

"Old Andrew Foster." We looked at him blankly. "You remember him. He was born in Brampton. Left it when he was quite young, I'll admit. But Charlotte, you've heard me speak of him, and Roy, you've met him a few times. He manages the movement of supplies for the CPR—the supplies the railway needs and the transport of difficult customer supplies." Neither Roy nor Aunt Charlotte displayed any signs of recognition. He continued. "He gets grain from more distant grain elevators; gets it to more difficult ports. He organizes special routes and processes when the usual ones won't do. He's quite clever."

Roy nodded. He had no recollection of the man. As few of us could quite fathom the difficulty of his position and none of us could fathom the name or the face, no one had a response worthy of the excitement of Uncle William's declaration. Finally, Aunt Charlotte asked Uncle William where he had seen Andrew Foster.

"Here in Brampton! He lives in Toronto but has family here. Wanted to see them before he heads off to Valcartier."

"Valcartier!" Roy said, the conversation now taking what he considered to be an interesting turn. "Is he enlisting? Isn't he a little old? I gathered he was your age."

"Thank you for that," Uncle William said. "Yes, he is enlisting, but not as a general recruit. He is going to be assuming a leadership role in a special division called the Canadian Army Supply Corps, or the CASC. His detachment within it is called the Railway Supply Detachment." John and Jim, who both loved trains, now became interested as well. "The division will be responsible for the movement of materials–guns, food, bandages, lumber, everything required—and to the movement of men from Canada all the way to the battle lines. It will also be responsible for the movement of men back again from those lines, including injured men. He needs smart men to join the corps—men who understand how to move materials and people."

"Ah," said Roy. "Now I understand why such an old man is enlisting. I couldn't picture him in a combat role."

Uncle William ignored that, knowing that of course there would be many older men serving in senior combat roles. "Roy that is exactly what you have been doing with grain in the past two years working part-time with me. I wonder if you shouldn't think of joining the division. Mr. Foster will be at Valcartier for the next month. You should meet with him there!"

The statement had an equal and opposite effect on two people at our picnic. Thinking that such a position would better keep Roy out of harm's way, Aunt Charlotte was quick to encourage him to consider the opportunity. For that exact same reason, Roy refused.

"Sounds like a desk job to me," he said. "No thank you. They need brave men on the battle lines; men willing to hold and shoot a gun. That's where you'll find me."

Aunt Charlotte's shoulders slumped a little. But only a little. She was not surprised Roy would take that position. When she heard what came next, she realized it likely did not matter. The positions were equally dangerous.

"A desk job? Well, I suppose, but the desk may well be at the battle lines—or very near them. Some of their work will be done in England, but much of the supply management will occur near the men in combat. The members of the corps carry a gun; they receive full combat training. Think about it. At the very least, meet with Mr. Foster when you get to Valcartier."

Of all those in attendance, the only one who seemed not to be following the conversation about the movement of war supplies and men was Ina. She had not uttered a single sentence during the entire meal. Her attention seemed focussed on something closer to our original picnic location. Jim noticed it too.

"Ina," he said as the women began to scrape the picnic dishes. "Go see if any of the McKechnies want to join our baseball game. We could use a few more players." Ina hesitated but then agreed. By the time she returned, ten minutes later, Jim and Roy had established the baseball diamond, employing four small burlap bags of sand.

Only Katie McKechnie accompanied Ina back to our location. Her sisters could not be convinced to leave their picnic blankets. With similar refusals to play provided by Father and Uncle William (there was never any suggestion that the ladies would play), we were eight players. Roy quickly divided us into two teams of four. Not the best, he declared, but we would have fun.

We did have fun—for about three innings. Jim and Roy, the two team captains, each hit a home run. Jim might have scored a second if Ina had not caught the ball he hit in his very glove, loaned to her while he was at bat. I stole a base, and so did Hannah. In the third inning, Bill hit a long ball, which bounced on the ground just behind Katie. Before she could retrieve it, she screamed. Running toward her, with a pack of eight boys in its pursuit, was a small pink pig covered in some kind of slime. John, who was in the process of stealing third base, did not look back. He ignored Katie's scream and would have made it to home plate had the greasy piglet not crossed his path. John went flying. The pig touched home plate, as did the eight pursing boys.

"Catch the pig," Ina announced, stating the name of the game they were playing. It had clearly gotten out of hand.

"I'm not sure that they will," Bill said.

"Say," I said to Ina as we watched the group recede in the distance. "Isn't that Michael at the back of the group?"

"I have no idea," Ina said, moving to check on John.

We played one more inning before our game was interrupted again. The piglet had doubled back and was once more running toward us. "Catch it!" the boys yelled. "Catch it!" I wondered how they expected us to do so, when I saw, approaching us from the other direction, a number of older men, one holding a leather halter and a towel. That man, who appeared to be a farmer, kneeled down on the ground before reaching our baseball diamond. Within minutes, he had the piglet in the towel.

"Suffice it to say, you lost the game, boys!" shouted the man with the greasy piglet. He and the other men began walking back to the church group near the parking area.

"I'm not sure we should go back," one of the church boys said to no one in particular.

"Don't go back!" Jim cried. "Harry! Michael! Sam!" he called, referring to those he knew by name. "Stay and play with us. We'll reconstitute the teams. The Methodists versus the Catholics. You good for a game?" They were. Introductions were quickly made, a coin was tossed, and the Methodists lined up to take the bat.

The remaining portion of our game took on a very different character. The St. Mary's team, being comprised of male members mostly the size of

Roy and Jim, assumed they would have a clear advantage over our team. In that, they underestimated the athletic abilities of both the male and female descendants of my sportsman grandfather, Jas Stephens. Our knowledge that the St. Mary's team members had not even been able to capture a piglet led to a high degree of confidence on the part of the Methodists.

Eventually, our little game became the entertainment for the rest of our family, a good number of the St. Mary's parishioners who came in search of their missing boys, and dozens of others at the lake that day. It was a good game, with each team leading at various points.

After nine innings, the score was tied and we agreed to end it that way. The most interesting aspect from my perspective was not the home runs made, the other runs earned, the fly catches, or the number of strikes. The most interesting aspect was a small event that occurred at first base about halfway through the game. The Methodists were at bat. The bases were loaded. There were two outs. Ina bunted the ball just beyond first base, which was then being manned by Michael. He slipped back to retrieve the ball as she ran for the base. He arrived back at it before she did, ball in hand. At full flight, she ran toward the base, where he caught her as she collided with him. I could not help but notice that his arms were around her approximately one second longer than necessary; that she blushed when she was ruled to be out; and that she smiled when our bases were emptied. As everyone else changed positions, I thought I was likely the only one to notice it. In that, I forgot the observant nature of my aunts.

* * *

We did not get home until about eight o'clock that evening. The day had been hot, and our house, so long closed up and empty, was stuffy. After opening the second floor windows, Mother and Aunt Charlotte joined Ina, me, Aunt Lil, Uncle William, and Father on our verandah. Jim had left for Millie's house. Aunt Rose, Hannah, and John were at their house. Bill and Roy were there too, packing their belongings in preparation for their departure the next morning. Aunt Lil sat on two of the four matching wicker armchairs. True to her word, Aunt Lil had not once the entire afternoon, despite the temperature rising to over eight-five degrees, removed her heavy jacket.

"The house will be cooled down in no time," Mother said as she and Aunt Charlotte claimed the last two armchairs. Father and Uncle William stood leaning against the railing, each with a pipe in hand. I was perched on a small stool next to Aunt Lil. Ina sat on the chaise lounge, her right leg causing it to swing gently back and forth.

Although our verandah was the location of many lively conversations, it did not appear that it would be so that evening. The activities of the day had deprived us of much of our remaining energy. Aunt Lil and Aunt Charlotte stared into the star lit sky beyond the verandah's roof. Eventually, Aunt Lil broke the silence by beginning a conversation, high on the outlandish scale.

"Ina," she said, "I am a little vexed with you."

"With me, Aunt Lil? What did I do?" Ina was clearly surprised by any suggestion that she would annoy her favourite aunt.

"Surely, dear sister," Aunt Charlotte interjected, directing her statement toward Aunt Lil, "this is not something to be discussed at this time." She furrowed her eyebrows and nodded slightly, identifying me and the gentlemen on the verandah as those who should not be present for such a conversation.

"I don't know what you mean, Charlotte," Aunt Lil replied. "I am certainly qualified to determine whether it is the appropriate time to speak about a matter with my niece." Although the conversation may have begun as one between Aunt Lil and Ina, by this point everyone on the verandah was following it.

"As you say," Aunt Charlotte conceded. "Sometimes discretion is the better part of valour, but I share your vexation, so do go on."

"I've upset both of you?" Ina cried. "But how?" Aunt Charlotte deferred to her elder sister.

"Dear Ina, it became very evident to me at the lake today that you have a secret you have been keeping from me. I'm hurt that you did not confide in me earlier."

"Confide in you?" Aunt Charlotte again interjected. "You are vexed because Ina kept a secret from you? Surely, Lillian, you are more vexed by the subject of the secret than by the fact that it was kept."

"The subject of it? Not at all," Aunt Lil replied.

Father and Uncle William looked at each other in complete ignorance. "What the deuce are you talking about?" Father asked irritably. "I'm concerned if Ina has caused either of you offence, but for the life of me I have no idea what secret she has kept from you."

"You have no idea, Jethro?" Aunt Charlotte asked. Father replied in the negative.

"You should know, Jethro, that Ina has a beau, and he is entirely unsuitable," Aunt Charlotte said in an upbraiding tone.

Mother rose from her chair, and after vacillating over who most required her support—Father or Ina—joined Ina on the chaise. I could tell that Mother was not completely surprised by Aunt Charlotte's accusation.

Uncle William turned to Father. "At times like this, I am most relieved to have only sons. I think I will take my pipe and go for a walk. Join me, Doc, if you like. It sounds like the ladies have this well in hand." Father hesitated only momentarily before following Uncle William down the remaining verandah steps. Ina shrank into Mother's arms.

"Charlotte, why do you say that he is unsuitable?" Aunt Lil asked. "He appears to be a nice boy. He comes from an old Brampton family." In those days, an "old Brampton family" was a proxy for a "good Brampton family." This was not to say that newcomers could not also be good Bramptonians—they just had to work harder to prove their worthiness. "Things like that don't matter to me," Aunt Lil continued, "but I know they matter to you."

"Yes," Aunt Charlotte replied. "They matter a great deal but…"

"His family is an old Brampton family. His great-grandfather was brother to John Lynch, one of Brampton's first settlers." In her history teacher sort of way, Aunt Lil laid out the key facts. John Lynch had settled in Brampton 1819. He was a great promoter of the area, prodigiously writing advice to early settlers as to what to plant, where to live, and what to build in order to make their life in the colonies a success. Together with his brother-in-law, John Scott, in 1839 he established a brewery and an ashery. Within fifteen years, he left that business and became a real estate broker and land conveyancer, coming to own great tracts of Brampton land. He advocated for the incorporation of the village and became its first reeve. He was an active justice of the peace for twenty-five years and was instrumental in bringing the railway to Brampton.

"None of that matters to me, of course," Aunt Lil concluded. "What matters is that he is kind to Ina, which he seems to be, and that he makes her happy, which he seems to do."

"I am glad you noticed that," Aunt Charlotte replied, in a scandalized tone. "Did you notice the team he played for today?"

"Of course I did. The St. Mary's team."

"Exactly. That young man is a papist. And a relation of John Lynch! Heavens. The Lynches aren't just any Catholics. They are the preeminent Catholics of Brampton." Then, demonstrating that she too was once a teacher, Aunt Charlotte continued. "Was it not John Lynch who in the mid-1860s donated the land on Centre Street for the construction of Brampton's first Catholic church—Guardian Angels—and its Catholic cemetery?"

I recalled what I knew about the Guardian Angels Church. It was burned to the ground on Orangemen's Day, July 12, 1878. The devastation of the fire was complete in part because the rope in the bell tower of the fire station was off its runner when the fire was first reported.

"But what is the harm if he is Catholic, Charlotte?" Aunt Lil queried. "Why should that matter? You are all Christians. I have never understood your commitment—or our brother's commitment—to this Protestant–Catholic divide." I looked at Ina. Her face was buried in her hands, resting on Mother's shoulder. I liked Michael Lynch, and I did not care that he was a papist. I also liked the new Ina—the Ina with Michael as a beau. She was much nicer to be with. She was almost kind to me. I did not relish a return of the old Ina—the Ina without Michael. So I ventured into the discussion, recalling facts I surreptitiously learned many years ago.

"I agree with Aunt Lil," I said. A minor could go very wrong in our family in disputing the position of an elder, but one generally had a hope of avoiding censure when the view was supported by at least one adult in the conversation. "There are other good Catholics in Brampton, and some of them are even of old families. And if Ina and Michael marry, then he will become Methodist." In Brampton, it was the custom that the husband joined the wife's church after they wed. Astonishment greeted my declaration. Even

Ina raised her head and uncovered her face to hear my oration. Believing I needed to educate my sister, mother, and aunts, I went on.

"Look at Mr. Gilchrist," I offered slightly louder, more confidently. "He was born and raised a Catholic. He became a Primitive Methodist later in his life, and look at all of the good things he did for Brampton. He was a town councillor and a Member of the Provincial Parliament and a businessman who employed many people. And he donated the concert hall to the town."

They continued to stare at me. I thought more examples were needed, so I continued. "And even though he was not Baptist, he donated the land down the street to that congregation for the construction of their church." The fact that he also donated the land for the Primitive Methodist Church did not seem particularly noteworthy, given that he was of that congregation. So I did not mention it.

They continued to look bewildered, and so I offered my last salvo. "And even though he was born Catholic, he donated the stone that was used for the construction of the Presbyterian Church."

At that Mother stood up. Mother was a model of tolerance. Many people told me that she was the sweetest person they knew. She certainly was the sweetest person I knew. Although she was sometimes stern with me, she was never cross. I knew that she did not share the prejudiced views of Aunt Charlotte and Father. As she walked slowly toward me, I rose to receive the embrace I was sure would accompany a compliment on my brave and principled stand.

But Mother stopped her approach too far away to take me in her arms, and her eyes, when cast upon me, were anything but proud.

She lifted her right hand and slapped me hard across the face. It was the first time anyone had ever struck me. My eyes filled with tears. My hand rose to touch my smarting cheek. "My dear," she said in a cold voice I barely recognized, "wherever did you get those notions? That man made no such donation to the Presbyterian Church. Don't let me or your grandfather ever hear you speak that way about that man again!" She turned and went inside, the screen door slamming behind her.

Ina stopped seeing Michael Lynch. When the Turners left for Winnipeg the next day, Ina went with them. It was a long time before I again uttered the name of Kenneth Gilchrist. But Mother's admonition never left me. "Don't let me *or your grandfather* ever hear you speak that way about that man again!" Had Mother just given me a piece in the puzzle that was the mystery of my grandfather and the Presbyterian Church? I did not know, but I was once again determined to find out.

Chapter 4

THE KNITTING CLUB

The declaration of hostilities that brought an immediate call to arms for men brought a no less immediate call for women. In the case of women, the call was for arms, or more particularly, *for* their arms and their hands. Though feminine hands could be put to many useful pursuits in support of the war, among my family and friends the initial pursuits revolved around sewing and knitting—neither of which appealed to me in the least.

As local militia regiments began to parade, waiting for their eventual muster, the president of the local Women's Institute sent a telegram to Colonel Sam. It announced the willingness of the Institute's members to immediately commence the creation of housewives (small cases to hold needles, thread, and other sewing notions), holdalls (shoulder bags to carry personal possessions), and stomach belts (that would similarly carry personal possessions, although at a different body location), all items found particularly useful by the local men who had fought in the Boer War. Replying through his director of clothing and equipping, Colonel Sam expressed his appreciation to the ladies of Brampton but advised that such items, should they be required, would be obtained through government contracts. He would gladly advise them if their services were required at any point in the future.

The Brampton women did not await his further advice. They knew nothing about the director of Clothing and Equipping's contractual processes, but they knew about men. They knew that those men Colonel Sam had committed to send overseas would have two feet, two hands, a chest, and a head, and they knew that those appendages would need to be kept warm and dry. Before the end of August, the Women's Institute, in conjunction with other charities, began the efforts that would eventually see the women of Brampton sew or knit over forty-seven thousand items for the men at the front. In achieving this, the Institute accepted the kind offers of time from some women, extended "invitations" to ladies who had not yet offered their time, and pressed into action women and girls who had not otherwise made offers or accepted their kind invitations.

Mother's involvement in the effort came primarily from her membership in the local branch of the Women's Christian Temperance Union. A supportive, although not a strident member of the WCTU, Mother had always been a willing foot soldier, occasionally hosting meetings at our home, participating in letter-writing campaigns, and contributing goods to support fundraising efforts. By 1914, the work of the WCTU in Peel County was largely complete, since the county, like hundreds of others in Ontario, was by then dry. Aside from suppressing any efforts to repeal the designation previously achieved by a vote of the electors and exposing to the authorities occasional illegal sales that came to their attention, the members of the WCTU were without a cause. With determination, they took on the challenge of keeping our men at the front warm. It would be some time before the WCTU members learned that the fighting men they sought to keep warm in their barracks and trenches with wares they worked so hard to make were being further warmed with shots of the liquid they had worked so hard to banish.

The prospect of joining her fellow WCTU members in sewing for the men overseas suited Mother well. She was, after all, an excellent seamstress, sewing nearly all of the clothes she wore and those worn by Ina and me. She knew that she was a far better seamstress than she was a letter-writing advocate for temperance. Sewing for the enlisted men suited Mother for another reason as well: she could participate in the activity without making any declaration as to her support or lack thereof for the war effort. No matter which camp one fell into (and to be clear, there were very few in the opposition camp), one wanted our enlisted men to be kept warm and dry. In sewing for the men, Mother did not have to be more supportive of the war than was her husband.

Mother assumed that I would share her enthusiasm to support our men and so invited me to join her at a party the Institute was hosting one afternoon in the third week of August. It would be the first of many such parties, all to occur on Thursdays. My summer days were usually occupied in part attending at-home teas or other social outings with my mother. Looking on this suggestion in the same way, I was initially indifferent.

"What kind of a party is it, Mother?" I asked. It was not a question of evaluating the invitation. Generally, I took the suggestions of my parents as instructions. It did not occur to me to reject my mother's invitation. I wondered if the party might involve making bandages or packing up cigarettes. I recalled hearing that the Women's Institute organized parties of this nature during the Boer War.

"It's called a cutting-out party. We're going to assist in the sewing of warm shirts for the men to wear under their uniforms."

I looked at her, dumbfounded.

"It's quite easy, really," she added.

"Mother," I said slowly, "you know that I can't sew."

"Yes, you've told me that for years, although goodness knows I began sewing when I was much younger than you, reapplying buttons, simple mending, even sewing straight lines with the machine." I could feel my temperature beginning to rise. She changed tacks. "But in this case, you will not need to sew. Others will do the sewing." The panic within me began to recede.

"All you need to do is fold the fabric in the right way, lay the pattern on the folded fabric, and then pin the three layers together and—"

"Pin the pattern on the fabric?" I interjected. My temperature began to rise again.

"Yes. Pin it. Using straight pins." Sweat began to form on my brow. "First you will pin the pattern in place, likely applying ten or twelve pins per shirt shape, firmly pushing the sharp pins through both layers of fabric and the pattern, and then bringing them up the other side."

I rested my chin on my fist. There was no other way to keep my neck erect.

"Then you use the large sewing shears, cutting the two layers of fabric as close as you can but not over the pattern." I moved my hand from my chin to my mouth. I was not sure I could keep my dinner down.

"Then you pull out all of the pins and put them into the pin cushion so that—Jessie, where are you going?"

I ran to the kitchen, through the pantry, and up the maid's stairs to the bathroom on the second floor.

"I'm sorry your dinner didn't agree with you," Mother said fifteen minutes later as I lay on my bed across from the bathroom. With Ina away in Winnipeg, I felt that I could truly call this bed that we ordinarily shared "my" bed. She was wiping my forehead with a damp cloth.

"Mother, I won't be able to go with you to the cutting-out party tomorrow," I said. "I won't be well enough."

"Nonsense," she said. "I'm sure it's just something you ate. By tomorrow you'll be as good as new. You'll see."

But it was not just something I ate. The fear I had of sewing shears, needles, straight pins, and pincushions was nearly pathological. It was also a secret—one of the few secrets in our family that was mine to keep. It arose on a summer day when I was six years old, also on a late August day, just before I began school. Bob Parker, the superintendent of the Peel County Jail, or the "Governor" as he liked to be called, took it upon himself once a summer to disgorge to the local teenagers the circumstances that led to the incarceration of one of the jail's inhabitants. The clarity of his oration and his penchant for details made his macabre accounts a highlight of the teenagers' summers. In addition to filling a good two hours of time on a summer afternoon, they provided the boys with an opportunity to demonstrate their bravery to a girl of their liking (the accounts never scared them) and the girls with an opportunity to sit closer to a boy of their liking (perhaps even taking his hand or arm). The Governor looked forward to the narrations as well, since they gave him an opportunity to describe to these near adults who were the offspring of the local ratepayers and hence his employers the depraved men he kept from their midst.

The recountings were not intended to be heard by young children. My father forbade me to listen to them. But on that sunny August afternoon, I succumbed to the entreaties of my friend Archie to hide behind the jail's concrete steps, located just down the road from our home, and listen to the Governor's account of the first occupants of Alderlea, the Italianate villa-style mansion, constructed in 1867 at the top of a hill that once included the lands later known as Gage Park. It was from that account that I learned of Mr. Gilchrist's contributions to Brampton's many churches, including the donation of the stone for the Presbyterian Church—a credit to which Mother took such great exception.

In addition to learning about its original owner, Kenneth Gilchrist, Esq., a businessman, politician, and philanthropist, we learned about one of his employees and that employee's two children. The employee, an Irish immigrant, came to Brampton in 1873. He was immediately hired to serve as the Gilchrists' gardener and mechanical man. Within a few months, he had married the Gilchrists' seamstress. They were married less than a year when he lost her in childbirth. The father and the two boys continued to reside in the mansion, working as groundskeepers and mechanics, until the owners decided to redecorate and replace all of the drapery made by the boys' deceased mother. The father bought a two-storey building not far from Alderlea. From its street level, they would operate a mechanical business fixing iron works and engines. They would make their residence on the second floor above the shop.

The father's plan only partly came to fruition. The dreams of the elder of the twins were haunted by his mother, who in his nightmares forced him to watch her sew. He realized that he could not leave the mansion. He agreed to stay on to carefully dispose of the draperies his father could not. But the nightmares did not abate. In his attempt to satisfy the mother that haunted him, he was driven to one act of depravity after another, initially abducting an eight-year-old girl from outside the local Anglican Christ Church and forcing her day after day to sew for him in the Alderlea attic. After a year of this torture, she killed herself with the large sewing sheers he had inadvertently left in her unsupervised space. Attempting to replicate the heinous exploit, his second victim died before being delivered to the attic. He was found out, captured, and jailed. In the process his clothes were torn. After confessing the intimate details of his life and his deeds to the Governor and announcing that his twin brother would take up the cause he was forced to abandon, he asked to be provided with some thread, pins, and needles in order that he could repair his clothes before facing the gallows. When the Governor next came upon him, his prisoner was dead, the straight pins puncturing his heart, like pins in a cushion.

The account would merely have been the subject of my nightmares had I not been personally acquainted with one of the surviving subjects. Although the Governor did not identify his prisoner or the prisoner's family members by name, I had no doubt who they were and where the father and surviving son lived.

Suffice it to say that I made no great contribution to the war efforts at the two cutting-out parties I attended. My hands were too shaky to hold the pattern in place, my fingers too clammy to push the pins through the pattern and fabric, my breathing too frantic to hear the instructions, and when my skin turned more shades of green than my Aunt Lil had in her entire wardrobe, I was on each occasion sent home. My contribution to the war effort would have to take a different form.

* * *

While my mother was an excellent seamstress, she was merely a fair knitter. In our family, we never had more sweaters, scarves, hats, or mittens than we strictly required, and the workmanship of those we had would never have been awarded prizes at the annual fairs. My mother's fingers, so precise at the keys of the piano and organ, failed her when it came to manipulating knitting needles, where they seldom followed the knit, pearl, skip, yarn over patterns she tried to follow. Her tension was not even. Her colour choice was poor. Frequently, our sweaters had one sleeve wider than another, were too baggy at the bottom, and too tight at the top. Dropped stitches that could barely be discerned when the garment was worked on became gaping holes with repeated wearing and washings.

Nonetheless, determined that none of our boys should have cold feet on her account, Mother began to knit socks. She was not alone in this. Whereas prior to the commencement of the war, a Brampton woman could happily sit in a parlour, a sitting room, or a veranda holding only a cup of tea or glass of lemonade, that became seemingly impossible by September 1914. Unless one was at a fancy soirée or at a dining room table, nearly every woman seen sitting would be seen knitting—usually socks, in various stages of completeness, supported by three short double-ended needles and a fourth one working its way into the position of one of the other three. For four years, the click-click-click sound of working needles accompanied nearly all of our conversations.

As for me, I recognized the difficulty one would have puncturing one's epidermis with a knitting needle—even the small knitting needles that produced socks. There was not, to my knowledge, a cushion that would support protruding knitting needles. I had never heard or read about the death of a man by knitting needles. Nonetheless, I was no more inclined to knit for the sake of our men than I was to sew.

I was not the only woman in our family who refused to knit or sew for this great cause. It was an aversion shared by my Aunt Rose, father's youngest sister, although for entirely different reasons. She had become a widow four years earlier on the death of James Darling, her much older husband, a successful businessman, local politician, and active community member. He left her and their two children, Hannah and John, well provided for.

Though Aunt Rose wore the black widow's weeds that were to be her uniform for the remaining years of her life, in most other ways she defied the stereotypical image attributed to widows of the time. In part this was due to her relatively young age. She was but forty-three when the sad status befell her. As a child, that age seemed quite advanced to me, but there were few among her peer group who claimed a similar situation.

She was also distinguished by her intelligence, particularly concerning financial matters. People about the town frequently spoke of it, although, again, as a child I did not see it. In fact, my perception was just the opposite. My earliest memories of my aunt were of her arriving at our house carrying an extra joint of meat, an extra basket of apples, an extra bolt of fabric, all purportedly delivered to relieve her from the errors she had made in her own purchases.

Most atypical about her persona was her strength of character. She refused to be dependent on others. She rarely sought their opinions, and when they were provided without solicitation, she was only occasionally guided by them.

Following Uncle James's death, my father briefly and happily assumed the role as the male head of her household. Father was confident that the death of

James Darling would leave Rose dependent on him for guidance on matters financial, political, and familial—a position he desired to hold. In this, he was severely disappointed. Within days of the commencement of her widowhood, it became clear that while Aunt Rose was prepared to receive her brother's advice and opinions, she felt no compunction to accept or agree with them. The improvement in my father's humour and the more generous approach to life he assumed on his brother-in-law's demise were dissipated measure for measure with each step my aunt took toward her own independence.

Aunt Rose's intelligence and self-confidence that proved a disappointment to my father were a marvel to her husband's executors. They proposed that Aunt Rose sell the large house on Wellington Street in which she and her two young children resided, his bakery business, and the numerous investment properties her husband held in and around Brampton. The family home was large and its upkeep prohibitively expensive, to their way of thinking. As for the businesses and investments, the revenue that could be garnered by more passive investments could, in their view, generate a more stable income from which she could support herself and her children. Aunt Rose would hear nothing of it. She and the children would remain in the large home. She would keep the bakery business and the farms just outside of Brampton, trusting them all to competent management.

In fact, those businesses produced enough income not only to support Aunt Rose and my cousins, John and Hannah, but also enough to allow her to make additional investments. As the years went on, Aunt Rose developed quite the reputation as a buyer, seller, and mortgagee of Brampton real estate.

"Rose, don't you want to join the other members of the Women's Institute in their efforts to bring comfort to our men?" Mother asked. We were sitting on the lawn side of the L-shaped verandah of Aunt Rose's home. Hannah and John were playing tennis in front of us. As usual, Hannah was winning.

"No, I am not!" Aunt Rose said with great conviction. This was not the first time the two sisters-in-law had had this conversation. "With my resources, I feel I should be making a greater contribution to the war effort. I know many women have only time to devote to the cause, but I have been blessed with other resources, and I think I would be of more use to the war effort if I properly employed them."

Any talk of her greater resources—which my father took to mean the money and capital that had once been her husband's—made my father uncomfortable. "What the deuce do you plan on doing, Rose?" Father asked. "You can't buy an army."

"No. I can't do that. But I can help create the things that an army needs."

"Are you going to become a munitions manufacturer?" Father asked sarcastically.

"Yes," she said. "Yes. I just might." We looked at her in astonishment.

"Really, Rose, I don't think one can equate the baking of bread and pies with the manufacture of army shells," Father said, referring to her bakery business.

"No. Of course, I know that. I won't manufacture them myself. I am considering going into partnership with an existing Brampton manufacturer."

"Heavens. What on earth could be produced for the war in this town?" Father asked, incredulous. "We manufacture footwear here, but I understand the contract to supply boots has been awarded to a company in Montreal. We make furnaces." In this he was referring to the Pease foundry managed by John Thompson, the father of my friend Jane. "I don't think they're going to need furnaces at the front."

"Exactly," Aunt Rose agreed. "But maybe one of those manufacturers would like to produce something required by Colonel Sam. If so, their factories are going to have to be converted. I have the capital to help them make the required changes."

"Surely the government will pay for that, Rose," Mother offered. "What would they need your money for?"

"That's just it. The government will not pay for the conversion of the factories. To be awarded a contract, you must prove that you have the capacity to make the goods; only after that will the government consider awarding you a contract. I have looked into it."

"What if you convert the factory—say, the Pease foundry into a factory that can make bullets, and after you do that, you are not awarded the government contract?" Father asked. "Or you get the contract and then the war ends before the contract is complete?" It was October. Barely three months into the war, it was no longer expected to be over by Christmas of that year. It was hoped it would be over long before Christmas of the next.

"That is a risk. A big risk. But that is the risk that business people across the country are taking. They are being compensated for that risk in charging higher than usual prices. If I invest in those enterprises, I will charge higher than usual interest rates."

No one knew quite what to say to that.

* * *

It was knitting—the bringing together of strings of yarn to form a warm and useful piece of apparel or houseware—that nearly tore apart the relationship between me and my best friend, Jane. It started when we returned to school in September 1914. Jane I were then in senior third form, the beginning of our second year at Brampton Central School, our "middle" school, a large school to our minds. Covered in brick, it was an oddly shaped building, reflecting the numerous additions that had been made to the original two-storey, six-sided structure built in 1855. In 1868, two single-storey wings were added, flanking the original structure to the east and the west. With over five hundred registered pupils, it was not surprising that in 1914 another wing was being added.

The school was almost the same distance from my house as the Queen Street Primary School I attended for the first four years of my education. But the middle school was located north of my home, on Alexander Street, just off Main Street. I was able to walk to and from it twice a day far from the intersection of Queen and George Streets, far from the Kelly Iron Works Repair Shop that housed the father of the vile boy who had abducted the two young girls and far from its stoop and the twin brother of the vile boy, a man-boy of indeterminate age, who grunted and gesticulated at me—and only me—every time I passed his stoop. While Scary Scott's treatment of me was not a secret—others had noticed it—only the two of us knew why he singled me out, a young girl with long, brown, curly hair like that of his deceased demonic mother. The two other people who knew were dead. One was the vile man in the jail who before turning his heart into a pincushion said his brother would become the vessel to continue their mother's maniacal mission to abduct young girls with curly brown hair. The other was my friend Archie, who took the secret with him to his grave.

Though I no longer required the accompaniment of a friend as I walked to and from school, I was rarely without it. My neighbour and oldest friend, Frances, generally walked with me the first half of the way to our middle school. At the midway point, the corner of Main and Nelson, we were often met by our friend Jane, who would always assume a position on one side of me. Frances, who had walked by my side to that point, would continue on the other side of me, unless the sidewalk became too narrow, at which point Frances would fall in behind Jane and me. The reverse occurred as we walked home from school, Jane and I always in front until we arrived at Nelson and Main, Frances beside me if space allowed. The placement rules were unspoken but well understood. I was certain that Frances, who had been my devoted walking companion the prior four years, thought nothing of it.

Jane took up the knitting of scarves just before we returned to school. She considered the hobby a particularly delightful way to make a contribution to the war effort. She loved gathering different colours and textures of wool and organizing them in what she called "cheerful but masculine" stripes. So taken was she with the pursuit that she suggested at one point in early September that we organize a school knitting club.

"We can meet after class in one of the school rooms. We could knit together for an hour. Think how much we could contribute to the war effort," she said. She was in no way deterred by my lack of enthusiasm for her suggestion.

"Aren't there enough women knitting in the town?" I asked. "Maybe we could contribute to the war effort in another way? I heard that during the Boer War, women rolled and packed cigarettes for the fighting men. Maybe we could do that."

She looked at me as though I was quite queer. "You'd rather work with smelly brown tobacco than pretty soft wool? And who would want the cigarettes? None of our boys smoke."

That was true. But the older men did—men like my father and uncles. Some men smoked during the Boer War. Surely, some men would smoke during this war. While Jane was not enamoured with the suggestion, it was enough to end the conversation about the knitting club—at least for a time.

My hopes to entirely quash the notion were put asunder by the admission to our class at the beginning of October of a new student. When Elsa Strauss walked to the front of our class to introduce herself, I was immediately struck by the thickness that exuded from every feature. Her ankles, covered as they were in black stockings, bore no definable shape below her mid-calf grey A-line skirt. Her arms completely filled the sleeves of her cream-coloured, collared blouse. The wool vest she wore added thickness to her chest. But the thickest features by far were those on and around her face. Her eyes were big, with heavy lids; her nose was pudgy; her lips were full. The only features of her face that did not seem thick were her ears, which were merely big. Their extraordinary protrusion from her skull was noticeable but highly useful, I soon learned, as they worked in combination with the thickest feature of all: her long, dark blond hair. Elsa seemed to be in constant competition with her hair, pushing it as she spoke behind one ear and then the other, generally losing the fight to control it. I wondered that her hair was not tied back—perhaps its volume defied even that. The entire effect, though, was not unpleasant. Her features, so different from the slight figures held by Jane and me, were attractive in their own way on her tall, sturdy frame.

In a voice that initially quivered she told the forty students in our class that she was from Shelburne, north of Brampton, where her father had been a potato farmer. Their move to Brampton the day before had been precipitated by his appointment as the chief vegetable propagator at the Dale Estate. Her family was living in an apartment on the top floor of the old Haggert Iron Works building at Nelson and Main Street, above the Main Street facing Brampton Dairy. She had one brother, Wilfred, who had volunteered for the first contingent on the first day volunteers were accepted. Having completed basic training at Valcartier, including a great deal of marching and working with muskets and bayonets, he was at that moment on his way to England.

As Elsa spoke, I thought of Jane and her introduction to our class two years earlier. Jane and her brother Douglas had just moved to Brampton from Toronto. As the two stood at the front of our class introducing themselves,

I had a premonition. This girl Jane, then a complete stranger to me, and I would become the closest of friends. My home would be hers, and hers mine. We would attend university together. We would stand up for each other when we each wed. We would be godmothers to each other's children. We would spend our twilight years together, two otherwise lonely widows. As Elsa spoke, I had no similar premonition. From the moment she uttered her first words to us, I determined that I liked her little. With each passing day, I liked her less.

In this it appeared I was not alone. As Elsa walked by my desk on her way to hers at the end of my row, Ricky Dyck, who sat next to me, turned to Allan King, who sat behind him. "Do you smell sauerkraut?" Ricky asked, fanning away the air in front of his face.

"It's revolting," Allan replied, sniggering. It was a refrain and a gesture that they were to repeat on a near daily basis.

Jane, full of empathy for the new student, felt otherwise. She sought Elsa out at both morning and afternoon recess breaks that first day. The three of us stood together in the large schoolyard behind the school while Elsa went on and on about her brother Wilfred, how he had stood in line at the barracks for three days waiting for the doors to be open to those wanting to enlist; how proud his parents were of him; what he looked like in his military uniform.

When Elsa was not telling us what Wilfred did, she told us about what Wilfred said. "You have to serve your country, that's what Wilfred says." "One can't show fear in the face of the unknown, that's what Wilfred says." "Activation without preparation is the surest means to defeat, that's what Wilfred says." I was hard pressed to think of someone I had never met that I found as irritating.

I told my family about Elsa later that day. We were in the sitting room, Father and Grandpa each reading the afternoon newspapers, Mother knitting as she waited for our meal to finish cooking. Millie had just dropped by to pick up some cut-out fabric with which to assemble shirts. She came in "just for a minute" and sat down on the little sofa beside me. I was glad to see her. Ever since Jim went back to school in September, we had seen her less. The reason lay not just with the burden of his studies but with the part-time job he had commenced in September with Dr. Mahoney, a dentist in Weston, a town southeast of Brampton. Father thought the experience of working every Wednesday afternoon and all day Saturday would be beneficial to Jim's future career as a dentist practicing in association with him.

For as long as I could remember, Father had punctuated his sentences about his future dental practice as one that would be shared with Jim. There had been no need to hope for that matter. It was a *fait accompli*. Father's hope with respect to the practice was that it would one day be an association of three: Father, Jim, and my cousin, John. On that front, some hope was required. Father was not able to exert his will upon his nephew in the same way he could his son.

If the cost was not an object, Father might have sent Jim away to Philadelphia to obtain a further degree in dental studies, following his own educational trajectory. But cost *was* an object. Father had barely been able to afford the four years of tuition and board expended thus far on Jim. He could not afford a fifth year in the United States. Furthermore, it was well understood that every year Jim spent at university delayed the day that Ina could commence her university studies. As a young man, Father worked hard to put his three sisters through normal school, thus qualifying them to become teachers before they wed. He would offer his daughters no less.

"But why can't Jim just practice with Father?" I groused to Mother when I learned that the arrangement with Dr. Mahoney would deprive us of Jim's company on Friday evenings and during the day Saturday. I did not consider asking the question of Father. Doing so might be construed as questioning his judgement. One did not question Father's judgement.

"Jim and your father are going to practice together for the next twenty years or more," Mother said as we stood in the kitchen canning tomatoes. "Your father thinks it will be good for Jim to gain experience with someone else before they begin their practice together. It's just for eight months. After Jim graduates next April, he will be living back home again—or at least," she said, looking around to be sure that no one could hear our kitchen conversation "—at least he will be living in Brampton again." As much as I wanted to see Jim every day, I actually hoped that he would not be living at home again. By that point, he and Millie would have been sweethearts for three years. Mother and I hoped they would become more than that when Jim completed his education.

"I see you've been active with the council," Father said to Millie, pulling his pipe from his mouth and dropping the newspaper.

"Oh, yes. We know that the mayor and the council want us to increase our employment numbers. They also want us to employ more men on a full-time basis—provide them all with a living wage, as they say. We're doing our best, but it's hard to both increase the number of employees and increase the hours we give to all of them. The flower industry has been hit as hard by this economic downturn as many other factories and businesses." The Canadian economy, which had been so strong in the first decade of the twentieth century, had begun to decline in the second. Although Brampton, with its growing manufacturing base, was less impacted than some communities, by 1914 it too was experiencing a downturn.

"Maybe the war will help you out in this area," Father said. "Nothing like a war to kick-start an economy."

"You may be right. We're making a few other changes in light of the war." Millie was very knowledgeable about the Dale Estate. In addition to being a member of the Dale family, she worked in its business offices.

"I know you are," I said proudly.

"What do you know, Jessie?" Millie asked curiously.

I then told Millie and the rest of my family what I knew about Elsa Strauss, her potato-growing father, and his new position at the Dale Estate.

"I guess there are no secrets in this town!" Grandpa exclaimed.

There are a few, I thought, looking at him.

* * *

Although I did not particularly like Elsa Strauss, she was soon to be one of my constant companions. On her second day of school in Brampton, Jane invited Elsa to walk home with us. Since the building Elsa lived in was situated at the very intersection where Jane joined and left Frances and me, she was with us the entire time Frances and I walked with Jane. Initially, as we walked along Main Street, Jane in the lead, Frances behind, I was able to maintain the coveted position beside Jane. Jane and I turned our heads while walking to hear Elsa tell us the latest news from Wilfred: how he had embarked on the SS *Tyrolia* at Quebec; how the ship had been escorted by cruisers throughout its voyage to England; how he had exercised two hours each day on the ship. "You have to be in shape to fight in France, that's what Wilfred says," Elsa intoned.

But when the subject of our walks began to change, so did the order of our pairings. As we began to discuss not what was being done by those in the first contingent but rather what we at home could do to assist them, Elsa began to jostle me to a position behind her. For these discussions, she fully required Jane's attention, and Jane fully desired to provide it.

"We should do something to help the fighting men," Elsa agreed when Jane raised the subject. "Wilfred and the men would so appreciate receiving a little something to comfort them. Perhaps we could take up a collection and buy some chocolate for them."

"Chocolate. That sounds nice," Jane said, turning her head toward Elsa then walking behind me. "Much nicer than the cigarettes Jessie suggested." The notion was greeted by gales of laughter from Elsa and Frances. I looked down at my walking feet.

"I was thinking of something that would require a little more personal involvement," Jane said. She had the avid attention of Elsa and Frances. "I was thinking that we should send the men scarves; scarves that we ourselves knit."

"That's a great idea," Elsa said, pushing her hair behind her ears as she moved ahead of me. "I know that Wilfred and the men would appreciate receiving scarves we make. We could make hundreds!"

"Exactly," Jane said, stopping and looking fully at Elsa then directly beside her. Frances, who nearly bumped into Jane, had the good sense to question the number.

"How would the four of us make hundreds of scarves?" she asked. Four of us, I wondered. Frances had never knit anything in her life, and she knew that I had not either.

"It won't be just the four of us," Jane said enthusiastically, finally seeing an opportunity to realize the vision that came to her a month earlier. "There will be many more of us. We'll form a club. The Brampton Central School Knitting Club. We can meet in the school after classes two afternoons a week."

Elsa thought the idea was marvellous. Frances agreed that was the only way to make hundreds of scarves.

"The club will need a president," Elsa declared.

Jane saw the wisdom in that.

"It should be you!" Elsa proposed.

Jane agreed, trying to look reluctant. "Of course, I will need a vice-president," she said. Elsa volunteered with no measure of reluctance.

Later that week, the Brampton Central School Knitting Club was formed, with many happy members. Frances and I, having demurred from actually kitting, were assigned the task of seeking donations of wool for use by the knitters.

Thereafter, as we walked home from school, Jane remained in the lead. Her enthusiastic vice-president walked beside her. I fell in behind. Frances walked to my side. "Don't worry," Frances whispered to me, "you'll get used to it." She well knew how it felt to be relegated to the position behind.

Chapter 5

MORE USUAL THAN USUAL

During those first long months of the war, while Mother was altering her routine for the sake of the war effort, constantly sewing and knitting, my father, with many opportunities to do much for the war effort, made a virtue of carrying on life as usual, and he did it superbly!

His commitment to do so arose not from his lack of enthusiasm for the war (although he certainly had little of that) or his frugality (although he certainly had much of that). Father's approach was inspired by God himself, delivered through the words of the Brampton clergy and thereafter promoted as a motto of the town.

Brampton in 1914 was a town of churches. They were all Christian and mostly Protestant. Our family worshipped at Grace Methodist Church, one of the two Methodist churches in our small town, which prior to the 1884 union of the Methodist churches was of the Wesleyan variety. Church was a big part of our lives. Mother was the church organist, Father the choir leader, and Grandpa a member of the choir. On a typical Sunday, our family attended church three times: once in the morning, for a sermon; again in the afternoon, for Sunday school; and then finally, in the evening, for a concert or a cantata. Our minister, Reverend J. Bruce Hunter, was a recent graduate of divinity from the University of Toronto. Mother and Father considered him to be young and modern, but at thirty-three years of age, he seemed quite old to me. Reverend Hunter was an eloquent and energetic sermonizer. His words, when delivered in a sermon, a lesson, or a prayer, provided spiritual direction for the week to come.

In August 1914, every minister in Brampton preached about the war. Patriotism was not anathema to the church. From the pulpit and in their writings published in our local newspapers, our clergy led us in prayers for those in peril at sea or on land; those who, through the ravages of war, were sick, or hurt or hungry or scared; those without hope; and those who were grieving. We prayed for liberty and justice and the time when all nations could dwell together in peace. We were commanded to make the sacrifices that would be required of us but to live, to the greatest extent possible, as we usually would. We were to conduct our business, attend our schools, purchase our wares, and support our communities as we always had. To do otherwise would be to grant a victory to the enemy. From the second half of the clergy's command—Father, who did not want to be unpatriotic—took his lead. The phrase "business as usual" became Father's sword and his shield, and he wielded it not just against the enemy abroad but also the ally at home.

* * *

Father's prediction about the costs of war, delivered at Aunt Rose's table the night the hostilities were declared, was right. Our first eighteen boys were barely sent off when our citizens were asked to contribute to the costs of the war effort. Whether the requests came from neighbours or businessmen, from family or friends, from the federal government, the provincial government, the county government or from the king himself; whether the request was for time to raise funds, resources to raise funds, or the use of his name to raise funds, Father was resolute. He would give the minimum required. He would not provide a penny more or raise a hand to assist in the raising of a penny more. His view was as illogical as it was consistent. He did not support direct appeals to citizens to pay for the war, because expenses like that should be paid for by government. At the same time, he was opposed to any increase in local taxes, provincial taxes, or the creation of new federal taxes. Yet Father somehow made a virtue of his intransigence.

I first saw him don his armour one day in late August. Father, Grandpa, and I were sitting on the verandah. Mother was inside the house, writing a letter to Ina. It was nearly nine o'clock. The moon was full, though barely perceptible behind a film of wispy clouds. The air was muggy, cloying.

Dampness hung around us. As we sat silently, lost in our own thoughts, we watched rabbits run across the street and listened to cicadas in the trees.

Our ruminations were interrupted by Mr. Mara, the town's mayor. He was on his way home from a meeting at the Mississauga Golf Course in the south end of Peel, he explained, as he climbed the stairs to join us on the verandah. A new committee had been formed about which he was extremely excited. It had resolved to create the Peel Patriotic Fund. The fund would be used to purchase insurance policies on the lives of the boys overseas to ensure their medical needs would be covered if they returned home injured and that their wives and children would be supported if they did not return at all. The Metropolitan Life Insurance Company had agreed to pay out up to $1,000 per man.

"The premiums are dear," Mr. Mara said, "but not too dear considering what these men may sacrifice. Based on the current projections of the number of men who will enlist, the premium will be $14,651. Doc, we are hoping you could help us raise that."

Grandpa and I looked at Father. I was fairly sure I knew what he would say. I don't think his answer surprised Mr. Mara either. "You know, Walt, I feel I've already emptied the pockets of our citizenry—all the money we raised to send the Excelsiors out west earlier this year. I just can't go back to them now and ask for more handouts."

"Oh, no need for that," Mr. Mara responded, quickly disabusing Father of the notion of a personal appeal. "We're going to charge the property owners; add it to their local taxes. Just an increase on the mill rate."

"Higher taxes?" Father asked, scorn riveting his voice.

"Yes," Mr. Mara replied matter-of-factly. "We'll put forward a by-law to approve it."

"Do you think the people will support it?" Father asked, somewhat shocked at the very levy he had predicted earlier in the month.

"Well, Doc, that's where you come in. Everyone knows how....careful you are about tax dollars. Your support for this levy will go a long way in helping us get the by-law approved."

"Walt, I think that my greatest contribution to the war effort will be made in another way." Father's gaze was not on Mr. Mara as he uttered those words. It was on the front door of the home of our friends, the Hudsons, who lived down and across the street from us. Mr. Hudson was just entering his house. He was likely returning from the same meeting at the golf course. "It has to do with the high school, Walt. You'll hear more about it later."

"Imagine!" Father exclaimed after Mr. Mara was well down the street. "To think that I would ever advocate for a tax increase. And to think that fourteen thousand dollars will be enough!"

"What is it that you propose to do instead?" Grandpa asked.

"I plan to do business as usual," Father said. With that he stood and went to see Mr. Hudson.

* * *

Father was not the only one abiding by the business as usual motto. Previously scheduled work laying electricity in the addition to my school was proceeding. The fall fair was held in September as it always was. A new jewellery store had a grand opening. It was all very patriotic.

What Father proposed was not only to do the things he usually did, but to do them better. The first activity that fell into that orbit was the Annual Brampton High School Amateur Athletic Sports Competition. The competition was a great delight to the high school students who were accorded an afternoon's leave from school to participate (in the case of the boys) and to cheer (in the case of the girls). The first such competition was held in 1892. Not a year had been missed since that time. One might have thought it sufficient in meeting the business as usual objective simply to hold the event again and to hold it in the same place involving the same events as had been the case the previous twenty-one years. The problem was that like many events that are held year after year, this event had become somewhat moribund.

One evening earlier that summer before the hostilities commenced, while Frances and I were untangling our skipping ropes on her verandah, Mr. Hudson told Father that he was considering cancelling the annual sports competition. Father, who never liked to see the demise of anything related to sports and athletics, expressed surprise.

"I think the competition may be a bit tired. The attendance keeps declining. The number of students competing is decreasing, and the number cheering them on has fallen off at an even greater rate. And the teachers—they aren't in their classroom and they aren't on the field. We're paying them half a day to socialize with each other. If the competitors did not have sweethearts, there would be no one there to cheer them on. I think the students would be better off staying in class."

"Let's think about that," Father said. "I don't want you to cancel it just yet."

"Are you saying that as a friend or as the chairman of the High School Board?" Mr. Hudson asked.

"Both," Father replied.

Throughout the late summer and early fall, as the leaders of the county pressed its council to approve the by-law to fund the Peel Patriotic Fund, as Brampton formed an artillery club and the Brampton armouries were formed, as Britain incurred war costs of $55 per second, and as Prime Minister Borden travelled the country promoting the war effort, Father, Mr. Hudson, and a host of other Excelsiors Lacrosse Club members organized the highly successful twenty-second Annual Brampton High School Amateur Athletic Sports Competition. Following much advertising, the issuance of invitations to community members and the introduction of some new races, the competition was held on the Rosalie Park grounds. Hundreds of men paid ten cents for admission, though no amount had previously been charged. Hundreds of women gained admission free. Dozens of competitors and all of the other students and staff watched and cheered the competitors in twenty-three different events, one of which was specifically designated for girls. It was all very patriotic.

A few weeks later, By-Law 455, a by-law to raise a patriotic fund of $14,600 to assist in the defence of the British Empire, to support soldiers from Peel and their families, was unanimously approved by the Peel County Council. It was the first in the province, and ultimately, when no more insurance policies could be obtained (there being so many more soldiers and family members than originally conceived), it became part of a national fund. It was not enough. It was not enough by far. Sixteen months later, the electors of Peel agreed to participate in the national patriotic fund, contributing $50,000 per year, the entire amount of which would be added to the local tax bill.

* * *

The next request Father received to assist with wartime fundraising came from an entirely different quarter. Being issued by a person we all held so dear and being accompanied by genuine tears, I thought it might actually succeed. The maker of the plea was Millie. It came in November 1914. It was made in our sitting room.

By that time, Millie was such a regular Sunday diner in our home that when we met before or after a meal, we gathered in the sitting room, a casual room reserved for family, rather than the more formal parlour. The frequency with which she dined with us arose not from the length of the courtship she and Jim enjoyed—although at over two years, that had something to do with it. No, it arose because Sundays in the hours between noon and eight o'clock in the evening were almost the only hours the two sweethearts had to share. Given his absence from his immediate family so much of the week, Millie's parents relinquished her to our society for some portion of those eight hours.

Two months into his part-time working arrangement, I questioned whether it really was beneficial for him. Jim worked for Dr. Mahoney two hours each Wednesday afternoon and six hours each Saturday. On the completion of his responsibilities Saturday afternoon, he took the train to Brampton from Weston, arriving home around six o'clock. In the first month of the arrangement, Jim would leave the house following our Saturday night meal to meet Millie. But as the weeks went by, Jim found himself too tired to socialize that evening, often retiring to bed before me. With those hours of sleep behind him, he initially was able to rise the next morning, eat breakfast, and attend church with the rest of our family. But as the weeks went on, he was unable to rouse himself initially for breakfast and then for morning church. It came to pass that he was always tired when he was with us and usually quite quiet. I was thankful that he perked up a bit when Millie arrived after her church service.

By November, I could not recall when Jim had last tugged one of my curls or called me "Little One." While he was sitting in a chair, I came to intentionally approach him from behind, dragging my locks over his shoulder, practically dropping them onto his rested hands. It did not make any difference.

"Why is Jim so tired?" I asked Mother one Sunday night as I watched his tall, thin frame disappear down Wellington Street on his way to the train station and his return to Aunt Lil's house in Toronto. "He goes to bed early, he gets up late. He hardly ever sees Millie." Ascertaining that we were alone, I asked, "Why would she agree to marry someone who has no energy to see her?"

"I wouldn't worry about that," Mother replied, confirming, as I just had, that no one could hear our conversation. "He has a lot of school work in his final years of study. Millie will understand. This is in her interest too." Millie came from a well-to-do family. We knew that she and Jim could not marry until he was established in his profession. These extra hours of work would help him become so.

One Sunday in mid-November, I became truly concerned. Millie was joining us for our meal that evening. In the hour beforehand, she and Jim were in our sitting room playing a game of cards. She sat on the little sofa, he on an occasional chair in front of her. A small table had been moved between them. Mother, Father, Grandpa, and I entered and exited the room at various times. I was alarmed when I returned to the room shortly before our meal to observe the two of them sitting on the sofa, Millie with a handkerchief at her eyes.

I feared the worst. She was upset with Jim and his lethargy. She had decided to end her relationship with him in favour of someone who was peppier and who had completed his studies. I thought back to a scene I had witnessed years before, when Millie was being courted by Clarence Charters and Dutch Davis. I was determined to stop any such transfer of affections.

"Millie! What is it?" I asked, rushing to the small sofa, squeezing in beside her. I looked cross at Jim then turned to her. "Are you hurt?"

"Oh, no. No, I'm not hurt, Jessie. Thank you for asking." She dabbed at her tears as Mother and Father, having heard the commotion I created, entered the room as well. "I'm just upset. Jim and I were speaking of those poor Belgians." We had heard about the poor Belgians for three months by that time. The Belgians were the first casualties of the war, with the

Germans invading their country early in August. The Germans had hoped to make a quick strike against France from that country. We read newspaper headlines of the accounts of the thousands killed, of the terror experienced by those living there, of their starving conditions, and of the bravery of the their countrymen. We were all moved in late September when we read the story of two Belgian telephone switch operators who had stayed at their posts while the town around them was being destroyed. Realizing that if they fled, important communications to Belgian military leadership and retreating troops could not be completed, they stayed at the switch, flames crackling and walls falling around them until the lines they utilized ceased to function.

"Do you think Ina would stay at the switch if the Brampton buildings around her were on fire?" I asked one night.

"Heaven forbid," Mother said. Both Father and Grandpa were confident she would. If those around her were struck by ravaging fevers, perhaps she would not. Ina had a phobia about contagion. But if the crisis involved falling walls and burning buildings, where lives were at stake, they thought she would stay.

That was nearly two months earlier. It was the news of the terror being inflicted on innocent Belgian men that now had everyone so upset. Those men were being killed as an example in order to scare or punish others in their towns for their brave acts and to deter the repetition of such brave acts.

"It is too frightening to believe," Millie said, continuing to dab her eyes. "Those poor people. Their houses and livelihoods destroyed. Some living under the command of the enemy, others trying valiantly to avoid it. All of them without enough food, clothing, and medical supplies. We have to do something." Mother noted the efforts to make and collect clothing for the Belgians that had been underway since August. Millie was proposing more.

She turned to Father, who sat in his usual chair next to the fireplace. "Dr. Stephens, we need to raise money to help them. We need a door-to-door canvass; a direct request to the homeowners. You could lead the effort."

"Oh, Millie, I'm not much one for asking people for money." He said it gently, seeing that she was in real distress.

"You asked people for money every day for the Excelsiors," she replied, thinking that he was just being modest. "Sarah and I would help you, like we did for the Excelsiors. Could you do that?" Sarah Lawson was Millie's best friend and the sweetheart of Jim's best friend, Eddie McMurchy.

"No, Millie. No, I don't think I could. But you do it. You and Sarah and others. As for me, my contribution to the war effort lies elsewhere."

"It's the Christmas Cantata, isn't it?" she asked.

"We can't miss it this year, of all years. In fact, I plan to make it extra special this year."

In reality, Father had been working on the Cantata every night since the completion of the high school amateur athletic competition in September. Seeing how the contribution of his time had resurrected an event over which he previously had no responsibility—how it had thwarted any plans the Germans might have had to disrupt life amidst the Allied countries—Father realized the blow that could be inflicted upon the enemy if he devoted an even greater amount of attention to an annual event that was entirely within his realm: the annual Grace Methodist Church Christmas Cantata.

Father was almost as passionate about music as he was about sports. In addition to directing the church choir and often singing with it, Father performed in amateur musical theatrics, including Gilbert and Sullivan operettas, which were his favourite, and other operettas that he wrote. Each year he produced at least half a dozen cantatas that were performed on Sunday evenings at our church. Always anticipated and well received was the annual Christmas cantata, though it rarely varied from year to year. There were, it seemed, only so many ways to produce a musical production about the birth of Christ. Ina, who had inherited our father's love of dramatics, often performed the role of Herod.

For Christmas 1914, Father desired to create a cantata that would be received with great acclaim, that would include the Christ story, but so much else as well. He desired to produce a cantata that would show the Germans and anyone else who mattered that Brampton was carrying on its business as usual. His object was well known to the church elders, who encouraged him heartily.

The production claimed hundreds of hours of Father's time, hours he spent conceiving the story line, identifying the characters, writing the dialogue and stage direction, determining the correct musical elements, writing original music and lyrics for two pieces, and working with the choir and quartet on the performance of the entire score. In the end, the cantata had all new characters. Gone was Herod. Ina, still in Winnipeg, was unavailable to play the role in any event. The new cantata included a wide cast of Christian, Greek, and secular figures, including six angels, four shepherds, Hope, Charity, a Goddess of Dreams, a Goddess of Love, Santa Claus, and a Frost King. A musical quartet and the church's choir provided the accompaniment. The cantata required a new stage backdrop, which Father conceived and others constructed.

Only six costumes of previous cantatas could be utilized. Mother was deputized to recruit church ladies to sew the new costumes, all according to Father's specifications. It was a harder task than would ordinarily have been the case given the prior commitments of the ladies to sew shirts with the cut-outs the Women's Institute produced at the Thursday afternoon courthouse cut-out parties.

The cantata was a godsend from my perspective, for three reasons. First, Father was so absorbed in the conception and execution of the cantata that he had very little time for the usual correction he provided over my life and Mother's. Even when he was home in the evening—bent over the reams of pages on our dining room table or picking away at the piano keys in the parlour—it was as though we were without his supervision. Second, the new cantata provided challenging new roles for me and Jane. Our years dressed as mute sheep were finally behind us—in fact, they were behind all of the children. The new cantata revolved around a journey taken and orated by two young girls, Jessie and her friend, Sophie. To the dismay of many children and their parents, there were very few roles for other children in the new cantata. Jane and I were honoured to assume those leading children's roles.

Finally, and most importantly, the new cantata, which required the participants to rehearse every Tuesday night during the months of November and December, provided me with an opportunity to be with Jane, whose family also worshipped at Grace Methodist Church, one night a week without the presence of Elsa, whose family did not. I so treasured that time that I elongated my efforts to memorize my lines. I delighted each time Father mandated me to spend more time with Jane practicing them.

By early December, adjustments were still being made to the costumes, backdrop, speaking lines and musical score, but with three weeks to the performance, Father was convinced it would be complete well beforehand. In fact, he could not recall a new cantata that was at that state of readiness that far ahead of its actual performance.

"It is going to be a triumph," he said one night at the dinner table, feeling quite self-congratulatory.

"I'm sure you are right," Mother said sincerely. "You have outdone yourself this time. The amount of effort will not go unnoticed. It will be a tribute to our church, our town, and our country. No one could ask more of you."

But it seemed someone could. The next Tuesday night, the gymnasium in which we were rehearsing was visited by a nonperforming member of our church. From my position, I witnessed Roger Handle, Father's friend and one of the church's elders, enter the gymnasium unannounced. Half an hour later, I also witnessed him leave in the same manner. In all that time, I never saw him smile. He said not a word to Father, who was so preoccupied with the production that he had not taken note of Mr. Handle's attendance.

I did not tell Father about Mr. Handle's appearance in the gymnasium, but three nights later, when he arrived at our house, I wondered if I should have. I sensed that he intended to criticize Father about the production. He seemed so unhappy while viewing the rehearsal. I had seen Mr. Handle interact with Father on two other occasions. The first time was when Father sought the mayoralty following my Uncle William's resignation from the post. Mr. Handle, after surveying the town councillors, advised Father that a bid by him would be unsuccessful. The second time was when Father's positions as the chairman of the High School Board and Water Commission were being challenged. It was Mr. Handle who laid out the plan for Father to recover his reputation and continue to hold those posts. Based on those experiences, I knew Mr. Handle was too savvy a man to criticize Father where a compliment would achieve the desired result.

The two men were discussing some matters about the town council when I entered the parlour carrying the glasses of water Father had requested. "Let me get straight to the point, young man," Mr. Handle said, changing the subject. Mr. Handle was the only person who called Father—who was his peer—a young man. Mr. Handle had nicknames for everyone he held dear. "We know how much work you've done on the cantata. Tickets are nearly sold out, and there are still two and a half weeks to go. The town is abuzz over the new production, but I've been asked by the elders to see if we could impose on you a little further. We have three requests."

Father stretched out his long legs, crossed them at the ankle above his white shoes, and settled back in his chair, clearly expecting the recitation of the list to take some time. I'm sure he was worried that one of the requests would be for money.

"First of all, we'd like a second performance of the cantata. We think that we can sell the church pews over twice." Father was quite amenable to that. Having put all of the effort into the creation of the cantata, the costumes, the set, the music, and having spent so much time in rehearsals, he was glad, and he expected the players would be glad, to perform it twice.

"But how will we complete two productions on one night?" Father asked. "It's ninety minutes long with an intermission, and we've already sold tickets for a seven thirty performance. We can't expect the children in the cantata to participate in another performance commencing at nine thirty."

"We quite agree. The second performance could be after Christmas, perhaps New Year's Day. We appreciate that some of your players may be away then. Do you have understudies?"

"Of course we have understudies!" Father replied somewhat indignantly. He took his role as producer and director quite seriously. He agreed to the New Year's Day second performance.

"The second request is that the proceeds from the second production go to the Red Cross Belgian Relief Fund." These were not funds to come from Father's pocket, so he did not object. He had reservations, though, as to whether people would be willing to attend on that basis. "There is only so much money our townsmen have to support these causes," he said. Mr.

Handle was confident that once word spread about the success of the first performance, there would be no difficulty selling tickets for the second.

"That seems settled then," Father said, his mood growing lighter. Mr. Handle had been in the house for twenty minutes at that point and had not yet asked Father to expend any of his own funds. In fact, Father was so relieved that he suddenly took notice of my presence on the piano stool.

"Jessie, what are you still doing here?" he asked sternly. "I do not believe you are part of this conversation."

I blushed. I was so transfixed by Mr. Handle's advocacy, I forgot my manners. I knew I should have left the room after serving the water.

"I wanted…to see…whether Mr. Handle needed any more water," I stammered, mostly truthfully. Mr. Handle often seemed hot and out of breath. He may have benefitted from another glass of water.

"Handle, would you like another glass of water?" Father asked.

When Mr. Handle declined, I was shooed from the room. Fortunately, the volume at which the two men spoke provided me with a perfect hearing of the remainder of their conversation from just inside the kitchen, where my manners were once again forgotten.

"And the third request?" Father asked, sounding a little bullish at this point.

"Yes. The third. We'd like you to add an opening act to the performance."

"An opening act? The performance is already ninety minutes long."

"Yes. We would like something a bit more patriotic." Now Father really was offended. He never liked it when others interfered with his artistic direction.

"A bit more patriotic? Our motto at this time is business as usual. The cantata is patriotic!" Father cried.

"We were thinking of something that might involve, perhaps, a flag or two? Perhaps an anthem? 'Rule Britannia'? Something like that?" As always, Mr. Handle was very calm.

"I'm sorry, Handle," Father said defiantly. "That is really not in keeping with the spirit of a Christian Christmas cantata."

"Young man, you have Santa Claus in there. A Goddess of Dreams. You've stepped a fair way from the book of Luke. In this year, at this time, you could go a little further."

"Perhaps," Father conceded, "but I'd rather not do that, if you don't mind."

"I've spoken to the elders. We insist. But if you're not up to it, we will find someone else who is."

The calm Father felt three days earlier vanished within moments of Mr. Handle's departure. "Get me some paper, Mother," Father bellowed as he set himself up once again at the dining room table. When we came down to breakfast the next day, the table was strewn with musical notes, stage directions, and costume drawings. I could see that the young children who were disappointed to lose their roles as animals would all have roles, and so would many of their older siblings.

At 7:30 p.m. on Tuesday, December 22, 1914, Mr. Duggan, the superintendent of the Sunday school, quietened the audience. Every pew in the church was full. With no more fanfare, he asked the audience, "Who's for the flag?" As he stepped aside, eight men in red British grenadier coats entered the sanctuary. Marching up the main aisle, each carrying a rifle, they began a patriotic chorus, one tenor singing the solo parts, the others joining in the chorus. As they positioned themselves in a semicircle on the makeshift stage at the front of the church, two figures emerged. The first, waving a large Union Jack, impersonated John Bull, the imaginary British recruitment officer. Then, waving a large Red Ensign, another man played Jack Canuck, the Canadian equivalent. The crowd applauded heartily as the eight men sang "Tipperary" while they marched back down the aisle.

From where I stood at the side of the stage, I could see Mr. Handle and Mr. Duggan nod at each other, obviously satisfied with the patriotic performance Father had arranged. It was just as they had hoped. The two men settled back in their pew, ready to watch with less enthusiasm the new Christmas cantata Father had created. For this they would have to wait.

Moments later, the choir began singing the first two verses of "Rule Britannia" as fifteen of the church's boy scouts marched into the sanctuary, variously wearing shirts of red, white, and blue. Their leader, waving a Union Jack, ushered them to one side. The choir ceased singing and the orchestra played the first chorus of the Belgian national anthem. Twelve children marched into the sanctuary, some wearing black shirts, some yellow, and some red, matching the colours of the flag of the Kingdom of Belgium being waved by their leader. The performance was repeated for "La Marseillaise" and then the Russian anthem. Finally, the last twelve children entered dressed in red, white, and blue, the final verse of "Rule Britannia" being sung again. Once all sixty children were at the front of the sanctuary, the audience stood with the children and sang the Canadian national anthem, many with tears in their eyes, Mr. Handle and Mr. Duggan among them. Standing directly across from them at this point, I heard Mr. Handle say to Mr. Duggan as they returned to their seated positions, "He really outdid himself, didn't he?" That, I am happy to say, was the consensus of everyone who saw the performances that Christmas season.

Later that night, long after the performance, I walked home from the cantata with Jim. We were both giddy with the success of the evening—happy for all of the players who loved their parts; happy for the town, which greeted the cantata so enthusiastically; happy for Father, who had poured his heart and soul into it. In my case, I was happy for one other reason too: my brother had been sufficiently rested to participate in the production, his classes and his work with Dr. Mahoney having taken a hiatus a week earlier.

"How did you like me in that British grenadier's uniform?" Jim asked, tugging a curl that had escaped my hat. "Don't you think I looked pretty handsome?"

"No," I replied. It was a look I never wanted to see. "I liked your singing, but I did not like the look of you in that uniform, and I definitely did not like the look of you carrying a gun."

"Really! I am surprised! I thought it was a look all young ladies liked." I had noticed a gaggle of girls around Jim in the reception that followed the performance. They backed off somewhat when Millie approached Jim and took his arm. I expected they all thought he looked quite handsome in the trim uniform.

"Did Millie like it?" I asked grudgingly.

"No," he admitted. "She didn't much like it either."

"Did you like it?"

"No," he conceded. "I really didn't." A huge wave of relief washed over me. "It was far too itchy."

The door-to-door canvass that Millie had advocated as a means of raising funds for the Red Cross Belgian Relief Fund took place three weeks following her discussion of it in our home. In early December, teams of men and women canvassed the homes of Bramptonians, seeking one dollar on behalf of each resident in the home. In this way, $3,244 was raised. With Ina in Manitoba indefinitely and Jim away at school all but one day a week, Father struggled over whether to give four dollars or six dollars to the canvassers. In the end, he gave five. Though fifty times that much was raised in the Christmas cantata he produced, he continued to think that his greatest contribution to the war effort in 1914 was not the money so raised but rather the actual creation of the new Christmas cantata. It showed the enemy, more than anything else, that Brampton was carrying on business as usual.

* * *

It was a different Christmas, that Christmas of 1914. It was different for many Canadian families. Our newspaper, the *Conservator*, said it best in a lengthy editorial on Christmas Eve:

> *...Christmas, 1914. In the years to come we shall remember it not only as a time of hideous strife, of cruel butchery and torture, of the slaughter of the innocents; a time when men, women and little children are starving and sorrowing because of their ruined homes, their wasted fields and trampled soil but as a time when men put aside their petty aims, their sordid ideals and arose as brethren, with one heart and one mind, to do what they could to aid the suffering and the despairing....*

In reality, the effect on our family was relatively minimal. For reasons unrelated to the war, we were without Ina. From the many letters sent to Mother by Aunt Charlotte and from Ina herself, we knew that she had settled in well in Winnipeg. Within days of arriving there, she found employment. The Winnipeg Supply and Fuel Company, originally formed in Ontario and known to Uncle William from that connection, seized upon Ina's experience as a telephone operator. While the orders for their coal, wood, brick, lime, clay, and stone products had historically been placed by mail, the company had come to realize how the order processing time could be expedited through the use of the telephone. Ina, a former Brampton switch girl, assumed the position with vigour.

Uncle William reported to Mother and Father on Ina's work ethic, a matter about which the company's owners, the Robertsons, always marvelled. Six days a week, Ina arrived by bus at their head office in the north end of Winnipeg, half an hour before the commencement of her shift, and stayed without fail a full half hour after its conclusion. When her services were not required on the telephone, she found orders to be typed, parts to be packed, mail to be opened, floors to be swept, counters to be dusted—anything that needed to be done. The office had never been so organized or so tidy.

When Ina was not working at the supply company, she was working within the community. Every night after work at the Winnipeg Supply and Fuel Company, she volunteered at the Broadway Church. There, with the support of two wealthy local merchants, the church had established a support centre for use by the troops. The men were welcome to wash and shave at the church first thing in the morning. Throughout the day and in the evenings, rooms were available for them to play billiards and in a separate room to write letters to their family members. It was to this latter room that Ina and other young ladies had admittance. There, the young women ensured there was at all times a sufficient supply of paper, pens, envelopes, cookies, and cakes. For the men that needed assistance in writing, Ina proved a competent secretary.

Though Father regularly expressed pride in Ina's work ethic, Mother and I knew that its near manic nature helped her contend with a wound not visible to the Robertsons with whom she worked or the soldiers with whom she volunteered.

It was a different Christmas for the Turners too. Aunt Charlotte and Uncle William still had Bill with them. As his parents insisted, Bill was at home, attending university. But when he was not studying law, he was studying to be a military officer. Earlier that year, a division of the Canadian Officers' Training Corps was formed at the University of Manitoba. The OTC, which originated in Britain over a decade earlier, was designed to expand the pool of military leaders beyond those born to a high class. The OTC promoted physical training and taught courses such as military engineering, military science, and tactics. Bill looked forward to the day when he could apply those skills in Europe as a lieutenant of a combat division.

As for Roy, we learned through the various letters sent by Aunt Charlotte and Ina that he had, as expected, joined his regiment on his return to Winnipeg in August. In a letter from him, we learned that he arrived at Valcartier on September 1st and that on September 23rd he signed his enlistment papers. In a letter from Uncle William, we learned that Roy embarked for England from Quebec City aboard the SS *Virginian*. It was from that letter we also learned that Roy had enlisted, not in a combat role as he had for so long aspired, but rather with Andrew Foster in the Railway Supply Detachment of the Canadian Army Supply Corps. In that posting, he was working to supply the troops to the front and to supply those troops with the ammunition, food, and other provisions they required.

Chapter 6

THE HOCKEY GAME

The first meeting of the Brampton Central School Knitting Club was convened the third week of October, 1914. The meeting was attended by eight girls who were experienced knitters, fifteen girls who were aspiring knitters, and two girls who had no desire whatsoever to knit but who wanted to appear to support the club's president. The meeting was held immediately after school on a Tuesday in the classroom of its president, Jane, still my best friend. At that first organizational meeting it was determined that the club would meet for one hour each Tuesday and Thursday after school was adjourned; that the initial meetings would take the form of lessons, so that all club members would have a basic skill level; that the object would be to knit scarves (it being determined that there were enough mothers knitting socks and that the abilities of the club members were best suited for basic knitting); and that each member would aim to produce one scarf per month, with the exception of the vice-president, Elsa, who was determined to produce four. Each club member was responsible for obtaining her own needles. Wool would be obtained through donations sought by the two non-knitting members of the club, Frances and me.

Having been relegated to a role of supply and equipping, Frances and I were not required to attend the Tuesday and Thursday meetings, except for the purpose of delivering the donated goods and ascertaining the quantities required to keep the club members in wool. While the twenty-three other club members knit, Frances and I, having obtained dispensation from our fathers to commence our homework and chores an hour later on those two days, sought donations of wool from mothers of the club's members, school teachers, church members, and eventually, merchants. Some days we received two or three balls of wool. Some days we received none. Some of the balls were large, never having been used. Others were small, clearly the remnants from a sweater made for a grandfather or a bonnet made for a babe. Some were tangled. One ball had clearly been the home to some form of vermin!

As we delivered the results of our scavenging exercise to the active knitters, Frances and I saw the growing lengths of the scarves being produced. We marvelled at the strange patterns the scarves were taking on. They were of various colours, with irregular widths of stripes. Some scarves were long and narrow. Some were short and wide. Some were wide in places and narrow in others. Many had a careless zig-zag shape to their borders—stitches clearly being unintentionally lost and added from row to row. "Our boys will never notice it," Jane whispered to me as I looked askance at Margaret Dawson's work. "Once it's wrapped around their necks they won't realize the odd colours or shape."

The girls issued their requests. "More navy if you please, Jessie." "Thicker wool if possible, Frances." We nodded in understanding, never bothering to write down their desires or even commit them to memory. The knitters would be provided with whatever wool we could collect. It was unlikely to meet their dictates. I soon concluded that supplying and equipping was almost as bad a job as knitting.

Nonetheless, between our scrounging efforts, as Frances and I called them, and the efforts of our knitters, the Brampton Central School Knitting Club had been successful in meeting its goal for the month of November. The first week of December, twenty-five scarves were delivered to the Women's Institute. To the knowledge of the club members, all twenty-five scarves were packaged and sent to England.

Only one thing would prevent the repetition of that accomplishment in the months to come. It was not a lack of commitment on the part of the knitters, for they were all quite devoted to the cause. It was not their lack of skill, although skill continued to be somewhat wanting. It was not the loss of a location in which to meet, our schoolroom always being available. No, the one thing that would prevent the delivery of a further twenty-five scarves—the one thing that would prevent the fair necks of our brave boys from being warmed—was an insufficient supply of wool.

"Jessie and Frances," Elsa said one Thursday in mid-December when the supply was nearly depleted, "have you truly spoken to all of the teachers in the school?" We had.

"Have you spoken to the Sunday school teachers at your churches?" We had.

"Have you spoken to your mothers and mothers of other club members?" We had.

"And the merchants in Brampton who sell wool?"

"Yes," I said. "Two times or more. They're starting to pretend that they're not in when we go into their shops."

"It's true," Frances said. "We saw Mr. Giffen run into his storage room when we walked into his shop the other day. I've never seen him move so fast. Then he pretended not to be there when we rapped on the storage room door."

Jane looked at Elsa. "We'll have to start the big campaign," she said.

"The big campaign?" I turned to Frances. She was equally mystified.

"Yes, the big campaign. At our meeting last Tuesday, we discussed the work that you two are doing. We know it is difficult work. So we have a plan to make it easier for the club to obtain more wool." Easier? She had my full attention.

"Yes, we decided that the scarves made in January and February won't be given to the boys. Instead, we'll sell them. The money made from the sales can be used to buy wool." That did seem easier, I thought.

"Where will you sell them?" Frances asked.

"At the hockey game," Jane replied.

In a town where hockey was played many times each winter week, in organized games, in shinny games, on ice rinks and streets, by young boys and older men, we all knew the game to which Jane was referring. It was scheduled to be played between the Brampton High School team and its chief rival, the Weston High School team, at the end of February. If this game was like those played before the war by these two teams, it would be the best attended winter sports event in the town.

The notion of selling the scarves at the game seemed a good one to me—particularly if the scarves were mostly red, black, and gold, the colours of the Brampton team. Hundreds of Bramptonians would attend the game. I could see that fifty scarves could easily be sold, so long as they were not too expensive. I began to imagine how much wool could be purchased with the proceeds. I began to imagine the many things I could do with my time if I was not spending it soliciting for donations of wool. Frances, who had a dreamy look on her face, seemed to be lost in similar happy thoughts.

"Wait a minute," I said, coming out of a near euphoric state. "How are we going to get the wool to produce the fifty scarves to be sold?" The lack of supply was the subject that had begun the conversation. To have fifty scarves to sell at the game, the club would need a lot of wool, and they would need it soon. Frances and I had no one left to approach.

"Oh!" Elsa said. "We forgot to tell you that. That's the second part of the campaign the club designed. We're going to knock on doors!"

"What doors?" Frances asked. "For what purpose?"

"Everyone's doors," Elsa said. "Everyone supports the war effort. No one wants our boys to be cold. People will be glad to give us wool if we ask. You know how happy our mothers are to do so."

I picked up on the word "us." "The whole club will do this then?"

"Heavens, no," Elsa said. "We need them to knit. You and Frances will continue with the scrounging." Seeing the look of horror on my face, she went on. "But don't worry. Jane and I will help you. The four of us will knock on doors on Monday and Wednesdays so that Jane and I can be with the club members on Tuesdays and Thursdays. We'll split into two groups. Jane will go with one of you, and I will go with the other." My anxiety was slightly relieved. In fact, I became slightly buoyed at the prospect. This would at least provide me with some time alone with my best friend. Ever since the knitting club had been formed, the only time I had with Jane without the accompaniment of the dreaded Elsa was in church and at church-related activities like the Christmas cantata.

The elation I felt was fleeting.

"Jane and Frances," Elsa continued in a dictatorial manner, "you two can go to the homes on the west side of Main Street. Jessie and I will go to those on the east side." She hesitated before she pushed the hair on the right side of her face behind a protruding ear and asked, "That's all right with you, isn't it Jessie?" Her big eyes danced with delight. She knew exactly what she had done. I could hardly object without hurting the feelings of Frances.

"It's fine," I said with the same lack of enthusiasm I truly felt.

Thus began my next wartime sacrifice: I spent two hours a week doing something I did not want to do with someone I did not at all like. It also began my real education about Elsa. As we walked to the streets we were to canvass, up the driveways and along the sidewalks; as we waited for doors to be answered and for housewives to go in search of remnants of wool; as we walked away from the houses, often with no additional wool in our bags, I came to know Elsa Strauss.

My lessons usually began with a plaintive observation about our relative positions within our families or within our town. "You're so lucky," she said to me the first day of our canvassing. It was the first week of January. I did not feel that lucky at the time. I was losing my best friend. I was being forced to spend two hours a week doing what felt like begging. Our country was at war, and though there were no hostilities on our soil, I continued to worry that might change.

"Why do you say that?" I asked, mostly out of politeness.

"You live in a big house. You have your own room."

I did live in a big house. I learned two Christmases earlier that my family had not always lived in it and that the burden of meeting the costs to maintain it likely explained, in part, my father's frequently poor temper. Elsa, on the other hand, lived in a small apartment on the top floor of a large building. The building, which had once been the offices and foundry of the Haggert Iron Works, was fully in view of the former Haggert residence, located up a hill and to the west. Known as Haggertlea, it was the house in which Jane then lived. The former foundry's tall mansard roof allowed its attic level to be used as apartments. Elsa had previously told us that her family's apartment was comprised of three rooms, two of them windowless bedrooms. From the dormer window of the third room—a combined kitchen, dining room, and sitting room—one could see and hear the activity on Main Street below.

We always referred to Elsa's apartment as the apartment above the dairy. This was because every child in Brampton knew the location of the dairy. We did not go there to purchase milk or butter for our homes. Those goods were delivered to our houses nearly every day. No, we knew the dairy because it was the place from which we purchased ice cream, a singular treat except when our mothers prescribed its ingestion as a means of warding off scarlet fever. While the apartment was above the dairy, it was not immediately above it. Two other floors separated the dairy and the apartment of the Strausses. They were occupied by a knitting mill and a box factory.

"I've only had my own room for four months," I said in reply. "Most of the time I share my room with my sister, who doesn't really like me." I hoped the conversation would stop there. I did not want to engage an intimate conversation with Elsa. I did not like her. I knew she had her own room. We had heard about it repeatedly in the fall.

"I don't have a room to myself anymore," she said as we arrived at the street I had selected to canvass that day. "I've had to move into the room with my parents." With her parents? I could not imagine having to do that. I wondered if her father snored, as mine did. Sharing a room with Ina seemed blissful in comparison.

"Why did you have to do that?" I said, too curious to ignore the comment.

"We've had to take in boarders. Apparently we need the money."

I was surprised at that. I had gathered from other remarks made by Elsa that her father was able to amply support his family with his earnings from the Dale Estate. Though I asked nothing further, she went on.

"Yes, it's a couple from Toronto. Mr. and Mrs. Boyd. They are working in the knitting mills. We don't see them much. Mother makes their meals. They take them in their room. We see them when they come and go from the apartment. The rest of the time it's as though they aren't there. But they are. And so now I don't have my own room."

Another day as we left school, set to recommence our canvassing efforts, she again told me how lucky I was. "Yes, I know," I said blithely. "I have my own room."

"No. I was thinking of something else." We knocked on the door of Mrs. Jennings, Elsa's lament temporarily delayed.

"You're so lucky that your family has a bakery," she said, adopting my preferred method of describing my aunt's bakery. "If you lived above the bakery, you would only smell freshly baked pies and bread and cookies. It would be so sweet."

She may have been right. Certainly, the aroma in the bakery was sweet. I had never been in the apartments above the dairy. "Does it smell bad above the dairy?" I asked, somewhat surprised.

"I don't think so. I've never had to hold my nose. But the Boyds moved out of our apartment at the end of January because of an odour." She sounded forlorn as she spoke. I gathered that their departure had not led to a restoration to Elsa of her former bedroom.

"Now we have two other people living with us. They're brothers. They work at the Hewetson shoe factory.

"Do they take their meals in their room?" I asked, recalling the habit of the Boyds.

"No. They eat at the table with us. A couple of days ago when they first arrived, they were quite nice, complimenting my mother on her meals, asking my father about the plantings at the Dale Estate, but now they hardly say anything to us. 'Pass the butter' is about all we hear. And when any of us says anything, they just glare at us. So now no one says anything while we eat."

I was slightly sympathetic. We had so much conversation at our dining room table. I could not imagine how uncomfortable it would be sitting at a table with no one speaking.

Another day, as we canvassed homes along Scott Street, her musings revolved around her brother. "You're so lucky, Jessie," she said. "Your brother lives near you. You see him every week."

I did not feel so lucky about my brother at that time. It was the second week of February. Jim had by then been working part-time for Dr. Mahoney for five months. Aside from the two-week Christmas break period in which he seemed to have a normal energy level, he continued to be afflicted by an undiagnosed sleeping sickness. Just the Sunday before, I had overheard him and Millie arguing about it. The two of them were supposed to see a picture at the Giffen Theatre the night before with Sarah and Eddie. The other three had waited for Jim at the theatre. He did not join them. He wasn't able to summon the energy to meet them at the theatre after he returned home from his Saturday shift with Dr. Mahoney. "But you saw the picture, Millie," Jim said. "What does it matter if I wasn't with you? It was dark in the theatre, and we weren't going to talk through it."

"That's not the point," she said. "I was looking forward to seeing it with you. We paid ten cents for your ticket, and you love Westerns." They had seen *Shotgun Jones*, a twenty-minute film starring Wheeler Oakman. "And your cousin John played the score. You would have loved it." In those days, no one talked while seeing a picture—least of all the actors. The music was performed separately by a live pianist. My cousin John, who was almost as talented a pianist as my mother, often provided the musical score.

"What are you going to do later this year once you've graduated and are practicing dentistry full-time? You will have no life—we will have no life—if it tires you this much."

"I know," he said. "I'll find out what's wrong. I will."

Elsa proceeded to tell me the latest on her brother, Wilfred. After five months of training in England, the Canadian troops there were preparing to leave for France. He would soon be on the actual battlefield in combat. Hearing that, I realized once again the wisdom of her observation. I *was* lucky. My brother was tired. If he could not find a cure for his sleeping sickness, he risked losing his girlfriend and his career. But he was safe at home in Canada. He was not at risk of losing his life.

* * *

By the middle of February, forty scarves had been produced for sale at the game. Ten more were in various stages of completion. The club was grateful for the wool Frances, Jane, Elsa, and I had been able to gather. Thanks to a donation of twelve balls Millie found in her attic that looked suspiciously like the single ball that Mr. Stork gave us from the inventory of his store, the club had more than enough wool to complete the scarves to be sold at the game. I felt I had made a good contribution to something that my best friend considered important.

Just as Frances and I were beginning to think that our work for the club was complete for a time, the club president and vice-president spoke to us about their latest idea. It was the most outlandish notion yet. The day before, when the club members were knitting, one of them commented on how much harder it was to knit scarves that were going to be sold rather than be given to the boys.

"So we came up with an idea," Jane said, clapping her hands and dancing on the balls of her feet, her straight long hair bouncing around her narrow face. We were standing outside the school during our morning recess.

"Yes!" Elsa vouched. "It was Jane's idea, but we all agreed it was the best idea yet."

Apprehension seized me. Thus far, every "great" idea pertaining to the knitting club resulted in me devoting more time to an activity I detested.

"We've decided..." Jane said, hesitating for effect, "we've decided...to donate the scarves we are knitting to the boys."

"The fifty scarves we were going to sell?" I asked, nearly dumbstruck.

"Yes!" Jane said, still jumping up and down.

My shoulders slumped. I sighed. No sales meant no money. I felt utterly deflated at the thought of the scarves actually going to warm those brave cold boys.

"I'm sure the boys will appreciate them," I said dolefully. I turned to Frances. "More begging, I guess."

"Yes," Jane said, "eventually, but not right away."

"Is the knitting club taking a break?" Frances asked hopefully.

"Of course not," Jane said emphatically. "No. We wouldn't do that. We wouldn't abandon our boys."

"Then how are we to delay our scrounging?" Frances asked.

"Because for a while we'll have the profits from selling the scarves." Frances and I stared at the president and vice-president of the knitting club, perplexed. We were standing in our schoolyard, our classes complete. The day was cold. It had been snowing all day. The flats area that formed the school's playground was a blanket of white. All the talk of scarves accentuated my chill.

"First, we're going to sell the scarves to the fans at the game, and then we're going to ask them to donate them back. Once we get them back, we'll donate them to the Women's Institute for the boys." She may as well have said "ta-da" before waiting for our applause.

"Won't they be used and dirty at that point?" I asked.

"That's the trick," Jane said. "They will have been used, but only for one hour. They won't have time to be worn out, and they shouldn't be dirty."

I considered that response. "You're going to ask the fans to donate them back at the end of the game?"

"Exactly!" A pile of snow fell off her hat as she bowed, the magic trick fully executed.

"So the fans will have paid the full price of a scarf to wear it for one hour?" I asked with some incredulity.

"Exactly!" A pirouette was performed.

"Who would ever ask them to do that?" I asked, fearing the answer as soon as the question left my cold lips.

It was all settled. Jane, Elsa, and two other club members would sell the scarves at the beginning of the game. Frances and I, each wearing a "collection hat"—a coned hat with a large piece of lettered cardboard— holding a donation box and hollering at the top of our lungs, would ask for the scarves back at the game's end.

"And we'll place some signs around the town ahead of time describing the arrangement," Jane said. That seemed more sensible to me.

"In fact, that's what we're going to do today," Elsa said. She took off her mittens in order to extract from her book bag four signs she had made the night before:

Show your support for our boys.
Buy a scarf from the Brampton Central School
Knitting Club for $1.00.
Support the Brampton team against Weston.
Afterward, donate your scarf back to the Knitting Club
so it can be sent to our boys.
Be a good Canadian!

It was not the most effective sign. There were a lot of words, and the writing was very small. She proposed we post them on notice boards at the post office and three of the churches.

"Will that be enough?" I asked. Frances and I would have a hard job retrieving the scarves from the fans if they could not read the signs before the game, either because the writing was so small or because they did not come into contact with one of the four signs.

Alas, no one saw the signs. We began our sign-posting efforts at the post office, located in the three-story rusticated brown limestone Dominion Building built by Grandpa in the prior century. Just inside the door, beneath the arched shape entryway, was a big board posting public notices. There were only a few people in the post office when we entered it. At the counter speaking to Mr. McCulla, our postmaster, they were oblivious to us at the notice board.

Elsa reached into her bag and extracted the four posters. She was about to hand one to Jane when her movements suddenly stopped.

"Hand me one," Jane said. Elsa did not move. Assuming that Elsa had not heard her, Jane repeated her request. Elsa remained inert. Her face turned beet-red. We were all warmer, standing inside the post office, but we were not that warm.

"Elsa, are you all right?" Frances asked. As Elsa tore up all four signs, dropping the shreds on the floor of the post office, we understood that she was far from all right. She ran out of the post office, Jane on her footsteps. Frances and I looked at the notice board. In addition to the yellowing signs advertising long past church bazaars and the fading signs advertising Christmas concerts, the board possessed a new sign. It bore that day's date.

Germans, Austrians, Hungarians, and Turks
Attention!
Every German, Austrian, Hungarian, and Turk is hereby
notified to report himself immediately at the station of the
local police to register as an Alien Enemy.

* * *

Finally, the day of the game arrived. My family was permitted to eat our noontime meal at a feverish rate that day in order to be sure that we could obtain a good viewing position for the game.

"Jessie," Mother said as she passed me a piece of cherry pie, "I assume you're going to be selling scarves prior to the game." Everyone in the family knew about the campaign of the knitting club, my efforts to gather wool to help its members meet their fifty-scarf objective, and its plan to sell those scarves at the game. "We'll save a place for you to sit with us during the game." The viewing of a game like this was a family affair in our household.

"Actually, no," I replied. "Other girls are going to sell the scarves at the beginning of the game. Frances and I are going to be collecting them at the end."

"Collecting them?" Mother asked. "It won't be much of a fundraiser if you have to return the purchase price at the end of the game." She chuckled at the naïveté of the notion.

"Oh, we aren't going to give the money back. We're going to ask the fans to donate the scarves back. Then we are going to donate the scarves to the Women's Institute to be sent to the boys."

My father looked at me incredulously. He was appalled. He was offended. He was so indignant about the scheme, he forbade me to participate. "I won't have a daughter of mine asking people to give up what they have just paid good money to purchase." It was one of the few times in my life that my father's edicts actually appealed to me. I was thrilled. Unfortunately, my relief at being prohibited from undertaking the enormous task I did not want to do deprived me of the good sense to take the minimal action I could have taken.

Once our meal was finished, Father, Mother, Grandpa, and I joined hundreds of Bramptonians and dozens of Westonians traversing the streets of Brampton to view the much-anticipated game. Dressed in our warmest coats and heaviest boots, our heads covered in wool hats and our hands, wool mittens and fur mufflers, we carried, or pulled on sleds, stools, or crates on which to sit, blankets to cover our legs and mugs in which to enjoy steaming hot chocolate.

Our destination was Smith's Pond, a large, roundish body of water at the top of our street. Fed by underground springs and situated in an undeveloped, slightly treed area, it was an ideal location for skating and hockey games, while also providing the town with a source of year-round ice. Named after the purveyor of that ice, Smith harvested its subzero yield, cutting and storing ice for sale throughout the year. Though once the graveyard for two runaway horses that were too heavy and vigorous for its thickness, by late February the frozen depths could easily support the fourteen skaters of the Brampton and Weston high school hockey teams.

Smith's Pond was principally accessed from two directions. Those entering it from the west side approached it from Wellington Street. On reaching the street's end, one descended to the park-like area below, treading a steep, snow-covered staircase of old tree roots and occasional stones. Only the presence of sturdy, upright trees and the handholds they provided made the descent possible in the winter. It was not the safest means of accessing the ice surface, but for many of the townspeople, it was the quickest.

The other point of access was from Centre Street on the east. From that road, one could meander down a gently sloping three-hundred-yard expanse to the pond's edge. People who lived on the east side of town and those who were wary of turned ankles accessed the pond area from the east side.

Although Father and I approached the ice rink from the more perilous Wellington Street side, Father preferred the view of the hockey surface from the east side. Thus, after safely climbing down the hill, we then walked around the frozen pond to sit with Grandpa and Mother, who had approached it the more cautious way. The walk around the ice surface was almost as treacherous as our descent to the area, obstructed as it was by many bushes, piles of snow plowed from the surface of the frozen pond, patches of icy well-trodden snow, areas of deep, untrodden snow, and a greater number of manmade hindrances. Benches for skaters to change and lace their footwear, fires heating cauldrons of hot chocolate and sleds, stools and wooden boxes of the spectators were all arranged in the area surrounding the frozen pond.

As Father and I walked to the east side of the pond, we passed not one but two tables of scarves. Jane and Elsa were at the first table—the one near the Wellington Street entrance. Underneath it, I could see the hat that Frances was to wear at the end of the game and the box in which she was to collect the donated scarves. Jane and Elsa seemed to be doing a brisk business.

When we finally reached the eastern side of the pond, we came into closer contact with the table staffed by Esther Jennings and Margaret Dawson, two other knitting club members. I waved as we approached them, noticing the hat and box I was intended to employ after the game. I could see there were only four scarves left to be sold.

"Should we buy a scarf?" Mother asked as we approached her. She was sitting on one of the boxes Grandpa had pulled on our sled.

"Why the deuce would we do that?" Father replied. "We know that they're only going to ask for it back when we leave." But others did not know that, since none of Elsa's signs had been posted.

As we took our positions on the sled and boxes atop the snow, I was delighted to see my friends Willie Core and Collin Heggie already sitting on boxes nearby.

"How do you think our team will do, Dr. Stephens?" Willie asked. My father's opinions on this subject were considered learned, given his experience as a past coach of the Brampton hockey team.

"It depends how disciplined they are," Father replied. He was never confident in a team he did not himself coach or manage. "And of course, it depends on how disciplined the Westonians are."

As the clock struck two o'clock, the teams appeared, walking toward us through the bushes at the north end of the pond. The Brampton team arrived first, its members laughing and jostling each other, a muddled mass in their gold school team jerseys, loose red knee-length hockey pants, and their thick black hockey stockings worn over their shin pads. Their leather skates were laced together and dangling over their shoulders. Their leather kneepads were askew. With glove covered hands they shook their sticks at the cheering crowd as they confidently made their way to the bench on the west side of the pond. Father despaired at their casual approach made all the more clear when the Weston team entered.

The Weston team members marched in unison toward their bench on the east side of the pond, each boy equally spaced from the one in front and the one behind. Their faces were devoid of expression. Their gloved hands tightly clasped their skates and sticks. They were all tall, with very long legs. I expected they were very fast skaters.

"Look at the size of their goaltender," Collin whispered. The player's position was clear by the wider stick he carried and the puck-stopping raised point that protruded midway along the blade of his skates. Like the other Weston players, he was tall, but he was also very fat. "His body mass alone will reduce our chances of scoring. He just needs to stay still, and half our pucks will miss their mark."

We all stood to sing "God Save the King" and then "O Canada" before the coin was tossed and it was determined which team would first occupy the southern net, and, by default, the northern net. Once identified, the teams, their skates finally donned, took their position on the ice, the Bramptonians Eustace McClure and Stewart Laird as left and right wing; Leo George and Art Gray as point and cover point; Dave Cormack as centre: Matthew Gomme as rover and Pete Armstrong as goaltender. Although the emerging Canadian professional hockey association had eliminated the rover position (a player who could freely traverse the ice), the local high schools, which had far too many candidates for each hockey position, chose to retain it. In a measure of modernity, the local high schools had adopted the new three twenty-minute period game standard, much to the dismay of Father and many others.

"I still like the two-period game the best," Collin said as Mr. Hudson walked onto the ice to drop the puck. "I never know where to sit for these three-period games. Until the coin toss, you don't know whether you'll spend more time in front of your team's net or the other team's net."

From the face off, Dave Cormack, Brampton's centre, took possession of the puck over the quick stickwork of his Weston centre opposite. With steely determination, Cormack and Matthew Gomme manoeuvred the puck toward the Weston team's net, making the obligatory passes before Dave, ignoring all the rules his coach had instilled in him, taking no notice of the whereabouts of his other five moving teammates—none of whom were in the position they were trained to hold—and being a good distance from the target of his efforts, shot the puck at the net. Intercepted by no less than four Weston team members, the puck was easily assumed by the Weston team's rover. As the Brampton team members scrambled to recapture it, the Weston team with a number of skilled passes handily moved the puck down the rink before their centre assumed full control. With his wingmen flanking him and not a Brampton defenceman in the vicinity, Weston scored the first goal.

The game improved for the Brampton team—but not by much. Eventually, its members assumed the formations they had been taught and were able to move the puck down to the Weston team's end, but no matter the number of shots they took on goal, they were unable to penetrate the net. At the other end of the rink, Pete Armstrong, who had to rely on skill rather than girth, allowed two pucks to enter his net in the first period and a further one in the second. At the end of the second period, Brampton was down three to nothing.

"It's going to take a miracle to pull this off," Father said as we sipped the hot chocolate we purchased for a penny a cup. Enterprising young people had arrived earlier in the day to prepare boiling cauldrons of the beverage above hot fires. For once, Father was pleased about the existence of a third period.

Mr. Hudson had obviously come to the same conclusion as Father. As we settled back onto our boxes, we saw the Brampton team huddled around their coach. Whatever he said to them seemed to work. The Brampton team came back to the third period as a mighty force. Within the first five minutes Matthew Gomme scored two goals. Five minutes later, Dave Cormack scored a third. At our end, Pete Armstrong, our goaltender, did not allow a single puck to enter his net. With five minutes to go in a tied game, one of the Brampton fans on the west side of the ice surface removed the scarf he had purchased an hour earlier from Jane and Elsa and began swinging it over his head. Within minutes, others on the west side joined him, the numerous spinning scarves creating a visual support for our team. Soon, nearly all of the scarves purchased at the beginning of the game were being used to spur on the local team.

Brampton fans who did not have scarves began to mimic the sound of the whirring scarves. Inspired by the support of their fans, the Brampton team members kept their eyes on the puck as they passed it from one to another. Scarves and people whirred. The puck moved down the ice, passing under and around the long legs of the Weston team members. *Whirr. Whirr,* the scarves seemed to sound. *Whirr. Whirr,* the fans shouted until with seconds left in the game, Eustace McClure of the Brampton team scored the final and winning goal.

Mother and Father leapt to their feet, clapping as loudly as they could through their woollen mittens. Willie and Collin stood and shouted, jumping up and down on their wooden boxes until Willie fell from his.

"Wasn't that amazing?" Willie asked, having regained his balance and standing beside me in the snow. I looked around—not at the ice where the players were gathering to congratulate each other. No, I looked around at those holding scarves.

"It is amazing. Truly amazing!" Those scarves, with their many dropped stitches, with their poorly darned in ends, with their badly blocked shape. "I was really afraid they'd fall apart," I said.

"Jessie, you should have more confidence in Brampton athletes!"

On the other side of the rink, through the melee of departing spectators, I could see a tall-coned hat and Frances below it, holding out her box and shouting lustily for people to contribute the scarves back for the fighting boys. Jane and Elsa, who were near Frances, noticed that I was nowhere near the table, below which was the matching paraphernalia. They began to wave to catch my attention, and when they did, they pointed at the table on the east side of the pond. All the way across the rink from me, we could not communicate with words. I turned my hands out at the elbow, palms up and lifted my shoulders, in a posture universally known to say: "Sorry, I can't." When they replied in a similar fashion, clearly meaning "What?!" I pointed to my father. We exchanged such hand signals before they realized that I was not allowed to assume the scarf-collection efforts on the east side.

Once this was understood, Jane left Frances and Elsa and began the long trek to the east side of the frozen pond. Jane was a fast runner, but it was a distance to traverse, and her path was impeded not only by the manmade and natural obstacles Father and I overcame earlier, but also by dozens of departing fans, many holding the hands of children, sleds, stools, and blankets. By the time Jane arrived at the east side of the pond, retrieved the box, and donned the cap, more than half of the spectators on our side had left. Jane was able to collect about a quarter of the desired number of the scarves.

"Sorry about that," I said, approaching her once the last scarf wearer had left.

"Sorry? Are you really sorry?" she asked. "You never wanted to collect the scarves, Jessie Stephens. You should have just told us that you wouldn't do it. Then I would have been here before the game ended."

"I did intend to collect them!" I said in my defence. "It was only at noon that Father learned of our plan and forbade me to participate."

I could tell she was about to say something about my father, but she restrained herself. "Tell me this, Jessie. Did your father also forbid you from telling me you were not allowed to participate?"

I cast my head down, saying nothing. He had not done that. She understood my silence. "Well, I have good news for you, Jessie Stephens. I know that your heart has never been in the knitting club. Now the rest of you is out too. Consider yourself a past member." Still wearing the ridiculous cone-shaped hat with the big cardboard sign and holding a partially filled box of scarves, she walked away.

Chapter 7

THE STRAUSSENHOFFERS

By the beginning of April 1915, it had been five weeks since either Jane or Elsa had spoken to me. I cared little about the loss of Elsa's society. I had never really liked it, although I confess that just before I lost it entirely, I had come to dislike it less. But Jane, I missed. The premonition I had when I first saw her three years earlier—that we would be life-long friends; that we would attend university together, marry together, be godmothers to each other's children—it would not come to fruition. She had not replied to either of my two letters of apology. There was nothing more I could do, Mother said, except be patient. "Jane is a nice girl," she said. "Eventually she will forgive you." Just when I was thinking she never would, something happened to change it all, and that thing had to do with Elsa.

The taunts that greeted Elsa on her first day of school the previous October persisted throughout the school year. Every day for six months, Ricky Dyck and Allan King asked if she was going home for sauerkraut or schnitzel; whether she had sauerkraut for breakfast; whether she took her schnitzel with marmalade. Whenever there was a strange odour in our classroom, one of them would turn and ask her if she was its source. Any time there was a setback in the war (and there were many), they would ask her what information she had about it. Elsa's reaction to every one of those questions was to turn somewhat red and to then talk about her brother and his experiences, whether at Valcartier, while crossing the Atlantic to England, in the Shorncliffe army training camps at Folkestone in Kent, in the trench training camp at Salisbury Plain, Wiltshire, or in the trenches in France.

One day in early April 1915, Elsa's reaction was quite different. To be fair to her, so were the actions of her tormenters. It was during the afternoon recess. The ditty that Frances, Esther Jennings, Margaret Dawson, and I were singing as Frances and I turned the rope and the other two jumped over it was interrupted by loud shouts on the other side of the playground area.

"We don't want you, and we don't want your sauerkraut aunt and cousins in this town! Go back home! All of you go back to where you came from!" I recognized the voices—they were the same voices that had been mocking Elsa for months, although in this case they were much louder, more threatening. I looked around. Ricky and Allan were twenty feet away from Elsa, who was standing with Jane near the wall of the school's west wing. The boys were not content to level their demands and move on. They continued to repeat them—loudly—while moving closer to Jane and Elsa, who were in equal measure slowly stepping backward.

"We don't want you, and we don't want your sauerkraut aunt and cousins in this town!" Their shouts took on an aspect of rage. What aunt, I wondered? What cousins? I did not long ponder that. Without a word, Frances and I dropped the ends of the skipping rope, leaving Esther and Margaret mid-jump. We ran to Elsa and Jane.

"Why don't you go back where you came from?" Ricky shrieked, practically baring his teeth.

"She's from Shelburne," Jane hollered back. "Do you want her to go back to Shelburne?"

"We want her to go back to Austria," Allan yelled as he continued to move closer to them. Jane and Elsa had moved back as far as they could go. They were nearly at the wall of the school. The distance between the two boys and the two girls was about ten feet. Frances and I slipped in to the gap, Frances flanking Jane's side and me flanking Elsa's. We assumed our positions just as Allan came face to face with Elsa. There was no need for him to holler the last salvo. She would have heard his whisper. "You're a filthy Austrian."

He put his hands on Elsa's shoulders, intending to push her. But Elsa was faster than him, and, we were surprised to see, stronger. Putting her hands on his shoulders, she pushed him away. The force applied was enough to cause Allan to step backward, lose his balance, and fall to the ground.

Ricky, infuriated by the assault on his friend, made a fist with his right hand, and intending to apply the maximum propulsion, pulled back his right arm. As it came forward to strike its intended target, my hand shot upward, pushing back not only his extended arm but his entire body. I too had an unknown strength. Ricky twirled before falling backward and landing on the ground beside his still prone friend.

Elsa, Frances, Jane, and I stared down at the two boys. Elsa spoke quietly, slowly, deliberately. "I am Canadian. My brother is Canadian. My mother is Canadian," she said. "I was born in Canada. My brother was born in Canada. My mother was born in Canada. My grandfather came to Canada more than fifty years ago. We are *not* Austrian!" Elsa turned on her heel about to walk away when a squeak emanated from the ground behind her.

"What about your father?" Allan asked quietly as the teachers arrived, one of them holding out a hand to help him up.

"Or your aunt?" Ricky intoned as another teacher helped to raise him.

Before Elsa could answer, we were separated, one teacher taking the boys, another taking us girls into the school and to the room of Mr. McHugh, the principal. After providing a report, the two teachers left us for their students. Frances and Jane were then asked to describe their version of the events. Their duty performed, they were directed to return to our classroom, their pleas to wait for Elsa and me rejected. "Miss Strauss and Miss Stephens will manage perfectly well without you," Mr. McHugh said. He always referred to the students formally.

Next to be dealt with were Allan and Ricky, whose conduct was found to be wanting in gentlemen. Allan received the strap twice, once on each hand. Ricky received it once. "But I didn't touch anyone," Ricky cried.

"Only because Miss Stephens's quick action prevented your hand from colliding with Miss Strauss's face. And gentlemen," he told the two boys, each of whom was fighting back tears, "if I hear any more sniggering about Miss Strauss from either of you, you will be back having this strap administered somewhere that will make it exceptionally hard for you to sit down." Once dismissed, they skulked out of the room.

"Now, ladies," he began. I feared the worst. The twosome who caused the least offence had been dealt with first. Allan and Ricky had received straps on their hands. What punishment was to be meted to Elsa and me? I began to quake.

"I saved you two to the last. Do you know why?"

"Because what we did was the worst?" I ventured. Elsa had actually shoved Allan, and I had struck Ricky's arm.

"I don't see it that way. Miss Strauss, you did push Mr. King, but you acted in self-defence. Frankly, I am amazed it took you this long to react to him. But I assume that this was the first time you actually feared for your physical safety." Elsa confirmed that it was.

"And Miss Stephens, your action was in defence of a friend. There will be no punishment for either of you—at least not by me. I require you, though, to tell your parents about this incident, and I require a note from them confirming that you have done so. You may leave now."

"Should we go back to class?" I asked. He looked at the mahogany clock on the wall, its bronze round Roman numeral face above its gently swinging pendulum.

"There's only an hour left. You are free to go home. I expect you will find Miss Hudson and Miss Thompson waiting just outside the door." We turned and saw the shapes of two heads receding from the heavily etched window of the door to his office. "You might tell the ladies that the next time they disobey one of my instructions, I will not be so lenient."

"I want to go home," Elsa said when we left the principal's office. She began to cry. We had never seen her cry.

"We'll take you there," Jane said.

With the rest of the students still in school and the four of us lost in our own thoughts, the eight-minute walk to the dairy was quiet but for Elsa's sniffles and Jane's occasional "there, there." We arrived at the door leading to the apartment prepared to say our goodbyes when Elsa turned and asked us to come upstairs with her. "My mother will want to hear what happened. She might not believe me."

For the first time, Jane, Frances, and I climbed the three dark flights of stairs to the top floor of the old Haggert Iron Works building. There, after passing a communal bathroom, Elsa opened the door to the Strausses' apartment. Light filled the hallway as we followed her toward its source.

"This one was my bedroom," Elsa whispered, referring to the room on the left. "The room I now share with my parents is here on the right." It was clear that neither room had a window. The main room, which ran the width of the apartment and about two-thirds of its length, was ahead. Looking out over Main Street, the room possessed a wooden table with straight-backed wooden chairs, a small sofa, and two upholstered chairs. A few smaller tables were scattered throughout. A large oval rag rug covered most of the floor. The faded wallpaper was beginning to peel in places. The large dormer window was uncovered. Sitting on the sofa were a small boy and a woman with a baby on her lap. Although their clothes looked quite normal, they had a foreign look about them.

Mrs. Strauss, who had been sitting on one of the upholstered chairs, rose as we entered the room. The tears that Elsa had mostly supressed as we walked home were released in torrents at the sight of her mother. Alarmed, Mrs. Strauss took her daughter in her arms and sought to calm her. Realizing Elsa was incapable of providing an explanation, Mrs. Strauss turned to us. She pulled her twelve-year-old daughter onto her lap, wrapped her in her arms, and invited us to sit down. Taking positions on two of the straight-backed chairs, we relayed to her the events of the afternoon, conscious somewhat of speaking about the people on the nearby sofa, who were obviously the referenced aunt and cousins. Seeing our discomfort, Elsa finally spoke—though in a near whisper. "Don't worry about offending my aunt and cousins," she said. "They don't speak English."

The tale related, we expected to leave, but Mrs. Strauss, so appreciative of everything we had done for Elsa, insisted we stay for some just-made vanilla crescent cookies.

"Mother," Elsa said, after eating the first cookie, "I want Jane, Frances, and Jessie to know our story. I told them how Canadian you are. Will you tell it to them?" After some encouragement from all of us, she agreed.

* * *

Elsa's mother had indeed been born in Canada. Elsa's maternal grandfather, Tobias Pichler, a short, stocky red-haired man, had immigrated to Canada from Austria in 1857, settling in the Forks of the Credit area in Caledon, where he began to work quarrying limestone. It was hard work, but it suited the industrious Austrian. In no time, he mastered the English language of his employer, Bill Hill, and gained the friendship of all of his fellow quarrymen, including another Austrian, Klaus Gruber, who had immigrated to the area nearly a decade earlier. Tobias was sad when two years into his work at the quarry, his friend Klaus left the employ of Bill Hill to take up farming in Shelburne, a community just north of Caledon. The one consolation—and it was a big consolation—was what Klaus left behind in Caledon: his sister, Lena, who a month earlier had become Tobias's wife.

Eventually, Tobias too left Bill Hill's employ. Within eight years of his arrival at the Forks of the Credit, Tobias acquired his own quarry operations, taking with him all of the know-how Hill had imparted and a good number of Hill's customers. Tobias's easy manner made him a favourite with contractors across Ontario, and his prices, at least ten percent less than those of his former employer, made him a desirable supplier. Tobias soon built Lena a large, two-storey home, clad in Credit Valley limestone. The home had a nursery area for four children, though initially there were not so many inhabitants. It had a separate dining room, a sitting room, and a parlour for entertaining. The home was the envy of their community and a far cry from what either Lena or Tobias had ever enjoyed in their younger days in Austria.

Klaus Gruber marvelled at the early and apparently easy commercial success of his brother-in-law. A slow, steady worker, Klaus had in the time Tobias bought his own quarry and built what Klaus considered to be a mansion, cleared only a quarter of his land and constructed a modest one-storey, three-room farmhouse. It took Klaus twenty years to put all twenty acres into production. By that time, he had all of the equipment he required—some manufactured by the renowned Haggert Foundry in Brampton. He also had a dozen chickens, three cows, six pigs, and four work horses to support his living and his farming operations. A second storey had been added to his house, complete with three bedrooms, although since Klaus never married, two of those rooms remained unoccupied.

One day, sixteen years after Tobias had purchased his quarry, Tobias, Lena, and their two children arrived on the doorstep of Klaus's small farmhouse. Tobias had lost the quarrying business and everything else he owned.

Klaus no more understood how Tobias lost the quarry than how he had ever gained it in the first place. Klaus moved back into the bedroom he formerly occupied on the main floor of his house. Lena and Tobias moved into the new second-floor bedroom. The other two bedrooms, never previously occupied, were taken up by Andreas, then fourteen, and Ingrid, then eleven.

When Tobias and his family first arrived at his farm, Klaus was not particularly in need of a farm hand. Klaus was still young—only fifty-one years old and in good health. It was just as well, since Tobias was not much of a farm hand. But for the next nine years, the two brothers-in-law rose at 4:30 a.m. each day. Tobias accompanied Klaus as Klaus milked and fed the cows, gathered eggs from the chickens, fed the pigs, chickens, and horses, changed the straw in the animal enclosures, and tilled, planted, and cleared the soil. Always by his side, Tobias attended to any small measure of the work with which Klaus entrusted him.

It was a surprise to everyone when Tobias, the stocky, fit former quarryman, died of a massive heart attack one day while carrying six eggs from the barn to the farmhouse. Klaus, then sixty, finally needed a hand at the farm. For a short time, he found the assistance he required in his nephew Andreas, who took up with enthusiasm the position his father had merely occupied. Klaus could see the value the young man brought to the farm as Andreas independently assumed all of the day-to-day jobs Klaus formerly attended to and many others that Klaus had delegated to occasional paid help. Andreas knew that value, too, and so after three years of such toil, he asked his uncle for a wage beyond room and board. Andreas was astounded when his uncle, fearing that he might have inherited his father's bad judgement about money, denied the request.

"You'll be paid in time," Klaus said. "In time you will be well paid."

Andreas, twenty-six years old and as impatient (if not as spendthrift) as his father, would not wait. He bid his uncle, mother, and sister *auf wiedersehen* and moved to a farm down the concession road, where the farmer was pleased to pay him a proper wage.

Klaus tried to carry on the farm without his nephew, but it had been three years since he actively operated it. The province was in a recession. Prices for produce began to decline, and yet his expenses continued to rise. Klaus thought he might have to sell his land. His exit from his life's work would be only slightly less ignominious than that of his spendthrift brother-in-law. He could hardly imagine it. Fortunately, he never had to take the step. His saviour was, surprisingly, not his nephew, who had worked the farm for three years, but his niece, who had simply benefited from that work.

Ingrid was twenty-three when her brother Andreas left their uncle's house. A pretty girl, she had her mother's milky white skin, blue eyes, striking facial features, and tall, solid figure. Though her brother Andreas had inherited their father's stocky frame, Ingrid had inherited his red hair, which was, thankfully, quite thick. "All the better to cover those ears of yours," her brother teased her.

Her father had always called her his *röschen*—his little rose. Her mother, who had wed at the age of twenty-two, and her uncle, who had never married, were worried that her looks and her sweet disposition would go to waste. Eventually, it was determined that Ingrid needed to be introduced to a wider field of prospective suitors. Arrangements were made for her to stay with the Mosers, Austrian acquaintances of Klaus, who lived in Toronto. Her uncle bought her a ticket. She entrained from the CPR station at Shelburne and disembarked at Toronto's Union Station.

Ingrid had never been to Toronto. She was concerned that she would not know how to find the designated meeting place within the large terminal. On exiting the train, she forced her way through the crowds of arriving passengers being met by friends and family and the crowds of departing passengers being sent off by friends and family. She passed men in uniforms pushing luggage on trolleys and men in uniforms announcing arrivals and departures.

Following the signs to the ladies waiting room, Ingrid finally arrived at the big clock on the wall next to it. Clearly, it was a popular meeting point. Eight people stood there, their backs to the wall, looking for signs of recognition among those approaching them. Ingrid peered at the group, searching for a woman wearing a black coat with a red scarf.

Every woman among them wore a black coat. Two of them wore red scarves! But neither of them gave Ingrid a second look. Just as Ingrid knew to look for Mrs. Moser in a black coat with a red scarf, Mrs. Moser knew to look for Ingrid in a green coat with a white scarf. Ingrid could see that no one else matched her description. Her mother had been right to select the coat, Ingrid thought, although her reasons for doing so had less to do with the coat being a beacon and more to do with how the colour complimented Ingrid's red hair.

Ingrid placed her back to the wall and stood with the other eight travellers. Within fifteen minutes, most of those people had been retrieved. Others had taken their place. Ingrid continued to wait. After half an hour, she began to worry. Her understanding was that the Mosers did not live far from the train station. She wondered what could be keeping them. Had she made a mistake in the designated meeting place? She reached into the pocket of her coat and extracted Mrs. Moser's letter. Then she saw it. There had been a transcription error. Ingrid's train had arrived on time at 5:59 p.m. The Mosers proposed to meet her at 9:55 p.m. They would not be at the clock next to the ladies waiting room for at least three hours.

Ingrid decided to explore the rest of the station. If she felt particularly brave, she thought, she would venture outside the station. As it happened, Ingrid did not get very far. She had only walked about twenty feet when she saw a uniformed man in communication with a traveller.

"English," the uniformed man was hollering. "We speak English here!" The uniformed man could not understand a word that the traveller said in reply. But Ingrid could.

"Can I help you?" she asked the traveller in perfect German. With her interpretive services, the traveller, who had arrived in Canada earlier that week and arrived at Union Station earlier that hour, learned that he had missed his connecting train. He would have to return to the station the next day at 4:00 p.m.

"Where will you stay in the meantime?" Ingrid asked the traveller after the uniformed man had left them.

"Here," the traveller said with resignation. "I have nowhere else to go." Elsa looked at the few hard benches nearby and nodded. She was about to continue her exploration when the traveller asked her to help him once more. "Could you ask that man if there's a place nearby to purchase a little supper?"

The uniformed man was then some distance away. After they pursued him, the uniformed man reported that there was a restaurant called Knapp's outside the station. She thought the conversation was at an end, but the uniformed man had more to say. She listened and then turned to the traveller. "He says that you have to pay for your food there."

The man rolled his eyes. "Tell him that I have enough money to buy a meal." He sounded indignant. She began to relay the message when he interrupted. "Don't tell him that I don't have much more than that!"

The traveller thanked her and began walking in the suggested direction. Ingrid watched him go and continued her own walk. She had not gone far when she heard someone running toward her.

"I realize," the traveller said, "that I will not be able to place my order. I do, as it happens, have enough money to purchase supper for two."

His name was Lukas Straussenhoffer—at least that had been his name a week ago. Thanks to the immigration authorities, his name was now Lukas Strauss. He was tall, with fair hair that was, despite his young age, already thinning on top. He had a roundish face with slightly chubby cheeks and a warm smile. He had immigrated to Canada from Austria with a view to joining his older brother Albert in the Canadian Northwest Territories—then an area comprised of all of Canada west of Manitoba save for British Columbia on the far west.

Albert, whose name had also been changed when he immigrated, was now known as Albert Smith. Answering a call of the Canadian government for European immigrants to help settle the territory, Albert had arrived eight years earlier and settled in a place called Belle Plaine, south of Regina. For ten dollars he purchased a quarter section of land—160 acres—and began to clear and settle it. Albert told Lukas that if he joined him in the territories and worked for him for three years, he would thereafter assist Lukas in purchasing his own quarter section.

Over the next two hours, Lukas told Ingrid about his life in Austria, and Ingrid told Lukas about her life in Shelburne. They sat on the wood spindle-backed chairs, their elbows resting on the white linen-covered table, long after the kitchen closed. Eventually, Lukas walked Ingrid back to the train station, to the area below the big clock, next to the ladies waiting room. She prepared to say farewell to this traveller. But there was no need. He asked if he could see her the next day. His train to Regina did not leave until late in the afternoon. The Mosers, who knew the purpose of Ingrid's visit with them, provided Lukas with directions to their residence.

The desire of Klaus to obtain a new farm hand, the desire of Lena to see her daughter wed, and the desire of Ingrid to be united with a man she loved were all fulfilled through that chance meeting in the large hall of Union Station. Unfortunately for Albert Smith, he would continue to be without family on his homestead in the Northwest Territories.

It did not take Klaus and his sister Lena long to discover the treasure that Ingrid brought to the Shelburne farmhouse. Lukas was a bright man with a kind disposition; he was responsible and hard-working. He learned English quickly, although he was never without the tell-tale Austrian accent. From his life in Austria, he had learned the essentials of farming in any climate. After a couple of years serving as Klaus's hand at the farm, Klaus, then aged sixty-five, retired once more from active farming.

Under Lukas's management, the farm thrived. Lukas was able to reap twice as many potatoes as Klaus had in the summer and fall, though he had reduced the acreage devoted to it. To diversify, Lukas began planting other crops too. He used his winters to construct buildings, extending the shed so that it could hold more equipment and the barn so it could hold more animals. Most importantly, though, Klaus used his winters to build greenhouses. In the third year that Lukas was on the farm, he was able to grow vegetables year round, from the fields in the spring, summer, and fall and in the greenhouses in the winter.

Ingrid and Lukas led a happy life on the farm, one beset by little tragedy save the day when the family lost their dear *oma*. Lena, Ingrid's mother, passed away in 1910 at the age of seventy-two. Klaus, Lukas, the children, and especially Ingrid cried for weeks. With her mother's sudden death, Ingrid realized how fleeting their life was. She began to require the children to spend time with their ailing uncle, quietly reading or playing near him or just listening to him tell stories of days gone by. Ingrid expected it would not be long before Klaus joined his sister in the little cemetery up the road. She tried to imagine what it would be like living in the house without her old uncle. She had lived with her uncle since she was eleven. She had kept the house for him for over seventeen years, her mother happily relinquishing the role when Ingrid married, and Lukas had been responsible for all of the upkeep and maintenance of his house. He had acted like its owner in almost every way.

As it turned out, there was no need to consider a life in the farmhouse without Klaus. Klaus's will was read in the spring of 1914, four days after his death, just after his body was joined with his sister's and brother-in-law's in the little Shelburne cemetery. That will, made just after the death of Tobias, left everything not to Klaus's niece and her husband, who had cared for him and the farm for over twenty years, but to his nephew Andreas, who had abandoned him and the farm immediately before that.

"There must be a mistake," Ingrid cried. "He wouldn't put us out of our home." Though they searched the farmhouse from top to bottom, no other will could be found. Andreas, who by then had his own farm, assumed title to Klaus's farm too. He invited Lukas to stay on as a farm hand and agreed to pay him in board—just as Klaus had offered to pay Andreas. Lukas demurred. Shortly after that, he, Ingrid, and Elsa moved to Brampton, where Lukas assumed the role of chief vegetable propagator with the Dale Estate. Wilfred had already left for England with the first contingent.

Chapter 8

SUCCESS

"And that is our story," Mrs. Strauss said. Elsa had left her mother's lap by that time and was sitting on the carpet at her feet. Frances, Jane, and I looked at each other. The account explained so much about Elsa and her family. But not everything. None of us knew quite what to say. Eventually, Frances whispered something to Elsa. "Mother," Elsa said. "They would like to know how my aunt and cousins have found themselves here."

"In that case," Mrs. Strauss said, "we'd better get a few more cookies."

"And some hot chocolate," Elsa said. With those indulgences served, she began again.

* * *

By October 1914, there were in fact three Straussenhoffer brothers in Canada. There was Albert, who went by the name Smith, the eldest brother who immigrated in 1884 to an area then known as the Northwest Territories and which by 1914 was part of the new Canadian province of Saskatchewan. There was Lukas, the middle brother, who went by the name Strauss and who lived above the dairy in Brampton. By this time, there was also Jakob, the youngest brother, who lived in Toronto and who went by the name he was given at birth: Straussenhoffer. Jakob considered himself the luckiest of the three brothers because when he immigrated to Canada in 1911 he had not allowed the immigration authorities to shorten his name. Earlier in 1911, Jakob resigned his post in the Austrian army, took up a position in its reserve, and then immigrated to Canada with his pregnant wife, Maria, intent on joining his brother Albert in Saskatchewan.

Life had been very good to Albert in the years since he settled in Canada. He worked hard as homesteader in Belle Plaine. By 1905, Albert was preparing to acquire a further quarter section of land when he received a handsome offer not with respect to the purchase of land, but rather the sale of it.

Albert took his oxen, his farm equipment, some pots and pans, the savings he had accumulated over the years, and the profits from the sale of his Belle Plaine land and moved one hundred miles further west to a new area opened for settlement. For ten dollars, Albert again purchased 160 acres—a quarter of a section—established an initial home of sod-like bricks and began to break the land. Albert had the resources to easily bring the required fifteen acres of land into cultivation in each of the first three years he owned it. In 1908, he acquired another 160 acres. He fenced his fields, acquired heads of stock, and built a barn and shelters for his equipment. By the time Jakob arrived in Canada, Albert was in possession of four contiguous quarter sections: 640 acres of land in all, an entire section. Now all he needed was family with which to share it.

* * *

The settlement of which Albert's section was a part had a name. Jakob took Albert's letter and showed it to his new wife, Maria. They were still in Austria, about to embark on their journey to Canada.

"Soo-kess. What odd names these Canadians adopt," she said to her husband in German. She knew the province she was going to live in was called Saskatchewan, named for a fast-flowing river of the same name. "What does Soo-kess mean?" she asked, passing the letter back to him.

He read ahead. "Albert says it is pronounced Suk-sess. It means *vohlstand.*"

"*Vohlstand*! How wonderful. Was it named for Albert? Based on his success?"

Jakob read on. "No. Apparently, that was the one-word reply given to another homesteader in the area when he acquired his land from the local railway company. After much negotiating, the railway company sent a telegram to the prospective purchaser with one word: success."

Maria looked at her husband blankly. "I like the Albert story better," she said. From that time on, whenever Jakob or Maria mentioned the name Success, they thought of the success Albert had in homesteading in Saskatchewan. They looked forward to the success that they would have there too.

Jakob and Maria would have been happily situated in Success by 1914 had it not been for three things: Jakob's particularly poor card-playing skills, a Canadian depression, and a world war. Jakob's troubles started on the ship that brought him and Maria to Canada. Fancying himself an able card player, Jakob engaged in some high-stakes gambling at which he lost badly. Thinking his luck had turned, he engaged in further hands on the train that brought them to Toronto, where the bets he placed resulted in his debts being doubled rather than eliminated. Being a man of honour, Jakob felt compelled to stay in Toronto, the location of his creditors, until his debts were paid. He flatly refused Albert's offer to loan him the funds required to retire the debts. Albert would have to wait six more months, Jakob said, to obtain the familial presence he had long wanted.

By Canadian standards, Toronto was a big city in 1911. Though its population was predominantly comprised of British stock, nationalities of every sort were located in many neighbourhoods. Jakob and Maria quickly found the Austrian community in the working class Ward area, not far from Union Station. With their meagre funds they rented a single ground-level room at the back of a big house. The advantages it provided in its own separate entranceway and its easy access to the back alley outhouse and laundry were soon discovered to be outnumbered by the disadvantages of the nightly noise, the cold of the winter that pulsated from the floors and seeped in under the doorway, and the ever-present vermin. But the room had a stove with which Maria could cook and which was frequently used to provide heat. The room was furnished, its ceilings and doors papered, and its floor covered in wood. It would do, they agreed, for the six months Jakob calculated it would take to earn the funds necessary to repay his creditors.

Unfortunately, the poor math skills that led to Jakob's losses at the card table applied equally to his home finance and budgeting process. Jakob had no trouble finding work when he first arrived in the Ward. Toronto was at that time a manufacturing centre, providing over sixty-five thousand jobs in the sector. Though he had no desire to spend his life working that way,

Jakob rather enjoyed his time at the Massey-Harris foundry, then the largest agricultural equipment maker in the British Empire. Each day, he walked the two-mile distance to the foundry on King Street, west of Bathurst, never wanting to incur the expense of a bus or an electric streetcar. He worked ten hours supporting the more skilled labourers manufacturing threshing machines and reapers. He was confident that the knowledge he was acquiring about the construction of the machines would make him more valuable to Albert in their actual operation.

Though he worked those long hours, the wages were not great enough, once amounts were deducted for food, lodging, and other necessities, to lay by the amounts required to quickly eliminate his debts. By March 1912, Jakob had worked for six months in Toronto. He wrote Albert and told him it would be another year before he would be able to travel to Success, Saskatchewan.

This time Jakob's math was correct, but one of his other assumptions was not. The wages that he had steadily received working at the Massey-Harris foundry began to wane. In 1912, the economy was on a downturn that would by 1913 become a national depression. As orders for goods dissipated, so did the jobs to produce those goods. With more men able to work than jobs to employ them, wages fell. By the end of 1912, Jakob was working fewer hours at the foundry and being paid less for the work he did. It might not have been so bad if his hours had been reduced proportionately with all other members of the work force, but as the number of jobs decreased, racial tension increased. The spelling of Jakob's first name, the length and composition of his last name, and his heavy German accent signalled him as a newcomer—a foreigner; a stranger. Work went to strangers only if there were no people of British or French origin to undertake it. Jakob sought other jobs to supplement his income from the foundry.

To make matters worse, in 1913 Maria suffered a miscarriage. Medical expenses were incurred. The costs of running their household were increasing. The amount available to pay his creditors was decreasing. Jakob wrote his brother again. He thanked Albert once again for the offer to loan him funds, politely declined them, and said he would require another year before he and his family could travel to Success.

While the prospect of joining his brother Albert became more distant, it was never far from the minds of Jakob and Maria. Every night when they tucked their son Jonas into bed, they told him about Success and everything they knew about it based on Albert's letters. In Success, they would live in Albert's farmhouse. They would have a separate room in which to sleep; a separate big kitchen in which to eat. The air would be fresh, the sunshine bright. Gone would be the bleak, coal-laden air of Toronto. The smell of growing grass would permeate the spring air. Jonas would run unrestrained through wild, knee-high grass, just as Jakob and Maria had run as children in Austria. He would chase the antelope, jackrabbits, and meadow larks. Apples, carrots, dark rye bread, and sausage would replace the constant watery soups and stews of their Toronto existence. Jakob and Maria rarely referred to the hailstorms, the grasshopper infestations, or the minus forty-five degree winter temperatures Albert had also described.

Every morning, when the family ate breakfast—watery porridge or tough old bread—they looked at the little map Albert had sent them. Jakob marked it with a red pencil, connecting in one long jagged line the route of the CPR that would take them west. With a green pencil he drew the spur that would take them along the new Empress Line from Swift Current to Success. Sometimes, when the family was filling in time, they made a little song about the cities and provinces they would enter as they travelled to their new home.

Jakob and Maria described Success so often to Jonas, they were not surprised that it was one of the first words he uttered. It was also one of the few words he spoke that were not German. Since Maria spoke no English, German was the language spoken at home. Jakob and Maria knew that Jonas would learn to speak English when he went to school—or from his Uncle Albert, who had been proficient in English before he left Austria thirty years earlier.

Jakob's letter to Albert sent in March 1914 announced the birth of his daughter, Clara. He didn't bother to speculate about when his growing family might travel to Success. Although he had paid down his debts to his creditors a little, there was still a large portion outstanding. He would not again commit to his arrival time in Success until he had settled his debts. He was hopeful the date would be a year hence, but having missed so many other projected arrival dates, he felt it best that he not make a further commitment.

It was just as well. Three months later, at the end of July, Jakob realized it would be impossible to pay his remaining debts. The jobs he was able to secure were too infrequent and paid too little. There were no more shifts available to him at the Massey-Harris foundry, or at the Don Valley brickworks, or at the Patterson candy factory, or at the William Davies pork processing plant, or at any other factory from which he had previously obtained work. On a good day, Jakob could find work shovelling coal or ash for a few hours. The dependence of the city on coal meant that there was always coal to be shovelled into trucks, cellars, and furnaces, and in the near reverse, ash to be shovelled from furnaces and refuse piles into trucks. The work was hard on the back and in the latter case the lungs, but Jakob would have happily done it every day, all day, to support his family.

Finally, in July 1914, looking at his beautiful wife and children, the squalor in which they were living, and the few coins he had to his name, Jakob realized that he had to put his family ahead of his pride. Maria cried as Jakob used half of his remaining funds to send a telegram to his brother. Albert responded promptly, sending funds to pay off the creditors and to purchase four train tickets to Success. Unfortunately, in the short intervening period between the request for the funds and their arrival, Canada made two declarations that prevented Jakob and his family from using them.

The first declaration was one of war. That alone would not have prevented the family from going west. The second declaration did. Pursuant to a policy of the Canadian government—instigated by Great Britain—all officers and reservists of the German and Austrian armies were required to report to the local police. The German sort were placed in detention. The Austrians were simply denied their freedom of movement. The British government did not want these men returning to their homeland and bolstering the combatant armies. Jakob now had the financial but not the legal means to travel to Success. He would not be able to join his brother until the war's conclusion. Everyone said that the war would be over by Christmas. Jakob and his family would have to wait until the New Year to travel west.

When they first moved into the street-level apartment at the back of the big house, Maria had Jakob erect a little shelf near their bed. On it she placed the two medals Jakob had been awarded while in the Austrian army: one for strategic foresight, another for bravery. Jakob had no interest in displaying the medals. He considered that part of his life to be behind him. But Maria was proud of what Jakob had accomplished in the army and wanted their son to be proud of it as well. At first, Jakob barely looked at the shelf. But when the funds came from Albert, Jakob chose to repurpose it.

The map that they looked at every morning was tacked to the wall above the shelf. The shelf was renamed the "treasure shelf," and added to it, beside the medals, were two jars. On one jar Maria glued a label with the word "Success" and a picture of the sun. It contained the funds Albert sent to purchase the four train tickets. On the other jar Maria glued a label with a playing card and a big "X." It was a reminder to her husband to stay away from such vices and contained the funds to pay off the creditors. Jakob could have emptied that jar immediately, paid the creditors, and be done with them. But he was concerned that his family might need some of that money. Five months—the expected duration of the war—was a long time to go without wages. He used the funds in that jar to dribble out payments to his creditors, to pay their rent, and to purchase their meagre food. He was determined not to dip into the Success jar. Every night as Jonas went to sleep, they looked at the little map above the treasure shelf and rhymed off the provinces and cities they would go through to get to Success. Then they looked at the two jars and the hope they provided. No one talked about the military decorations.

Jakob continued to search for work. But with more than a hundred thousand people expected to be out of work in the winter of 1914–1915, those who were enemies of the country were the last to be hired and the first to be fired. Jakob exhausted all of the funds in the creditors jar. Eventually he began to dip into the Success jar. Finally, in December, with no funds left in the creditors jar and with few funds in the Success jar, Jakob asked his brother for help. But in this case, the help he sought was not from his brother Albert in Success, Saskatchewan, but rather from his brother Lukas in Brampton, Ontario.

* * *

"So that is why you had to take in boarders?" I asked.

"Yes," Elsa replied, giving her mother time to sip some chocolate, which had long ceased to be hot. "Starting in January, we had to take in boarders so that my parents could support my Uncle Jakob and my Aunt Maria and their two children."

We deduced that the woman on the sofa with the two small children, both of whom had fallen asleep beside her, was her Aunt Maria. "But where is your Uncle Jakob?" Frances asked. He had not been mentioned by Allan and Ricky in their demands earlier that day.

"Just wait," Elsa said. "You'll hear." Mrs. Strauss continued.

* * *

Lukas was not offended to receive the request for financial assistance from his brother. Lukas had offered to assist his younger brother many times. The problem was that by the time Jakob made the request, Lukas, then off of the Shelburne farm, had no resources with which to provide it. Nonetheless, he had to help his brother and his family. He considered his assets. The furniture within the apartment above the dairy constituted nearly all of his worldly possessions. He didn't think any piece of it would fetch much, even if Ingrid let him dispose of it. But as Lukas watched Elsa rise and walk into her bedroom, a thought came to him. If Elsa slept in the same room as her parents, the other room could be let to boarders. In that way, the Strauss family of Brampton could support the Straussenhoffer family of Toronto. In short order, Elsa was relocated and boarders were found—boarders that paid in advance.

Jakob found a third jar for the increasingly crowded treasure shelf. Beside the jar with the word "Success" and the picture of the sun, the contents of which were slowly diminishing, beside the jar with the picture of the playing card and the big "X," which was completely empty, a jar was added with a label on which was drawn a heart. From January until April 1915, that third jar was full at the beginning of each month and empty toward the end.

Jakob spent his days with the other Austrian men in the area, moving from one apartment to another, complaining about their circumstances and considering their options. Initially, they were not all required to register with the authorities. Only those like Jakob who were officers of the Austrian army or who were members of its reserve were required to do so. Just a few fell into that category. But by December 1914, that changed. At that time, over 300,000 people of German origin and over 129,000 people with roots in the boundaries of the former Austro-Hungarian Empire were living in Canada—five percent of the Canadian population. Many, like Albert and Lukas, had come to Canada at the specific urging and at the expense of the Canadian government as it sought to settle the territories and the new provinces. Practically overnight, they were enemies within their new country.

Though Canadians were urged to be kind to foreigners, many of whom had lived in Canada for years, from that day in December 1914, Germans, Austrians, and others were required to register as enemy aliens and to carry a parole card. After completing an undertaking to abide by the laws and to report at the specified intervals (weekly in the case of Jakob and monthly in the case of Maria), their names were placed in a large registration book, updated following each report.

Their treatment infuriated most of the Austrian men in the Ward. Many, especially those who had been in Canada for a number of years, had come to think of Canada—not Austria—as their home. Their allegiance was to the Maple Leaf, not the Edelweiss; to the king, not the emperor. They had not felt as Austrian in years as they had as a result of their enemy alien designation.

"I'd have never thought of harming this country," some said, "until it chose to harm me!" But that was mostly talk, Jakob knew. None—or few—of them really wanted to harm their new country. They just wanted to get on with their lives. They were as eager as everyone for the war to end quickly—possibly more eager than some.

But the war did not end quickly. As it went on, their attitudes began to change. Some of the men laughed at the undertaking not to break the law. "If they won't let me work to earn a piece of bread for my family, then I am going to steal it." That they did. Others talked about leaving the country. If they were going to be called enemy aliens, they were going to act like them.

"You go through the States," one of them said one afternoon when they were meeting in Jakob and Maria's apartment. That alone was contrary to the *War Measures Act*. There were now restrictions on the ability of enemy aliens to speak, associate, and move together. Maria had cleared the treasure shelf of the money jars before the men arrived, as she did each time they met in their one-room apartment. "That's what you do. You go to the States, then you get passage to Italy and from there passage to Austria. You join the army, and then you show these king's men what enemy aliens really look like!"

"But what if you get caught trying to enter the States?" another man asked.

"Then you get put in detention and made to work for the railways," the American schemer replied. "At least you get a wage to support your family. That's more than we have."

At various times, Jakob asked the authorities if it would be possible to travel within Canada—if he could transfer his reporting obligations to another reporting station. Usually he was told that such a request was out of the question. One time though, in February 1915, he was told it might be possible. Further details would be provided the next week. Jakob returned to Maria jubilant.

Jakob's hopes were dashed the next week. His request would be considered, he was told, but only if he provided details about where he would be going and with whom he would be staying. His brother Albert had not registered with the police authorities in Saskatchewan. Having been known as Albert Smith for over thirty years, and having been a good English linguist even before he came to Canada, Albert had no intention of declaring his Austrian citizenship to the authorities. Jakob was certainly not going to expose him. He again reconciled himself to staying in the Ward for as long as the war endured.

But by the middle of March 1915, Jakob was becoming desperate. He had gone through three months of payments from his brother Lukas. The amount provided was not enough to support Maria and the children, though he knew it came at a cost to his Brampton family. He was dipping into the Success jar more and more. There was no end in sight to the war. He had heard stories about Austrians that had left Toronto surreptitiously. Jakob wrote a last letter to Albert. For the next three weeks, as his family stared at the jars on the treasure shelf, Jakob stared at his military decorations. His hope, he now realized, would come from those medals he had lost interest in and not the jars and their dwindling contents.

Albert's reply provided Jakob with everything he required. Applying his full military voice, he ordered Maria to ask no questions. Going to a second-hand clothing store, he bought himself, Maria, and Jonas each a new coat, hat, and pair of boots. For Clara he bought a pretty dress with smocking at the top, black tights, and a pretty knit sweater, bonnet, and booties. Gone were Jakob's *lederhosen* and collarless jacket, Maria's embroidered blouse and dirndl skirt, and the children's *strümpfe* leggings, knit by Maria. Jakob bought a handbag for Maria and a solid case for himself. On their way home, they bought four loaves of fresh bread and eight apples. It had been a long time since they purchased so much food at once. It was their family's night to access the communal bathing facilities. Jakob instructed Maria to take special care with herself and the children. He asked her to curl her hair. That night, after they put Jonas to bed, Jakob told Maria the plan. In the morning, they packed their few possessions and emptied the remaining funds from the jars on the treasure shelf, depositing them in a special purse Jakob tucked away in the inside pocket of his new coat.

"Should we take the map, Papa?" Jonas asked.

"No, Jonas. We won't be needing that any more."

"What about your medals?" Maria asked.

"We will leave them behind too," Jakob said. "They've served their purpose." That they had. They reminded Jakob that he was an officer of the Austrian army. He had been decorated for strategic foresight and for bravery. He was no longer going to cower to the Canadian authorities; he was no longer going to subject his family to life in the hovel of their one-room street-level apartment. Jakob issued the final instruction to his German-speaking family. It was the most important instruction of all. For the next two hours, they were not to say a word. Not a single word. Maria and Jonas indicated their agreement. There was no need to obtain such a commitment from the nonspeaking Clara. The cries of babes were not of a particular language. As they walked out of their Toronto home for that last time, Jakob leaving first, holding the hand of four-year-old Jonas, Maria slipped back and swept the medals into her new handbag.

Jakob was glad that the day was overcast and foggy. The coal soot clung in the air, further obscuring the three smartly dressed English-looking people walking down Bay Street. Once in Union Station, Jakob extracted the four tickets Albert purchased. It would have been impossible for Jakob to purchase the tickets himself. With his accent, he would most certainly have been asked for identification. His status as an enemy alien and the restrictions on his travel would have been revealed. After looking up at a large sign, he led his family to the area assigned to those departing on Track 3. Two dozen people were already in line. Jakob and his family took their place at its end. He put the suitcase on the ground at his feet, let go of Jonas's hand, and then took Clara from Maria. The train was due to depart in thirty minutes. He assumed they would board it within fifteen minutes. They waited. Soon there were more people in line behind them. They waited.

When the train was five minutes away from its scheduled departure time and still not in the station, Maria looked at Jakob, her eyebrows crossed. "What's going on?" they seemed to ask. "I don't know," his shrugged shoulders silently responded. They waited. Clara began to squirm in Jakob's arms. He gave her back to Maria. They waited.

Jonas became restless. Another boy had left the line to bounce a ball. Soon another little boy joined him. Finally, a man ahead of them flagged down a man in a uniform.

"The train is delayed," the uniformed man announced. "It will not arrive for at least half an hour." There was a general shuffling as people moved positions—without leaving the line. Jonas tugged his father's hand and then pointed to the boys playing with the ball. "Could he play with them?" his eyebrows asked. Jakob shook his head. Jonas's head dropped. He moved closer to his father. They waited.

The woman ahead of them had finally run out of things to discuss with the woman in line ahead of her. She turned to Maria. "I am going to Regina," she said, "to visit my sister. Where are you heading?" Maria did something she had never done before. With her fingernails under Clara's leg, she pinched her daughter, hard. The child screamed. The woman understood that Maria's attention had to then be focussed on her crying child.

Another half hour passed. The uniformed man returned. "Ladies and gentlemen," he said, "the train will be arriving in fifteen minutes. We will begin boarding in twenty minutes." *Just twenty-five more minutes*, Jakob thought. No one in his family had said a word in over two hours. They just needed to stay quiet until they were settled in the private sleeping compartment Albert booked for them.

Finally, the train entered the station. Within minutes, those leaving the train paraded by those waiting to succeed them. Travellers at the head of the line began to pick up their bags. They called in their children. Jakob kept his eyes forward, willing the line to move; willing his family, along the platform to Car 5 and into Sleeping Compartment 4. They would be in it any minute now.

"Come on, Freddie," a man ahead of Jakob hollered to his ball-playing son. Two other boys had joined him in the long wait.

"One more throw," Freddie said as he looked at the boy positioned between him and his father. The boys had been playing catch without incident for quite some time. They were not positioned far apart. Their throws were really lobs. But that last lob of the ball, that last lob to be made before Jakob and his family boarded the train, that last lob was fateful. It was more a throw than a lob. The aim was somewhat wide. The boy intended to catch it, but having just been called by his own parents to rejoin the line, was distracted. The ball's full force, not lessened by any intervening object or any great distance, landed squarely on the head of a boy not playing with the ball, a boy whose attention was firmly fixed on his father.

"Ouch!" Jonas hollered clutching his head. "*Ses tut weh*!" ("That hurts")

It was as though a bomb had detonated. All the waiting travellers stopped talking. Those ahead of Jakob and his family, whose eyes had been positioned on the platform ahead of them, looked back. The uniformed man stopped inspecting tickets. He walked slowly to Jakob, who was holding Jonas next to him, rubbing his head.

"Your papers, please," he said.

Jakob, Maria, and the children were taken into a small room. Only Jakob could understand the questions being asked; only he could answer them. Maria tried to be strong, for Jakob's sake. She reached into her handbag and slipped something into his pocket. He put his hand in his pocket and clutched his medal for bravery. It was true, he said. He was trying to make his way to the United States, with Austria being his ultimate destination. The fact that their tickets had Swift Current, Saskatchewan as their destination? He thought his family members would be less easily detected if they went west before going south. The name of the state to the south of Saskatchewan? Jakob, Maria, and Jonas had memorized the provinces, not the states below them. Jakob pictured the map above the treasure shelf. "North Dakota," he said calmly, particularly happy that Albert had planned to meet them in Swift Current and had not sent the connecting tickets to Success.

"It's a long way out of your way," one of the officers said before looking at the two other officers in the room.

"Makes me really confident that we're going to win this war," another officer said jovially. They all laughed.

Two hours later, Jakob was arrested. The contents of his pockets were confiscated, including not only the four train tickets and his army decorations, but also the money in the purse he put in his coat pocket earlier that day—the remaining funds from the Success jar; the funds he planned to return to Albert on their arrival in Saskatchewan. The authorities had a right to confiscate all of Jakob's possessions. They took one look inside his case and gave it to Maria. Three hours later, Maria and the children, in their fine English-looking clothes, were back in their dark, cold, street-level room. They would not be there long. As Jakob had instructed, with her last remaining funds Maria sent a telegram to Lukas. The next day, she and her children moved to Brampton. Once again, Albert would be without a family member in Saskatchewan. He would however continue to farm unmolested. Thanks to Jakob, the authorities knew nothing of Albert Smith or his relationship to the Austrian internee, Jakob Straussenhoffer.

* * *

The events of the day and the relating of the story of the Straussenhoffers affected me greatly. The story itself stayed with me for years. I felt that I knew each member of Elsa's family. I came to love them all—well, nearly all. I had no love for her Uncle Andreas, who had essentially robbed her family of their home in Shelburne. Specifically, the story and the events of the day affected me in three ways.

First, when the day commenced, I had in Frances one kindred friend. As I left the apartment above the dairy late that afternoon, having received warm embraces from Jane and Elsa, I realized I had three. Jane had been kind to and protective of Elsa for eight months. In the future, I would assume a similar posture.

Second, the order of our walking foursome returned to its natural position. The next morning, Frances and I met Jane and Elsa at the corner of Nelson and Main, as we had each school day before the late February falling-out. As we began the familiar walk north on Main Street, Jane in front, Frances behind her, Elsa gave me a little shove. It was a kind shove. It was a shove that said, "Thank you. I appreciate what you did for me yesterday." From that day on, as our foursome walked two by two, I walked in front, beside Jane, Frances and Elsa walking behind us.

Third, for the first time ever, I was the lead orator at our dining room table. It took me all of the main and the dessert courses that night to relay to the best of my ability the story told in such detail by Elsa's mother. My mother, my father, and my grandfather were captivated by it throughout my entire telling—until the very last. "Oh, and one other thing," I said before Mother and I rose to clear the table. I had deliberately saved this one part until the end. "Grandpa, Mrs. Strauss told me that you and Elsa's grandfather Tobias were friends." I wasn't sure which person to watch while I made the statement, but I chose my mother, who reacted predictably.

"How ridiculous," Mother said, "to think your grandfather would be acquainted with an Austrian stone quarry owner." She threw down her napkin. "I now wonder if we should believe any part of the story." But I had seen the look on Grandpa's face earlier when I mentioned the name Tobias Pichler. I knew that the friendship between a contractor and a stone quarry owner was not that ridiculous at all.

Chapter 9

JIM'S GRADUATION

April 9, 1915 was a noteworthy date in our family. It was the day we gathered to celebrate the long-pursued admission of my brother Jim to the Royal College of Dental Surgeons of Ontario. A momentous accomplishment for any person, it was considered especially significant for Jim, whose entry to the Royal College had been anticipated by our father practically since the day Jim took his first breath and whose initial pursuit of it had been forestalled by illness. The stomach and headache-inducing malady, which no doctor could diagnose, required Jim to withdraw from his first year of dental studies just six weeks after they began. Father insisted the condition was pneumonia. After pressing the case with the Royal College, Father arranged for Jim to be readmitted to the program as a freshman a year later, in September 1911. Jim's last year of dental studies saw a return of an unknown malady—this one inducing the need for copious amounts of sleep. The condition, which lasted the better part of six months, left as quickly as it arrived following Millie's threat to seek a romantic attachment elsewhere if Jim could not summon the strength to see her on Saturday evenings.

The significance of Jim's successful completion of dental college was so great that it was deemed appropriate to be commemorated twice. Consistent with the tradition that had been established when the Royal College of Dental Surgeons was first formed in Ontario as an independent school, its graduates were honoured in a ceremony admitting them to the profession. Commencing in 1888, when the school became affiliated with the University of Toronto, its graduates participated in a second university convocation ceremony the following month at which the degree of doctor of dental surgery was conferred upon them. While each graduate was expected to attend both ceremonies, there was no expectation his entire family would do so. No expectation, that is, except in families like ours. A large Stephens party assembled in the auditorium of the dental college to attend the first of the two ceremonies. A cadre of us would return six weeks later to attend the second.

Concerned that we not miss a minute of that first ceremony, under Father's direction we arrived in Toronto at the dental college a full hour before the program began. We had the distinction of being the first to enter the auditorium within the four-storey brick building located at the corner of Huron and College Streets, gaining us admission to the first row of seats behind those reserved for the graduates. We were all there: Mother, Father, Grandpa, Aunt Rose, Hannah, John, and Millie. Even Ina was with us, having returned from Winnipeg earlier that month, nearly restored to her old self. The only local family member absent was Aunt Lil, who deemed the tiresome laying of hands and longwinded addresses too tedious for her attendance.

As we waited for the ceremony to begin, we reviewed the program and its list of thirty-nine graduates—all but one were male. I contemplated the six speeches to be made and wondered if Aunt Lil was correct in her assessment of the dearth of stimulation they would provide. But while others, in contemplating the outcome of the day's events, could only raise their spirits with the prospect of Jim's admission to the profession, a few of us had something further to consider. That morning, as I sought assistance in the placement of my new hair bow, I overheard a private conversation among Mother, Father, and Jim in the tower of my parents' bedroom.

Mother had her hand at the back of her top bureau drawer. I recognized the small black box she extracted since, at my behest, she had shown it to me on a number of occasions. She opened the box and displayed the contents to Jim.

"Grandpa gave this to me just after your Grandma Brady died," she said to Jim. "He hoped you might ask for it one day. It's a garnet. Grandpa gave it to your grandmother on their twentieth wedding anniversary, when his business was booming. He wasn't able to afford anything like this when he married her—or, as I think about it, for any significant anniversary after their twentieth. She offered to sell it many times. He wouldn't hear of it." She pulled the ring out of the box and held it to the light, looking at it wistfully. Returning it to the box, she made the lid fast and handed it to Jim. "It will make Grandpa very happy to see it on her finger. You know we already love her like a daughter."

"It's going to be quite the day for you, son. A day you will always remember," Father said, patting Jim on his back.

Jim thanked Mother and Father and put the box in his inside jacket pocket. It would have been noticeable if the jacket fit him better. Hanging lankly on his five-foot-eight-inch, one-hundred-and-forty-pound frame, the single-breasted wool blazer had once been Father's.

"Where and when do you intend to ask her?" Father asked.

"Tonight, after the party," Jim replied. "At Gage Park. In the bandstand."

"Won't it be dark?" Mother asked. "And cold?" Although there had been no new accumulations of snow in more than a month, the ground continued to be strewn with hard, greying clumps of ice that refused to give way to spring. It would only be just above freezing that night.

"Not really," Jim replied. Mother was entirely transfixed as Jim described to her the elaborate arrangements he had made for the propitious event. Father, having listened to the first couple of sentences, turned his attention to his sock drawer, the contents of which were apparently in need of straightening.

I was about to enter the room and throw my arms around Jim, but his next words caused me to turn back around the curved wall that separated my room from my parents' room. "You won't say anything to anyone, will you?" Jim asked. "I want her to be surprised."

"Of course not," Mother and Father said in unison before Mother added, "but we will be looking for a full report in the morning."

It was all I could do to contain my delight as I entered my parents' room a few minutes later. For once, I revelled in the tangles Mother sought to eliminate from my hair. The painful pulls kept from my face an all too knowing smile.

* * *

While others read and reread the program, waiting for the ceremony to begin, I stared at Millie, who was sitting beside me, and in particular her left hand. I imagined the teardrop-shaped garnet on her thin ring finger. I contemplated how it would look on her wedding day as she held a dangling spray of Dale roses in front of a long ivory gown. In time, Millie noticed the direction of my gaze. She thought that it was focused on her purse, resting on her left side. "Is it that noticeable?" she asked. "I'd hoped I could give Jim his graduation gift at some point today without having to go home to get it." Until that moment, I had not noticed the rectangular object pushing out against the flat front of her black leather bag.

"Most people won't notice it," I said, truthfully enough while also managing to avoid disclosure of my actual thoughts. "What did you get him?" I asked. I knew it would pale in comparison to what he was going to give her.

"It's not much, really," she said modestly. She opened her bag and pulled out a wooden case. Inside it, laid in felt grooves, was a pen and pencil, each made of matching dark balsam wood. The wood was inlaid with a brass panel engraved with "James G. Stephens, DDS, RCDC." Following the letters were two lacrosse sticks with a rose in the space above where the handles crossed each other. I admired them.

Jim did not receive many presents to commemorate his graduation. Father had laid out a great deal of money over the years to assist him in acquiring his degree. Aunt Lil had provided him with reduced rate room and board. Mother organized a graduation party. Jim insisted that everyone had done enough for him and that no presents were warranted. Within our family, only Aunt Rose ignored the plea, presenting him ten days before his commencement with a camera. Jim and I spent many hours together reading its directions, pressing buttons, turning knobs, inserting, and removing film and taking pictures in various lights. We were ready to capture the images of the day.

Eventually, the ceremony commenced. We received ten minutes of welcoming words from the chairman of the board of the Royal College and then another fifteen minutes of welcoming words from its registrar. When we felt we had been sufficiently welcomed, we received similar greetings from the president of the university, who after fifteen minutes advised us that he would be addressing us again in six weeks' time when we reassembled at the university's convocation.

Father's friend, Dean Willmott, the big white-haired man who came to tea at our home one evening nearly four years earlier and who spoke then of nothing but dentistry, was the next to speak. At seventy-eight years of age, his presence was still commanding, although I wondered whether he was a little frailer than when I had last seen him. Within the first two minutes, he laid out for us the subject of his discourse. Over the next forty-five minutes he proposed to enlighten the audience on the evolution of the dental profession in Canada; to describe its evolution in focus from the mechanical aspects of eating and speaking to chemistry and biology and their contributions to oral health; and the relationship of dental disease to disease more generally. He proposed to describe the latest developments in the profession, including the use of *sonoform* as a local anaesthesia.

"Ladies and gentlemen," he began, "it is hard to imagine that any profession anywhere in the world has made as many advancements in so short a time as has our dental profession in the Province of Ontario. Why, it was not long ago that charlatans were pulling teeth under circus tents in front of hundreds of onlookers as a method of entertainment. It was not that long ago that teeth were pulled by uneducated barbers. It was just five years ago that the connection was drawn between unsterilized equipment and oral infection."

* * *

"Isn't it too bad that Aunt Lil missed that speech?" I asked Millie as I vigorously joined in the audience's polite applause at the conclusion of the oration.

"Yes, I'm sure she'll deeply regret her decision not to join us," Millie replied with what I took to be a surprising note of sarcasm. I gathered that the students were not that enamoured with the dean's remarks either.

"Can you believe that windbag?" a graduate in front of us said to the fellow beside him, loud enough for everyone near me to hear. "Why would he think that topic would be of interest to our family members?"

"Like I always say," the fellow graduate replied with equal volume, "the old man's going a bit daft."

A military man spoke next. He was short in stature, with a thin face and a surprisingly low voice. He paid special tribute to the Canadian Army Dental Corps that had recently been formed to support the eight-month-old war effort. He described the military dental clinic that had been established at the Canadian National Exhibition grounds, the first of its kind in Canada. In addition to providing dental services to the base of army personnel, the members of the corps were involved in the review of candidates wishing to enlist in the Canadian Expeditionary Force. Just as a recruit could be rejected for armed service due to having flat feet, so he could be excluded for having bad molars. Initially, a determination as to whether recruits were orally fit to serve was made by physicians or drill sergeants who considered a loss or decay of ten or more teeth to be a disqualifying condition. They were in this uninformed way barring many men with good oral health and admitting many with bad oral health. The involvement of dentists was sure to improve the selection process for recruits. Members of the corps would also serve overseas. There they would assist in the reduction of oral health problems including not just usual issues of decay but also the emerging problem of trench mouth, an acute disease that incapacitated large numbers of soldiers.

The dentists serving overseas were not posted in isolation. McGill University had created a medical unit known as No. 3 Canadian General Hospital. Due to arrive in England the following month, it was comprised of thirty-five physicians, seventy-five nurses, two dentists, and over two hundred other healthcare providers, including many dental students.

The military man ended his speech with a plea for others to take up the cause. "Other universities are following the lead of McGill. Queen's University in Kingston is well in process, and so, importantly, is the University of Toronto. It is my sincere hope that No. 4 Canadian General Hospital out of the University of Toronto will be deployed within the next month or two. Four members of your class have volunteered to be among them."

"Four?" I heard the loud boy ahead of me say. "Macdonald, Atkinson, and MacNevin. Who is the fourth?"

"Probably has his numbers wrong," the boy beside him said. "He should stick to counting rounds of ammunition."

"For the sake of God, the king, and the country, I ask all of the graduates to consider this noble and so very badly needed service. You are young. You have your whole lives ahead of you. Make this sacrifice now for your country—for a year, or maybe less. Then go back to your families and begin the career you have long planned. The country will be better for it! *You* will be better for it!"

While some family members clapped enthusiastically at the conclusion of the military man's remarks, a number of them, like most of the graduates in front of me, appeared to be looking at their knees or the knees of their neighbours while they politely applauded. It reminded me of times in school when I did not want to be called upon to answer a question or to participate in an exercise in front of all of the other students. If the teacher did not catch my eye, I might not be singled out. I assumed that those graduates who were motivated to serve God, king, and country had already indicated their intentions to do so. The others did not want to be caught by the eye of the military man.

The final speech was given by one of the graduates. The valedictorian recounted the tribulations of the "mob" who beset the college four years earlier; the trials they suffered at the hands of the sophomores; the retribution they as sophomores visited on the freshmen; the hours they spent perusing *Gray's Anatomy*; the teeth they learned to manufacture, first with mud, then with vegetables and ultimately with ivory; their athletic pursuits; the holidays they took (possibly the most of any year?); and their socializing. To knowing chuckles, he observed the changes in their physiognomies over those four years: the addition of a few bristles, the graying of hair, and the adoption by some of a matrimonial status.

Mentioning not a word about the war or any military pursuit, he ended with some rousing words: "We have borne the burden and heat of the day—we have weathered the storms of uncertainty and doubt and withstood many trying ordeals—all to the end that we may be fully prepared for the faithful discharge of our duties in connection with a noble profession."

Dean Willmott's talk of oral sepsis and mastication was forgotten, and the call for patriotic action was entirely banished from thought. The graduates stood to applaud the words they had longed to hear: that they were but one stage-walk away from pursuing the profession they had so long sought. The families, who had in many cases sacrificed much to enable them to do so, joined in the ovation.

In that spirit, the graduates left their seats to begin the "laying of hands," as Aunt Lil referred to it. In the time-honoured way, each walked across the stage, shook hands with the dean, received from him a word or two of wisdom, and then accepted a rolled and beribboned diploma before exiting the stage on the opposite side. The ages-old ceremony with all of its pageantry could not, following those rousing words of the valedictorian, contain the enthusiasm of most of the graduates. Flashing wide, well-tended, toothy smiles and waving at the audience, thirty-seven male graduates and one female graduate—Mary Elizabeth Livingston Nicholson—bounded across the stage to embrace their new profession. Only one crossed the stage in a truly formal matter, the head always looking forward; the face in repose; the pace, even and unhurried. The difference was obvious and slightly unsettling until Father whispered to our large party, with great pride, that Jim's procession was the only one that accorded the ceremony the level of respect and solemnity it deserved.

Jim's new camera was much in use following the ceremony as families coalesced and the graduates moved from one group to another, singly and in packs, to meet the families of their chums and to pose for pictures. Jim seldom left Millie's side, his classmates flitting to him rather than him to them. Mother and Father's pride swelled with each classmate met, all of whom referred to Jim as a true friend with a sincere soul, a boy held in high esteem by one and all. Jim's natural bashfulness was apparent as he took each compliment silently, with a slight smile and bowed head.

The celebrations continued later that day in Brampton. Mother served a large supper for all who had travelled with us to and from Toronto for the celebration, as well as for Jim's closest Brampton friends and some of our neighbours. Once the cold meats and cheeses and the Queen Street Bakery breads and cakes were consumed, Father called for the attention of all assembled.

Although I had never known Father to make a two-minute speech when one of twenty minutes duration could be made, his emotions for once got the better of him. Before succumbing to them, however, he was able to remind everyone that it had been nearly fifty years since his parents, Jas and Selina Stephens, immigrated to the small village of Brampton—a community then of less than a thousand souls but with much promise. They saw the opportunity in that village and were determined to plant within it long roots on which successive generations of their family could establish themselves and thrive. A sturdy tree with four large limbs had been grown there in Brampton's Peel plain. Two branches remained, each thriving. He glanced appreciatively at Aunt Rose before casting a look of derision at Aunt Lil, who had left Brampton for Toronto in her early twenties. I knew that Aunt Charlotte, who left with her husband and two children eight years earlier, would have received the same glance had she been present. Father only wished that his parents were then alive to see his eldest child about to embrace his heritage, to start his own profession in the building they had purchased, to build his life in this community they had helped bring to fruition.

It sounded like he intended to go on, but after a few unsuccessful efforts he stopped, looked up and said, "I think we have heard enough long speeches for one day." Instead, he reached behind him and clasped from the sideboard a long, thin, gift and handed it to Jim. A hush fell over the room as Jim took the object out of the luminous fabric in which it was wrapped.

Addressing all assembled, Jim said, barely above a whisper, "It's a new sign…for the door of our building."

The room erupted into applause as he hesitantly held up the black-and-white sign. "Dr. Jethro G. Stephens, D.D.S., R.C.D.S.," and below it in the same script, "Dr. James G. Stephens, D.D.S., R.C.D.S." I noted that there was room at the bottom of the sign for the engraving of one more name.

While the new sign may have been a surprise, there was of course no surprise in the arrangement the sign declared. Jim joining Father's dental practice had been preordained for almost as long as Jim's joining of the profession. The installation of the new sign was to be one of the few actual physical changes to the Stephens Building at that time. Father had determined that for the first few years of their business association, he and Jim would alternate the use of Father's dental furniture and equipment, with Jim using it initially to perform more elementary procedures and to assist Father in performing those more complex. Eventually, our cousin John, who was then eighteen and about to enrol in dental college, would join the practice as well. The son and two grandsons of Jas and Selina Stephens would operate from their building the largest dental practice in the area. The front apartment would be converted from a residential apartment into additional office space. The income that could be generated by three dentists practicing in the entire second floor space would more than offset the rent lost from the front apartment and would be realized with significantly less inconvenience.

"I suppose you are confident that the university will confer the degree next month," Jim said, referring to the degree of doctor of dental surgery represented by the "D.D.S." on the sign.

"I have it on good authority," Father replied. Everyone applauded. "We'll get that installed tomorrow," he said, pointing to the sign. "And an identical one will be installed at the top of the stairs."

"Thank you, Father," Jim replied in a slow, hesitant manner, "for this sign and for all it represents, and for the sacrifices you have made to enable me to attain the degree displayed. I hope that you will always be as proud of me as I know you are today."

He stopped, looked down, collected himself, and then continued. "To the rest of my family and Millie, thank you for the good meals, the good advice, the understanding, and the welcome diversions you have provided from my studies." There were a few chuckles before Jim began again.

"Finally, I would like to thank our friends and neighbours for coming today, and especially for supporting me and my family over the past four years." I wondered if every graduate had to extend such thanks to their friends and neighbours or if the words were only necessary by virtue of Father's actions two years earlier. "It is never easy to start a new phase of one's life, no matter how prepared one is for it. I know that you will support me and my family in its new course, just as you have in the past." He stopped, reached for Millie's hand, and looked down again.

"That was a bit glum," Aunt Lil said to no one in particular. She had agreed to join us for this part of the celebration, notwithstanding the likelihood that she might have to listen to a speech or two. She then led the guests in three hearty rounds of "Hip hip hooray!"

It was nearly ten o'clock when the last guests departed. Aunt Lil left with Aunt Rose to spend the night at her house before catching the first train back to Toronto the next morning. Jim announced that he was going to walk Millie home, and Mother came to usher Ina and me upstairs to our bedroom.

"No, Mother," I said. "Please let me stay and help you tidy up." I wanted to be awake when Jim came home, to be among the first to congratulate him on his betrothal.

"Whatever are you thinking, child? Look around you. Mrs. Fenton, Aunt Rose, and I were cleaning up throughout the evening. The only things left to deal with are three teacups. I assure you I can manage those. You too, Ina," she said. "Up to bed."

Ina was about to object. She didn't normally retire so early. She had resumed her job as a telephone operator on her return to Brampton earlier that month, frequently working a later afternoon shift. She did not need to rise early. But it had been a long day for all of us, so she complied with Mother's direction.

We slowly ascended the stairs. While Ina turned at the top to enter our room, I took a slight detour into Mother and Father's. Before the westernmost tower window, I stared down toward the park. The bandstand was well out of my sightline, as I knew it would be. I joined Ina in the room that was once again shared between us.

When we were both in bed, Ina ruminated, "I don't know what the hurry was. Why was it so necessary that we come up here at this hour? I'm still wide awake."

How interesting, I thought. For once, I knew something about Jim that Ina did not. I wondered whether I was bound to keep the proposal a secret at that point. I had made no promise to do so. Only Mother and Father had made that commitment, and they had only agreed to keep it until Jim actually proposed.

I was tired, I conceded, and as I did so, I recalled my many unsuccessful efforts to stay awake in anticipation of hearing about a desired event. My best hope of staying awake was to continue talking.

"Ina, do you really not know why Mother sent us up here now?"

"I have no idea."

"I do." I waited for effect. "It has to do with Jim."

"Jim? What about Jim?" I considered lording the secret over her, as she had done to me so many times before. I considered requiring her to utter excessive compliments as the price of my revelations; to threaten to keep them in confidence if I was not fully satisfied. But I did not have the ability to do so. I was bursting to tell someone the exciting news. I heartily wished it could have been someone I actually liked to share secrets with—someone like Frances or Jane, but I had not seen Jane that day, and I hadn't seen Frances at a time when I could make the disclosure.

"It has to do with Millie, too," I said disgorging the entire secret in less time than it takes to snuff a candle. It would have been impossible to make Ina eke it out of me. "He is proposing to her tonight. Right now. In the bandstand."

"Tonight? Are you certain?" she asked, clearly surprised, and, I could tell, somewhat skeptical. "But how do you know?"

"Mother gave Jim Grandma Brady's garnet ring this morning before we went to Toronto. I walked into Mother and Father's room as she was giving it to him. But he asked Mother and Father to keep it a secret, as he wanted to surprise Millie."

"Yes, of course he did. And in the bandstand. Isn't it rather dark? And cold?"

"Not really. Did you notice Sarah and Eddie leave the party a little early tonight?"

"How could we miss it? Jim begged them to stay longer. But no, Sarah had a headache. Honestly, he should take up with someone of heartier stock—and with a less irritating voice!" Years ago, Millie and Frances told me that I would come not to notice Sarah's irritating voice. They were right. I had long stopped noticing its scratchy din.

"She didn't really have a headache. And Jim didn't really want them to stay. They had to leave an hour earlier than Jim in order to get the bandstand ready. At this very moment," I said, repeating the description Jim provided to Mother and Father earlier in the day, "it is bathed in the light of twenty-one candles—one on each side of the steps leading up to the platform, twelve on the circular ledge around the perimeter of the bandstand, and one large lantern on a blanket in the middle of the floor. Also on the blanket are twelve long-stem Dale roses—and not the rejects from the flower dump, but twelve flawless roses."

"What colour and variety?" Ina asked. Mother had asked the same question. Every Bramptonian knew the colours and varieties of the Dale roses.

"Champagne. American Beauty varietal."

"Very nice. Go on."

"Decorating the bandstand, draped from the top of each pillar and connected to the top of the next, is a length of white tulle." I think he would have had the Citizens Band playing a piece by Chopin if he could have found a way to arrange that and keep the proposal a secret.

We lay there in silence, picturing it all. "I want to stay awake until he gets back," I said.

"Yes, I want to do that too." It was unusual for us to want the same thing, to be similarly engaged in any activity not mandated by our parents. How strange, I thought, that I was about to obtain by marriage the sister I had long desired when the one to whom I was borne twelve years earlier was finally beginning to feel kindred. We lay back on our pillows, waiting for the sound of a door opening. We waited a long time.

* * *

The early morning sun was seeping into our bedroom when I awoke. Reaching over, intending to slowly raise the blind, I lost my balance. The tug on the porcelain knob that hung from the blind's lower edge was so hard that on letting go, it spiralled noisily up around its roller. I shuddered, expecting Ina to roar with protest at her brusque awakening, but the promise of the previous night's events eliminated that usual response.

"It's morning," I said. "I fell asleep before Jim came home."

"I did too," she said, to my great relief. I could not bear the thought of her congratulating Jim before me, particularly when I had been the first to know of the felicitous event.

Dressing quickly, we noticed as we left our room that we were the last occupants of the house to rise. All of the other bedroom doors were ajar. Jim's bed was made. His room was neat and tidy. Cast in the glow of our brother's certain joy, we started happily down the stairs when we were struck by a racket louder than the madly spiralling window blind—the banging of piano keys. Mother played the piano for two purposes: one was to practice hymns to be played in church, consistent with her role as its organist. The other was to relieve stress, disappointment, and ire.

"Mother, what is it?" we asked as we hurried into the parlour. The tune emanating from the keys was not a church hymn. Neither expecting nor receiving a reply, we ran through to the sitting room, which was devoid of any person, and then to the dining room. In that room we found two people. Father sat in his usual position at the head of the table, his uneaten toast on a plate in front of him, staring at the flowered china pot that held his favourite strawberry jam, a cigarette between his fingers. Grandpa sat in his usual position on the far side of the table, assuming a similar pose, the heavy white-and-green leaf motif pot containing his favourite marmalade the object of his attention. Jim's usual seat was empty. There was a napkin strewn across the plate that had been his. A piece of cut apple could be seen underneath the napkin.

"Father," I asked, "what's happening? Where is Jim?"

Obtaining no reaction at all, I turned to Grandpa, who offered no reply either. I looked at the table at which the two men sat. A small arrangement of flowers left over from the party the day before was positioned in the centre. Salt and pepper cellars were scattered about. But there in front of Mother's place near her half eaten toast was one item I had never before seen at our table.

Though we had not yet received answers to any of the questions posed, I asked another, more pointed one. "Father," I asked, "why is Grandma Brady's ring here?" My voice was laced with panic. There was no reply.

"Father," Ina asked sternly, "where is Jim?" Father did not look up from his jam pot.

Ina and I stared at the two men. Mother hammered out her moronic music in the parlour. I walked into the kitchen. As I suspected, Jim was not there.

"Grandpa," I pleaded, trying to rouse him as I returned to the dining room, "where is Jim?"

He looked up slowly. "On his way to Toronto. He left a few minutes ago."

"To Toronto?" Ina asked. "Why?"

"There is something he feels he must do."

"What is it he feels he has to do, Grandpa?" The only answer came from the black and white keys two rooms away. Dread spread through me.

For once, Ina's instincts and mine were in unison. We turned and ran for the front door. We were down the street, across the Wellington Street Bridge, and halfway up Main Street when we realized we were too late. The first train out of Brampton chugged across the overpass with Jim and Aunt Lil onboard. We walked home slowly, tears streaming down our faces, our arms wrapped around each other.

None of us attended the convocation ceremony of the University of Toronto six weeks later. A notation on the program indicated that four members of the 1915 class of the Royal College of Dental Surgeons were on active service with the Canadian Expeditionary Force. My brother, James Gershom Stephens, was one of them.

Chapter 10

PAULETTE

That long day following Jim's graduation, while Mother played her gloomy strains and Father and Grandpa stared at the breakfast things, we all hoped that Jim would change his mind before he reached the enlistment centre. We were certain that the notion to enlist had come upon him quickly—within the eight hours between his ill-fated proposal to Millie and his announcement at breakfast the next morning. We hoped it would leave him with equal rapidity.

Aunt Rose, who joined our waiting circle on seeing Ina and me walk back from the train station, unusually in tears and even more unusually in an embrace, agreed that a change of heart was certainly possible. But whether his heart would change before he began the formal enlistment process was another matter.

"It was that damn recruiter," Father said when he finally began to speak. "He put that idea in Jim's head. I don't know why Willmott let him address the graduates yesterday. There were enough other speeches. The students are right, he is becoming daft. There were those graduates, all ready to begin their profession, to build practices, to improve the health of their communities, to marry and have children—why was it necessary to talk of war and—" He was going to say "death," but the recruiter had not actually done so, and Father couldn't bring himself to say the word that was the natural extension of war.

Grandpa and Aunt Rose echoed those sentiments. None of us wanted to say what we really suspected. Jim had not succumbed to the recruiter's implorations. His decision to enlist surely arose from his love for Millie—or more specifically, her rejection of that love. If he couldn't have a life with her here, we assumed he had chosen not to have any life here. None of us would suggest he had chosen not to have any life at all.

"It's Millie's fault," Ina said, finally uttering the words. "What kind of a girl is she? Agreeing to be his sweetheart through the poorest years of his life and then refusing him when he was about to be in a position to actually support her? I never liked her. But I didn't think she was capable of being this mean."

Father had a different perspective. "I was always surprised that those Dales would let her see Jim. 'Not good enough.' I expect that's what they told her. 'Not rich enough. Go get yourself a commission in the army. Become a war hero. Then maybe we'll consider you good enough.' See if I ever buy another Dale rose. Don't hold your breath!" He was on a tear now.

Aunt Rose disagreed. "Oh, I don't think that can be it," she said. "If the Dales had considered it an unsuitable match, they would have had Millie break it off years ago. Do you think there is someone else? I would never have expected it. She seemed so devoted to Jim. And yet what other explanation can there be?"

"Maybe the ring was too small," suggested my cousin Hannah, who had joined us. Grandma Brady's garnet ring still sat on the dining room table. To be fair, it did look small sitting on its own in that black box. But on Millie's delicate fingers, I was confident it would have looked lovely.

"Maybe he won't pass his physical examination," my cousin John offered. "How good are his teeth?" Father glared at him, never so sorry, I think, for insisting upon good oral hygiene for his children.

"Let's just hope he comes to his senses and returns home before it's too late," Aunt Rose said.

Variations on these themes followed until I could take it no more. I ran to my room and threw myself on my bed. I was not sure what upset me more: the terrible things they were saying about my beloved Millie; my sense of loss for a sister who was so nearly my own; the pain I felt for Jim's broken heart; or the dread I felt about his enlistment. But I knew this: Millie was not the duplicitous, superficial, or mean person of those speculations.

I thought of the many kindnesses she had showed me over the years, the numerous occasions on which we laughed and how she bolstered me when others did not. I thought of the time, years ago, when I came across Jim and Millie and Eddie and Sarah in the tree at the Forks of the Credit; the many times she located Jim for me when he was working at the Dale Estate; the night I sat with her waiting for news of the lost Archie; and the little bouquet she helped me make and cast into the Etobicoke Creek the day of Archie's funeral. I thought of how she arranged for me to participate in the hundred-acre bicycle ride, though I was young and Ina had forbidden me to do so, and how she worked with Father to sell the tags to raise funds to send the Excelsiors west. I thought of the beautiful writing instruments she presented to Jim the day before. I did not know why she refused Jim, but I was certain it was not for any of the speculated reasons. I cried until I fell asleep, hoping that when I awoke, Jim would be back, his senses restored. I could barely tolerate the loss of Millie as a potential sister. I could not lose Jim as an actual brother.

Jim did return that night, but without, it seemed, his senses. He realized he owed his family an explanation, although the one offered was not very satisfactory. He had for quite some time been considering joining the Canadian Army Dental Corps. He had a skill set that the expeditionary force required. He did not have any patients of his own. Father had not yet altered his practice to accommodate him. Clearly, he had no children and was not married—although he had until that day wished to be so.

He passed his physical examination and received the first set of inoculations. He let it be known that no amount of persuasion would alter his course, to which he was now intellectually and morally bound. He refused to discuss Millie or what happened the night before except to ask us not to speak about her ever again in his presence. He returned to Toronto the next morning to commence six weeks of training with the second contingent, then quartered at the Canadian National Exhibition grounds.

For the next few days, we functioned in a daze. On the third day, Father vacillated between being mystified and angry. He ordered me to stop crying, an edict to which I could easily accede, as I had not a tear left in my body to shed. He ordered Mother to stop playing the piano, a directive with which she complied, her fingers too sore to continue pushing the keys. The new signs for the dental office were put in the cellar. Grandma Brady's beautiful ring was returned to Mother's bureau, though it sat atop the polished surface rather than resuming its former position at the back of her top drawer.

Eventually, we came to accept that Jim was in training to go overseas; that he would become a member of the expeditionary force; that in a matter of weeks we would say goodbye to him, not knowing if we would see him again. Eventually, we came to accept that Jim's name would be one of the names we would have to look for on Mr. Wood's lists of the dead, injured, and missing.

The boys in training for the Canadian Army Dental Corps were provided with two hours off per evening and one day off per week. Many men spent that free time with their sweethearts. Some of those sweethearts had held that distinguished position for many years. Some of the sweethearts had newly achieved the status. Many of those who were not yet wives were planning on becoming so before their beaux set sail. There was no shortage of girls willing to assume those roles. Wearing pretty dresses with hemlines well above the ankle, assuming alluring poses and adopting an always gay disposition, they gathered at the Dufferin Street gates of the training grounds, waiting for an invitation past the guarding sentries or for an escort away from them to the nearby coffee shops and cinemas. The girls were very alluring—too alluring, it seemed, for Jim to resist.

So it was that within seven days of proposing to join with Millie in holy matrimony, Jim became caught in the embraces of one Paulette Flynn, a tall, thin brunette from Toronto with poor manners and even less grace. Four years younger than Jim, she had what I considered to be a painted appearance. Her long, thin nose ended in a little ball that was accentuated by rouge applied heavily in circles where her cheekbones protruded in similar small orbs. The make-up, applied in almost equal intensity to her chin and forehead, gave her an exceedingly colourful look, especially combined with the shiny red affixed to her pouty lips.

We had the dubious pleasure of meeting Paulette on three successive Sundays when Jim brought her home to Brampton on his days at leisure. Each occasion was cause for greater concern. On her first visit, she established the habit of calling the adult members of my family by their first names—something then considered the height of disrespect and poor breeding. Not even Grandpa or Father were spared this peculiar conduct, although Grandpa was then eighty years old. As for Father, the nomenclature was particularly galling given that since he became a dentist over twenty-five years earlier, no one had called him by his Christian name other than his then deceased parents, his three sisters, and, occasionally, his wife.

I did not believe Paulette's naming customs sprang from disrespect. She did not look down on our family. On the contrary, she seemed quite impressed with what we had. No piece of furniture, book, knick-knack, or length of linen was above her appreciation. "Oh, Mary," she would intone to Mother. "I so adore your silver service. The pattern is so like my mother's." She saw more of these items than most guests did since within each room she entered she felt free to open every curio and chest drawer, to lift the glass doors of every bookshelf, and to peer inside each urn and candy dish.

She constantly draped herself over Jim, sitting so close to him while on the sofa, she was nearly on top of him. On the third Sunday she was with us, she called Jim by her pet name: "lover." She spoke that day openly about her future with Jim, weighing aloud the relative merits of marrying him before he commenced or after he returned from overseas service. I noticed that Mother lost her appetite that night.

I tried not to draw comparisons between Paulette and Millie—there were too many, and to itemize them would only diminish my already poor regard for Paulette. But in one respect I revelled in their differences. Paulette would have nothing to do with me. She ignored me completely.

During her second Sunday with us, as she made her way through our things, I suddenly became terrified about Grandma Brady's ring, which was still in its black box on Mother's bureau. The thought had no sooner occurred to me than Paulette announced the need to use the washroom. We had only one, and it was on the second floor. Springing from my chair in the sitting room, I bounded up the maid's stairs and flew across the second floor hallway, prepared, if necessary, to physically restrain her from entering Mother and Father's room. It was not necessary, but that night I begged Mother to remove the ring from her bureau and hide it in a place that would not be known to either Paulette or Jim. Mother did not disagree with me, but she did ask why I was quite so insistent.

"Mother, if Jim doesn't have that ring, he won't be able to marry her."

"Oh, child, I wish it was that simple. Neither this ring, the absence of the reading of the bans, or the lack of our consent will stop such a marriage from proceeding if the two of them are intent on it." I thought back to the remarks made by Aunt Rose and John the day after the graduation. Aunt Rose hoped that Jim would return home that day, having come to his senses. John suggested that Jim might fail his physical examination.

"Mother, do you think that Jim has truly lost his senses? Is he becoming daft? When they gave Jim that examination to join the corps, did they check his head as well as his feet and teeth?"

Mother smirked and then asked me to elaborate. "How could Jim take up with a girl like that?" I asked. "And so soon after he proposed to Millie?"

"I've been wondering the same thing," she confessed. "I have a few theories. I don't think he is becoming daft, but I think he may be scared. She may provide him with a diversion from the enormity of the decision he has made. He may think that she will keep him connected to home. I think those boys all want a girl back home to pray for their safe return; to send them love letters; to give them a reason to return; to give them succour before they leave."

I thought about that. I didn't see why he needed a girl to do any of those things. We could keep him connected to home. We would pray for his safe return, send him letters, give him a reason to return, and support him before he left. "What are your other theories?" I asked.

"That he is mad at Millie or that he is trying to forget her."

I thought each theory was plausible, but I didn't think that any of those possible explanations was a good reason for Jim to take up with Paulette.

After Paulette's third visit with us—the "lover visit" as I came to think of it—Father asked Jim not to bring her to Brampton the following weekend. It would be his last before he departed. Father said that Mother did not want to share him with anyone other than the family for the better part of the two days he would be with us. Jim, realizing that he had caused his parents enough heartache, did not object. But he let it be known that his relationship with Paulette would be governed by their feelings for one another and not by the feelings of his parents toward her. Mother and Father's efforts to conceal their aversion had not been successful.

By mid-May, the members of the No. 4 Canadian General Hospital of the Canadian Expeditionary Force formed by the University of Toronto were at full strength and ready to embark. The dentists within that division numbered 151. Fifty-three of them, including Jim, were given the rank of lieutenant. Supporting them were nearly one hundred undergraduates or experienced laboratory men, all of whom held the rank of sergeant.

Jim came home to Brampton the weekend before his division left for Montreal and thence England. It was decided that our family would see him off from the Brampton train station the Sunday afternoon before his departure. Mother said she did not want to shout her final goodbyes over the din of the hundreds of others who would be gathered on the train platform in Toronto. She did not want to be jostled and pushed by other people seeking one final embrace from their sons and brothers. Moreover, she did not want to share that farewell with Paulette. It was still not clear to us whether Paulette would merely be part of Jim's Toronto send-off party or also part of his future. It was agreed that Ina would travel into Toronto with Jim, and she and Aunt Lil would represent the family at the send-off there.

That Saturday night, our house was filled with well-wishers. Jim's dearest friends, Eddie and Sarah, and their parents, members of our church, people with whom Jim went to school, those with whom Jim worked at the Dale Estate, the Governor and his family, who came from their apartment on the top floor of the jail, Aunt Rose, John and Hannah, the rest of our neighbours, the members of the town council, our pastor, the members of the senior and junior Brampton Excelsiors, and the Young Men's Debating Society, and dozens of others, all came to wish Jim Godspeed. Mother, Father, Grandpa, Ina, Jim, and I stood in the parlour, greeting all of them. To my mind, the only person missing from our gathering was Millie. But we had not seen her since the day of the graduation. She did not come to visit us, and none of us ventured near the Date Estate. When it appeared as though our paths might cross as we walked down the same street or found ourselves in the same room, one of us took a different route or found an excuse to go to the other side of the room. I missed her terribly, but I did not know what to say to her, and, it seemed, she did not know what to say to me or to anyone else in my family.

While the tidings of the others in my family to our assembled guests were warm and tender, I confess mine were on the cooler side. Though I knew I should have been appreciative of the solicitations of our neighbours and friends, I was in fact, resentful. I said how happy I was to see each person, but I was not. At Mother's request, I passed around little dishes of sweets to make our guests feel welcome. In reality, I wanted nothing more than for them all to leave. Jim was my favourite sibling, dearer to me than any other family member. He was my confidant, my champion, my inspiration, my companion. He understood me better than any other family member.

I knew that every moment the guests spent with him was one moment less I had with him. Every sentence they exchanged with him was one less that I could. As I walked from person to person extending the dishes, I reviewed the catalogue of things I wanted to tell Jim before he left; the questions I needed him to answer before he embarked. Jim would be gone for an indeterminate period. I did not know when I would see him again. I did not know *if* I would see him again.

The things I had to say to him and ask him about were not things of which I would ordinarily have spoken at that time. They were things that would have been revealed, as he often said, when I was older. I feared that by the time I was old enough for those matters to be divulged, he might be too far away to communicate them. I knew that when I really needed the answers to my questions, he might not be able to provide them.

I wanted to tell him, for instance, that I had decided to start playing hockey. Our family seemed to excel at that sport, and Father was anxious for me to become more athletic. A girl's hockey league was then forming in Brampton.

I wanted to tell him how much I admired Mary Elizabeth Livingston Nicholson, the lone woman in Jim's graduating class the previous month. I needed to know from Jim how she fared in that position; how I could tell our parents of my desire to become a dentist; how I could obtain Father's support in that; how I could tell Father that I did not want to be a public school teacher.

I wanted to tell Jim that in four more years, if the war was not yet over, I would enlist too. I would find a way to do so, even though I was a woman, and I would find him. I wanted to tell him that I had grown an inch in the last month and that I was not sure he had noticed.

I wanted tell him that I was sweet on Collin Heggie, and I thought that our family physician's son was sweet on me too. I wanted to tell him about a film I had seen at the Giffen Theatre a few months earlier; how it displayed people walking on the moon; and how the image still made me laugh.

Then there were the questions. I would ask him why our family could not enter the Presbyterian Church and what had made Grandpa "others destroyed." I would ask him where he was all those times I could not find him at the Dale Estate. I would ask him why Mother thought that Mr. Gilchrist had not donated the stone to the Presbyterian Church.

I would ask Jim why Millie had refused to marry him and whether he was going to marry Paulette. I wanted to know whether he loved Paulette, and if so, what he could tell me about her that would allow me at least to like her. I would ask him how he could have loved Millie so intensely one week and then so shortly afterward love someone so entirely different. Thinking back to a conversation I overheard between Grandpa and Jim the night Jim was assaulted outside St. Mary's Catholic Church following the meeting of the Young Men's Debating Society, I would ask him what fight Grandpa had intervened in that led Jim to suggest their situations were so similar.

Mother indicated in her at home cards distributed earlier that week that we would be receiving guests until ten o'clock that night. I counted the minutes to that terminating hour, reciting the things to tell and ask Jim, picturing the two of us on the little sofa in the sitting room talking long into the night. I estimated it would take us two hours to get through all of those matters. Unfortunately, the enthusiasm of our guests for Jim's attention could not be contained. By the time the final guest departed at half past eleven, Jim was exhausted. Rather than being the last in our family to retire, he was the first. The tightly shut door to his room made it clear that the long conversation I desired would not occur that night.

I rose early the next morning, not wanting to miss a single opportunity to speak with Jim alone. I dressed for church and waited in the parlour for him to come down the stairs. I wanted to catch him before he joined the rest of the family at breakfast. My stomach growled as I waited. By the time he came downstairs, breakfast was served. There was no time to speak alone.

We would soon be walking to church. Possibly, I thought, he and I could leave for church early and walk there on our own. But Ina appeared to have the same idea, and asking him first, the two were out the door before I finished clearing the breakfast table, as my responsibilities required. Ina's manoeuvre, given that she would have Jim alone with her on the way back to Toronto, struck me as particularly vexing. The fact that Ina did not know of my desires for private time with Jim was irrelevant in my castigations.

As I walked to church with the rest of my family, I sifted through the things that I wanted to tell and the questions I wanted to ask Jim, identifying those public matters that could be raised in front of others. About a fifth of them fell into that category. I could raise them at dinner—if Father would indulge me. The noontime meal would only last an hour. I would sit with Jim in his room afterward, discussing the more private matters while he packed up his few things. If I was organized, we could get through most of the matters over dinner and in the half hour in his room afterward.

Jim ate his last meal in our home before he embarked in full uniform. His loose-fitting graduation ceremony jacket had been replaced by a long, form-fitting brown wool coat, cinched at the waist with a wide brown leather belt. Underneath it he wore a taupe-coloured dress shirt and a tie of the same colour, but darker. His trousers were met at the knee by funny *puttee* bandages that wound around his legs and over the top of his boots. His hat, with its firm brim, sat on the ottoman next to the wall behind his chair.

There were just six of us at the table for that final send-off meal: Mother, Father, Grandpa, Jim, Ina, and me. Aunt Rose had declined to attend, wanting us to have Jim to ourselves for this last meal in Brampton. She, Hannah, and John would join us at the train station at two o'clock, half an hour before Jim's train would depart for Toronto.

With every mouthful of that meal, I contemplated the matters to be raised. But while we sat at the dining room table eating Jim's favourite dishes, my lips uttered no words. It was not that Father invoked his usual "children are to be seen and not heard" rule. I think he would have welcomed almost any conversation at that meal—regardless of who commenced it. It was not that I could not find an opportunity to speak in an otherwise full discourse. The six of us ate in near silence, our compliments to Mother on the tender roast of pork, the crisp roasted potatoes, the sweet young carrots providing the only dialogue between the quarter hour chimes of the grandfather clock in the hallway. There were, it seemed, no military battles for Grandpa to speak of; no marvels regarding the telephone switch that Ina could recount; no military trivia for Jim to relay. Even Father could not find a subject to discuss, although he could usually be relied upon to complain of the imposition of new or higher taxes, of which there were quite a number.

With every opportunity, I could utter not a word of what I longed to discuss. Though my mouth opened several times, it closed each time around a fork full of food. The water I drank to lubricate my larynx served only to spawn sweat from my brow. Partially, I felt that even the public matters I had designated to be discussed in front of my family were actually too private to raise. Partially, I worried that raising them would annoy Father and possibly the others too. While I thought Jim would understand my immediate need to discuss these things at that time, the others might deduce that in raising them then, I had concluded there would never be a later opportunity to do so, a possibility that no one in our family was willing to acknowledge.

I resolved to wait—to discuss the private matters with Jim while he packed, as I had planned, and to corral him into walking with me to the train station, where I could speak with him about the public matters. Even if others overheard us as we walked, with less attention on me, I could raise at least some of them. With that plan in hand, I resigned myself to eating in silence.

But that silence did not last long. It was broken by a quick rapping at the front door while we ate Mother's vanilla snow pudding. After confirming that none of us were expecting visitors, Jim rose to answer it. A few moments later he reentered the dining room. There was something he needed to attend to. He would leave then and meet us at the train station in an hour—at two o'clock, half an hour before his scheduled departure. We could not imagine what he needed to do, but we could hardly restrain him. Jim gathered his bag, which, unbeknownst to me, he had already packed, and left the house, his bowl of pudding half eaten.

"Do you think it is Paulette?" I asked. "Would she have come to Brampton?"

No one had an answer. The ease with which I anticipated eating Mother's dessert was quickly replaced by panic. Afterward, as I helped Mother clear the table, I reconstructed my list of things to say and questions to ask. I struck a few. I wouldn't ask, for instance, why Millie had refused him. I had asked him that question three weeks earlier and was told that I was too young to understand. I expected he would not find I had gained sufficient additional maturity in the interim. We would have half an hour at the train station. I condensed my list of matters that could be discussed in front of others to one that could be processed in ten minutes. Surely, I could speak with him alone for a further five minutes and get through at least a few of the questions I hoped he would answer privately.

The bells of St. Paul's tolled two o'clock as we arrived at the CPR station. There were only a few people on the platform. Old Mrs. Grafton sat on the bench next to the station, half covered by the shade of the roof's overhang as she awaited the southbound train that would bring her second cousin from Orangeville. A little farther down the platform, Mrs. Beck and her daughter Kathryn waited to board. They were on their way to visit Mrs. Beck's mother in Toronto.

I looked both ways down the track for Jim. I had begun to formulate our five-minute private conversation. I narrowed my list to three items.

As we waited, I could not help but think how different this occasion was from the last time we had come to this station to say goodbye to Jim. A mere ten months had passed since more than a hundred cheering fans joined us to send the boys off in their quest for the Mann Cup while the Brampton Citizens Band played in the background. The speeches by the mayor and others encouraged the boys to play well, to be polite, not to smoke or swear, to reflect well on Brampton. It was less than a year. It was another age.

Aunt Rose, John, and Hannah joined our quiet group around five past two. "Where is Jim?" Aunt Rose asked.

"We don't know," Mother replied, exasperated. "Someone came to the door as we were finishing our dinner. He said he had to attend to something and that he would meet us here at two. I guess he's running a few minutes late. I hope he gets here soon. I think we all have some last-minute things we would like to say to him."

Another five minutes passed. Still no Jim. I could feel my ten minutes of public conversation and my five minutes of private conversation slipping away. I was becoming more anxious.

It was a quarter past two. John offered to check for Jim at the far ends of the station platform. He ran to the north end and then back. There was someone coming, but it wasn't Jim.

I abandoned the notion of spending time alone with Jim. It was clear there would not be enough time. But I was increasingly anxious. What could be keeping Jim from his family, I wondered. I could only think of one person he might consider more important than us at that moment, and what he would be doing with her was too horrendous to consider.

Huffing and puffing along the platform came Tom Mara, our mayor. "Hello, Doc. Mary. Rose. Children. Sorry to be so late. I know this is hardly the send-off we gave to the eighteen boys last August, but I wanted to come and again wish Jim Godspeed," the mayor said. It was indeed a far different send-off than that formed by the fifteen hundred people who gathered the previous August just after the war was declared. We were a party of thirty, if you counted Mrs. Grafton, the Becks, and the smattering of others who had arrived on the platform to travel to Toronto or some point along the way. There was no one from the Dale Estate waving a Union Jack. The Citizens Band was not leading the crowd in the singing of "God Save the King," "The Maple Leaf," "O Canada," or "Rule Britannia."

"Where…" The mayor looked around. "Where is Jim?"

Mother provided the same explanation she had provided earlier to Aunt Rose. John ran to the other end of the platform.

Father was becoming agitated. As much as he had not wanted his son to enlist, having made the decision to do so, Father expected Jim to excel in his position and certainly to be on time for his departing train. Father was about to leave the platform in search of him when John hollered from the south end of the platform that my brother was on his way.

It was two twenty-five. Jim ran down the platform to join us. Following him at a slower pace were two other people. For once, even Ina was happy to see Sarah as she and Eddie accompanied Jim to our party. Based on their sombre countenances, it was clear that their goodbyes had been said.

In the distance, we could see the bright headlight of the train coming toward us from the north.

"Well, none of us likes long goodbyes, do we?" Jim asked in a light tone. No one replied. He was right, but clearly on this occasion, we all would have liked one slightly longer than what we were about to receive.

He shook hands with the mayor and then gave each of us a final tender embrace. When he got to me, he bent over and lifted me up, pulling my chest to his and spinning me around. I wrapped my arms about him and leaned into his neck, inhaling his usual musky scent before noticing that it had been combined with the sweet fragrance of the most delicate flower of the Dale Estate. Millie's distinctive perfume clung to Jim's wool uniform.

As he held me, I thought of all the things I wanted to tell him; all the things I wanted to ask him. I opened my mouth, and for once that day, in his presence, words were emitted. "I love you, Jim."

"I know you do, Little One." He lowered me back to the ground and gave one of my ringlets a tug. "I love you too." My anxiety dissipated. Maybe there was nothing more that needed to be said. Maybe everything else was too great or too trivial.

Earlier that afternoon, Father had asked that we all contain ourselves when Jim embarked. He thought it undignified for anyone to be crying at the station. We obliged as long as we could, but there was not a dry eye on the platform as Jim ascended the train.

A strong gust of wind blew onto the platform as the train left the station, forcing my damp handkerchief out of my hands. It sailed high up in the air before landing behind us, near the station. As I ran to retrieve it, I saw another crying figure just beyond the station. Seeing me moving toward her, she retreated farther away. In a moment, Eddie and Sarah rushed past me, taking the heaving figure in their arms.

* * *

Immediately before Jim boarded the train, he gave Mother an envelope. She opened it as soon as we arrived home. In it were two documents. The first was a copy of the standard form last will and testament each recruit was required to complete. Jim had provided for all of his worldly goods, such as they were, to go to Mother. The second was a direction regarding his paycheque. Jim would be paid a regimental allowance of $1.35 per day, an allowance of $0.15 for each day he was in the field, a monthly separation allowance of $29.50, and a clothing allowance of $13.00. He directed that all such amounts should be paid to Mother. By these two documents we came to understand that Jim's relationship with Paulette was over.

Chapter 11

THE CABAL

Expected and unexpected diversions took hold of the inhabitants of our home in the weeks following Jim's embarkation for Great Britain. Predictably, Mother could be found most often in the parlour on her piano bench, her fingers making their way over and over her entire melancholic repertoire. Grandpa could most often be found in his favourite chair in the sitting room, next to the parlour, one of his many newspapers in hand, poring over every article pertaining to the Great War. Father resumed his dental practice during the day, continuing his work as the chairman of the High School Board and Water Commission as required. In September, Ina commenced her undergraduate studies at Victoria College at the University of Toronto, becoming the first of Aunt Lil's female boarders.

As for me, my time in those early days, when not in school, was principally spent in three places. The first was Jim's room. Alone there, sitting on his bed, inhaling his lingering musky scent, I stared at the objects that were so dear to him: his drawing paper and instruments, including the new pencil and pen Millie gave him on the day of his graduation; the camera Aunt Rose presented to him for that same occasion; a growing compilation of developed photographs; a stack of completed sketches; and shelves of books and magazines. On the top of his glass-faced bookshelf, I stared at the assortment of items he had acquired through the years, including numerous model cars and countless athletic trophies. Occasionally, I wondered what would become of all of this if Jim did not return from the war. I knew from the contents of the envelope he gave Mother before he boarded the train that they would initially become Mother's. But what would she do with them after that, I wondered, before admonishing myself for ever contemplating that Jim might not return home.

When not in Jim's room or at school, I could in those early days generally be found on our verandah, waiting for a letter from Jim or at the post office making inquiries about the receipt of one. Mr. McCulla, our aged Peel County postmaster, was well known to me. In addition to being a member of our church, he was also a renowned local personality, having once been the secretary of the board of health, the clerk of the town, and afterward a Conservative Member of Parliament. He'd lost his seat in the last decade of the last century for failing to take a hard line stance on a bill that made him most unpopular with the Orangemen of the time. He was well in his eighties when he oversaw the post office during the war, generally holding his command from behind the counter. Though he left most deliveries to younger stalwarts, he prided himself on making some deliveries every day.

"Good day, Jessie," he would say to me whenever he saw me. "Are you without cares today?" Until Jim left for England, my answer was nearly always, that I was indeed carefree. But in the days after Jim's departure, my response was slightly different. "I will be carefree, Mr. McCulla, if you tell me you have a letter from Jim."

"I'd so like to take away your cares, Jessie, but I'm afraid I have no letter from Jim at this time. But soon I will. Mark my words." For twenty-eight days, two or more times a day (Sundays excluded), Mr. McCulla and I engaged in the same exchange. While I sat on the verandah at noon and half past three in the afternoon, while I stood at the counter of the big post office building at eight in the morning and half past five in the evening, I imagined the correspondence Jim and I would exchange. The weeks, days, hours, and minutes of time together that this war had deprived us I was confident could largely be made up in a full and lively written exchange. I knew that our letters would be read by censors—but I knew that the things I wanted to tell Jim and the answers I wanted him to impart were not military secrets. While I did not want our writings shared with our kith and kin, I cared not if they were read by army personnel.

Finally, one morning in late June, a full four weeks after Jim departed, Mr. McCulla approached our house and without inquiring about the state of my cares announced that he had something to entirely relieve me of them. It was a thin enveloped addressed to Dr. Jethro Stephens, Brampton, Ontario, Canada. The stamp on it bore a picture of the king and noted that it cost one penny. It had been posted from England.

"Gracious child!" Mother said, trying to calm me as I ran into the house calling for her. "It's just a letter. You have not received a pound of gold!" But I felt like I had, and what is more, I knew Mother felt like she had too. Though she tried to dampen my enthusiasm, she took that letter, put it in the small pocket of her apron, near her heart, and would not remove the letter or the apron even while preparing to sit at the dinner table.

Father too tried to downplay his elation at receiving the letter, insisting that we finish our noontime meal before it was read. Consuming the victuals with uncommon speed, we all silently calculated that any resulting indigestion was well worth the reduction in time between the meal's commencement and the reading of the letter. With the plates cleared, Father summoned the delivery of a letter opener. After anxiously obliging, I returned to my chair at the table so quickly, I nearly missed its seat. "Calm yourself, Jessie," he said. "There are a few more formalities to attend to."

I could not imagine what they could be and was beginning to regret all the quick action. My stomach hurt. I was not sure if that was because of the speed with which we ate or my anticipation of the reading of the letter.

"First of all," Father said, "your Mother would like to say a few words."

Mother? Mother never made speeches, though perhaps a few words uttered to one's husband, father, and daughter did not quite constitute a speech.

"Thank you. Yes, Jessie, I wanted you and Grandpa to know that based on your father's good suggestion, I have prepared a special basket in which we will lodge all of the letters and cards that Jim sends home." She reached under the table and pulled out a large wicker basket the sides and handle of which were covered in red and blue cloth. "The colours you will see match the Red Ensign, which, being our flag, I thought somewhat patriotic. Blue is Jim's favourite colour, and of course, red is the colour of our hearts. I will put the basket on the chest in the front foyer so that we will see it many times a day, and we can all have ready access to what I expect will be a great accumulation." Before leaving for Britain, Jim had promised Mother and Father that he would write home once a week, so Mother spoke those last words with great confidence.

"Thank you, Mother," Father said, "and befitting the importance of our communications with Jim, it is my desire that we develop a certain formality pertaining to them. Specifically, all letters and cards to and from Jim will be read at this table with all of us present, after the meal which succeeds the delivery of his correspondence to us or precedes the posting of our correspondence to him. Whether his letters are addressed to one, two, three, four, or five of us and whether our letters be written by one, two, three, four, or five of us, the treatment shall be the same. This," he said pointing to the letter then in Mother's hand, which at that point felt as though it had been delivered days earlier, "I am confident will be the first among many. Mother, may I please have the letter."

The letter was passed from Mother to Grandpa and then from Grandpa to Father.

"It is dated May 30, 1915 from Shorncliffe and reads as follows:

Dear Mother, Father, Grandpa, and Ina (assuming that you come home at some point and read this, Ina),

Just a note to let you know that I have arrived in England and that all is well. The train ride from Toronto to Montreal was uneventful save for the loss of my hat. The boys on the train were a merry lot, including not only the members of the No. 4 General Hospital Division but also many recruits on their way to Val D'Or for basic training. They left us at Montreal, but as we boarded the SS Corinthian, *we were joined by a number of other army recruits who had completed that training and were on their way to join the expeditionary force. The crossing to England was cold and stormy, with not just a few people experiencing the sea sickness Grandpa oft described to us regarding his first crossing fifty-eight years ago. Of course, we completed it in considerably less time, and there were no crying babes or hungry rats on this ship nor prejudiced bullies on the shore!*

We arrived in England on May 27 and were moved to St.
Martin Plain, part of the Shorncliffe Camp in Kent. This camp
has been used for military purposes since the late 1700s. We
will stay here until we are ready to be shipped to the front. I
do not yet know when that will be but will keep you apprised,
as I am able, of course.
I miss you all already.
Yours affectionately,
Jim

"Gracious," Father said. "I wonder what happened to his hat." I
wondered what happened to his hat as well. I also wondered what prejudiced
bullies he was referring to. But in reality, I was far too preoccupied with
matters raised earlier in the letter to focus on those near the end.

"Isn't that good to hear," Father went on. "You see, Mother, all that
moronic music and for what? He is fine. We must go on with our lives.
That's what I've been telling you. And that is what this letter confirms. Jim
is fine. I've read about Shorncliffe. He may well be there for quite a while.
What do you say, Grandpa? Aren't you cheered by this letter?"

Grandpa opened his mouth to reply, but before he could, I interjected.
"Father, could you please read it again?"

"Ah. Well, certainly. It isn't very long. 'Just a note—'"

"No, Father, if you don't mind—from the salutation."

"From the salutation. Yes, I noticed there was something a bit odd
about that—"

"Please just read it, Father—faithfully."

Father cleared his throat and read. "'Dear Mother, Father, Grandpa
and Ina (assuming that you read this at home, Ina).' Now Jessie, I know
what you are wondering. I expect that Jim was just so excited to report
to us that he inadvertently forgot to list you. I am sure he meant to. You
see he wrote this long bit for Ina. He was likely so caught up in that, he
accidentally forgot to list you."

Mother, also anticipating my feelings and knowing that Father's explanation would provide no comfort whatsoever, tried a different tack. "Jessie,

I expect that Jim intends to send you a separate letter—one especially for you. That is likely why this one is not addressed to you."

"Why could he not have addressed this one to me too?"

"As I say, I expect because he had a separate special one for you. Just be patient. You'll see."

Shall I describe the feelings I endured that day and in the days succeeding it? Shall I describe how I felt as each day passed with no further communication from Jim—none for me especially, or for the family in general? My heart hardened. Why had I wasted all those hours waiting for the mail to be delivered? Why had I so frequently inquired at the post office? Why should the first letter to arrive not even be addressed to me when it was me—me and only me—who had made those twice daily inquiries at the post office, who sat diligently, day after day, waiting for its arrival? If there was a separate letter for me, why had it not arrived? What was I to do if it ever did arrive? How could Jim and I have that lively, loving, illuminating dialogue that I sought to take the place of the conversations unspoken in the days and hours before his departure? How could I tell him the things I wanted to tell him? How could he provide the answers I longed to obtain, when Father proposed to read all of our correspondence at the dining room table?

Jim should have made time for me before he left. He should have found the time. He should have done that. If he loved me so much, why had he not done so? He did not make the time. He did not find the time. I knew he loved me, but he could have tried harder. He could have. He didn't. I became mad with Jim.

With my heart growing harder, I ceased waiting for the deliveries of mail. I made no further inquiries at the post office. I stopped going into Jim's room and sitting on his bed. I no longer looked at his drawings, his photographs, his books, his awards, or his memorabilia. I brushed my hair so hard and wound it so tight, there was not a stray curl available to long for a tug.

Thus, I was almost surprised when Mr. McCulla stopped me on the street near the end of June, more than a week after we received Jim's first letter. It was a Saturday, and I was on my way to visit Jane. "Whoa, Jessie," Mr. McCulla said, halting my determined effort to pass him without comment. "Jessie, are you carefree? I have something to make you so. A postcard from your brother, Jim. I just left it with your Mother. Addressed specially to you, it was. Didn't I say you'd have a fine correspondence? I expect you'll want to run right home and read it and send him a reply. He'll like to hear from you."

I thanked Mr. McCulla. I thanked him profusely. Then I lied to him and told him I was running a pressing errand for Mother but that I would look forward to reading the card as soon as I could. I spent the entire afternoon with Jane looking for a four-leaf clover. The old lawns of Haggertlea were quite extensive.

I had no intention of reading the card Jim sent me and even less intention of replying to it or to any other letter or card he sent. Mother had already replied to the first of Jim's letters. As instructed by Father, her reply was read aloud before being mailed. She had asked me to jot a little note at the end of hers, but I refused. Since she had suggested in the body of the letter that my note would follow, she felt compelled to explain its absence. She made a notation about the extensive amount of studying I was undertaking for my upcoming examinations. It was a true, if not particularly relevant fact.

Mother concealed the arrival of the postcard until we had concluded the night's meal. At that time, with great fanfare, she announced the correctness of her explanation for the odd salutation of Jim's first communiqué. His card to me had in fact been the first correspondence sent home. For some reason, however, it took longer to arrive at its intended destination. "There," she said, extending it to me, "don't you feel better?" Without waiting for an answer, she asked whether I would like to read it aloud.

"No, thank you," I said, my hands remaining firmly crossed in front of me.

"No?" she asked doubtfully, extending the card farther toward me.

"No, thank you, Mother."

"Would you like to read it to yourself first?"

"Now, Mother," Father interjected, "that is not the way it's to be done."

Stymied, she tried another approach. "Shall I read it then? Would you like me to read it aloud?"

"You may if you like, Mother. It's up to you."

She and Father exchanged glances.

"Hear! Hear!" Father said. "What is this malarkey? Why don't you want to hear what your brother has written to you?"

"I just don't. That is all, Father."

"Well, that is among the least considerate things I have ever heard. I'm so glad that your brother cannot hear you. Mother, if you will pass the card to me, I will read it aloud.

> *May 19, 1915*
> *Miss Jessie Stephens, Brampton, Ontario*
> *Dear Jessie:*
> *This is the boat we are on. It looks pretty fine, doesn't it? We are having dandy weather and a good sail. My cap fell out of the train window yesterday near Kingston, so I'll have to wear my balaclava cap until we get to England. It is just the thing for the boat. It isn't very cold yet, but we will get it colder when we get farther down. We are just going to pass a big boat. It is a merchant's ship.*
> *Yours affectionately,*
> *Jim*

I could see the picture of the SS *Corinthian* on the front of the card as Father read from the back. I tried not to listen to his words.

"Ah. That's what happened to his hat. You see, Jessie, it was written before the letter he wrote to the rest of us. Now, you'll be a good girl and write a reply to him this evening. I will look forward to it being read tomorrow after breakfast."

There was, however, no letter for Father to read the next day after breakfast, or after any meal that day. There was no letter for Father to read any day that week. There were also no visits between Jane and me that day. There were no visits between Jane and me any day that week. Until I wrote my brother a reply to his letter, I was required to spend each evening—other than those during which I attended church—sitting at our dining room table, paper, pens, and ink at the ready.

Jim's correspondence became more regular after that. A letter was delivered addressed to all or any of Mother, Father, Grandpa, or Ina about once a week, and cards came addressed to me alone once a month. As Father had stipulated, they were all read aloud to all of us—no matter to whom they were addressed. Though I never read a single one myself, I learned through this process that Jim continued to be stationed in Shorncliffe, where he was providing dental services to the many men stationed there. He was doing well, and by early September he received three separate promotions, first to corporal, then to sergeant, and finally to staff sergeant.

In his various letters, Jim inquired after me. He congratulated me on the results of my examinations, once communicated, but those matters, like all others pertaining to me, he derived from the correspondence of others. Throughout that entire long summer of 1915, I went to not a single concert in the park, had not a single bicycle ride around the hundred acres, swam not once at Snell's Lake, and picnicked not a single time at the Forks of the Credit. I rarely saw Jane, Frances, and Elsa, save for when Jane happened to be at the same church service or when any of the three of them were at the same war support function Father mandated me to attend. I spent each morning attending to household chores, each afternoon sitting quietly on the verandah reading the newspapers or a text approved by Father, and every evening at the dining room table with my unused supply of letter writing paper, pens, and ink.

I suspected that Mother and Grandpa did not approve of Father's approach to my recalcitrance. In Father's absence, they each offered me inducements to change my course. Mother promised to bake my favourite cookies. Grandpa offered to tell me more about some of his building projects. Their efforts were in vain.

With confinement not producing the desired results, Father also tried different approaches. "I saw your friend Elsa Strauss earlier today," he said one summer day. "Her brother Wilfred is overseas. Writes him each week, that's what she does. A letter a week to a brother overseas. That's what a good sister does."

When peer pressure did not produce the desired effect, he tried guilt. "Hate him. I suppose that's what you do. You hate him. Why else would you not write him?" Of course, I did not hate my brother. I loved him. I knew he loved me. But he had treated me wrongly, and the resentment I felt continued to fester.

At the end of July, my parents stopped asking me to write to Jim. They realized that there was a problem and that perhaps they could have some role in its resolution. "Tell us what the difficulty is," Father pleaded, feigning, if not truly experiencing, heartfelt concern. "Just tell us. We will see if we can fix it. If you tell us, you can leave this table; you can leave this house. You can enjoy your summer."

But I was resolute. "I can't tell you. It's between Jim and me."

"You say that," Father said accusingly, changing his earlier considerate tone. "But clearly it's only a disagreement in your mind. Jim has no idea why you are not writing to him, as you well know."

Mother suggested that for a time I be allowed to correspond directly with Jim, to communicate privately what was upsetting me. Father dismissed that proposal as absurd. There was nothing that I should keep secret from my own parents. He was right; it *was* absurd. I was in no temperament to write Jim, whether my correspondence was private or otherwise. Thus, July turned into August, and I continued my detention.

Completely flummoxed by my unwillingness to write Jim or explain why I would not do so, Father devised his own theories on the matter. "It's the suffragists, isn't it? Here I have been allowing you to read the newspapers during the day. You have fallen into the thinking of the pacifist lunatics, Sylvia Pankhurst and the like. No more. Mother, from now on in addition to sitting at this table in the evenings, doing chores in the morning and sitting quietly on the verandah each afternoon, Jessie shall, until she writes her brother, be denied access to the newspapers." Actually, I was sympathetic to some of the causes promoted by Sylvia Pankhurst—including her position on women's suffrage—but her pacifist views had no bearing on my stance.

Father's vociferous reaction to Sylvia Pankhurst was due to the fact that by that point in time her pacifist views were so entirely contrary to his own. The war that in his mind had begun as Britain's war had as a result of Jim's enlistment firmly become Canada's war. The June 1915 sinking of the *Lusitania* and the accompanying loss of Canadian lives (including the lives of some from Peel County) solidified his new way of thinking. The feverish devotion to the cause that since the outbreak of the war in August 1914 had gripped most Bramptonians finally gripped him. The rancour with which he once held those so firmly devoted to the war he now reserved for those who were not.

In fact, Father's support for the war became so fanatical, it repressed his long-standing opposition to tax increases and to wartime fundraising—at least for a time. Thus, when Richard Blain, our Member of Parliament, J.R. Fallis, our Member of the Provincial Parliament, and other leading men in Brampton joined in August 1915 to form a Peel Civilian Auxiliary, Father became an active member of its executive. Meeting weekly in the concert hall, next to the Carnegie Library, the men took on the responsibility for raising additional funds to support the medical needs of Peel County's men in the 74th Battalion.

Working with the Red Cross, the Auxiliary determined that its first major activity would be the raising of funds from the Peel citizenry through a countywide canvass. The Auxiliary used as its example a similar exercise conducted in the fall of 1914—the one that inspired Jane and Elsa to have the high school knitting club undertake a door-to-door appeal for wool. It also had as an example an appeal conducted earlier that spring in honour of the birthday of King George V. As that milestone approached, the king announced his wish to receive no presents for himself. Rather, he asked every person in the British Empire to contribute to the war effort a number of coins equal to their own years of life. From nation to nation, women of all ages canvassed door upon door, distributing envelopes one day and then returning a few days later to collect them. In this manner $455 was raised in Brampton alone, all of which was used to purchase supplies and equipment for the overseas hospitals.

By contrast, the campaign to be organized by the Auxiliary for the fall of 1915 was to be conducted on a single night: October 21, 1915, Trafalgar Day. It would seek a considerably larger amount from the residents of Peel County and would accept cash or pledges of cash. It was hoped that $10,000 would be raised. The canvass itself would be preceded by a massive effort to raise awareness of the campaign, recruit and train canvassers, print the necessary instructions, pledge forms, receipts and other documentation that would comprise the canvass kits, allocate streets within the county to different canvassers, and canvass captains and coordinate the retrieval and tabulation of results.

Though the amount to be done to make the campaign a success was monumental, Father never shrank from it. Not since he assumed the presidency of the Excelsiors in the team's quest for the Mann Cup had I seen him filled with such zeal. The only thing that irritated him about the campaign was the lack of enthusiasm it sometimes received from others. One night in late August, his frustration with the lack of support for the campaign crossed with his frustration at my noncommunicative state with Jim. "I need twelve men to distribute pamphlets next week, and how many have volunteered? Six. And there you sit at this table, Jessie, for hours and hours every night doing nothing, wasting time in your foolhardy stubbornness and fomenting pacifist plans."

Once the words were uttered, the method of escape from my incarceration was determined. He stopped, looked at me, and then continued. "Jessie, from now on you will spend your nights in service to the war effort. School will commence next week. You will return from your classes every day and complete your studies and your piano practice. In the evening, your activities will be dictated by me, based on the needs at that time of the Peel War Auxiliary." I tried not to show how well that suited me. I was pleased to do anything I could to help Jim and his fellow soldiers at the front.

Over the next six weeks, the campaign was promoted. Advertisements were published in the local paper. Pamphlets were distributed and flyers were posted. Public meetings were organized and held with guest speakers both from near and afar. A great patriotic meeting was held three days before Trafalgar Day at St. Paul's Methodist Church. Canvassers were recruited, trained, and provided with the necessary kits. Memberships in the Red Cross Society were sold as further support for the effort. A headquarters was assembled to receive the completed canvassing kits. In all of this, Father was active, and by correlation, so was I. The day after Trafalgar Day, the Auxiliary announced with great fanfare that with the generosity of all of the residents of Peel County and a few special donations by leading businessmen, the $10,000 campaign target had been met.

The canvass kits had barely been collected and the donations hardly counted when the Auxiliary announced its next campaign with a goal of $50,000. But in this case, the amount would not be raised by voluntary donations. Rather, it would be raised through a tax on property owners, payable for five years. The actual $50,000 would be borrowed immediately by the local government. Auxiliaries across the country were applying pressure to their local councils to raise their local mill rate—or tax rate—in order to support similar taxes. The tax would be dedicated for the provision of medical supplies to the men at the front. In mid-October, the executive of the Auxiliary strategized for an entire evening on the methods by which they would convince the local councillors that this was an appropriate undertaking. Since the Auxiliary included nearly all of the local councillors, Father thought the four-hour meeting somewhat excessive. Also, while his enthusiasm for the war had not dampened, his old opposition to tax increases was beginning to reemerge.

"And that is all they discussed," Father complained to Grandpa the next night while the two sipped tea and I cleared the table. "There was no discussion about whether it was the right or wrong thing to ask for; whether the amount was not stupendously high; whether hardworking Peel County residents could afford to pay a further $50,000 in taxes. There was simply a discussion of how to get it approved by council.

"It's that Liberal, William Lowe," he said, referring to one of the Auxiliary members. "All he talks of is money. Always quoting that Albertan R.B. Bennett—a good Conservative, if you can imagine—but a rich one, I expect. All he talks about is money. 'If you can't enlist, then pay, pay, and pay some more.' As if money could buy the war's victory. It's not money the army needs—its men! That should be our focus.

"Of course, I voted in favour of the motion to approve it. I didn't want to be the lone dissenter. It needed to be unanimous at the executive committee level. There will be a further vote of the Auxiliary as a whole in January. But I did question at one point whether this was to be our sole purpose: to raise money."

"What was the reply?" Grandpa asked, finally finding an opportunity to speak.

"There was none! It was as though I was speaking to a wall. No one even acknowledged my question, let alone provided an answer."

But it became clear over the next few days that some Auxiliary members had heard Father. The following week, a number of the executive committee members and a few other Bramptonians approached Father. They complained that the Auxiliary's mandate was too narrow. A wider focus was required, particularly in one area: recruitment.

When the war commenced, recruitment was not really a concern. But by mid-1915, with death, injury, disease, and capture all playing their part, recruitment had become a priority. To that date, 3,500,000 soldiers worldwide had been killed and 8,000,000 wounded. Canada had deployed over 60,000 men and had a further 49,000 in training. The Empire required 10,000 reinforcements a month, and recruiting was falling off. Brampton, Father and others concluded, was not contributing the number of men its population suggested it should. The rectification of this deficiency was determined to be the objective of the Enlistment Committee of the Peel Civilian Auxiliary, or the Cabal as they liked to be known. Joining Father in this group were eleven men, including Mr. Hudson and Mr. Thompson, Frances and Jane's fathers, as well as Father's chief strategist, Mr. Handle. The focus of the Cabal, which met around our dining room table every Tuesday night, was the 126th Peel Battalion—Peel's second battalion then being formed—and in particular Company A within it. As Father's underling and retinue, I became the committee's secretary.

For the next three months, the men discussed the actions to be taken to increase enlistment among Brampton's population of nearly four thousand. Various options were discussed. One man proposed an increase in education about enlistment, the making of more speeches and the distribution of more informational brochures. Others proposed methods by which support of the Allied cause could be more clearly demonstrated through the distribution and display of pro-British signs and flags. The committee considered creating role models for the boys by advertising the names of particularly popular young men that had enlisted, like those from the junior Excelsiors and other sports teams or by publicizing how well Brampton boys performed in their recruitment tests. Knowing the power of money, the committee considered better communicating the pay one could expect to receive as a private ($1.10 per day), a corporal ($1.20 a day), or a sergeant ($1.50 a day), with "room" and board provided on top of that. Identifying the influential members of the community, the committee considered making appeals to third parties like employers, teachers, and family members who could impart additional pressure on those eligible men. Finally, the committee considered the extent to which its efforts should target specific potential recruits, perhaps embarrassing them into enlisting. In the end, the Cabal agreed to proceed by degrees. Only if their broader, more general appeals to increase recruitment were unsuccessful would they resort to the more direct personal and potentially embarrassing pleas.

At the end of a meeting in mid-November, as I was tidying my papers on our dining room table, Mr. Hudson approached Father. All of the other members of the Cabal had left. "Doc, I want to speak with you for a moment if I could about the commitment of the Auxiliary to the band of the 126th. The Auxiliary committed to raise $700 to purchase their instruments. A number of band members have purchased their instruments on the understanding that they would be reimbursed. The Auxiliary appears to be a long way from raising the money—its efforts being directed elsewhere, as you know."

"Bill, stop right there. You know I've taken a stand against the Auxiliary's continued focus on the raising of taxes and other strong-armed fundraising tactics."

"I know that well—but Doc, you understand the importance of a military band. You also know how to fill a sanctuary. I'm hoping that you'll consider holding a concert at Grace for this good cause. I understand the band is about to get some new leadership and that some of your own choir members are joining it."

Father looked at the table. He did not say no.

"Will you at least think about it, Doc? The missus and me, we are doing as much as we can. But I'd sure appreciate it if you and Mary would help us in this."

Mother entered the room as Mr. Hudson was finishing. After he left, Mother told Father that she would be willing to participate in such an event, if Father chose to do so.

Over the next month, each evening after my homework was done and the piano practiced, and all day on Saturdays, I worked with Father to print signs, post flyers, distribute flags and signs, and organize informational meetings—all to further enlistment.

Initially, the Cabal members were buoyed by their success. The Brampton recruitment numbers appeared to be increasing in the latter part of November and early December. But by the end of December, with the recruitment numbers again on a downward wane, the Cabal members became disheartened. They concluded that the supportive signage and the educational campaign were insufficient. At the end of December, the committee agreed to proceed with the next phase of its campaign, initially utilizing the local newspaper. The first advertisement would be directed at employers. I wrote out the words agreed to by the Cabal. They were to be delivered to the *Conservator* the second week of January.

> *Is it a square deal for an able-bodied man of military age to*
> *hold a job which can be filled with:*
>> *(a) a returned soldier*
>> *(b) a boy*
>> *(c) an old man or*
>> *(d) a woman*
> *when your Battalion needs men? Apply at the armouries,*
> *Brampton or St. Helen's Barracks in Toronto.*

Before he left that meeting, Mr. Hudson again approached Father. "Doc," he said, "have you given any further thought to holding the concert? If our recruitment efforts are successful, the Battalion will be ready to go and the band will not have enough instruments. Those it has will have been purchased with funds the owners could not afford to part with."

"But what about the dance at the armouries in mid-January?" Father asked. The armouries, just down the road from us—next to the fire hall and not far from the Carnegie Library—had only recently been constructed. It was one of fifty-six armouries built by the Department of Militia and Defence across the country. Mrs. Hudson was on the organizing committee for the fundraising dance to be held there later in January. "Will it not raise the necessary funds?"

"I'm afraid not. Ticket sales are going well, but we still expect to be at least thirty dollars short. We know that you can raise that amount at a minimum through a concert. We could advertise it at the same time that we are advertising the dance. The events would appeal to different people and have different prices."

Father again looked down, saying nothing.

"You'd fill those pews, Doc—you always do. You'd have them filled with men and women, girls, and boys of all ages—it couldn't hurt our recruitment efforts either." He chuckled as he said those last words.

Father, who had been staring at his papers, looked up suddenly. "You're right. It could help our recruitment efforts, couldn't it?"

"Now, hold it, Doc. No one is suggesting that you actually engage in recruitment efforts during the concert."

"No, of course not," Father assured him.

"It's just that your presence as the leader of the concert and the unofficial leader of our Cabal would mean that the Cabal's objectives will indirectly be supported."

"Precisely," Father confirmed. "Quite so. Let me speak to Mary. We may just do it."

For the remainder of the month, in addition to attending and carrying out my secretarial duties for the Cabal, I helped Father and Mother organize the concert scheduled to occur the evening of Tuesday, February 1, 1916, two weeks after the dance at the armouries.

* * *

Letters from Jim continued to arrive at our home, and letters to Jim continued to be sent. While many were addressed and read to me, none were sent by me. "You are still holding this grudge, are you, Jessie?" Father asked one day in January.

"Yes, Father. I am." My family had come to understand that I was indeed mad at Jim. Though they had no idea the reason, they were convinced it was unjustified.

"Well, there will be more war work for you to do. It seems to me that your Saturdays are not fully occupied."

* * *

As the day of the concert neared, I worked with Father to complete the program for the night. Thirteen pieces would be performed: nine by our choir, conducted by Father with Mother at the organ or piano; one by a guest soprano; one by a guest tenor; and two duets performed by the guest soloist and the guest tenor. There would be a twenty-minute intermission, during which refreshments would be served in the church hall. Most of the funds to be raised for the instruments would be realized from the ticket sales revenue, but Father also agreed to make a general appeal for donations at the end of the performance.

Jane joined me at the church's doors the night of the concert to sell the few tickets that were not sold ahead of time. It was too cold a night to require ticket holders to assemble outside. The pews began to fill at half past six. At seven o'clock, the performance began.

Father welcomed everyone to the concert in support of the band of the 126th Battalion. Turning his back to the pews, he raised his baton, the choir stood, and Mother pushed out the opening strains of the first piece.

The ticket holders were in great spirits as they gathered for refreshments in the hall during the intermission. Though Mother and the performers utilized the time available to rest, Father circulated among the crowd, accepting the many compliments bestowed. It was just before intermission ended when I noticed Mr. Handle extricate Father from a group of Mother's friends. The two men had only a few minutes to discuss their apparently confidential matter before Reverend Hunter performed his only official responsibility of the evening, ringing the bell to sound the end of inter-mission. Everyone returned to the sanctuary, leaving Jane, me, and two other girls to clean up the refreshment dishes.

The four of us returned to the sanctuary in time to place the collection buckets at the main doors and to hear the choir in a rousing concluding piece. As the performers bowed, the entire audience rose to its feet to cheer them. It was gratifying to see the special prolonged ovation extended to Mother, as the chief instrumentalist, and to Father, the concert's producer and conductor. As I watched the crowd look on them in appreciation, I was reminded again of how far Father had come in two and a half years in reacquiring the respect and admiration of his fellow citizens.

Eventually, Father raised his hands and using his baton, motioned for the audience members to return to their seats. They chuckled as they were led in this choir-like fashion. Turning to the actual choir behind him, Father repeated the gesture. With everyone's attention, he began to deliver the remarks I had written pursuant to his dictation earlier in the day. He described the role of the military band, how important music was to both comfort and motivate our troops; how it instilled steadfastness and strength, morale, and valour; what instruments were required by the band and how far the proceeds of the ticket sales from the concert would go to acquiring them. He followed the prepared lines well, I noted, needing only to announce the presence of the buckets at the main doors, when his speech suddenly took a varied course. Instead of dismissing the audience with a request to fill those buckets, his oratory began anew.

"Ladies and gentlemen, that was to have been the end of my formal remarks, but I am afraid I cannot stop there. As you know our country, our empire, the world as we know it, is involved in a momentous battle—an epic battle—against tyranny and oppression. Many men and women of Brampton have long been involved in efforts to support our men at the front. The women have been collecting necessities, knitting socks, sewing shirts, and raising funds. Men and women alike have been reaching as far as they can into their pockets to purchase the medical supplies that are needed to help our injured boys. Tonight you have done the same to bring our boys what only music can uniquely bring. But ladies and gentlemen, that is not enough; it is far from enough. We will not win this war with gifts to the boys at the front. We will not win this war with new socks. We will not win this war with more bandages or even with more music. What we need to win this war is more men.

"Look around you. Who do you see? There are over five hundred people in this sanctuary. I will tell you who is here." I froze at that moment. I knew the lists that the Cabal was starting to create—lists of men they considered to be eligible to enlist; men of the right age and physical fitness.

Please, Lord, I silently prayed. Please do not let him announce the names of the eligible men in the room.

"I will tell you who is here. There are mothers. Raise your hand if you are a mother." Slowly, very slowly, the hands of nearly a third of those assembled were raised.

"Yes, there are mothers. I will tell you who else is here: there are sisters. Raise your hand if you are a sister." Most of the women in the church raised a hand. "What about sweethearts and fiancées? Raise your hand, young ladies, if you have a special lad in your life." About a fifth of those gathered did that. I was relieved he was not calling on the eligible men.

"Thank you, ladies. Now here is my message to all of you." He waited until he had everyone's attention. "Let them go! Let them GO! If you are a mother of an eligible young man—let him go! If you are the sister of an eligible young man—let him go! If you are the fiancée or sweetheart of an eligible young man—let him go! Is it right? Is it right, I ask you, that sons of other mothers should be fighting in the trenches when your eligible son is not? Is it right that brothers of other sisters should be in Europe when your eligible brother is not? Is it right that beaus of other young women should be serving their country when your beau is not? It is not right! It is not right! It is not right!" His face reddened with each exclamation.

"And the last of you, the men in this audience, the eligible men. Is it right that you are at home enjoying a concert with your mother, your sister, your sweetheart, when your fellow countrymen are doing their duty by enlisting?" He was leaning forward as though lecturing to a single man standing in front of him. At that point, one man (displaying an extent of bravery that some would suggest far exceeded his nonenlisted status) attempted to quietly leave the church.

"Richard Gardner," Father hollered, pointing at John, who had almost made it to the north door at the back of the sanctuary. "Richard Gardner, I am not finished speaking to you. I am not finished speaking to any of you! Eddie McMurchy," he called out, pointing to Jim's best friend, "I am not finished speaking with you. John Darling," he called out, pointing to my cousin, who had the misfortune of coming home from his dental studies in Toronto for the weekend, "I am not finished speaking with you! You and your friends! We need two hundred and twenty-nine men to complete Company A of the 126th. We have secured one hundred and eighty-five."

His face was nearly puce, but then he paused. His weight, which had been hoisted on the balls of his feet, settled down. He began again, his feet firmly planted on the floor, his voice barely above a whisper, his complexion returning to its normal pale state. "Forty-four more men. Forty-four more men. That is what is needed. Do not leave it to your neighbour to complete the company. Do not leave here tonight, men—do not leave here tonight without resolving to fill that company. Brampton needs you," he said, his voice rising again. "Peel County needs you!" The volume of his voice rose again before ending in a final crescendo, his body once again extended towards the pews, his face again reddening. "Your country needs you. DO YOUR BIT! Enlist!"

The audience sat in stunned silence. People had come to enjoy a night of nice music and contribute some loose change. No one was prepared for that diatribe—least of all those singled out. Father had to lift his baton to signal that people were free to leave. Once that was understood, they left with extraordinary speed. Though Father moved to the back of the church to speak with anyone who wished to congratulate or thank him—no one did. In a very short time there were only four of us left in the church: Reverend Hunter, me, Mother, and Father. Even Grandpa had hurried out.

"Come along, Jessie," Mother commanded. "Your work here is done for the night. My work too." She grabbed my hand and marched me out.

"Up to bed, Jessie," Mother said as soon as we returned to our house. "No delays. Up to bed, immediately."

I could tell that she did not want me near her when Father got home; that she did not want me to hear their conversation. It did no good. Since she rounded on Father as soon as he entered the foyer and since I deliberately left the door to my room at the top of the stairs open, I could hear them quite well.

"How could you? How could you do that?" she demanded. "You misled people! You invited them to a night of music, not to a public shaming. And who did you shame: people who for reasons of which you are not privy have determined that they cannot now or will not now enlist.

And you used me. You used our entire choir. And those guest soloists. None of them devoted the time and effort to prepare for and perform this concert under the pretense you had in mind. None of them! And to carry out this campaign in a church. Did you see the look on Reverend Hunter's face as you went on? Mortification: that was his look. Mortification. That is how I felt too.

"And those boys! How could you humiliate them so? It was beneath you. Your own nephew. Jim's best friend. You owe them better! Jim made a decision to enlist. I still do not fully understand that decision, but it was his decision. His. No one else's. No one forced him to go to war. He chose to. Who are you to deprive others of the right to make that same choice? Who are you to do that?"

There was silence for a moment. Then Father spoke. He spoke calmly, shocked I expect, since Mother had never, to my knowledge, ever spoken critically of him and certainly not in anger. But she was clearly angry now.

"Are you quite through?"

"Almost," she said, still defiant. "I am almost through. If I had more time to think about this, I might have much more to say, but I do have one more thing to say: you owe this town an apology. You owe it to the town, to John, to Eddie, to Richard Gardner, to Reverend Hunter, and to all of those women and girls. I don't know how you are going to do it. But you will have to find a way. We live in this town, and I won't have us ostracized. I won't go through that again. I will *not*!"

The next thing I heard were her feet stomping up the stairs, their bedroom door slamming, and the lock on their door turning. It had been two and a half years since I heard that sound.

I fell asleep that night contemplating all that had occurred that evening. The most remarkable thing had not been Father's diatribe, which he had so thoroughly inflicted upon a church full of music lovers. Rather, it was the actions of my mother that struck me so. I had never seen or heard her stand up to Father that way. Even in the time of the Johnston affair, Mother had not lashed out at him; she had merely retreated.

Mother's capacity for surprise struck me again the next morning, when I rose to another unfamiliar sound. Like the harsh words of the night before, it too emanated from the foyer. But this time, Mother was crying. I could hear Grandpa trying to soothe her. Slipping out of bed, I crept down the hallway afraid to think of what could have upset her so much that her piano could not console her. Peering down the stairs, I saw Mother leaning against Grandpa, wrapped in his arms. "He'll die now," she sobbed. "I know he will." My heart stopped. I became faint. Tears began to fill my eyes. *He'll die! Jim will die.* My heart stopped. *He will die, and he will die with me mad at him, not knowing that I love him.* In a daze, I made my way slowly down the stairs. Before I got to the last of them, Mother began again, her words slowly escaping between her sobs.

"I never intended for this. I didn't! Two family members at war! How can this be happening?"

"There, there," Grandpa said. Grandpa, with all his advanced years, still towered over Mother. His back to the staircase, her head against his chest, neither saw me descend the last of the steps. A letter lay open on the chest next to the basket of Jim's letters.

It took but a moment to read.

> *Wednesday February 2, 1916*
> *Mary,*
> *I have left to enlist. This is my apology.*
> *Jethro*

"He won't die," Grandpa said. "Well, eventually he will die, as we all will. But he won't die in this war."

"How can you be so confident? Men are dying every day over there. Every day. And he is old. He isn't as agile as the younger men. It will be even more dangerous for him!"

"He won't be going over there, Mary," Grandpa said, "for exactly that reason. He is too old. He is fifty-three years of age. They will never send him, and he knows that. He knew it when he wrote that letter. They will assign him a role here in Canada. I wouldn't be surprised if he is stationed in Toronto and if he comes home for dinner once a week. Just wait. You'll see."

"Are you certain?" she asked, pulling her head back to look at his face.

"Quite. He isn't the first fifty-year-old wanting to do his bit."

"When will he let me know?"

"By that note, I gather he isn't too pleased with you?"

"We had words last night. Well, I had words. For the first time really."

If Grandpa overheard them, he was too polite to say so. "In that case, I expect it may take him a few days before he relieves you of the anxiety that note was intended to cause." As they both turned to look at it, they saw me, tears running down my face.

"Oh, Jessie," Mother said. "You've seen the note. Don't be upset. Grandpa says it is nothing to be alarmed about." They reached out and pulled me to them. "We will miss your father, but he'll be safe," Mother said, professing in that moment all of the confidence she had lacked moments before. "Don't be upset."

* * *

Reflecting on that moment I first read Father's note, I confess I felt no alarm. Maybe that was because I read it at the same time that I heard Grandpa's reassuring words. Maybe it was because I was simply so relieved that it was not Jim's demise Mother was foretelling.

The house was quiet the rest of the day. Although it was not her at-home day, Mother set the dining room table with the tea things and two large plates of cookies and bars, in case anyone came by to condole with us. No one did. While the tea, cookies, and bars sat on the table untouched, Mother sat at the piano. I noticed, though, that the notes expounded were more a lament than the torrents of sorrow they had sounded the prior spring after Jim had enlisted. In the hopes of receiving a telegram with word from Father or of being some use to Mother, I stayed indoors that day and the next, even missing school.

The solitude of the first day was relieved the second when our door saw a steady stream of visitors. The first was Mr. Handle, whose thick legs crossed our threshold early the Thursday morning. Demonstrating once again his vast knowledge of people and facts, he called to advise Mother that Father was being posted at the Canadian National Exhibition grounds in the rank of captain. Not wanting to cause Mother any embarrassment for his possession of information that by all rights she should have had first, he took pains to say that he had this advance knowledge from a reliable high-up source. He was certain Father would communicate it directly, likely later that day or the next, when he was at liberty to send a telegram.

After thanking him for conveying the information, Mother asked for confirmation of a certain aspect. "Mr. Handle," she said. "I gather that you have come across this information from a confidential source."

"Indeed, I have, ma'am."

"Mr. Handle, you've been of such good service to me, relieving me of a great deal of worry. If it isn't too much, though, I wonder if I may ask of you one thing?"

"Of course, it would be my honour to provide any comfort to you that I am able."

"I am glad to hear it. I would be so grateful, Mr. Handle, if you would do me the honour of disclosing that confidential information as soon as possible to absolutely everyone with whom you come in contact."

Mr. Handle hesitated not a moment. "It would be my pleasure, ma'am." Then he turned to me, sitting in the chair next to the sofa on which Mother sat.

"Young lady, you've provided invaluable services to the Cabal over the last few months. While we will find another location to meet, we would be honoured to have the benefit of your continued services, if you would be willing to provide them."

"I'm afraid that will not be possible, Mr. Handle," Mother interjected before I could reply. "With her father and two siblings out of the home, I think I shall be requiring Jessie's available time for the foreseeable future."

"I quite understand, ma'am," he said to Mother before turning toward me. "Then let me just thank you, young lady. You did excellent work. The first advertisements we wrote will be published as planned, but I am happy to say that as a result of your father's impassioned plea two nights ago, recruitment has taken a turn for the positive. If it continues, it may not be necessary to place the final advertisements."

Mr. Handle was as good as his word, and his word was widespread. That afternoon—Mother's usual at home day—others began to call. Fresh tea and coffee were made and the cookies and bars of the prior day were retrieved. Caller after caller came to express support for Mother on hearing of Father's enlistment, though many of the visitors fell into the camp of those without sons, brothers, or beau eligible for enlistment.

Among the visitors was Reverend Hunter. To him alone did Mother issue an apology. She assured him that none of the performers expected the concert to include any sort of clarion call. "Indeed," she said, "I am not sure that my husband knew one would be made. Something seems to have galvanized him partway through his prepared address."

"No need to apologize, Mrs. Stephens," Reverend Hunter said. "It's not a sacrilege to speak of the war in our church. We are not Papists, are we?" He was referring to the edict issued by the Pope the year before in which he forbade Catholic priests to pray for either side in the conduct of the war. "Your husband has done us such good service for so many years, we must forgive him his unconventional approach. We know he spoke from his heart. In fact, there are many who believe his words were right and needed to be said—somewhere. Perhaps not there! In any event, they hit their mark. I have decided to enlist myself."

"You, Reverend Hunter? You are going to enlist? To fire a rifle?" Reverend Hunter was then thirty-five years of age, the father of a toddler.

"I am going to enlist, but I hope the only thing I will fire is bit of brimstone. As soon as a replacement can be found to tend my flock here," he patted Mother's hand at that moment, "I will join the infantry as a padre, in the hopes that in my prayers and intercessions, I will bring the Lord's divine comfort to our men at the front."

Late in the afternoon, with the last guest departed, Mother was back at the piano. I sat down on one of the slipper chairs near her. Without my Cabal duties, I felt somewhat at a loss of what to do. Eventually, Mother stopped and spun on her bench to face me. The tears that I had never seen her issue until the day before spilled forth again. It was as unfamiliar a sight as I had ever seen, and it had the effect of inducing the same waterworks in me.

"Mother," I said, seeking to check mine, "how would you like me to assist you with Father gone?"

"Well, that depends, Jessie," she said. She retrieved a handkerchief from her pocket and took it to the corners of her eyes. She waited a few moments, composing herself.

"Jessie," she said, starting again, "there is a limit on the emotional trauma any one person can endure. I have a son at war, a husband who will be living in barracks with the armed forces in Toronto, and a daughter living away from us in that same city. I cannot continue to tolerate the discord between you and Jim or, should I say, of you toward Jim. Can you please tell me what he has done to bother you so?"

I looked down and said nothing, anger coming to the fore.

"It has been eight months," Mother said, her voice unsteady. "It has been more than eight months. Many of the men overseas do not live half that long. How can you carry on this way knowing that we could lose Jim at any time? That he could go to his grave out of favour with the sister that always gave him so much affection. You are very young, Jessie. You will have many years to carry that guilt. Decades. Please tell me what is wrong so that I can help fix it."

Still looking down, I summoned the many reasons I was mad at Jim. I was mad that he came too late to the train station for me to tell him all of the things I needed to tell him, to get answers to all of the questions I needed answered. I was mad that he was not home to shield me from my father—if Jim had been at home, I would not have spent the last eight months in Father's servitude. I was mad that he was not at home pursuing a dental practice that I longed to pursue. I was mad that he was not with Millie, who I loved like a sister. I was mad that he was not with me to tug my curls and call me "Little One." I was mad that I could not see what he was drawing and know what he most cared about at that time. I was mad that he might die and leave me.

But I could not articulate those feelings. Some could not be put in words. Others could not be put in words shared with Mother. But I did want to end it. Mother was right. How could I live with myself if Jim died not knowing that I loved him? I had realized the morning before that I could not continue on this course. I wanted to read for myself the letters my darling brother had written to me. I wanted to look at the postcards he had chosen for me. I wanted to write to him.

"It's...." I started. How could I say it all? It would sound so foolish. Jim had not meant to exclude me from his presence before he left. In my heart, I had come to know that.

"It's just that..." Really, I had sat with him two evenings before he left. I could have spoken to him then. I could not find the way to tell him those things at that time. How could I say them now to Mother?

"Yes?" she prompted.

"It's just that," I looked up and then gathering all of my courage, blurted out, "He left everything to you! If he dies, you will get everything! Even the camera!" I said, referring to the gift Aunt Rose had given Jim in honour of his graduation, creating a source of resentment that I had barely acknowledged previously. "And you..." I inhaled unevenly, and then accused, "you don't even know how to use it!" My chest heaved with the wracking sobs I had suppressed for over eight months.

"That's it?" Mother asked, calmly and somewhat skeptically, ignoring my histrionics. "All this, over a camera?"

"Yes," I said, holding fast to my excuse. "I love that camera. Jim and I learned to work it together. And now it is just sitting in his room, with no one using it." I continued to sob maniacally.

"If he had just given you the camera before he left, we could have avoided all of this?"

"Yes," I lied.

"I think I need some air," she said. "Why don't you go to your room now and get some rest. I will reflect on how to best use your services in the weeks to come."

* * *

Three weeks later, a large advertisement appeared in the *Conservator*. Under a three-inch-high caption, the paper listed the names of the eighty-nine Brampton men who enlisted in A Company 126th Battalion and the twenty-four Brampton men who tried to enlist but were declared medically unfit.

It asked the reader where his name appeared and then urged him to put himself right by enlisting, being rejected and securing a medical certificate or proving that it is impossible for him to enlist. It was the last of the Cabal's advertisements.

The following week a telegram was delivered to our house. *Jessie*, it said. *The camera is yours. Love, Jim.*

Chapter 12

THE INTERNEES

The rapprochement with Elsa that had been imposed on the belligerents Ricky Dyck and Allan King in February 1915 came to an end one fine afternoon at the end of May 1916. It came without any hostile actions on the part of Elsa. It came without the excuse of misunderstanding her words. It took the form of an ambush—a physical and verbal assault that struck Elsa and her three compatriots as they left school late that Tuesday afternoon. Our teacher, Miss Fallis, had asked Elsa, Jane, Frances, and me to stay to help organize tables for a bake sale to occur the next day. We walked the short distance between our school and Main Street, speaking about cookies and cakes. As we turned onto Main Street to begin walking south, we noticed how empty the street was. We assumed it had to do with the lateness of the hour. As we continued in our usual two-by-two formation, with me and Jane in the front and Frances and Elsa behind, we contemplated bars and candies. "There won't be candies at the bake sale," Frances said to me.

"We sell candies at my family's bakery," I said, referring to the bakery owned exclusively by my aunt. "Maybe someone will contribute candy to the sale tomorrow." The proceeds of the sale were going to the Red Cross. I was thinking about the oatmeal cookies Mother had agreed to make that day as my contribution when the silence of the street was broken.

"Go back home, you dirty Kraut! Go back home!" It had been so long since we had heard those cries, I had almost forgotten them. I turned to face the two assailants running toward us, each holding a bucket in one hand and a red grenade-like object in the other.

"Run!" I said. It was too late. The first tomato hit me on my chest. The second hit Elsa on her back.

"Run!" Jane echoed. We ran. The apartment above the dairy, a block away from the site of the ambush, was the nearest of our homes. The onslaught continued as we ran. Words and tomatoes flew.

Nearing the apartment, two grown men ran toward us. I considered flagging them down to help us, but they seemed almost as menacing as the two boys chasing us. We continued to run toward the dairy, surprised and relieved that the physical and oral assault had abated.

The street-level door to the dairy was just ahead of us. Strangely, it was open. We ran full speed into it before being stopped abruptly by an object on the ground at the base of the stairs. Elsa, right behind me, screamed. As our eyes adjusted to the darkness inside the stairwell, Jane, Frances, and I took in what Elsa had moments earlier discerned. Splayed on the ground before us was her father. Dr. Heggie was leaning over him. A large rock lay near the door.

"Girls," Dr. Heggie said, "help me lift Elsa's father. We need to get him upstairs." To our relief, the words were no more expressed when Mr. Strauss began to rouse. With our help, he was able to walk up the stairs.

After gasping at the sight of Mr. Strauss, Elsa's mother and aunt helped him to lie down on the sofa in the apartment's main room. A clean wet cloth was applied to his head. Dr. Heggie, who had been walking back to his office at the time of the assault, and who naturally had with him his large black bag, prepared to administer stitches. Ice was secured to prevent later swelling. Only once those matters were attended to did anyone take notice of the red-blotched dresses of Elsa, Jane, Frances, and me.

"Rotten tomatoes," Elsa said, beginning to cry. "Why did this happen?"

In the main room of that little apartment above the dairy, crammed with Dr. Heggie, Mr. and Mrs. Strauss, Elsa's Aunt Maria and her two children, Elsa, Jane, Frances, and me, Mr. Strauss told us why.

* * *

By the spring of 1916, Canada had been at war for nearly two years. Despite the headlines of the local paper that declared success after success, it had to be said that the prosecution of the war on the battlefields was to that point merely fair. In late April, the loss of Canadian men in Ypres was so great, we were urged to fly our flags at half-mast. The prosecution of the war on the Canadian home front was not much better. Canada had, by that point, come to understand the full measure of its required contribution. Just as the twenty thousand men Prime Minister Borden first offered to Britain were woefully insufficient, so were the initial offers of wheat. Belgium and France were unable to feed their people, so many of their farmers having been converted to fighters, so much of their farmland having been converted to killing fields. Britain had a similar loss of food producers and a growing number of colonial armies to feed. They all looked to Canada to supply them. Canada may have been able to meet vastly accelerated food production quotas, but her farming efforts had been compromised by the loss of so many of the men Britain sought to feed. Over two hundred thousand Canadians were then under arms. The Allies needed Canada's farms to be more productive at the very time they deprived her of the men to make them so.

The situation created an opportunity for the Dale Estate—an opportunity its trustees identified in the first days of the war. Those trustees rarely let a business opportunity pass them by. Trustees, rather than directors, operated the large greenhouse operation in Brampton because the business of Harry Dale, the son of the founder of the business, was placed in the hands of his trustees on his demise in 1901 and because the trustees had never parted with it. Among the trustees was Tommy Duggan, the managing executor, who began working with Harry Dale in 1885 as his accountant.

By early 1916, Tommy Duggan and the other trustees were congratulating themselves on the decision taken in the first months of the war. Hiring Lukas Strauss to lead the effort to convert a portion of their greenhouse operations from the cultivation of flowers to the propagation of vegetables was considered quite far-sighted. Though the production of vegetables was not likely to be as profitable as the production of flowers, the trustees were prepared to devote a large percentage of their greenhouse real estate to vegetables, if that was required by king and country. It was somewhat ironic, they thought, that when the Dale business began in Canada in 1863, the concern pertained to the growth and sale of vegetables not flowers. Edward

Dale, the founder of the business, was a garden vegetable grower. Through his greenhouses he had, by the late 1860s, created a thriving year-round business selling potatoes, cabbages, cauliflower, asparagus, celery, radishes, and lettuce. It was his son, Harry, who convinced his father to add flowers to his greenhouse production. Before long, the quantity and profitability of grown flowers exceeded those of vegetables.

Tommy Duggan knew that the estate could return to the production of vegetables, but he knew that to continue to produce flowers, which were highly profitable and at the same time to help the nation, the estate was going to have to grow the vegetables efficiently and produce the maximum quantity of vegetables in as little greenhouse soil as possible. Special knowledge and techniques were required. That was what impressed him about Lukas Strauss. After their first meeting in Brampton, Tommy travelled to Shelburne to see Lukas's greenhouses. He was somewhat impressed by their construction. He was entirely impressed by their production. In very little space, Lukas was growing volumes of uniformly good-sized, tasty vegetables.

"How soon can you start?" Tommy asked. Lukas feigned uncertainty on the matter; he had many things to take care of before leaving the farm, he declared. Tommy offered him a bonus if he could start by the beginning of October. Lukas, who had already told Andreas he would be out of the farm by the end of September, readily agreed.

Lukas's initial foray into the growing of vegetables in the Dale greenhouses was small but successful. Lukas was given two men and assigned to Greenhouse 10, an older, smaller four-row greenhouse. By December 1914, Lukas and his men had produced a row of vegetables. The beans, carrots, and potatoes they planted had thrived. The cabbages and cauliflower did not fare so well, but Lukas thought that with a different placement, they would do better in the next planting season. Tommy Duggan was pleased and ordered an additional row in the old greenhouse to be available for the next planting, although Lukas had asked for three more rows. Tommy was not yet ready to devote the entire greenhouse to the vegetable operation. What if the success of the first planting was a fluke? An entire greenhouse without either flowers or vegetables would generate no revenue. Lukas hid his disappointment and consoled himself with the knowledge that if the winter planting was a success, Tommy would surely provide him with the entire greenhouse for the spring planting.

Unfortunately, Lukas was not able to secure that additional planting space in the spring. The cabbages and cauliflower did no better in the winter planting, and the beans produced in the winter were thin and short. Only the carrots and potatoes flourished. Lukas tried to understand it. He reevaluated the conditions of the greenhouse. He studied the daily notes he made of the greenhouse's temperatures and the penetration of the sun's rays, of the water content, temperature, and volume, and of the condition of the soil. The problem, he determined, was the soil. It had so long been used to cultivate flowers, it was desperate for the change brought on by the first planting of vegetables. But having given so much to those first vegetables, it was now depleted. Lukas instructed the men assigned to him to rotate and enrich the soil.

The crop of vegetables produced in the spring of 1915 was bountiful. Every vegetable was produced in excess: big white cauliflowers, thick, orange carrots, leafy cabbages, firm, fleshy potatoes, and long green beans. In the summer of 1915, with the Empire's demand for additional vegetable production increasing, Tommy Duggan gave Lukas all four rows in Greenhouse 10. For the fall of 1915, Tommy allowed him into the newer bigger greenhouses, giving him first one long row there, then two. For the winter of 1916, he gave him three. By that time, the need for more vegetables from producers had been identified, and the price to be paid for them by the government was rising. Tommy could see that the Dale Estate could meet its duty to king and country and turn a fair profit by growing vegetables, as long as they continued to be produced in the volume Lukas had recently achieved. Starting in the spring of 1916, Tommy would devote all of Greenhouse 10 and seven rows in the large greenhouses to vegetable propagation. There was only one problem. It was a problem that Lukas and Tommy had predicted.

The growing of vegetables in a greenhouse—particularly the concentrated form of growing practiced by Lukas—was a labour-intensive activity. To maximize growth in quantity, the plants required constant tending. In addition to the usual matters of watering and weeding, plants had to be both moved and removed to ensure the good plants could grow and thrive. Had all of the men involved in the cultivation of the flowers been available to assist in the propagation of vegetables, Lukas may have been able to manage. But they were not. As the war went on and as more and more men enlisted, succumbing to the entreaties of the patriots or in response to their own heartfelt desires, the number of men available to work in the greenhouses was decreasing.

Tommy could hardly believe that only two years earlier he was being admonished by the town for providing an insufficient number of full-time jobs; that people had been begging him to provide a living wage to the people of Brampton. By 1916, he was hiring every person—full- or part-time as they chose—who came his way. Even doing so, he did not have enough men to fully tend the rows of vegetables and the rows of flowers. He wanted the vegetable operations to be a success, but he would not create the conditions for that success at the expense of the flower operations. The vegetable operations were temporary. They would end when the war ended. The flower operations would continue indefinitely. He would do nothing to jeopardize the quality of the flowers produced by the Dale Estate or the reputation it held. The first call on manpower was therefore directed to the flower operations.

Lukas was considering how to address that labour shortage one February night in 1916. That spring, he would be planting his largest greenhouse vegetable crop since he joined the Dale Estate sixteen months earlier. He knew he needed more men to make the planting a success. At the nearby table in the apartment above the dairy, Elsa was working on her homework. On the floor in front of Lukas were Jakob's children: Jonas, just four years old, playing with a wooden train, and Clara, nearly two, holding a big top. Maria was reading aloud in German a letter she had received that day from Jakob.

"How exhausting for poor Jakob," Ingrid said when Maria finished. "Laying railway ties is hard work."

"He doesn't mind," Maria said. "He's happy to be working and able to support us once more." Between the monthly stipend Jakob received as a prisoner of war for the support of his family and the wages he received for working on the railways, he was earning more as a prisoner of war than he had earned since his first year in Toronto. The international Hague Convention to which Britain, and therefore Canada, subscribed, prohibited prisoners from doing work that was for the advantage of the government or for private entities, unless they did so voluntarily. When they did, they were required to be paid for that work at the same rates of pay as the country's soldiers were paid for noncombat work. The work could take the form of government initiatives like the laying of rail lines or the cutting of trees or commercial endeavours for private concerns.

"He finds it very hard on his back, though, particularly in this cold weather," Maria said.

"At least he is here," Ingrid said.

It had been a year since Jakob had been arrested and detained as a prisoner of war. Like other Germans, Austrians, and Turks taken into custody in the Toronto area, Jakob was first interned at the Stanley Barracks, the six stone buildings constructed by the British in 1840 as part of the New Fort York. The buildings were, by 1914, a part of the many buildings on the grounds of the Canadian National Exhibition. The barracks were distinguished from others by the high rows of barbed wire that surrounded them and their adjoining exercise yard. The Stanley Barracks were intended to hold prisoners of war on a temporary basis before they were sent to larger camps like the one at Fort Henry in Kingston, in eastern Ontario, to which Germans and Turks were most often sent, or the work camp in Kapuskasing, in northern Ontario, to which members of the former Austro-Hungarian Empire were most often sent.

There were at that time over sixty internee residents of the Stanley Barracks. Jakob was by then the longest internee resident. All of the other men who were interned when he first arrived had been sent to other camps. The explanation for the exception in his case lay with Jakob himself. The commanding officers liked the short Austrian reservist. He was pleasant to be with, he followed the orders he was given, and best of all, he had a manner with the other internees that resulted in them following those orders too. This was the case, it seemed, whether the other internees saw their allegiance to their new country or the old. By the time the internees reached the Stanley Barracks, there was an equal number in each camp.

Jakob realized early on that the conditions for all of the internees would improve if they cooperated where they could and acted collectively. In exchange for providing a generally compliant group of inhabitants and a mostly productive work force, Jakob obtained comforts for the men above and beyond those to which they were strictly entitled. The standard-issue cots were, as a result of Jakob's efforts, topped with decent mattresses; the three blankets mandatorily provided were not threadbare; the food, required to be of a certain nutritional level, was also tasty; the monthly visits with their family were a little longer than required.

"You are right, Ingrid," Maria chimed. "At least he is here."

That was when Lukas got the idea. Surely those internees would rather work in a greenhouse than on a railway line. This could solve his labour problems. It could help the government meet its food production quotas. It could be a model to be replicated in other communities. The ability to have Jakob living and working just up the street from the dairy—well, that was just another benefit.

Lukas spoke to Tommy Duggan about it the next day.

"Would they allow it?" Tommy asked.

"I don't see why not," Lukas replied. "We would have to make an application. We would have to describe the type of work they would be doing, the hours, and the pay. We would have to provide their lodgings—they couldn't be taking the train to and from Toronto every day. And we would have to ensure that their living accommodations were secure."

"What do you have in mind?" Tommy asked

"Greenhouse 13," Lukas announced with some fanfare.

"Greenhouse 13! It's barely a greenhouse!" Tommy exclaimed. It was true. So much of the glass on it was broken or missing, the most plentiful material on it was wood. It had not been used in a decade. For some time, Tommy had been waiting for an excuse to burn it down.

"The carpenters can cover it in plywood, put on a tarp-style roof. That will be fine for May to September. If the arrangement works out and the war continues, we can put on a better roof before winter. It has water. A couple of showers and toilets can be installed. We can buy a dozen army cots and a long harvest-style table. We will have to arrange for food to be delivered. I can think of a few women who would take this on as their patriotic duty."

"Their patriotic duty? To feed the enemy?"

"To feed those producing vegetables required by the Allies," Lukas corrected.

"You might do better to appeal to the pocketbooks of the dear women," Tommy suggested.

Tommy was not convinced that the proposal was viable, but he liked the enthusiasm of his director of vegetable operations, and he couldn't think of another way to obtain the necessary labour.

"Will the other trustees approve of this?" Lukas asked.

"You leave that to me," Tommy replied before convening a meeting of the trustees later that day. Though they shared Tommy's reservations, they authorized the making of the application and the renovation of Greenhouse 13. The estate needed to be ready to receive the internees as soon as the application was approved.

* * *

"When will we tell them?" Lukas asked Tommy one day when they were walking from the Dale business office to the greenhouses. The application to employ the internees had been submitted. Lukas and Tommy were waiting to obtain approval. Every week, they lost two or more men to the war. The number applying to work at the estate was low by comparison.

"Who?" Tommy asked.

"The other workers. The staff in the office." They had all seen the carpenters working on Greenhouse 13. They were under the impression that the sleeping quarters would be filled by high school boys brought in from Toronto for the summer—an impression of which they were not disabused. No one wanted to lie about the matter, but the trustees did not want the true identity of the intended workers disclosed—at least not until their application had been approved. They were not sure the information would be well received, and they did not see the point of upsetting the applecart if the application was not successful.

* * *

A colonel from the Stanley Barracks came to Brampton. He was impressed by the application the Dale Estate had submitted. He found the amount of work to be done sufficient to keep the internees occupied and the living conditions entirely adequate. The authorities were looking for new ways to occupy the time of the internees. Too many internees were becoming depressed from lack of activity. When they became depressed, they didn't bathe; when they didn't bathe, the other internees and many of the guards complained. The expense of keeping the internees was spurring a movement in the official circles to close down a number of the camps. If the internees could be sent to work for entities that provided food and board, so much the better. The only real concern the authorities had about the application of the Dale Estate pertained to the person who had completed it, the man proposed to oversee the work of the internees (including very likely his brother) and its greatest proponent: Lukas. Technically, Lukas himself was an enemy alien. Because he was not an officer of the Austrian army or a member of its reserve, as Jakob was, Lukas was merely required to report monthly to the local police department.

Eventually assured of Lukas's patriotism by Tommy Duggan and the local police and on the condition that at least one other employee of the Dale Estate have a role in the supervision of the internees (a role Tommy readily agreed to assume), the application was approved. Seven internees would be delivered to the estate the following week. If others subsequently expressed interest, the number might in the future be increased to twelve.

"They can't come soon enough," Lukas said to Tommy as the colonel left Brampton. Both were disappointed that there would only be seven men, not twelve—those seven would have to work more hours than Lukas had contemplated if they were the only men to be working in Greenhouse 10. But they were pleased nonetheless. At that time, Lukas had the most rows in vegetable production and the least men per row he had had since arriving at the Dale Estate. In addition to the four rows in the smaller, older Greenhouse 10, twelve long greenhouse rows were now fully within the vegetable operation. He and his dwindling team of men worked longer and longer hours keeping the beds tended, but they were simply too few to provide the care needed. Good plants that had the potential to be great plants were not flourishing.

"When will we tell the others?" Lukas asked.

"What others?" Tommy asked.

"The other workers. The office staff."

"I've been thinking about that," Tommy said somewhat hesitantly. "I've concluded it would be better if we say nothing about this arrangement for a time. Why don't we wait and see if the internees work out; whether they are willing to stay; whether we are willing to keep them?"

Lukas looked at Tommy in astonishment. "But surely people will notice. The plumbers, the carpenters, the electricians, the deliverymen, the ladies who are cooking for them. Many people will come into contact with the internees."

"They will but you heard the colonel: they all speak English. They will be dressed in black slacks, white shirts, and wearing ties, just as all other Dale Estate workers. As long as the internees do not fraternize with the other workers—and we will see to it that they don't—I don't see how the other workers will know anything about the arrangement."

Lukas and Tommy had already agreed that the internees would work in a single greenhouse under the supervision of Lukas. The old Greenhouse 10 had been designated—the greenhouse Lukas first used when he arrived at the Dale Estate in 1914. Unlike the newer greenhouses on the property that were built contiguously, under a common roof, Greenhouse 10 was a separate building. Other men who had been working under Lukas's direction for the last year would tend to the vegetable-growing rows in the newer greenhouses, overseeing, as available, more traditional sources of labour.

"Given the proximity between Greenhouse 13 and Greenhouse 10, at least initially, the other workers will have no knowledge of the arrangement," Tommy said.

"But..." Lukas stammered. "Others now know. The police know."

"They won't say anything. I'll have a word with them. And you," he said pointedly to Lukas, "will continue to say nothing of this—to anyone!"

It was an absurd notion, Lukas thought. But Tommy was the boss. Lukas demurred, sad that he would not be able to tell Maria how close her husband would be to her.

"I don't know why you think there will be such resistance," Lukas said, though he was resigned to Tommy's edict. "The vegetables being produced will feed Canadians, Canadian soldiers, and Canadian allies. Why will the workers care that the vegetables are being grown by internees?"

"Prisoners of war," Tommy said. "They are prisoners of war. They are our enemies. They will be working in close proximity to people who have family members who have been taken prisoner by our enemies; who have been harmed by our enemies; who have been killed by our enemies. I know you are not my enemy, Lukas. I know you don't see your brother as an enemy. But our workers—well, they may not see this the way you do."

* * *

The internees—all Austrians—arrived the next Monday before morning light. Tommy and Lukas met them in Greenhouse 13, shaking hands with each of them as they arrived. An extra-firm handshake was extended by Lukas to the brother he had not seen in over a year. An opportunity for a more intimate greeting would follow, they both knew. Tommy welcomed the men and described the arrangements. He issued three firm directions. First, only English was to be spoken at the estate. Second, the internees were not to fraternize with any other workers. Third, under no circumstances were they to disclose the fact that they were prisoners of war. The breach of any of these directions would be considered grounds for dismissal. The internees nodded in understanding. Tommy turned to Lukas to lead the men to Greenhouse 10 and teach them the ways of the Dale Estate.

The first day was long. Lukas had seven dedicated workers, a matter that pleased him, but they were seven untrained men. Only Jakob and one other man had any experience growing plants. As the day went on, Lukas wondered if the plants were not being more harmed than helped by the arrival of the internees. Some plants were being overwatered, others underwatered; some underpruned, many others overpruned.

Two of the men new to planting had an understanding of science. They told Lukas that morning that they were looking forward to working with the soil and plants. The others expressed no similar enjoyment, but by the end of the day, two said that the work was better than laying railway ties.

One man did not even approach the plants. His name was Hermann. He was short and squat. He didn't work. He didn't talk. For the entirety of that first day, he just stood and watched others. "Does he speak English?" Lukas asked Jakob at one point. He wondered if he would have to speak German to better instruct him. Tommy Duggan would not like that.

"Happy speaks English," Jakob replied.

"Happy?"

"That's what we call him. He is, as you can see, not happy at all. Really, none of us are, but most of us have realized that the days pass faster and we can be of more value to our families if we do the work assigned. You will probably have to terminate him after a few days. That's what all the other employers have done."

Jakob spoke to Hermann, urging him to get closer to the plants, to start watering those near him. Hermann just stood there, looking blankly ahead, never replying. Lukas would have to consider what to do about him.

Tommy Duggan came into Greenhouse 10 four times that first day, twice in the morning and twice in the afternoon. He inspected the internees, though he could not provide any useful directions. The man who knew so much about financing, marketing, packing, transporting, and selling flowers and vegetables knew very little about growing them. But his attendances in Greenhouse 10 provided Lukas with an opportunity to check on the vegetable growers in the other greenhouses.

Lukas was looking forward to the second day. With a full day under their belt, he was confident the men in Greenhouse 10 more fully understood the growing methods. It was not too late to save the plants that had been roughly handled the prior day. The second morning began well enough. The men told Lukas they were satisfied with the cots and other conveniences provided. The food that had been delivered to Greenhouse 13 while the men were working in Greenhouse 10 had been quite satisfactory.

Six of the seven men performed well during the prebreakfast shift between seven o'clock and nine o'clock. Happy—or Hermann—on the other hand, was as still, quiet, and nonproductive as he had been the day before. Lukas walked around him, resolving to speak to Tommy about him later that day.

It was just after they returned to Greenhouse 10 after their breakfast that queer things began to occur. The first was the delivery of a load of fertilizer—a load that Lukas had not ordered. What made it all the more strange was that it was delivered by two men. Fertilizer was generally delivered by one man—since one man alone could easily push the wheelbarrow that held it. The two men had a good long look around Greenhouse 10 as Lukas was shooing them out.

Then just before noon, two carpenters entered Greenhouse 10. "We're here to tend to the repairs, Mr. Strauss," one said while the other surveyed the greenhouse.

"What repairs?" Lukas asked. "I haven't ordered any repairs."

"Let us just look around," the one who first spoke said, walking up one aisle of the greenhouse. "Maybe there is something to be repaired that you don't know about."

"I know my greenhouse," Lukas replied curtly. "I assure you there are no repairs to be made. You can be on your way now, if you please." At that point, the man was halfway up the long aisle of the Greenhouse 10. His coworker was back at the entryway.

"Say," shouted the one back at the entryway, loud enough to be heard by his coworker and everyone else in the greenhouse, "did you hear that the Allies beat those Krauts yesterday? Killed ten thousand of those slimy dogs in France. Picked them off one by one in their trenches, straight between the eyes." He looked around for a reaction.

"They were the lucky ones. They took another fifteen thousand prisoner. I hear they plan to put them all in pig pens, have 'em eat pig food, and if they don't eat it they can just starve."

He again looked for a reaction.

"Thank you for the news report, Mr. King," Lukas said. He had read the papers the night before and saw no such account. He knew Alfred King and his fellow carpenter, Richard Dyck. They were his least favourite of all of the estate's employees. He considered them ignorant and brutish. "I am sure there are repairs for you to attend to in another greenhouse, if you will just be on your way."

"Pig pens is all those people are worthy of being the sons of—"

Alfred King did not have an opportunity to finish his sentence. Happy, the one internee who had said and done nothing for a day and a half, suddenly revealed the full extent of his English comprehension. He lunged for King. It took two men to pull him off the carpenter.

Alfred King, who had sustained no serious injuries, stood back from Happy, then being restrained by Jakob and one of the other internees. "I will be on my way now, Mr. Strauss," King said calmly as he dusted off his sleeves. "I will leave you to these filthy Austrians. You seem to fit in perfectly well with them."

By two o'clock that afternoon, a crowd began to gather at the Dale Estate. It was a small crowd, initially—maybe only ten people, mostly men. By two thirty it had grown to one hundred. It included many men who worked for the Dale Estate, and it was loud. "Send them back!" the crowd shouted. "Send them back!"

At three o'clock, before a crowd of two hundred people, including a number of police officers there to protect the internees cowering in Greenhouse 10, Tommy Duggan announced that the experiment intended to produce more food for Canadians, for Canadian troops, and for Canadian allies, was at an end. The Austrians would leave the estate that night.

The people got what they wanted. But for some it was not enough. When Lukas left the estate at four o'clock that afternoon—a departure made at the insistence of Tommy Duggan—two thugs followed him home, jeering the entire time. Lukas was at that time forty-eight years old. A number of pounds had been added to his tall frame in the years since he first met Ingrid at Union Station in Toronto. He was not a man easily to be trifled with. But thugs, being essentially cowards, were not deterred by his height or girth. After following Lukas and calling him names as he walked the half-mile distance to his home, the taller one threw a rock at Lukas's head as he entered the stairway leading to his apartment above the dairy. He collapsed at the threshold, just as Dr. Heggie was walking by. Taking in the scene, Dr. Heggie scolded Alfred King and Richard Dyck, who would, he said, be reported to the police.

* * *

That was the last day Mr. Strauss worked at the Dale Estate. The trustees were not pleased with Tommy Duggan. Duggan was not pleased with Lukas

Strauss. It would take the Dale Estate a long time to recapture the goodwill lost with this experiment. They had spent a lot of money renovating and equipping Greenhouse 13. They had received exactly one and a-half days of service from seven men (even less when you consider how little Happy did). Tommy Duggan decided to burn Greenhouse 13. Its best use, he decided, was firewood. But before demolishing the building for that purpose, he terminated the employment of Mr. Strauss.

Mr. Strauss's efforts to find other employment in Brampton were as unsuccessful in the summer and fall of 1916 as his brother Jakob's had been in Toronto in the fall and winter of 1914. Of the two brothers in Ontario, now only Jakob was working—though intermittently. The episode in Brampton had a cooling effect on the ability of the authorities to place the Stanley Barracks internees. Major-General Otter, the director of the Canadian internment operations, ordered a review of the process by which the Dale Estate had been selected as a suitable location for the employment of the internees.

Elsa told us that her father had few regrets about bringing the Austrians to Brampton. He continued to think that doing so was the right thing for the Dale Estate and the right thing for Canada. He believed that Canada would soon be facing a real shortage of vegetables. Perhaps, he thought, if the people of the town had better understood that, if they and the other employees of the Dale Estate had been better prepared for that eventuality and the nature of the temporary workers, they would have reacted differently.

His actual regrets were twofold. He very much regretted not telling his sister-in-law about the presence of her husband in Brampton. Mr. Strauss was duty-bound to keep the fact a secret. He knew that Maria could not have seen Jakob in any event, but after the Austrians left Brampton, he could see how much it would have meant to Maria to know that for thirty-six hours her husband was working and residing half a dozen blocks away from her. In a similar vein, he very much regretted not having had the opportunity for familial discourse with his brother. Their remarks to each other in those two greenhouses were perfunctory. In his effort not to display favouritism to his brother, Mr. Strauss thought he was likely too formal; too distant. He had thought there would be opportunities for private discussions in the future. He had thought there would be many opportunities for them. Instead, the two brothers exchanged one embrace as Lukas was being led away from Greenhouse 10, as the police were moving in to protect the internees. "Take care of my family," Jakob said to his older brother.

"They are my family now too," Lukas replied.

The internee stipend that Jakob sent to his wife Maria every month could no longer be set aside for their future. Maria's offers to Lukas to contribute to the expenses of the household were now accepted. Those payments, plus the payments being sent home by Wilfred, had to support the two families.

Elsa's references to Wilfred and his wartime activities, which had been so prevalent in her first months in Brampton, returned to the fore. They correlated completely with her security or lack thereof in her new community. Thus we heard such nuggets as: "You have to get your rest on a furlough if you're going to be up to the task in the trenches" and "you have to be respectful to the local people to reflect well on Canada." But hearing the "Wilfred-isms" now with Elsa as a friend, though completely without utility to us, was not quite as irritating as it once had been.

Our school routine changed again in the fall of 1916 when Elsa, Frances, Jane, and I entered high school. Like most students, we had long looked forward to our tutelage in the institution attended by every high school student in Brampton and points well beyond. I had heard many stories about the goings-on there from my two older siblings and their friends. Frances, the daughter of the school principal, knew even more lore. Together we sought to enlighten Jane and Elsa, who had no similar vantage point. On many occasions in July 1916, the four of us would stand on Church Street in front of the two-storey building, staring at its tall, arched windows and the big, square three-storey tower in the centre. It did not matter to us that the school was nearly forty years old; that it had no gymnasium; that it did not have modern plumbing; that part of it had actually been condemned. We imagined what it would be like to walk in its wide halls, to climb its tall stairs, to move from one classroom to another as we took different courses, to play sports in its yards, and to conduct experiments in its science rooms. It was a good thing we had such vivid imaginations. The four of us were actually to see very little of the school. By January 1917, Elsa had left Brampton and the school had burned to the ground.

The circumstances of Elsa's departure, though sad for us, were happy for her as she described them to us in December 1916, four months into our high school years. At the end of November, Elsa's family was visited by her mother's brother, Andreas, the man who had refused to pay Elsa's father to farm the land formerly owned by her Uncle Klaus; the man who had inherited that land under a twenty-year-old will. Elsa's family had not seen him in two years. Her mother was surprised to receive a letter from him requesting the visit.

Andreas arrived a week later with a heavy-set, round-faced woman who had recently become his wife and who prodded him to speak when he began to flounder. Andreas explained that he had never lived in the farmhouse that the Strausses had vacated. He was happy in the farmhouse he had built years earlier on the lands he first owned. After the Strausses left the farm, he let out their farmhouse.

The new tenant occupied the same bedroom on the main floor of the farmhouse as was occupied by Klaus for most of the years he resided there. Though the tenant lived alone, he was not without companionship. Each night, the tenant was visited by a mouse. It took the tenant a number of weeks to find the mouse's den, but when he did find it—in a cavity at the base of the wall behind the bedroom's large chest of drawers—he also found a black metal strongbox with the letters "K. G." painted in gold on its lid. The tenant removed it and took it to Andreas.

"What was in it?" I asked excitedly.

"Two envelopes."

"To whom were they addressed?" Frances asked with enthusiasm.

"One was addressed to my mother. In it was a will made five years before my Uncle Klaus died. He left the farm to my parents. The other envelope was addressed to my Uncle Andreas. It was full of cash—all of the wages he should have been paid over those three years he worked for Uncle Klaus, and a tidy sum in addition."

"When did this happen?" Jane asked indignantly. "How long did he have the box?"

"About a year. He really wrestled with what to do about it. But he heard of our plight a couple of months ago and realized what he had to do."

"Your father must be furious," Jane said. We knew how difficult the past months had been for the family. The Strausses could have been on the farm all of that time.

"My parents are just so happy that we can return to the farm. They don't seem that mad. We'll be leaving as soon as school breaks for Christmas next week."

"What are you going to do when you get back to Shelburne?" Jane asked.

"I don't know. Enrol in the Orangeville High School, for a start."

"Aren't you nervous about going to a new school?" I asked. I knew I would be.

"My old Shelburne friends will be there, so I am not too nervous about that." It was hard to believe that Elsa had only been with us for a little over two years. Of course, she had in Shelburne all of the friends she had made in the years before she moved to Brampton. "But I will miss the three of you and the members of the knitting club." We echoed the sentiment.

"What about your aunt and cousins?" Frances eventually asked.

"They'll come with us. They have nowhere else to go, and of course there's no reason for them to stay near Toronto." Indeed there was not. For Mr. Strauss was not the only Straussenhoffer to relocate that month. Two weeks earlier, Jakob left the internment camp within the grounds of the Canadian National Exhibition. The authorities had conducted a complete review of the Stanley Barracks. Arrangements were made for all of the internees there to be relocated. This time there was no reprieve for Jakob. He, along with all of the other Austrians, including Happy, were sent to Kapuskasing, a town over five hundred miles north of Toronto, where they would work in the mines.

* * *

A few weeks later, Jane and I stood staring at the smoking remnants of the high school we had so long sought to attend, inexplicably incinerated the night before. The old school could not be saved, despite the response of the fire brigade and its innumerable firefighters, who pulled the reels holding the hose through heavy snow all the way from Main Street. The hose, once in place, could not bridge the distance between the nearest hydrant some three hundred yards away and the tall flames reaching high into the midnight skies. The new fire alarm system that provided specific sounds for fires in four specific districts of the town, that had recently been installed by the Northern Electric Company at some expense and tested with great success, was to no avail in saving the school.

As we walked away from the smoking embers near the one partially standing wall, moving through the dozens of people similarly paying respects to the old building—some silently, some speculating at its cause, some in tears—I thought of another fire a year earlier. That one, in February 1916, claimed the lives of seven people and Canada's beautiful Parliament building. The headlines reporting on it asked whether the fire was the work of the enemy. Indeed, at that time nearly every major calamity—a fire, an explosion, an industrial accident—was a suspected act of enemy sabotage. I turned to Jane. "It's a good thing that Elsa's family is back in Shelburne now," I observed. She concurred.

Chapter 13

THE AEROPLANIST

The summer of 1916 brought to fruition the desires of two people close to me: Aunt Rose, who had long sought to use her resources to further the war effort, and Eddie McMurchy, who had long wanted to follow his best friend Jim to the defence of king and country. In some ways it was a surprise that it had taken so long for Eddie to follow Jim into the expeditionary force. Jim's enlistment so much earlier than Eddie's marked only the second time that their paths had diverged in any meaningful way, the other being Jim's participation in the Brampton Excelsiors. From their youngest days, Jim and Eddie shared every classroom, friend, club, and sport. Together they abandoned their weekend and summertime play for responsible part-time and summer jobs. They attended the same university, where they lived in the same boarding house. They adopted as sweethearts two girls who were, like them, the best of friends. We knew how much Eddie longed to join Jim—to join the many Brampton boys—overseas. For a reason many people did not understand, he could not do so until the summer of 1916, almost two years into the war.

It was not long after Father enlisted that the efforts of the Cabal came to a successful conclusion. By early May 1916, Company A of the 126th Peel Battalion was at full strength, its band fully equipped. Company A had not long departed when recruitment efforts in Peel began anew, this time for a full eleven-hundred-strong military battalion. With the Cabal having been decommissioned, the campaign to complete the 234th Battalion took on a decidedly gentler tone, appealing purely to patriotism, with only the occasional request for family members to influence eligible men in their midst.

In addition to those who left with Peel companies, men left individually to join specialized corps such as a construction battalion, also then being raised in Peel, or the Canadian Army Supply Corps that Roy had joined. Eddie was interested in joining a specialized corps. To do so, he needed the resources of people like Aunt Rose.

By the end of January 1915, Aunt Rose, who had been an early and avid champion of the war, had still not found a way to use her resources to advance Canada's position in that conflict. Father thought the idea of her investing in a Brampton munitions or other war-related industry ridiculous. He was sceptical that the manufacturers in the town would obtain military contracts, and even if they did, he did not believe they would require Aunt Rose's money to do so. In the former respect, Father was quite wrong; in the latter respect, he was quite right.

John McMurchy, Eddie's uncle, was the first industrialist Aunt Rose approached about the use of her resources for wartime procurement. Mr. McMurchy had recently acquired the old tannery property on Queen Street East, which he had converted to a woollen mill. Aunt Rose met with him in September 1914 to ascertain whether he would be interested in utilizing his mill to produce wartime supplies. She was heartened to hear that he was and that he had already begun to consider the article that could best be produced by his mill. Delighted, Aunt Rose shared with him her thoughts on the matter. "Blankets," she said. "Woollen blankets will be very much in demand for use by the troops in all aspects of their service. They would be required by the men while in training in Canada, while in training in England, while in active service, and on the trains and boats on their way to active service. They would require blankets at the front and while in positions behind the lines; even while in hospital. In short, every man would require a blanket every single day." When she finished making her proposal to him, Mr. McMurchy apparently uttered one word.

"Socks!" Aunt Rose resounded in complete dismay when reporting the conversation to us later that week. Mr. McMurchy laughed at her suggestion that there were enough women in town producing socks. His woollen mill was going to produce 38,000 dozen pairs—a hundred times the number that were being produced by the good ladies of Brampton, he told her, and he would be well paid for his efforts. He was already in discussions about it with Richard Blain, our Member of Parliament, and with Colonel Sam's clothing and equipping department.

His cost to produce the socks would be less than some manufacturers, thanks to the dispensation granted to him by the town allowing him to operate his mill with electricity he himself produced. As for capital to convert the mill to the production of socks, he was certain he had enough. "If the government contract doesn't come through, Rose, I may just call you. I'll have to convert to something else at that point. There aren't enough people in this country to purchase all of the socks I plan to produce."

Aunt Rose thought she would have more success with the second manufacturer she planned to approach. She had the notion that the Pease foundry, managed by Jane's father, John Thompson, could be converted from the manufacture of domestic furnaces, for which there was a limited demand, to the manufacture of shells, for which there would, for as long as the war continued, be unlimited demand. But hoping not to be similarly rebuffed, she rehearsed her proposition in front of Father and the rest of the family the night before. After she stated her case, not once but twice, Father asked her why she thought she would be successful; what gave her the idea that John Thompson would be interested in converting some or all of his foundry to the production of munitions.

To answer that, Aunt Rose reached into the newspaper bin next to the fireplace. Extracting that day's *Conservator*, she opened it to an advertisement and passed it to Father. Father read the advertisement aloud:

> *Be Prepared*
> *Preparation is very often the dominating factor in success.*
> *Preparation has enabled Germany to hold practically all of*
> *Europe at bay during the past three months of fierce warfare.*
> *Unpreparedness has cost Great Britain millions of dollars*
> *and prolonged war and bloodshed…winter is coming again,*
> *as surely as the sunsets every day, and with it will come the*
> *troubles and misery of former years unless you prepare.*
> *Now is the time to look into the heating problem, investigate*

the different systems on the market to determine to get the
best... Your local dealer will gladly demonstrate to you all
of the qualities and superiorities of Pease Heating Systems
and supply you with explanatory literature. Branches in
Hamilton, Winnipeg, with head office in Toronto, Ontario,
and manufacturing works in Brampton, Ontario.

"I see your point," Father said. "If these are the lengths to which they must go to sell a furnace, they may be open to the manufacture of other items at this time."

Aunt Rose's preparation for the meeting with Mr. Thompson stood her in good stead. Her delivery, she told us afterward, was flawless. Her case was strong. It was so strong that Mr. Thompson entirely agreed with it. Unfortunately, Mr. Thompson had come to the same conclusion himself earlier that fall. By the time Aunt Rose spoke to Mr. Thompson in late November 1914, Mr. Thomson had already begun his conversations with Richard Blain and with Colonel Sam, completely bypassing Colonel Sam's clothing and equipping department. In fact, Aunt Rose caught Mr. Thompson just as he was preparing to leave Brampton for New York, where he was meeting with a prospective machinery provider. He would need money to purchase that equipment and to make some changes to his factory, he conceded. Aunt Rose momentarily fancied herself as an armaments financier, but Mr. Thompson's next words made short shrift of that notion. Mr. Thompson had already secured from the mayor a commitment for a $43,000 loan from the town. The loan, which he would not be required to repay for twenty years, was on terms that Aunt Rose could not replicate, even if she had that much capital available. A by-law providing for the loan would have to be approved by the electorate, but given the number of jobs the refitted foundry would produce, neither Mr. Thomson nor the mayor had any doubt that it would pass. Mr. Thompson expected to receive an initial order for a hundred thousand shells. It would take thirty men working for eight months to meet that order. He expected other orders would follow.

Aunt Rose was dejected. It was not long, though, before other Brampton businessmen heard that she was willing to invest in enterprises supplying goods to be used by the expeditionary force. Soon men were coming to her. "It's a good thing she has two nearly grown children living with her," Father said one day that winter. "The stream of men coming and going from her house would make a harlot blush." Mother swatted his arm.

But none of the other opportunities tempted her: the proponents were unrealistic about what they could manufacture; their business cases were too poor; they had insufficient business experience or poor credit history. The worst were those who did not require an investment at all but rather wanted access to her connections—such as they were. "Maybe you should just join the other members of the Women's Institute and take up knitting," Father suggested one day. "The men overseas do appreciate the socks and shirts the ladies are making."

It was a conversation at our dinner table one Sunday night late in 1914 that set her on her eventual course. Aunt Rose, John, and Hannah were at our house that evening. Ina was still in Winnipeg. Jim and Father had just returned home from a rehearsal for the Christmas cantata. They brought Eddie with them. Since Millie was not able to be with us that night, Mother invited Eddie to stay for the meal. While we were eating our stew, Grandpa made an observation about an article he read in the paper that week.

"I see that the motor league is going into partnership with the aeronautic supporters. I thought that was quite interesting." The motor league had been formed at least a decade earlier when the first cars appeared on our streets, but it was still considered a fairly new association.

"I'd have thought they would focus on their core mission before venturing into other modes of transportation," Father, always the contrarian, remarked. "What does a motor league have to do with aeroplanes?"

"Aeroplanes do have motors in them," Jim observed.

Father allowed that. "But I don't think those are the motors the league members intend the association to deal with." He was speaking only theoretically. Not owning a car, he was not a member of the league.

"They seem to have realized the value of flying machines to the war effort," Jim said. "I'm glad someone has."

"It seems too fantastic to me," Father replied. "Flying machines. Flying machines. It's all we ever hear of. It is just a form of entertainment."

Father was right about the entertainment value. For years, the papers had reported on one exploit after another as aeroplanes accomplished increasingly daring feats. As Canadians, we were all proud of the Aerial Experimental Association, formed in 1907 by Alexander Graham Bell and four young airmen, two of whom were Canadians. Before building the Silver Dart in 1909, Canada's first "heavier-than-air" flying machine, the Aerial Experimental Association produced and flew in the United States two planes that broke records, flying in one instance 318 feet and in another just over 1,000 feet. Public interest burgeoned as the flying machines—flown by airmen and airwomen—were able to fly longer, faster, and higher.

I remembered the day we went to the Canadian National Exhibition in Toronto to see Count Jacques de Lesseps fly his Bleriot plane *La Scarabee* over the exhibition grounds. My whole family attended, except for Aunt Lil. Aunt Lil's attitude about aeronautics was only slightly more progressive than her attitude toward automobiles. Aeroplanes were at least not pushing horse-drawn carriages off the street. "It flew twenty miles at a speed of seventy miles per hour," Jim told Aunt Lil later that afternoon back at her house.

"You're lucky it didn't hit a nearby building and land on your head," she cried. There was no opportunity to tell her that flying at a minimum height of fifteen hundred feet, no building was likely to have been hit. Aunt Lil had a different view of stationary planes. Later that summer, she joined us to view the airplane assembled on the fifth floor of Toronto's preeminent retailer, Eaton's.

"I think they are more than entertainment," Eddie said in response to Father's claim. "They are legitimate instruments of war. I've read that twenty aeroplanes can eliminate an enemy's communications lines. They can be used to scout and report on enemy movements quickly and safely, and really, what else can be used to combat the Zeppelins currently striking the British navy ships? Some British aviator recently conducted a bombing test on a model battleship. He had a ninety percent strike rate."

"And they are more cost-effective," Jim chimed in. "I read once that it costs at least $12 million to build a battleship. A modern aeroplane costs on average $6,000. If someone was willing to invest in them, we could have two thousand aeroplanes for the cost of a single battleship. We could win the war with those alone."

"Maybe that's what you should do with your resources, Mother," my cousin John suggested. "You could be like Mable Hubbard." John was referring to the wealthy wife of Alexander Graham Bell. Hubbard financed the Aerial Experimental Association with $35,000 of her own funds.

Aunt Rose appeared to contemplate that for a moment. "No. I don't see how I could do that. We don't have any aeroplane manufacturers in Brampton. I will say, though, the situation is a bit of an embarrassment." We all looked at her.

"Do you know," she said, "when the war was first declared, Colonel Sam offered to send aviators as part of the first contingent. The British asked us to send six aviators. We were only able to provide two. Of the two that went with the first contingent from Valcartier, one returned home almost immediately afterward, and the other was killed while taking his first solo flight in England."

"That's exactly what the motor league is trying to address!" Jim said. "It's hoped that the club will train men to be available for the defence of Canada and the entire British Empire. But first it has to create a team of experienced aeroplanists and mechanics."

"It may be a good cause," Aunt Rose conceded, "but I can't see who would actually want to fly one of those things. Practically every day the papers report tragedies involving airmen." She looked at the boys at the table.

"Don't look at me," her son John said, repeating the words spoken at Aunt Rose's table the prior August. "Apparently I am too young to enlist."

"Don't look at me," Jim said. "I have no intention of enlisting. I have important dental work to do, don't I, Father?" Father nodded.

"Don't look at me," Eddie said, providing an explanation similar to the one provided by our cousin Bill. "I don't have the funds to pay for the training."

But even though none of the boys said they wanted to fly, and though Aunt Rose had not expressed any interest in personally advancing the cause, the conversation planted seeds in the minds of two people at that table.

* * *

In the spring of 1915, while Jim was enlisting in the No. 4 Canadian General Hospital, Eddie was investigating joining the British Royal Navy Air Service or the Royal Flying Corps. Jim's eventual announcement to our family that he had enlisted coincided with an announcement by Eddie to his family of his plans. But where Jim was able to independently pursue his means of enlistment, Eddie was not. The Imperial War Office wanted qualified airmen to join their two flying corps. Eddie needed to obtain flight qualifications before enlisting. Those qualifications did not come cheaply. He could not obtain them without a source of income (and the time to earn the necessary funds) or support from his father. Eddie's father refused to provide the financial support. "Go and join the infantry, if you must," his father said. "It's much safer. We want you to come back after the war." While Jim received basic training before leaving on the SS *Corinthian* and afterward at Shorncliffe, Eddie began work at his uncle's knitting mills, hoping to save enough money to pay for and receive his basic air flight training before the war ended.

It was investments like the one Aunt Rose ultimately made that enabled Eddie to receive the qualifications he required, for just as Eddie left that conversation at our house with a seed planted for a future military role as an aeroplanist, Aunt Rose left with a similarly germinated mind.

In late January 1915, her resources having been rejected by both Eddie's uncle and Jane's father and no other local industrialist having made a proposition for their use that she considered reasonable, Aunt Rose turned her sights in another direction. What Brampton needed, she came to believe, was a flying school. Flying schools needed land. Aunt Rose had plenty of that. Once again, she began meeting with men, but this time instead of receiving them in her premises, she was received in theirs. She met with the mayor; the town councillors; J.R. Fallis, the local Member of the Provincial Parliament; Richard Blain, the local Member of Parliament; educators, military men, and the president of the motor league. All were intrigued by the proposal—some enthusiastic—but not a single one of them would support it without the support of one person. That one person was not a pilot, or a banker, or an insurer, or a by-law officer. That one person—the linchpin to the entire scheme—was the well-known Peel philanthropist, William Gage. Over a decade earlier,

Gage had purchased a portion of the lands owned by financially troubled Kenneth Gilchrist and donated them to the town of Brampton for the purpose of creating a large park.

"William Gage?" Father said one Saturday afternoon as Aunt Rose was apprising us of the status of her inquiries. "Why would the support of a book publisher be necessary to the creation of an aero club?"

"Apparently he has made the creation of such a club, and the training of airmen his great cause."

"I see. But if it is his cause, why would it be difficult to obtain his support?" Father asked.

"The thinking is that there cannot be too many of these schools. He is well along in supporting one outside of Brampton," Aunt Rose explained.

"Rose, you know lots of people," Mother said. "Can you not find someone equally prominent who would support a school in Brampton?"

"I don't think so," she said. "He's created a foundation to support young airmen. He has on its board the most prominent people you could think of, including the Duke of Connaught." The Duke of Connaught and Strathearn was Queen Victoria's third son, then the Governor General of Canada.

"Maybe you could approach Sir John," Mother suggested, referring to John Strathearn Hendrie, the Duke of Connaught's provincial counterpart but no actual relation to him.

"William Gage has already done that too. He has the support of all of the provincial lieutenant governors. They're working with Doug McCurdy of the Aerial Experimental Association to create the school. The federal government is going to provide them with the land—one hundred acres near Lakeshore and Dixie Road—at Long Branch."

After hours and hours, days and days, and months and months of meetings, Aunt Rose came to the reluctant conclusion that she was once again too late. Efforts were too far along for the creation of the Long Branch flying school. A time might come for a Brampton flying club, but it had not yet arrived.

"What can I do?" she asked William Gage one day, conceding that her vision for a club in Brampton could not then be realized. She told us about the conversation later that night.

"Make a monthly donation to my foundation," William Gage answered.

"A donation?" Aunt Rose asked. "I had wanted to make an investment."

"It will be the best investment you ever make," William Gage replied. "It will allow us to train the airmen we need to win the war."

* * *

Donations like those made by Aunt Rose and hundreds of others made it possible for people like Eddie to obtain their Canadian flying qualifications. Eventually, the Imperial War Office agreed to reimburse airmen for the costs of their training—$350 per airman—and to provide a weekly stipend for trainees. But for boys whose families could not afford the initial outlay or for boys like Eddie whose families could afford it but were not willing to make it, the funds of the Canadian Aviation Foundation allowed them to obtain the training required. The funds of the foundation facilitated the contribution by Canada of some of the greatest flying aces of the war.

The air school, named after one of the Aerial Experimental Association founders, Glenn Curtiss, commenced operations in May 1915. It immediately had fifty-two students—far less than the number who desired to attend it. With the knowledge of the financial support available, Eddie added his name to the list of aspiring students. Eventually, his name was called. Like all students of the school, he completed his initial two hundred minutes of training on airboats flown from Hanlan's Point in the Toronto Islands of Lake Ontario. Thereafter, he moved on to land training, launching, and landing planes out of the Long Branch Aerodrome. With fifty hours of experience and his certificate in hand, Eddie was by July 1916 ready to follow Jim to England.

* * *

An intimate group met at the CPR station that morning to bid Godspeed to Eddie. It was a far cry from the throngs that met on the same platform six weeks earlier to send off the 229 Brampton men who formed the A Company of the 126th Battalion. Eddie was on his way to join those men and the nine thousand others then training in Niagara. It was hoped that the boys would leave the Niagara training camp for England at the end of the month. Having finally learned the name "Valcartier," our troops were no longer sent there for training.

Neither the cool temperature of the dawn nor the sleep we sacrificed to be with Eddie at seven o'clock that morning diminished our support for him or the solemnity of the occasion. With Eddie, who was dressed in his military uniform, were his mother and his sister. His father, who had never supported his son's choice of enlistment, refused to attend. The father and son had a short, private send-off the night before.

Ina was there. Home for the summer following the completion of the first year of her university studies, she was easily able to arrange her schedule at the local telephone switch to be in attendance. I do not think she had ever stopped loving Eddie—even while she was besotted with Michael. Of course, she would never say so. Her attendance at the send-off was for a good friend; her brother's friend. "Jim would want that," she declared.

Father considered coming home for the train station send-off but thought better of it. Mr. and Mrs. McMurchy had not forgiven him for singling out Eddie at the concert the night before Father enlisted. Mother stood on the platform, making a brave face while apologizing to Mrs. McMurchy for Father's "unavoidable" absence. She said some kind words to Eddie and then stood slightly back from him, joining the cadre formed by Grandpa, Ina, and me a short distance from Eddie.

Sarah and Millie were both at the station, of course. Sarah stood next to Eddie, crying profusely. Millie stood on the other side of Sarah, trying to calm her.

"He'll be fine," Millie kept saying to her. "Look how well he's been trained. He has his airman's certificate."

"That isn't the same as actual combat experience!" she wailed, looking at Millie and then at Eddie—anyone who would agree with her and require him to stay home and receive further training. She had so hoped that Eddie's father would have stopped him from going.

"You think anyone can shoot me down, Sarah? Knowing how fast I am? How well I aim? How well I fly? You won't even have time to get your hair cut before I'm back." He ran a hand through her shoulder-length brown hair. "I'll be home for Christmas," he said confidently. Speculation that the war would be over by Christmas of 1916 ran rampant earlier in the year. A conjecture as to the war's ending by any British resident passing through Peel County or any Peel resident returning from Britain, based on what was being said in the "best-informed circles in Britain" was sufficient to constitute a near certainty—no matter how little connection the speaker had with those actually in the best-informed circles. It occurred to me, as Eddie made the pronouncement, that it had been some time since I heard anyone so confidently predict a near end to the war.

"Do you really think so?" she asked Eddie hopefully.

"I thought so when I told you that last week. I thought so when I told you that last night. I think so now." Eddie chuckled.

"All right, Eddie McMurchy," Sarah said, almost defiantly. "I won't be cutting my hair again until I see you. You'd better come home soon. It grows fast!" He kissed her forehead before turning to speak to his sister, who had joined him on his other side. That was all it took. His head turned away from her for a second, and Sarah lost her composure again.

Millie tried to help bring her friend's emotions in check. "Sarah, I'm so confident that Eddie will be home by Christmas, I too will pledge not to cut my hair until I see him again."

"You would do that?"

"Of course I would," Millie said. "It will be very little sacrifice. My hair could use a three month grow. I think it is a little too short." Millie's hair looked exactly the same length as Sarah's. But I could see she was trying to help her friend. She was being kind to Sarah—as she always had been to me. It was awkward being so close to her and only exchanging polite greetings. It had been fifteen months since she and Jim had ceased to be sweethearts, but I still missed her.

John McMurchy, Eddie's uncle, was at the send-off. His woollen mill was by then running around the clock, with fifty or more employees working to meet the sock orders of the military. He handed a pair to Eddie as he approached him to say farewell. "We're all proud of you, Eddie," his uncle said. "Your father most of all, though he won't admit it. Be brave. But be careful. There's a lot here for you to do when you return."

Jane and her parents were there too. The Pease foundry then had thirty men also working multiple shifts manufacturing small parts of equipment to fit into shells, readying itself for the eventual construction later that year of complete six-inch-high explosive shells. The conversion of the factory to produce shells had been more of a challenge than Mr. Thompson had anticipated. The foundry's cash flow was, and would remain, tight until the first shell was produced in December of that year. Though the circumstances were well known, Aunt Rose never spoke of them to Mr. Thompson. Despite the early hour and the financial pressures he was under, Mr. Thompson came to the station for the send-off. He had a great deal of respect for Eddie and the other airmen being trained in the province. He didn't want to miss an opportunity to express his admiration and appreciation.

Major Sheriff, who had recruited and trained Company A of the 126th, was there, standing with A.H. Milner, the mayor. They approached Eddie. "You're the second," the mayor said. "So far it's just you and Douggan. The only aviators Brampton has produced. I know you'll do us proud." Mr. Milner was referring to C.R. Douggan, a Brampton boy who had returned home from England just six weeks earlier after falling three hundred feet from his aircraft. Though he wanted to return to the flying corps immediately, the doctors insisted he first recover from the shock of the plunge.

Sarah, who had momentarily regained her composure, lost it again. The mayor quickly moved away.

"Will she not stop wailing?" Ina said, too loudly, considering how close we were standing to Eddie, to be considered the whisper she pretended it was. "Her voice is even more irritating through tears. Honestly, he'll think she has no confidence in him. No man needs to be sent off that way." With that, Ina strode to Eddie, practically pushing Sarah towards Millie as she came between the two sweethearts.

"Now, Eddie, this is not going to be goodbye for us. I know that. No one is better suited to fly an aircraft than you. Remember all those talks we had on the verandah about wind and weather and pressure and turbulence? You know those systems, Eddie McMurchy, and that is what will make you a great pilot. And when you get back, I hope you'll join me on the verandah and tell me how you shot down plane after plane of those attacking Germans. You'll do that, won't you, Eddie?"

He looked beyond Ina at Sarah, weeping into her hands, Millie at her side, an arm around Sarah's shoulders. He took a breath, looked into Ina's eyes, and said, "I will do that, Ina. That is exactly what I am going to do. And when this war is over, I'll be back on your verandah, waiting for Jim to come home from his dental practice, filling in time with you, reminiscing over those very things." He looked back at Sarah and then at Ina. "Thank you." He gave her a long embrace.

My farewell was quicker and less poignant. "Eddie, will you see Jim when you're over there?" I pointed vaguely to the east.

"Certainly I will, Jessie. And do you know what I'll tell him when I see him?"

"No. What will you tell him?"

"That I tugged a ringlet of his favourite girl." He gave one of mine a little pull.

"Thanks, Eddie. I needed that. Say hi to Jim for me. Tell him I miss him." He reached out and gave me a big hug. I couldn't help but notice then how solid Eddie was. He'd filled out a lot since Jim left. At twenty-five years of age, he was a full-grown man with broad shoulders, a thick neck, and a large, square head. The dimple on his chin that seemed so faint when he was younger had developed into a full clear "Y" when his lips were closed. His eyes were as tender as always.

I've never forgotten the actual date of Eddie's departure. It was Jane's birthday. After watching the train leave for Toronto, Mrs. Thompson asked me if I would like to join her family that night for a celebratory meal—a dinner, as we had all begun to call our evening meal. Mother approved, and I arrived at the Thompson house at four o'clock that afternoon. The birthday dinner, consumed two hours later, was taken in the dining room of Haggertlea, above their long, sloping lawn, looking down over the old Haggert Iron Works building. Afterward, Jane opened her gifts, which included a Columbia record given to her by her brother Douglas. His mother admonished him for bragging about the price he paid for it. "I got it on sale for eighty-five cents," he gloated. "It was regularly one dollar!"

Her father's sister sent her a fashionable new dress from New York. We looked aghast at the dress, with its high, deep waistband and large front pockets.

"Put it away," her mother said. "You can wear it in a few years' time once it is fashionable here in Canada." We had a hard time imagining it would ever be so.

After listening to the new Billy Murray record on the gramophone and playing a number of hands of gin rummy, I began to organize my things to leave. It was nine o'clock. With Father away, I no longer had to abide by a ten o'clock curfew, but we had risen particularly early that morning. I was tired.

"Would you like Douglas to accompany you home, Jessie?" Mrs. Thompson asked. "I don't think you should walk home on your own this late."

"No, that's not necessary," I replied. Douglas had moved on to playing cribbage with his father. "It's still light out." Jane walked me through the rotunda and opened the front door to let me out. With my cardigan in hand, I walked into the cooling summer night. I had only gone a few steps when I heard the door open again.

"Jessie!" Jane said, running toward me. "We didn't decide what we're doing tomorrow!" We stood on the semicircular drive and discussed the two options we had for the next day. One was to attend a summer social at the church. Lemonade and cookies were being sold in support of the Red Cross. The ladies at the church were always looking for a "pair of younger hands" to help them with the serving and cleanup, but we had not yet committed to attending. At the same time, in the courthouse, a new group of girls—the Girls Club—was meeting. Its objective that day was to prepare packages for the Brampton women who had gone, and who were soon to go, overseas as nurses or as aids to nurses. Comprised of my cousin Hannah and other high school-aged girls, we thought it a real honour to be invited to join them. Their efforts in support of nurses and nurses' aids were to be funded by a group of fifty men who had agreed to donate one dollar a month to their support. The packages, once prepared, would be distributed by the Canadian Red Cross. We spent some time discussing the pros and cons of each option.

By the time we decided to join the older girls at the courthouse the next day, it was nine thirty. The sun had set. It mattered not. I was not afraid to walk in Brampton in the dark, with the exception, of course, of the area near the Kelly Iron Works Repair Shop, which I was afraid to walk in during the dark and the light. I had no intention of walking near it that night or at any other time it could be avoided. As I walked along Nelson Street to Main, toward the old Haggert Iron Works building, now the home of the knitting mills, the box factory, and the dairy, I thought of Elsa in the apartment on the top floor. She had not attended the send-off at the train station. Ever since the Austrians had left the Dale Estate, Elsa and her family had been living reclusively. Her father left the apartment a couple of times a week to search for work (a fruitless endeavour), to register with the police, or to pick up groceries and other necessities. Aside from her occasional physical reports to the police station, always taken with her brother-in-law, Elsa's aunt never left the apartment. Since the school term ended in June, Elsa left the apartment only to see Jane, Frances, and me in our own homes. She never went to concerts at Gage Park; she never walked with us through the flats; she never went swimming or bicycling with us.

I was thinking about which home she could next visit as I approached Main Street. Frances was away and would not be home for another week. Jane had Elsa and me at Haggertlea a few days earlier. With Father away, I was now able to have friends into my house. I began to run through the activities I had planned for the week ahead to ascertain an available day to host Elsa and Jane. But as I turned the corner, I ceased to think. The only thing my mind could process was a scream. It was a loud scream; a scream that hurt one's ears; a scream that hurt one's throat. As it sounded, my body began to shake; my knees began to buckle. The scream was mine.

"It's all right. He won't hurt you. The words were spoken by a man about Father's age. He spoke softly, soothingly, repeating the words over and over. Seeing their failure to produce the desired effect, he turned to the person beside him and hollered. "Scott! Remove your hand now!" My right shoulder, which had been locked in Scott's vice-like grip, was released.

"There," the man said once my shoulder was free. "I'm terribly sorry about that. It is his way of saying hello."

I couldn't reply. The scream had sapped all of the elasticity of my vocal cords; all of the muscle control within my neck.

"I don't think you should walk home on your own. Shall we walk you there?"

The question released my vocal cords and neck muscles. The last thing I wanted was for them to know where I lived. I shook my head. "No. Thank you. I'll be fine," I said as I backed away from them and turned to walk south on Main Street, in front of the old Haggert Iron Works building, past the dairy and the doorway to the stairway to Elsa's apartment. I briefly considered alighting the steps to the apartment above the dairy. I knew that Elsa would be home; that her family would take me in. But I didn't want to explain to them the reason for my terror.

"Come along," I heard the man say. "Let Miss Stephens be on her way." Their footsteps receded as they turned the corner off of Main Street and began walking up Nelson Street, tracing in reverse the steps I had just taken.

Clearly out of their sight, I proved right the earlier concerns of Mrs. Thompson: I could not walk the remaining fifteen minutes home. I ran all the way, wondering how the father of Scary Scott knew who I was.

Chapter 14

THE INVALID

Though Father no longer lived with us on a daily basis, we continued to see him, usually once a week. Most often he would come home by train wearing his "civvies"— his regular clothes, generally sporting his signature white patent leather shoes. If his visit was to be of a short duration—perhaps simply for three or four hours—Father might travel home by car, driven by one of the army personnel. At those times, he would arrive in full dress uniform looking every part the officer he was. Nothing made him happier than taking his meal with his family inside our house while a car and driver waited for him outside.

At those times, our conversations with Father nearly always revolved around the war and any current or impending battles. For months, he spoke about the "big push" that was to be the turning point in the war—the point at which the Allied forces would take the offensive, leave the trenches, and begin to reclaim the captured territories of Belgium and France. Over the course of those discussions, we heard about the enormous losses of men to gunfire and poison gas as they sought to claim a hill, a ridge, or a few yards of muddy turf, sometimes with success.

Although the conversations referenced such places as St. Eloi, Mont Sorrel, Fromelles, and High Wood, as did the conversations in many Canadian homes, our conversation also referenced such far-flung places as Lake Doiran, Kosturino, Mazirko, Karajakois, River Struma, and Serres. These places in and around Greece were not top of mind for most Canadians—indeed, the names of these places rarely appeared in local newspapers. But these places were known to the British, who sent a small force to the area in the wake of the Gallipoli debacle. While they arrived too late to be of any assistance to the British Allies-supporting Serbians who had been attacked by the German Axis-supporting Bulgarians, they stayed in Greece to help ward off any similar attack against Allied Greece. These places were known to my family because from October 1915 through to September 1916, Jim was posted in Salonica, Greece. Along with other Canadian Army Dental Corps personnel, their mission was to fill deficiencies within the British forces. News about the war activities in that theatre was provided to us by Father, who went to great efforts to receive it and from letters sent home from Jim.

From Jim's letters, which were still read aloud at the dining room table (once when received and then again when Father came home for a meal), we learned that Jim's days were not spent in cold, wet, rat- and lice-infested trenches or in the various camps behind the lines, but rather in a warm, dry, arid, desert-like area. Surrounded by hills, Jim slept each night in a tent next to a parade ground about four and a half miles outside of Salonica. The people of the area were a mixture of Turkish, Macedonian, Greek, and Bulgarian. Mostly poor, living in squalid conditions and employing a rudimentary method of mule transport, they practiced a thriving commerce selling the troops shaving cream, among other things, for three times the cost at home. The work of the Allies in Salonica was chiefly comprised of laying barbed wire around its hills (creating what became known as a "bird cage") and defending themselves from the very occasional Bulgarian or Austrian airstrike. In his spare time, Jim and his friend and fellow officer Freddy rode bicycles up into the mountains, past the former Balkan war trenches and the armed French guards.

The comparatively carefree ease with which we led our lives thinking that our Jim was safe from harm's way came to an end with news in August 1916 that his life hung in the balance. As Jim provided dental services in Salonica to the members of the four British divisions, which, together with Serbian, Russian, and Italian Allied troops, successfully warded off a summer invasion of Greece, Jim was struck with not a bullet but rather dysentery. The telegram, delivered to Father at his barracks in Toronto, advised that Jim had been admitted to hospital in Salonica on August 4,

1916 and was seriously ill. In Brampton, that first telegram was followed by days of waiting for further reports, eating the many dishes prepared by our neighbours, and reading all we could about dysentery.

Unfortunately, we all knew something about dysentery. "Didn't Sir Frances Drake suffer from dysentery?" I asked Aunt Lil, who had come home with Father the day he received the telegram.

"The bloody flux. Indeed, he did," confirmed Aunt Lil, the history teacher. "It was the end of Drake in 1596 in Puerto Rico. Struck him while he was attacking San Juan. It's claimed the lives of others you've heard of too: King John of England in 1216 and King Henry V in 1422. Those are just the well-known victims." She went on as though we were in a classroom, completely oblivious to the horrified looks on our faces. "Its victims suffer extreme abdominal pain, diarrhea—their feces mixed with blood and mucus—dehydration, fever, headache. Thousands die of it every year in..."

"Yes, Lil. Thank you for that informative lesson," Father said, cutting her off before she provided more disturbing details. "I think we will wait for further particulars from Dr. Heggie." Hannah had gone to fetch him. Aunt Rose and Hannah had run to our house shortly after seeing the army car drive up our street midafternoon.

"How could this be, Dr. Heggie?" Mother asked, for once not descending the cellar stairs to retrieve a jar of pickled beets to pay him for his services. The visit, it was acknowledged, was of a neighbourly nature. "He had his inoculations before he left Toronto. How could he have contracted dysentery?"

"The inoculations would have nothing to do with this, Mary," Dr. Heggie replied. "There is no inoculation to ward off dysentery. He would have become infected through something he ate, or if he rubbed infected hands next to his mouth or nose. He may have come into contact with it through one of his patients.

"No matter how it got into his system, it has attacked his intestinal lining, bringing about fever, pain, and swelling. If the infection is serious, and we understand that Jim's is, it could also affect his immune cells, which will make it difficult for his body to fight this or any other infection. It could also inhibit the absorption by his body of the necessary nutrients. Bacteria could enter his bloodstream, leading to the death of cells throughout his body."

I began to wonder why Father had sent for Dr. Heggie. I had never been so unhappy to see him.

"You may take some comfort in knowing that if Jim survives this—and there is certainly a chance he will—he will be discharged from the army for medical reasons. He will be sent home and could lead a full and normal life—a life with all his limbs, which of course is more than can be said of many of our returning men."

"Is there something that can be done?" Mother asked imploringly.

"They will try to keep him hydrated to have it run its course. As for those of us back here, ladies," he said looking at Mother, Aunt Rose, Ina, Hannah, and me—he seemed to know better than to look at Aunt Lil— "you can pray. Doc, in a few days, you should return to Toronto. Try to get Jim moved. If his condition was caused by contaminated water—well, for that and other reasons, it would be best to get him back to England."

Seeing that there was nothing more he could do for us, Dr. Heggie took his leave. Standing in the tower within our parlour, I watched him walk down the street, the always present black bag in his hand. How, I wondered, did I ever think it could hold a baby?

We did pray. We prayed at home and at church. We prayed on our knees; on the floor; in front of our beds; in our beds; at the table; in the garden. We prayed by ourselves and with others; with acquaintances and with near strangers alike. We prayed that Jim would be invalided back to England. We prayed for a full recovery. We prayed for a full discharge. While we prayed, we waited.

Although we had no further news, after three days of waiting, Father returned to his barracks, taking back to Toronto with him his eldest sister. Aunt Lil, who ordinarily spent far too little time in Brampton for my liking— always leaving before I was ready for her to depart—outstayed her welcome on this occasion by about two and a half days of the three days she was with us, constantly rhyming off other famous victims of dysentery and the circumstances of their demise.

Finally, sixteen days after the first telegram was delivered to Father, a second one arrived. This one announced that Jim had been admitted to the military hospital in Malta, where he was in isolation.

Father apprised us of the development that night. The car and driver waited for him while he briefly returned home that evening. "It isn't England. But it is British. It is most assuredly a better-equipped hospital, a more sterile environment, than the one in Salonica. It's only temporary. They will keep him there until he has fully stabilized."

"Is he stabilizing?" Mother asked hopefully. "Do you have any news on that?"

"The telegram doesn't say," Father replied. "But I am quite confident that he is. According to the telegram, he is once again within the ranks of the No. 4 Canadian General Hospital, and he has been recommended for commissions. Why would they make that change or recommend him for a commission if he was not expected to live and serve?"

"Serve? Can he not be honourably discharged, as Dr. Heggie suggested?" That was all she asked. We all knew that near dead servicemen were often recommended for a commission.

"They may," Father said. "But I expect the army will want him to stay on. A fine young man like Jim—they need men like him. But I suppose it will be up to Jim."

My heart sank. Up to Jim? If it was up to Jim, I knew exactly what he would do. My prayers increased threefold. I continued to pray for his full recovery. I continued to pray that he would be transported to England. I now prayed that he would choose to come home.

For the next four weeks, Mother, Grandpa, Ina, and I lived in a stupor. We barely went anywhere. The commencement of my high school career, to which I had looked so forward, barely registered with me. Like Elsa, I attended school. I did not engage in it. Jane and Frances restrained their excitement around the two of us as Elsa ended each day relieved at not having been persecuted, and as I ended each relieved that our family had not received a telegram. Mother played the piano incessantly, always reciting gloomy refrains. She drove me to my room to do my homework. Even Grandpa needed respite from the dirge-like strains. He expanded the hours he reserved for reading in his room to include not only the evening but also the afternoon. "At least you are at school during the day," my eighty-one-year-old grandfather whispered to me. "If Jim doesn't get better soon, I'm going to have go start building again." Ina managed to start her second year of studies at Victoria College at the University of Toronto, but her attendance there was, like mine at high school, perfunctory at best.

Finally, at the end of September, Father received word that, having travelled on two of His Majesty's ships, first the HMS *Formosa* and then the HMS *Aquitania*, Jim had been admitted to a war hospital in London. He was on the mend, but since he was suspected of being a carrier of dysentery, he was required to recuperate there for at least two months.

"Two months," Mother said. "Can he not come home and recuperate here surrounded by his friends and family?"

"Not unless you want to subject everyone on his returning ship and your friends and family to the scourge," Father said. "He'll be in good hands in the British hospital. He should be out by Christmas."

"Christmas," Mother said longingly. We all pictured Jim home in time for Christmas 1916.

"Say," Mother asked. "What hospital is he in? Wouldn't it be wonderful if Jim was in the Perkins Bull Hospital?" Perkins Bull, a lawyer and financier, was a Brampton native. His family operated the world's largest Jersey cattle business on one thousand acres of land at the south end of Brampton. The land was almost half a mile from the four corners area of the town. One day, years earlier, Frances, Archie, and I had walked to Derry Road in search of space not contaminated by scarlet fever. We walked by the dairy farm and discussed a rumour then being circulated that the farmland would be sold for the purpose of constructing homes. We laughed at the very thought of anyone, aside from a farmer, living in a house so far away from the centre of town.

In 1912, Perkins Bull left his brothers Bartley and Duncan to operate the family's Jersey operation and relocated his immediate family to London, England, to further his personal business interests. He and his brother Jeffrey were living there in 1914 when the war was declared. They both sought to enlist, but only Jeffrey succeeded. Perkins, at two hundred and sixty pounds in weight, was considered too fat to serve. In those days, the army could be choosy about who it accepted within its ranks.

Perkins Bull returned to his wife Maria and their seven children, all under the age of sixteen, and considered what he could do to support the war effort. By the summer of 1915, Maria recognized the need for a location in which Canadian officers could convalesce. Since their home was too small to accommodate all who required such care, they leased a vacant home adjacent to their own, refitted it with modern heating, lighting, and plumbing, and installed a table that could seat forty-four men and the beds on which those men could sleep. One afternoon, while their neighbours were otherwise occupied, they moved in the first occupants. It was the talk of Brampton.

"Being a suspected carrier of dysentery, I am sure Jim would not qualify for convalesce there," Father said. Mother was disappointed that Jim could not be with some people from home.

* * *

Once Jim was ensconced in the military hospital, life took on a greater air of normalcy. I was finally able to enjoy the high school experience I had so long anticipated. The miasma of my first weeks behind me, I began to take note of my surroundings, my fellow students—most of whom were new to me—my new teachers, of which I now had a different one for most classes, and my subjects, which included Greek, Latin, and a number of sciences. Mother resumed her usual amount of piano playing and a more diverse selection of tunes. Grandpa returned to reading his newspapers in the sitting room in the afternoons.

In early October, we received our first letter from Jim since he left Salonica. He apologized for not writing earlier, but until the middle of September he had been too frail to even hold a writing instrument. The few times there had been volunteers or nurses able to write letters for him, he had been too weak to dictate them. But that was behind him. He was feeling stronger every day. He told us how much he loved and missed us and said that he would be home once he was fully recovered. Until then, he promised to write soon and regularly.

"How wonderful! It is just as Dr. Heggie said it would be," Mother cried, espousing the heartfelt feeling of our entire family.

"What do you think Jim will do when he comes home?" Mother asked Father when he was next home. Father had closed his dental practice when he enlisted. "All of your equipment is in your office. Could he reopen the practice?"

"Let's not get ahead of ourselves," Father said. "If Jim does come home before the war is over, the dental corps may have a role for him in Toronto with me." Mother visibly bristled at the word "if." "In any event, we should wait and see if he actually does come home early. Just because he is entitled to does not mean that he will. He was weak and tired when he wrote those words. Let's see how he feels a month from now." Whether Jim felt any differently a month hence we never really knew, for Father forbade us from asking the question, and in the regular letters Jim sent home, he never wrote of the future.

From Jim's letters, we learned that he was staying in a military hospital called Addington Park Hospital. It was located in Croydon on the grounds of a palace, which for most of the nineteenth century had been the home to six bishops of Canterbury. The special purpose of the three-hundred-bed hospital was to accommodate patients who had enteric diseases—diseases of the intestinal tract, like dysentery and typhoid. By segregating those convalescing from enteric disease and subjecting them to regular tests, carriers could be identified and contagion limited. Jim was tested frequently. Some test results were positive; some were negative. He could not be discharged until his test results were continuously negative.

Jim's life at Addington Park was quite sedentary. He spent much of it sitting in the hospital itself or in the surrounding park. Walks were permitted on the grounds of the park and to a nearby post office. The food served at the hospital was good, though—he was at pains to state—not as good as Mother's. Without taking anything from the quality of Mother's cooking, we all acknowledged that he would likely consider any food to be good at that time, given that he had consumed nothing but liquids while in isolation in Malta and in the ship hospitals.

Jim read the local newspapers thoroughly. His letters to me often took the form of a social studies lecture, setting out information about Britain he thought would interest me. He told me about people working in munitions factories, including women; how they had to wear wooden shoes while they worked and could not wear anything metal including jewellery or hairpins for fear that sparks would be created and explosions occur. The fear, it seems, was not merely theoretical. He told me that the skin of the people working with trinitrotoluene in those factories took on a yellow hue. I wondered if Mr. Thompson should have the same concern for those working in his factory and set my mind to look for yellow-skinned Bramptonians.

He told me about the developing food shortages. Between German U-boat strikes on Allied transport ships and a bad harvest in Britain in 1916, there was such a shortage of potatoes and other vegetables that poor people in Manchester, Newcastle, and Glasgow were suffering from scurvy. The government was encouraging girl guides and women to start farming. It was even promoting a new fashion trend for women: overalls! In fact, food was becoming so scarce that hotels, restaurants, and clubs were ordered to limit the number of courses that could be served as a meal to two or three. We laughed when we read about the enforced "simple life" that described our regular routine.

In response to my letter telling him about the treatment of the Austrian internees and the Strauss family, he told me about the anti-German sentiment in England, which heightened following the sinking of the *Lusitania* in May 1915. All men of German and Austrian descent who were living in England, who were of military age and who were not British citizens, were placed in internment camps, purportedly for their own safety as well as that of England.

Although Jim's letters home were regular and full of interesting tidbits about life in Britain, we were soon to learn that the information they provided about Jim himself was somewhat deficient. The better information we received about his life in London we acquired not from Jim but from Ina. In early October 1916, a letter was delivered to our house addressed to my sister. She opened it when she arrived home from Toronto that weekend. It was from an acquaintance, Anne Gomme, who was serving in London as a nurse.

"You remember, Jessie," Ina said after reading the first such letter. "The Girl's Club prepared a package for her in August." I did remember. There were not that many trained nurses in Brampton, and the number who were serving overseas was an even smaller subset.

The army had set up a separate corps for female nurses. Though they were officially called "nursing sisters," they were mostly referred to as "blue-birds" for the colour of their blue uniforms and the long white veils that draped down their backs. The nurses, who were fully commissioned officers, tended to soldiers who were wounded, sick, and convalescing, whether they were near or far from the front, in every theatre, in makeshift temporary hospitals, on hospital ships, and in hospitals in England and elsewhere. Only fully trained nurses were eligible to serve. In addition to having to have the requisite nursing credentials, successful applicants had to be of strong moral character.

"How long has she been serving?" Mother asked.

Ina looked down at the letter in her hand. "She enlisted in January 1915 and went overseas shortly after that. She served on the continent until mid-July. She is serving the last six months of her two-year posting at the convalescent hospital in Croydon."

"Her last six months? Is she coming home after that?" Mother asked.

"Yes," Ina replied. "She promised her father she would only serve for two years, and as her two younger brothers have just enlisted, she feels she needs to come home and be with her parents, as she had promised."

"Her brothers? Is Matthew Gomme her brother?" I asked, thinking of the Brampton High School rover in the 1915 hockey game. I knew he had a twin brother.

One could not blame Mr. Gomme for taking the position that his daughter's tenure as a nursing sister should be limited. Many fathers, I am sure, thought such a tenure should be nonexistent. Nurses and doctors were no more exempt from the dangers of the war than many of the soldiers. I remembered reading one newspaper article about a Toronto doctor who was on a train that was shelled by Germans. A nurse who was accompanying him had her nose shot off.

"How did she come across Jim?" Mother asked.

"She had been at Addington Park for a couple of months when she heard a new Canadian had been admitted. She inquired and heard that he was from Brampton. She couldn't believe that it was our Jim. She's promised to keep an eye on him for us."

Mother barely had an opportunity to say how wonderful that was when Father, who was also at home, spoke up. "Jim does not need anyone to keep an eye on him."

"Of course, you are right about that," Mother replied. "But it will be nice. What does she look like? I can't picture her."

"She has blond, curly hair arranged around the nape of her neck. Wide smile. Big eyes—blue, I think. A small nose. She is about my height. A little thinner," Ina conceded. "A pretty face." But for the fact that her hair was curly rather than straight, the description matched that of Millie.

"Was she at the graduation dance at Haggertlea?" I asked. The faces and dresses of all the women there had been indelibly impressed in my memory. Two years earlier, Jane, Frances, and I had a near bird's-eye view of the members of Ina's graduation class and their partners as they twirled in the salon-turned-ballroom.

"No. She was ahead of me in school. I knew her best from the time we worked together at the switch."

Fortunately, both Jim and Anne were regular correspondents. Each wrote weekly, but Jim's letters arrived earlier in the week, in part, we suspected, because they were so much shorter. They would have taken less time to write. Anne's letters came later in the week, always addressed to Ina, with whom she developed a fast friendship over the course of the weeks that became months. We had to wait for Ina to return home from Aunt Lil's each weekend to learn their contents. Anne's letters to Ina were warm and detailed. They spoke of current events and of future events. Ina shared with us all aspects that pertained to Jim. "I don't think she would mind," Ina said. "Why else would she tell me these things?"

In his letters, Jim told us that the Addington Park Hospital provided entertainment in the way of a concert or a film each night. In her letters, Anne told Ina she accompanied Jim to those shows.

Jim told us he spent many hours in the park's gardens, sitting on its stone benches, studying the statuary and the increasingly leafless trees. Anne told us that whenever she could she accompanied him on those outings, covering his legs with blankets to keep him warm.

It was based on Anne's letters that the women in our family continued to expect Jim's early return from the war. Though Jim never spoke of the future or his aspirations, Anne spoke frequently of her future back in Brampton, and her references were repeatedly to "us" and "we."

"Don't you think it's odd," Father asked one Sunday, "that in his letters home, Jim has never once mentioned Anne?"

Ina, Mother, and I did not think that at all odd. Based on Jim's history with women—Millie's refusal of his proposal and his obviously poor judgement concerning Paulette—it did not strike us as odd in the least that he would want to keep this liaison secret from us until it was more firmly established.

"He is drawing her, after all," I said. At least, we thought he was. I knew this was the surest way to determine Jim's passion. I had over the years determined his passion for hockey, lacrosse, trains, cars, and eventually, Millie from the drawings in Jim's sketchpads.

On Jim's arrival at Addington Park, Grandpa sent him a sketchpad and pencils. In his letters home, Jim told us that he was sketching the flora and fauna of the park. Anne's letters corroborated that, but in addition to those drawings of which he made no secret, she told us he was also surreptitiously drawing female facial features. He drew noses, ears, cheeks, lips, and foreheads. She felt confident that they were hers. But since they were never combined all in one—since there was never a head and a face or eyes and hair—she was not positive. Furthermore, since he always turned his page over when she approached, she felt she could not ask him about them. As the months went on, she became convinced that the facial features were hers and that he was practicing sketching them in order to surprise her with a complete portrait at Christmas.

By the beginning of December, Jim was pronounced cured of dysentery. He was free to leave Addington Park and go to another hospital for his final recuperation. We were thrilled to hear that he had made a request to be transferred to the Bull hospital and that he had been accepted. He would be transferred there on December 13th under the charge of one of Addington Park's highly competent nurses. From Anne we learned that she was that highly competent nurse and that she too had applied for and received a transfer to the Bull hospital. "We are always pleased to have Brampton nurses and voluntary aid workers on our staff," the Bull hospital matron told her.

In his letters, Jim described life in the Bull hospital, located on Heathview Gardens in Putney, near Wimbledon. His room overlooked the park between that house and the Bulls' Tudor-revival house known as Wynnfield. Dinner was taken between eight o'clock and ten o'clock. Over those two hours, the guests were entertained not only with delicious food (limited to three courses) but by great oratory as Perkins Bull and his guests regaled those in attendance with their views on the politics and culture of the day. Speculation about military and naval matters was strictly off limits, not only because it was illegal to discuss such matters publicly, but also because the host would not tolerate any discussion that might harm the mental or emotional health of the convalescing patients. Perkins Bull's exuberance was infectious. Dinners were often followed at the Bull's Wynnfield with dancing in the ballroom or singing around the piano. Although everyone knew the words, Jim was called on occasionally for a solo reprise of his 1914 Christmas Cantata performance as a British Grenadier singing "It's a Long Way to Tipperary." No one left an evening in poor spirits. Mother was happy to hear that those were the only spirits available in the Bull home and hospital—alcohol being strictly prohibited.

In the Bull hospital, the convalescing patients had much more liberty than those in the Addington Park hospital. Jim described attending shows on the Strand, a mere forty-five minutes from the Bull hospital. One letter included a lengthy description of a visit to a music hall. Over the course of a number of hours, he had seen singers, short plays, magicians, escape artists, acrobats, jugglers, and a trick dog.

"A music hall?" Mother said, appalled. "I can't believe he would step into one of those establishments. I am sure they serve alcohol. Please tell me he did not take Anne with him!" Since Jim had never mentioned Anne in his letters home, it was not possible to ascertain from his account whether he had done so. But the next letter from Anne made it clear that he had. Although she did not say that she had attended a music hall, she did mention attending a show with Jim where they saw a trick dog.

"I'm very disappointed in him," Mother said. "It's bad enough that he would frequent such a place, but to think he would expose a young lady to it! Well, it's beyond me. Ina, Jessie: do not speak of this. I fear for the young girl's reputation."

"I've been looking into this since you last mentioned it," Ina said. "Music halls are all the rage in London. They're supported by the military men and their female friends. I don't think they have the stigma there that you think they do."

"Stigma or not," Mother said doubtfully, "is it right for young people to be engaged in something so frivolous while their countrymen are dying on the fields of France and Belgium?"

"It's probably what keeps many of them in those trenches," Grandpa said. "The knowledge that in a few weeks' time, they will have the opportunity for some frivolous entertainment."

Father concurred. "Given all those young men are exposed to, it's probably quite therapeutic." Mother was not convinced.

We were all disappointed that with Jim's long recovery, he could not be home for Christmas with the family. We later learned that in fact he *was* with family. Both Bill, who had enlisted earlier that year and who was then posted to Seaford, England where he was a sergeant with the 196th Battalion, and Roy, who was serving as a sergeant with the 1st Depot Supply Column, were in London for three days over the Christmas week. The Bulls were gracious enough to include them in their Christmas celebrations.

On December 28th, the last night of their furlough, Bill and Roy took Jim to see a concert. Jim's account of it was, of course, perfunctory. We read Anne's detailed account of it one Saturday night at a dinner with Grandpa, Aunt Rose, Hannah, and John. The concert was performed by Laura Cowie, one of the most popular singers of the time.

"Laura Cowie!" Hannah exclaimed. "They saw her perform!" We had all heard her songs on the gramophone.

"Yes, but that's not all. Towards the end of the show, there was a surprise guest appearance by—" Ina looked for the name, "Vesta Tilley."

"Vesta Tilley? Have we heard of her?" Mother asked.

"I have," Grandpa replied. "She's a satirist." When Mother still could not place her, Grandpa added. "She sings the Blighty song."

"'I've Got a Bit of a Blighty One,'" Mother said knowingly. Someone had performed it at the Giffen Theatre during a recent fundraiser for the Red Cross. The song was about a soldier being treated like a prince while in a military hospital suffering from a sliver, while his comrades were suffering in the trenches. We had all thought it quite hilarious. Ina continued laughing.

"What's so funny?" I asked.

"Oh, my. Apparently, she changed the words in the song. The soldier wasn't being pampered in the hospital while suffering from a sliver; he was being honourably discharged for having a hangnail." Her gales continued. We all joined her in laughing at the image.

Only Grandpa did not join us in the mirth. "And Jim was there?"

"Yes, she says he was," Ina replied, attaching no import to the question.

"She mocked the soldier who left service due to a minor injury?" Grandpa confirmed.

"Yes, it appears so." Our laughter began to recede. Eventually it stopped altogether.

"I don't think you should expect Jim home any time soon," Grandpa said.

"There's a big difference between a hangnail and dysentery," Mother said defensively.

"There is at the time they are experienced," Grandpa conceded. "There isn't that much of a difference after the skin is healed and the intestine is clear of infection." The room became very quiet.

"She's their best recruiter," Grandpa said. "She invites young boys and grown men on to the stage. She asks each man if he will enlist. If he doesn't say yes, she has a young boy pin a white feather on his lapel. If Jim saw her perform a Blighty hangnail song, well, as I say, he won't be coming home now."

Ina received a final letter from Anne. It was her last letter sent from London. She had just finished packing her trunk for her return voyage. The trunk included her uniform—two sets—her "civvie" clothes and trinkets she had accumulated over her two year period of service, including small gifts from soldiers. Among her most treasured gifts was a drawing given to her by Jim on Christmas Day. His eye captured every detail. His hand brought each detail to life. The fine strokes and bold strokes were exquisite. He had completely captured the essential nature of the subject. She would frame it when she got home and keep it near her always, a reminder of the best three months of her two years away. Someday it might go in a gallery. Surely, no one could ever draw a greater likeness of the park between the Bull family's Wynnfield mansion and the Bull hospital. She was too proud to describe what Ina knew to be her broken heart.

After spending two and a half months in Addington Park War Hospital and a further month in the Bull Hospital for Convalescing Canadian Officers, Jim was given a choice to return home with an honourable discharge or to resume his duties with the Canadian Army Dental Corps serving in the elevated position of captain. Jim chose the latter. He was posted to St. Martin Plain, Shorncliffe, England.

* * *

The next month, my family and various townspeople met again at the CPR station, this time to send off my cousin John. By February 1917, though only a year and a half into his dental studies, John was declared adequately trained in the profession to serve with the Canadian Army Dental Corps overseas. In order to meet the ambitious objective of the Royal College of Dental Surgeons that called for one dental surgeon to every five hundred men in service, the college had condensed its curriculum. Whole classes were going straight from the lecture theatre to the war theatre, and John was among them.

In June 1917, Aunt Rose told us that John, serving with the CADC at Shorncliffe, had been promoted to sergeant. In a letter from Aunt Charlotte, we learned that Bill had applied to join his brother Roy in the Canadian Army Supply Corps. At Bill's own request, he had reverted to the rank of private and was posted at Seaford, England waiting for his transfer. I thought back to the gathering in Aunt Rose's dining room the night that hostilities were declared. The Turners were with us. Aunt Lil made a surprise appearance—an apparition prophesying the tide of war devouring our boys. Nearly three years later, she was proven right. Roy, Bill, Jim, and John were all serving overseas, though none in combat roles. Even Father, who had not been part of her ominous prediction, had enlisted. Uncle William, still a civilian, was devoting most of his working time to the movement of grain to feed our troops and our allies. The tide of war had caught up all of our men. I only hoped that when it broke, it would expel them all intact.

Chapter 15

THE FARMETTES

It is perverse that these years between 1916 and 1918—these years many Canadians would describe as the worst of their lives—were for me, in some respects, among the best. With Father not living at home, my life took on a previously unknown sense of ease. In those years, while the Canadian men at the front lived cold and wet, surrounded by mud and rats, their feet sore and infected, their stomachs content with the simplest of meals, their nerves frayed, their hearts longing for their loved ones, I carried on a life more in keeping with the average teenager of my time than any previously experienced.

For two years, I attended teas, fêtes, and dances. I watched motion pictures and live entertainment at the Giffen Theatre. I attended evening concerts at Gage Park (sometimes being permitted to stay until they concluded, an indulgence never permitted when Father was at home), entertained friends (not only on our verandah as I had hitherto been generally limited but also indoors), and experienced my first beau (we first held hands while watching a touring carnival and last held hands a week later at a touring vaudeville program). With a gaggle of friends, I rode my bicycle near and far. I attended local fairs and Saturday night dances. I played hockey, a girls' league having been formed, and travelled with the team to places as far as Georgetown and Milton, ten and twenty miles, respectively, away from Brampton.

Of course, the war touched nearly every one of those activities. The teas, fêtes, and dances were almost always fundraisers in aid of the war. Dance lessons that may not have otherwise been available until our later years were thrust upon the only agile generation in town with an equal number of properly matched partners. As we road our bicycles outside the centre of town, it was often to chase the craft of pilots in training who would dip their wings to us as they flew overhead, readying themselves to fly overseas. The fall fairs were filled with activities aimed at transforming the way those at home lived while the country was at war. At nearly every sports event, including our girls' hockey games, collections were taken up for the Red Cross.

We raised money for the war effort just by doing the things we ordinarily did—except it cost us more to do so. Any activity, no matter how ordinary or unique, how exciting or droll, how solitary or companionable, was a wartime fundraiser in support of our men overseas. In this way, we raised money to pay for medicines, medical care, and ambulances. We continued to raise money to pay for wool to be knit into socks and for foodstuffs and other niceties that could be included in care packages for soldiers and nursing sisters and female voluntary aid workers. To Jane's dismay, we even raised money to pay for cigarettes. The tobacco companies advised us in one advertisement after another that nothing gave a soldier more comfort in the trenches or in the hospital bed than the presence of Canadian tobacco.

The war transformed nearly every aspect of our lives, from what we ate, to what we wore, to what we read. No day was complete, for instance, without a visit to Mr. Wood's Main Street jewellery store located next to Mr. Thauburn's CPR telegram office. Posted on his window were the day's listings of the dead, injured, and missing in action. While the immediate family of the affected soldier would have been apprised of that status by a personally delivered telegram, the rest of the town learned of it from the public posting. The inclusion of anyone close enough to be called an acquaintance (and in a town of less than four thousand, many were) dictated a woman's cooking and baking schedule for the foreseeable future and the visiting schedule for all as we sought to support the afflicted family. As the war progressed and the campaigns of the Canadians in Belgium and France became more daring and successful, the lists on Mr. Wood's window grew and grew. Those great victories in Passchendaele and Vimy Ridge all came at a cost. Since the men from Brampton fought in companies together, our town's losses were rarely of a solitary man.

But by 1917 there were two other roles for those of us who could not fight. The first related to general conservation. With the country and the Empire about to enter its fourth year at war, we were, it seemed, running out of everything. Government edicts urged us to refrain from using fuel—particularly coal—unless absolutely necessary. People were discouraged from using their cars on Sundays in order to reduce gas consumption. As for food, the avoidance of waste was an even greater priority.

Women were urged in the name of their heroic husbands, sons, brothers, and fathers to take a food service pledge to avoid waste and to evidence that commitment by posting "FSP" signs on their windows. Not a single ounce of food was to be wasted. As for the food to be consumed, we were, at a minimum, to reduce our consumption of meat and wheat and preferably to entirely avoid white bread, beef, and bacon, all of which were to be saved for our men overseas and our allies under siege. Oatmeal, corn, barley, or rye flour were to be substituted for white bread and fish; peas, lentils, potatoes, nuts, and bananas were to be substituted for beef and bacon.

The money coming into our household during the war was not insubstantial. Between the two separation allowances paid to Mother and the portion of Father's and Jim's pay directed toward her, our household income greatly exceeded the amounts realized in the depths of the drought we experienced following Father's liaison with Mrs. Johnston. Nonetheless, Mother felt the need to economize. As a result, although she was never a leader of civil causes, she was one of the first to take the food service pledge, displaying not one but two FSP cards in our windows: one on the Wellington Street side of our house and another on the Chapel Street side. Our household became meatless and wheatless every day of the week except one—the Saturday or Sunday on which Father came home for dinner, often wearing the same uniform as those for whom the sacrifices were being made. Mother felt no compunction about serving a piece of beef, a slice of white bread, and a piece of cake when he was with us.

Father was generally in fine spirits when he returned home. He was always happier when he was held in high esteem by his peers, and the

Canadian Army Dental Corps held him in particularly high esteem. Though he entered the armed forces as a captain, in October 1917 he was promoted to a major. The pay raise and the additional responsibilities and respect well suited him. In addition to working at the exhibition grounds, he began working at the Central Military Convalescent Hospital in Toronto.

The second obligation placed on those staying at home was related to the first. In addition to aiding the war effort by avoiding waste, meat, and wheat, those of us at home were also urged to produce our own vegetables. As a result of the war, arable European fields that would have produced a healthy harvest and lush fields that would have satiated grazing livestock had become the tunnelled labyrinths of hundreds of thousands of men; the burial grounds of the world's most precious commodity; the resting points of land mines and poisonous vapours.

In 1914, Britain had relied on imports for eighty percent of its wheat and forty percent of its meat. A bad harvest in 1916 and its own shortage of farming labourers had only exacerbated that need. The proliferation of the German U-boat attacks that were responsible for the loss of over five hundred thousand tons of shipping in the month of March 1916 alone had so reduced the amount of food being successfully delivered to the island that the British government had declared the food situation a crisis. With the nation's food supply deemed sufficient to meet three or four weeks' needs at most, a formal rationing system was introduced.

At home in Canada, in advertisements in newspapers, the government recounted historic military campaigns lost due to the starvation of troops and their kin. It asserted that the key to the success of the Allies was the abundance of food.

Canadians, therefore, were urged to supplement what could be grown in our vast breadbaskets of the west and the rich farmlands of the east by utilizing our own gardens to meet our personal needs and allowing as much of the professionally grown harvest as possible to support the forty-five million Allied troops and the British and European citizens within the Allied nations. In short, we were told that if we could not go, we were to grow! The problem was that there were not enough with the experience to grow who did not go. The shortages in Canadian farm labour that existed before

1914 were greatly exacerbated by the war. By August 1917, with 424,456 Canadians having enlisted, there were simply not enough farm labourers available in Canada to work our many farms. A new type of farmer—an urban farmer—had to be developed.

To assist us in meeting that goal, a committee was formed by the Peel Agriculture Society, the Brampton Horticulture Society, the Board of Trade, the Public School Board, the Boy Scouts, the Girl Guides, and the Women's Institute. The committee sponsored meetings at the Giffen Theatre featuring government specialists who provided instruction on growing a vegetable garden in town. The *Conservator* ran a series called the "vegetable garden campaign." Every man, woman, and child in the town was urged to produce.

"Look at this ad," Jane said to me one day in April 1917.

> *If you had a garden in prior years, can you not put in two to three times as much this year? If you want to grow vegetables and have no land, some will be provided to you.*

"It is clearly our duty to grow vegetables. Where do you think we can do this?"

I really had no idea. Our backyard was small, and its grounds were rarely touched by sunlight. Grandpa's beloved rose gardens at the front of our house had already been sacrificed to the war effort. There was precious little space available, but what there was, Grandpa had cleared and planted it with vegetables at the first call to hoes. If the plants were well tended throughout the growing season (and I was confident Grandpa would tend them well), and if the carrots, beans, beets, and tomatoes produced were carefully picked and canned (and I was confident that Mother would can them well), I was certain we would have enough produce to feed our family of three for at least a month or two.

Haggertlea, Jane's house, provided more opportunity for us to do "our bit"—a phrase regularly used to denote what all good Canadians should be doing. The big mansion had been fully subdivided by that time, leaving to the road facing aspect of the Thompsons' house a semicircular driveway and an ornamental lawn. We thought it unlikely that Mrs. Thompson would consent to its conversion to a vegetable garden. Its small size would have limited the quantity of vegetables that could be foraged there to only slightly more than what Grandpa could gather from my family's former rose gardens. The property in front of Haggertlea, looking down over George Street and Main Street beyond, held much more promise because most of its wide terrain continued under the Thompsons' control.

Standing on the Haggertlea balcony and looking down toward George Street, Jane and I calculated the availability of at least half an acre of land. We retrieved a piece of paper and a pencil and began plotting our garden. We considered and then abandoned the seigneurial system of early Quebec that we studied in school. Although the Etobicoke Creek ran in caverns underneath much of the downtown area near Haggertlea and ran exposed next to the main street further beyond, it had no physical connection to Haggertlea. We were without the central river from which all long-narrow seigneurial plots ran. Over the next hour, we developed a comprehensive plan for the planting of many vegetables and flowers. Jane was sure that her mother would want to see flowers as she looked out her bedroom window toward George Street. Reviewing the newspaper articles in the "Vegetable Garden Campaign" and calling on lessons learned in science classes, we determined the number of rows we would plant and the approximate yield we would generate.

We assembled a list of farm implements that would be required and a schedule for hoeing, planting, tending, and picking, considering the time and effort that would be required to convert the steeply sloped, undulating lawn into a garden. We revelled in the knowledge of the real contribution we could make to the war effort. The next Saturday afternoon, with our plan in hand, we went to speak with Jane's father. In great detail, Jane explained the plan to him. She showed him our diagram, our lists, our schedules, and our expectations. She showed him the advertisements and articles in the *Conservator*. "All we need, Father, are a few gardening implements and your approval to convert the lawn into a garden. The government will provide the seeds if you cannot afford them."

"Can't afford them? Girls, the seeds are the least of our problems. Approval and some gardening implements? That's all you need?" We nodded vigorously.

"Where is the water going to come from? You can't think you can carry watering cans up and down that hill, do you?"

We stood silently, sheepishly. Of course, we had noticed that we had no river running through the centre of our plan—hence the abandonment of the seigneurial system—but we had not considered how we would irrigate the large area.

"What of the terrain? Do your articles say that crops can be grown on hillsides?" The articles had, we conceded, recommended flat areas.

"Girls, I admire your spirit. I really do. But it won't work. Now, if you want to help the war effort, why don't you help me out with my munitions contract?" By 1917, the shell-producing operations were on steadier financial ground than had been the case a year earlier. The foundry had begun to make deliveries of shells and accordingly had begun to receive payments. Mr. Thompson now had other problems.

"Take a look at this ad that I plan to place in the *Conservator*," Mr. Thompson barked, pointing to a piece of paper. Written on it were the following words: *Farmers and others: We will buy your cast iron, scrap from old mowers, etc.*

"I need iron. Any kind of iron. I have a hundred thousand shells to produce for the Canadian army, and I need iron. Perhaps you two could spend your summer holidays knocking on the doors of all of the businessmen and homeowners in Brampton to see if they have any cast iron to sell. Now that would be patriotic. And I know that from your wool collection efforts you have experience canvassing. Why don't you think about that?"

We did think about it. We thought about it a great deal. Mostly we thought that a door-to-door canvass for cast iron would be even worse than a door-to-door canvass for wool and a dreadful way to spend a summer.

"The Empire badly needs food," Jane declared a month later. "That is what the *Conservator* says. It doesn't say that there's a shortage of ammunition."

As we walked up Wellington Street toward my house, passing the Baptist church, the courthouse (still serving as our temporary high school), and the registry office, we silently contemplated where we could find a spare piece of land to cultivate. Our thoughts were interrupted as we approached the jail, when I nearly tripped over a ball.

"Throw it here, Jessie!" Frances called. She and Hannah were playing tennis on the large grass court beside Aunt Rose's house. Though it was only May, the day was uncommonly warm. Frances and Hannah were getting an early start on their summer time tennis games, an activity they both enjoyed.

While I ran down the street to retrieve the rolling ball, Jane pulled out of her pocket the paper on which we had drawn our plan to cultivate Haggertlea. "You know," Jane said after I had thrown the ball back to Frances, "if we eliminated the flower garden on our plan and reduced all other plots by a quarter, we might be able to generate enough produce on this side lawn of your aunt's house to feed a few families for the year. The lot is flat, and look at that water pipe," she said, pointing to the side of the house. "Your aunt is very patriotic. She has a son overseas. No one uses this lot except for Hannah and her friends. They could play tennis somewhere else. Let's speak to your aunt."

Jane and I smiled and waved at Hannah and Frances before inviting ourselves into Hannah's house to deprive her of the pleasure of her favourite recreational activity for the balance of the war. To our great satisfaction, Aunt Rose entirely endorsed our suggestion as to how the lot should be used. To our great dissatisfaction, she took a different view as to who should cultivate it. "You are just girls," she said, "with no growing experience whatsoever. And you still have two months before you are done school for the summer. How can we deprive our fellow citizens, and, by extension, our troops of any carrot, bean, or tomato we could reap from this lot? Perhaps we should ask your grandfather, Jessie, to oversee this project. He's a skilled gardener. He may well be able to use your assistance once the two of you are out of school. It will likely be too much for him on his own."

Grandpa thought the idea of turning Aunt Rose's side lot into a garden a capital one. He readily agreed to oversee its production. It was, as Aunt Rose suspected, too much for him to personally tend on his own. But rather than waiting for Jane and me to work the land at the end of our school days or on weekends, Grandpa made other arrangements. With the cooperation of the Governor, the inhabitants of the jail across the road from Aunt Rose's house provided the necessary labour. There appeared to be no shortage of eligible felons!

It was the confluence of these extreme needs—for food and for farm labour—that struck Jane, Frances, and me one hot early August day in 1917. We were sitting on the curb across from Aunt Rose's house beside the jail, watching the Governor and Grandpa oversee the weeding of the large garden that was formerly Aunt Rose's side lawn.

"I want to thank you again, Jessie, for suggesting that your cousin's tennis court be converted into a garden. It is a lot of fun sitting here and seeing which weed has the good fortune to escape the plucking hand of a convict." Frances had developed a biting sarcasm.

"It isn't quite as exciting as watching Hannah wallop you at the net," Jane said, rightly coming to my defence. The conversion of the tennis court into a vegetable garden had, after all, been her idea. In previous summers Jane and I, her brother Douglas, and our friends Douglas Gordon, Collin Heggie, Morley Burrows, and Willie Core sat on those very steps watching the two girls challenge each other. But that summer, the boys were working long days on farms. We rarely saw them.

"It's strange not having the boys with us, isn't it?" Frances asked.

"Strange and unfair," Jane countered. "They are out on the farms saving an empire, and here we are taking a break from yet another social tea. They're getting status as 'Farm Service Corps' and being presented with medals for their work, and we're getting pats on the head for pouring tea without spilling it. At a certain point, can't the women of the town just empty their change purses and give every copper, nickel, dime, and quarter they have in them to the war effort? Must we really hold successive garden parties, tea parties, bake sales, sales of any sort, dances, and sewing bees to separate them from their money? Can we not attend a single concert or parade without having to hold a bucket and collect donations?"

"You're just tired," I said. She did sound tired. We had helped out with at least three such wartime fundraisers a week since our summer holidays began. Jane, Frances, and I were very popular in our mothers' circles. We distributed flyers and invitations, set up chairs, made and served tea, set and cleared tables, collected contributions, and washed dishes. At fourteen years of age, we were old enough to handle the fine china and crystal without breaking it and young enough to have no gainful employment. "And we are helping the war effort."

"We are raising two or three dollars a day! How much is that helping? The boys are going to feed an army! And we could do what they're doing! We're strong. You saw Frances's backhand before we shut down her tennis court." Jane looked sheepishly at Frances before continuing.

"And they need people on the farms. Did you see the headline today? It said it would be criminal—*criminal*—to lose a sheaf of wheat for want of labour. We have a record crop of wheat, and there is a danger that it will die fallow in the fields. Why can't we help harvest it? Why can't our bit be a bit more of a bit?

"Three weeks—they want three weeks of labour from more boys. It's just enough time to get the wheat out of the fields and then return to school. And if we could do that, we could help feed an army and not have to pour another cup of tea or serve another piece of cake this summer. Or any summer!" We were once again hoping that the war would be over by Christmas; it was the fourth such Christmas for which we had held out this hope.

"But they'll never let us do it," I reminded her. "The ads call for boys and old men. They're not looking for women and girls to work on the farms."

"I know they aren't," said Jane peevishly. "But sometimes you have to show them what they aren't at first looking for. Eventually they'll see what it really is, and they'll think it was all their idea. Look at the suffragettes." Frances, Jane, and I had been watching with great interest the Canadian suffragettes, Mrs. Nellie McClung and Miss Francis Beynon on the Prairies, as well as our own Dr. Stowe-Gullen in Ontario. Our parents and many others considered them to be unpatriotic and their ideas a menace. Only Aunt Lil would speak about them with us as though the women were heroines. That all changed, though, when it was realized that granting those women what they sought could actually advance the war effort.

Jane continued. "Men didn't think women should have the right to vote, but then the suffragettes took action, and lo and behold, giving women the right to vote is exactly the ticket—at least women who are related to men at the front." In Canada, women had been given the right to vote in the upcoming federal election if they were related to a man in service. While the ostensible reason was to allow them to exercise the franchise that their loved one could not, it was well understood that the measure was likely to garner votes in favour of the exertion of all necessary military efforts to bring a successful conclusion to the war. The thinking was that those who had invested the lives of their loved ones in the war would very likely support conscription and military spending. Although those measures were supported by Robert Borden's government, they were also supported by some within the caucus of the former prime minister, Wilfrid Laurier.

"It does seem strange to me," Frances observed, "that women should have the right to vote but not the right to contribute to the war effort in the way they think best."

Listening to Frances and Jane that day sitting in a place so often occupied by Archie, Frances, and me, it occurred to me that in this threesome, Jane had become Archie: the strident one; the daring one; the one willing to push boundaries. Frances was still Frances: able to appreciate a good argument, to consider it and adopt the position that seemed right. Eight years had passed since Archie and I sat in this very spot listening, at his urging and against my reservations, to the Governor's story about Alderlea, the seamstresses, and the two brothers. I was still the conventional one; the timid one; the follower. I may have developed a stubborn sense, but I was not yet a leader. I decided it was time for a change.

"Why don't we just go?" I asked. "The boys get picked up for the farms from the four corners every morning at seven. Why don't we just go there too? We could wear overalls and pin our hair up under our caps." I had had plenty of experience pinning my hair under my hat in the years I walked past the Kelly Iron Works Repair Shop. "The drivers will think we are boys and take us with them to the farms. We will leave our hats on all day and not say a word. No one will know that we are girls." As soon as the words left my mouth, I realized their idiocy. We would be in the trucks and working in the fields with our closest male friends. Of course they would know who we were, even if we were mute all day. I thought that I might be able to work an entire ten-hour day without talking, but I was quite certain that neither Frances nor Jane could. By the perplexed looks on their faces, I could see that they had come to the same conclusion.

"You're right. A disguise will not work. And really, why should it be necessary?" I asked. I recalled Jim telling me that in England, Girl Scouts were overseeing agricultural allotments and that over a hundred thousand British women were wearing overalls and working on farms, members of a "Women's Land Army."

"Jane, your Father is advertising for boys and girls to work in his foundry, and Hewetsons is doing the same thing. If girls can work in a foundry or a shoe factory, they can work on a farm in the fresh air." I was quite emphatic in my conclusion.

"Yes, my father is willing to hire girls, but so far there have not been many Brampton parents who will let their girls work there."

"Right. It's a question of permission. We should not go in a disguise. We should go as girls, though we may have to wear overalls and hats because that is the proper attire. We can work on a farm if the farmer welcomes us and if our parents let us."

Mother was now making most decisions pertaining to my wellbeing, but I knew she would not make a decision like this. We agreed that it would be best if we all sought the permission of our parents on the same day. Since Father was expected home on the Saturday of that week, we delayed our request until then, spending our time between fundraising at social teas and properly preparing our case.

I decided it would be best to ask Father directly, but to do so in a location where my position could be taken up by Grandpa and Mother, if they were willing. I was not certain that my mother would be supportive, but my grandfather rarely denied me anything that was reasonable, and I had concluded that this request to support our troops and our allies in what they needed most was reasonable. Amazingly, so did Father. We were, of course, at the dining room table. I waited until Father had a bowl of ice cream in front of him, a dish that was a favourite of his, though no favourite of mine. However, his consent was not provided until he first tested my resolve.

"You understand that if you make a three-week commitment, you will have to meet that commitment? You understand that the farmer will be relying on you to clear the fields? You will be working outside for ten hours a day, no matter the weather. You will get blisters on your hands. You will have to rise at six in the morning six days a week." When I confirmed my understanding of all of those points, he agreed, but on two conditions: Mr. Thompson and Mr. Fenton also had to approve, and a farmer had to be willing to take on the three of us together.

It came as a bit of a surprise that all three fathers agreed to our plan. That Saturday night, we took their acquiescence to be an indication of how great the war need was. By the next day at noon, we understood their acquiescence to be an indication of how unlikely they thought it was that any farmer would have us. We met outside on a bench after our morning services and reviewed the outcome of our inquiries. Between us, Jane and I had spoken to six farmers at Grace Methodist Church that morning. Frances had spoken to seven farmers at the Presbyterian Church.

"How did you speak to so many?" we asked her in astonishment.

"I get straight to the point, I guess."

The speed with which one got to the point mattered not. None of the thirteen farmers we spoke to would have us. As we sat in silence, considering how best to proceed, three men in their Sunday best walked past us in deep discussion. Each man was tall, nearly six feet in height without counting the four inches added by his hat. Though the day was warm, each man, having just been in church, wore a three-piece suit. Their suits were well cut. Their brown shoes were highly polished.

"Acres, I have acres that may as well be fallow if I can't get the wheat cut and moved," one of the men said to the other two. The others nodded. "To be honest, cutting it isn't the problem. That new thresher does a fine job mowing it down. But someone has to gather it on to the wagons. I keep asking for more boys. There are no more to be had."

"Rather makes me wish we hadn't sent away those Austrians," one of the men said. I knew that he was Tommy Duggan, the managing trustee of the Dale Estate. Jane, Frances, and I had thought the same thing over the past year. Would the people of Brampton have drummed Mr. Strauss's workers away from the vegetable growing greenhouses if they had arrived in Brampton in 1917 when the shortage of food was obvious to all? Maybe they had arrived a year too early.

We looked at each other. "Isn't that Mr. Lowe?" Frances asked me. I was expected to know all of the politicians in the county. I generally did.

"Yes, it is. And he has a number of farms: one in Snelgrove and one or two north of there, I think." William Lowe had only recently become our Member of the Provincial Parliament. The consummate Liberal standard-bearer in Peel County, he had lost successive federal and provincial elections before winning a by-election in 1916—an outcome that surprised even him. His predecessor, the very popular Conservative J.R. Fallis, a livestock broker by profession, had been accused of improperly profiting from a sale of horses to the government in the early days of the war. He resigned his seat, put his case to the electors, and sought reelection. His contribution to the 126th Peel Battalion of the $1,880 of profits realized from the transaction was insufficient penance to the voters. In a by-election where he placed his conduct before them, the electors chose William Lowe, another livestock broker—the first Liberal parliamentarian elected in Peel County in over ten years. It was hard to know what annoyed the voters more, the fact that Mr. Fallis had profited from the transactions, or the fact that his work on the remount commission formed by Sir Adam Beck to oversee the purchase of six thousand horses had prevented others from similarly profiting. Possibly, it was a bit of both.

The men said nothing to us as they passed us. We were not too surprised. They were deep in conversation, and we were nonvoting minors.

Jane jumped off the bench first. "Mr. Lowe! Mr. Lowe!" she called after him. The three men stopped. "Mr. Lowe, on behalf of all Ontario women, I want to thank you for your support for extending to us the right to vote." Following the federal example, the provincial government had extended the franchise to women. The initiative of the provincial government led by Sir William Hurst had been approved unanimously by the ruling Conservatives and the opposition Liberals alike.

"That was very far-sighted and liberal of you."

"Why, thank you, young lady, I do believe that women should have every opportunity to exercise a franchise..." And then, seeing the quizzical looks on the men with whom he stood, he qualified the statement. "Particularly at times like this when women are contributing so much to the war effort."

"Yes, that is our thought too!" Jane said, seizing on the sentiment. "Mr. Lowe, we couldn't help but overhear that you are short of men on your farm; that if you have no more assistance, your crops will be lost. We read in the paper this week that it would be a crime—what with the Allied forces and their livestock needing every sprig of vegetation that is grown—it would be a crime if your fields went fallow. Isn't that so, Mr. Lowe?" He could hardly disagree.

"Mr. Lowe, we believe that we may have a source of labour for you. Three able-bodied people! They could start tomorrow."

We started the next morning, clothed in overalls borrowed from Jane's brother Douglas. Father was at first disbelieving that any farmer had taken us on, but when he heard the identity of our employer, he rolled his eyes. "Only a Liberal," he said.

At the end of the first day on Mr. Lowe's farm just north of Brampton, we felt tired but triumphant. At the end of the second, we felt sore but satisfied. At the end of the third, we began counting down the remaining fifteen days. We were tired, sore, and calloused. For a myriad of reasons, we hoped the war would be over by Christmas.

Chapter 16

ARMISTICE

The war to end all wars ended in 1918 on the eleventh day of the eleventh month. The hostilities that had claimed and maimed millions; that had challenged the natural order of life; marriage and death for a generation; that had drained the coffers of the combatants ended at the eleventh hour of that day. The proclamation of that peace reverberated across the Earth. It was proclaimed in Brampton in the early morning hours.

"Dot! Dot! Dot! Dot!" I heard as I awoke from a deep sleep.

"Dot! Dot! Dot! Dot!" I sat up, confused, wondering from where the sound came and what it signalled. It awoke Grandpa and Mother too. They stood in front of the open door of my bedroom—the halfway point between their two rooms.

"What is that noise?" I asked groggily.

"We aren't sure," Grandpa said, coming into my room. He went to the window next to my bed and lifted the sash. The storm window had been reinstalled the previous month. He lifted the small board at its base exposing three large circular vents to the outside.

"Dot! Dot! Dot! Dot!" With the sash lifted, the sounds were louder.

"It's coming from the north," Grandpa said, looking over the roof tops toward Queen Street, "from the Dale Estate, I expect." Then, looking down at the street below he exclaimed, "Ladies, get your coats and boots. That whistle is sounding peace!"

"Is it really peace this time?" I asked. A false report of the ceasefire had circulated four days earlier. While it led to a joyous afternoon celebration, we were crestfallen that evening to find that our celebration was premature.

"We'll have to go see," he answered, "and I wouldn't bother getting changed. It doesn't look like anyone else has."

I threw my legs over the side of the bed and joined him at the window. Our neighbours were pouring out of their homes, their winter coats over their nightgowns, their pajama bottoms tucked inside their boots.

Arriving at the four corners area a few minutes later, there was no doubt that the peace for which we had all long prayed had been realized. A bonfire was burning in the middle of the intersection. Dozens gathered around it in an effort to stay warm and to obtain sufficient light to read the one-page pink extra the *Conservator* staff were distributing—a broadsheet citing the earlier announcement of the US State Department and the signing of the armistice earlier that morning.

The shrilling Dale horn that first awakened us soon brought about a chorus of other horns and whistles as the other Brampton factories joined in the proclamation. With the arrival of dawn, most of us returned home, filled our stomachs with hot porridge and tea, changed into more suitable attire, and returned to the four corners with a noisemaker appropriate for the occasion—often a spoon and the lid to the pot just used to cook our oatmeal.

There was no school that glorious Monday. Instead, we attended services and celebrations. Three special church services were held that day. One was held in the street that morning, led by the Salvation Army. Two were held that afternoon: one in Christ Anglican Church and the other in St. Paul's Methodist Church. There were two parades, the afternoon production led by the veterans and the schoolchildren, and the evening production led by the town businesses.

Wherever the crowd moved, oration occurred. Samuel Charters, father of Jim's friend Clarence and our new Member of Parliament, and L.J.C. Bull, a brother to Perkins Bull, our new mayor, were the font of many of those speeches. But ordinary people—the people who had lost one, two, or even three family members to the Great War—they spoke too and with heartfelt eloquence. They spoke by that early morning bonfire and later up the street, where another crowd gathered, later still in the concert hall, and finally in Gage Park, where a tree was planted as a tribute to the Brampton men who made the supreme sacrifice. They spoke of the imperative of war and the glory of peace; of what it meant to lose a loved one in the great cause; of what had been achieved. We applauded and banged our noisemakers.

When we were not listening solemnly to a bugler's rendition of the "Last Post," we were lustily singing "God Save the King," "O God, Our Help in Ages Past," "Onward Christian Soldiers," "God Save the King," and "O Canada." We sang until we were hoarse.

Father, Aunt Lil, and Ina all came from Toronto, arriving at various points in the day. We hugged each other as we hugged friends and strangers alike—often several times throughout the celebrations. We thanked God that it was over; that the killing had stopped; that Germany had been defeated; that our allies could live in peace; that our lives could return to normal.

But throughout the day, as I celebrated with all those who had been affected by the war—and everyone had been affected in one way or another—as I listened and prayed, as I sang, clapped, and pounded my porridge pan lid, as I marched and walked and hugged and laughed, I could not help but think that this peace—this praiseworthy peace—had come too late. It had come too late for the 1,698,000 dead French soldiers. It had come too late for the 996,000 dead British soldiers. It had come too late for the 67,000 dead Canadian soldiers. It had come too late for Jim, of whose demise we learned three months earlier.

* * *

It was all I could do to concentrate on my book as I sat on our verandah that hot Sunday afternoon, the eighteenth day of August 1918. I was physically exhausted from the contribution Jane and I were once again making to the war effort. The food shortages identified in 1917 had not been ameliorated, notwithstanding the extensive public education and prodding vegetable garden growing efforts of that year. Renewed pleas for increased food production and decreased food consumption were made in 1918. Although farm labour campaigns were still aimed at boys, there were growing numbers of "farmettes"—town girls—contributing to this effort. Mr. Lowe, so impressed by the spirited offer Jane, Frances, and I made to him in August 1917, sought us out in the spring of 1918. We feigned feeling flattered by the request, summoned our patriotic spirit, and more than tripled our contribution to the 1918 farm-focussed war effort, committing to work on his farm Monday to Saturday the entire months of July and August.

That August day, in addition to being physically tired, I was emotionally drained. Father had been at home with us for the prior day and a half. The equanimity Mother, Grandpa, Ina, and I had all come to enjoy while he was away was always disturbed when he came home for more than a single meal. It was an effort to revert to the formality and discipline he was used to—his expectations for which had actually increased since he joined the army. Our lapses were met by harsh words.

Only the frequent interruptions provided by Ina, who sat beside me on the verandah that afternoon, prevented me from falling into the slumber I knew that Grandpa and Mother were then enjoying in their rooms.

With her weather journal on her lap, Ina was recording the near-record-level temperatures of that month. "Did you know it was ninety-five degrees two Mondays ago and 101 last Thursday?" she asked. I knew. In the fields, it felt like 120 and 150. Ina had never lost her interest in climate matters, although fortunately it had been many years since she had converted our verandah into a scientific weather station. It had also been a number of years since she had written a weather column for the local newspaper, but with a Bachelor of Science degree nearly in hand, she was preparing to teach the subject until she entered a matrimonial state.

"It cooled down a bit, of course. But yesterday, the mercury rose again and now today...." She turned her back to the large thermometer she carried onto the verandah earlier that day. "It's inching up there again. With so little wind, and the pressure so high, it feels hotter than it actually is." I could vouch for that. "It will break soon," she offered. "A storm is coming." I looked up again, skeptically. There was not a cloud in the sky.

"A storm. From the east. By later this afternoon. Tonight at the latest." She resumed writing in her journal. I sincerely doubted it. The biggest thing separating us from the heavens above was a heavy haze.

In the end, it was not Ina's observation of what was above the ground that jarred me from my semiconscious reading state. Rather, it was her observation of something that was on it. "Heaven save us!" she said with a start. "Isn't that Mr. Thauburn walking up the street?"

I stole my eyes from the pages of my book and glanced toward the intersection of Main Street and Wellington. Ina's eyes were better than mine. I asked her whether Mr. Thauburn, the CPR telegram agent, had an envelope in his hand. Mr. Thauburn walking up a street with no envelope in hand could be expected to be paying a social call or attending to some matter of civic, athletic, religious, or business purpose. Mr. Thauburn walking up the street carrying an envelope in hand was there on CPR business, and the news he came to convey was quite possibly very bad.

Of course, Mr. Thauburn knew the content of every telegram that was sent to or sent by a Brampton resident. He felt no compunction to personally deliver telegrams regarding such day-to-day matters as the purchase and sale of livestock, birthday greetings, and holiday reports, all of which he was perfectly able to place in a sealed envelope for the punctual yet impersonal delivery by one Johnny or another. But where the telegram imparted knowledge of the demise or near demise of a family member of one of Mr. Thauburn's acquaintances (and he was acquainted with nearly everyone in Brampton), he felt it necessary to personally deliver the telegram in order to immediately bestow the solicitations such knowledge required. Over time therefore, Mr. Thauburn personally delivered to the people of Brampton hundreds of telegrams proclaiming the deprivation or near deprivation of life. It was lore within the town that every time a telegram of this nature tat-a-tat-tatted into his telegraph machine, he rendered an audible sigh and said to whichever delivery boy was about, "Ah Johnny, the Lord is claiming another. You mind the shop. I have sad news to impart."

With that, he would take the flimsy piece of paper, embossed with the emblems and conditions of the CPR, place it in a manila envelope, don his hat, and depart for the home or workplace of the addressee. Having hailed the intended recipient to the door, he would commence with words known all about Brampton: "Mrs. Elliott, I am afraid I have sad news to impart. The Lord has called out for your dear brother Hank." Condolences would be offered, another family member or nearby neighbour summoned, instructions obtained about telegrams to be sent in reply, and Mr. Thauburn would return to his premises.

Once the people of Brampton understood the practice of Mr. Thauburn, it became obvious to them that whenever he walked up a street with a single envelope in his hand, his purpose was to convey particularly bad news. As a harbinger of ill intelligence, even the more sturdy Bramptonians would begin to perspire as he approached their houses, envelope in hand. After a period of personally delivering only ill tidings, it became clear to him that for the health and safety of his beloved citizenry and his own social acceptance, it would also be necessary for him to deliver particularly happy personal reports. Thus, Mr. Thauburn adopted the practice of also delivering telegrams heralding marriages and births. The people of Brampton then knew that his presence on their street with an envelope in hand was likely to stir strong emotions for someone, but whether those emotions would be happy or sad, while readily speculated upon, could not with any certainty be known.

For twenty-three-year-old Ina, who feared every chill as a calling to her grave, every sneeze as a potential epidemic, and every telegram as a sure announcement of our brother's demise, the sight of Mr. Thauburn on our street had been, on each occasion over the last three years, a death knell for poor Jim. While I shared a degree of her anxiety, the habit that I and the rest of my family had adopted of dissuading Ina of her every paranoia forced me always to vouch for another reason for Mr. Thauburn's presence. On that day, like all others, I sought to offer an alternative explanation.

"I can't be certain," she confessed in response to my question regarding the presence in his hands of an envelope. "His hands are at his sides, so he could be carrying an envelope."

"He *could* be," I replied, taking my usual contrary stand, "but more than likely he is coming empty handed to pay a call on Mr. Peaker. I think that the two of them are planning a fundraiser for those new tank vehicles they are using at the front."

Ina turned and glared at me. "You know what's been happening at the front, Jessie. How can you be so confident the news is not bad?"

Earlier that month, the Allies commenced a huge offensive. We read the reports in the papers each night and knew that the Canadian troops had ended their four-month post-Passchendaele hiatus and that our rejuvenated, replenished, and reorganized "shock troops" were actively involved in the August campaign. They were now, so far as we knew, solidifying their victories.

"Ina, the battle has been over for eight days now. And we don't even know whether Jim fought in it," I reminded her in a tone of reassuring calm. Inwardly, I felt every bit as terrified as Ina sounded.

"Well, of course he fought in it," Ina snapped. "You think that they would post him to France, put him in charge of a platoon, and then tell him to sit out? Of course, he's among them." I could not argue with that. Jim had been posted to the very region of the present conflict. After his recovery from dysentery at the end of 1916, Jim practiced dentistry with the Canadian Army Dental Corps in Shorncliffe, holding the position of captain, which was granted to him on his return from Salonica. But in October 1917, after ten months in Shorncliffe, he was transferred to the London area. While there, seeing what he considered to be the greater needs of the war effort, he left the Canadian Army Dental Corps. Reverting to the rank of lieutenant, by April 1918 Jim and the platoon he led were in the fields of France.

"Still," I said, "you don't know why Mr. Thauburn is on our street. He may be here on a matter of business relating to his store or that fundraising campaign—"

"No. He isn't. I can see it now. There is an envelope in his hand. This is very bad news! Very bad! I know it! You can't be that successful in a battle and not incur casualties and...deaths. Twenty thousand Germans were captured. Miles of land were liberated. That comes at a cost. I know it." Her voice began to vibrate. She was speaking at an unnaturally high octave. She closed her weather journal and stood.

"Ina, you know no such thing." I continued to be outwardly calm while willing Mr. Thauburn to turn into the path of a house before ours—or to walk past our house. "You saw the prime minister's cable from London reprinted in the papers during the battle. He very clearly said that the Canadians had obtained all their objectives and that their losses were unexpectedly light."

"Light but not nonexistent! Oh my. He is still walking toward us. Should we wake Mother?"

"Of course not," I said with false confidence. We were both watching him. I could see that his walk was not spritely.

He was almost to Aunt Rose's front walk. There were four houses between Main Street and our house and a further two dozen beyond ours. There were any number to the north and south of our house, extending both ways along Chapel Street. "It may be that his news is bad, Ina," I rationalized. "But surely it may be intended for someone else. If the news was to be delivered to us, Mr. Thauburn would have approached us directly from Chapel Street. Why would he walk to us in this indirect manner from Main Street?" The route I proposed was not really any more direct. Inwardly, I repeated over and over, *Stop before us or after us; before us or after us.*

"Oh! You're right, Jessie! The Lord be praised! Mr. Thauburn has walked up to the home of...our...aunt." Although Ina tried to sound concerned in that final stanza, there was no doubt that the overwhelming sentiment expressed in that sentence was one of relief.

Closing my book, I watched Mr. Thauburn walk the short distance from the sidewalk to Aunt Rose's verandah, climb the stairs to its landing, and knock on her front door. Aunt Rose had no family members in a position to bear children, and so it was highly likely that the telegram Mr. Thauburn was delivering to her brought bad tidings. Yet it was hard to imagine what they would be.

In November 1917, her son John had returned to Canada. While it was conceivable that he could have been fatally wounded in a chemist accident at the Toronto dental office in which he was then working, it did not strike me as likely. Could something have happened to Aunt Lil? Might she have had that collision with an automobile she always feared? Could she have fallen into one of her vats of green dye? As terrible and preposterous as both of those scenarios were, I confess that they provided me with the same relief I detected in Ina's voice seconds earlier. Relief it was not Jim. Relief Jim was safe. I had been willing Mr. Thauburn to go to any house other than ours. I had not really willed him to go to Aunt Rose's house, but between her house and ours, I confess that, like Ina, I was greatly relieved that Mr. Thauburn was at hers.

"Ina, maybe we should get Mother," I ventured. Mr. Thauburn was now inside Aunt Rose's house. "Aunt Rose may need consolation."

But before Ina could reply, the front door of Aunt Rose's house opened again, and Mr. Thauburn, Aunt Rose, and Hannah exited it. I breathed a sigh of relief. Aunt Rose was not in pieces; nor was Hannah. Whatever the content of the telegram, it could not be that bad. The three of them walked down the steps from the verandah, Aunt Rose at the helm, Hannah behind her, and Mr. Thauburn behind Hannah. I assumed that Aunt Rose and Hannah were now coming to our house to share their news, since as soon as they reached the sidewalk at the end of their front walkway, they turned toward us. But where Mr. Thauburn should have bid them good day and turned in the other direction, he instead assumed a lead position in their slow three-person procession. In Mr. Thauburn's hand there appeared to still be an envelope. The telegram he came to deliver had not been left with Aunt Rose.

Perhaps because it would otherwise be too much to absorb, time eases us into these shattering realities. It stops for a few moments so that those about to experience or witness a true tragedy can prepare themselves. In this way, the soldier who had not previously seen the face of his enemy or the fatal shell midair sees with perfect clarity the bullet aimed at his chest and the assailant from whose gun it was ejected. The impatient horseman who chose to preemptively cross the railway tracks rather than wait for the locomotive to pass sees before he is struck the horror in the conductor's eyes and every marking on the front of the engine. The child who lost her footing playing on the wrong side of the bridge sees every rock and tree trunk upon which she will fall; every bar of the railing she should have grasped before she breaks a leg in the crash on the ground below.

It was in this time-frozen state that I watched the party of three approach us: Mr. Thauburn, the look of concentration on his face, as though preparing to make a speech; Aunt Rose, still wearing the widow's black, sombre, sad but not obviously devastated; Hannah behind her, a willowy, attractive young woman now, her eyes cast down, not wanting to catch ours, a large handkerchief in hand. It took them a minute at most to reach our house. Ina, who had collapsed into her chair when their destination became clear, and I who slowly assumed a similar position, were mesmerized. Gone were Ina's questions and declarations of ill tidings. Gone were my false reassurances. We said nothing as they came closer and closer. Tears streamed down my face as the threesome crossed the road and reached our front path. "Jessie," Aunt Rose said softly, "where is your mother? Your grandfather?"

"Upstairs. Asleep," I managed.

"We need to go wake them," she said in that same soft voice. "Mr. Thauburn has a telegram for your parents." In his hand was an unopened envelope.

When I did not move, Aunt Rose walked by us to enter the house and wake Mother herself. But in the end, there was no need. Ina's primordial scream was sufficient to wake anyone sleeping within a two-block radius.

* * *

The telegram that Mr. Thauburn delivered to our house that day was one of fifteen delivered to local families that week. The success of the Amiens battle took a disproportionate toll on the boys of Peel, with the lives of five men claimed—all from Brampton—and ten others wounded. Among the dead was Major Jeffrey Bull, the brother of Perkins Bull, who had so generously kept and entertained Jim in his London convalescent hospital and the brother of our new mayor.

The events of the week that followed those telegram deliveries cannot be easily recounted. Just as time did us the favour of slowing down in order to allow us to more gently absorb the impact of the pronouncement of Jim's death, it did us the further favour of accelerating the minutes, hours, and days that followed. I recall the anguish of my mother, who in addition to experiencing the loss of her eldest, dearest child, was tormented by the lack of knowledge of the circumstances surrounding it. I recall the anger of my father, directed primarily at the Canadian military and its failure to abide by the standing instruction to notify him in Toronto rather than Mother in Brampton of any "adverse event" and his resulting declaration never again to wear the uniform of a military man.

With greater clarity, I recall my own alternating feelings of abject despair and profound disbelief. When I was not in torrents of tears over our loss; I was in a fit of near denial over their cause. The "sincerely regret," as we came to call that fateful telegram that brought only distress to the rest of my family, brought me both sorrow and doubt.

> *Major and Mrs. Stephens. Sincerely regret to advise that*
> *Lieutenant James G. Stephens was killed in action the 10th day*
> *of August 1918 in the defence of his country. He led his men*
> *valiantly to his death on the third day of the Battle of Amiens.*

I read it over and over, thinking that doing so would bring some reality to the pain that had entirely enveloped me. The reason for my doubt lay in part in the bundle of letters that filled the basket Mother had lovingly made—the letters below the sincerely regret, in which Jim described the day-to-day events of his life at war. Their ordinary nature hid the real dangers he faced, though we were not oblivious to them. Our newspapers regularly published pictures of Allied men in action, positioned in the trenches, crossing bridges, riding in train boxcars, and perched in the new tanks that were charging on German trenches. We read reports of life in the trenches based on letters or interviews of local boys. We knew that the Allied troops took shifts looking "over the top" and that they were in constant danger from bullets, grenades, poison gas, and air bombardment.

Yet Jim's letters home were written as though he was at a distant summer camp. If he felt in any danger, he never let on. Several times after the "sincerely regret" was deposited in the basket, I reached below it to extract letters written in Jim's familiar hand. There was the letter he wrote on Mother's Day, a few months earlier. He described the little white flowers that had been given to him by a young girl he met on the road. He promised to press them and send them home to Mother when they were dry. He described the pretty countryside a little distance from his trench and the scenery that reminded him of beautiful English landscapes. In June, he wrote about a visit he had with our cousin Roy, who came to see him on a motorcycle. Both Roy and Bill were then serving in the Mechanical Transport Company attached to the 1st Canadian Division. Roy had just been promoted to warrant officer.

In July, he wrote about the Brampton boys he saw earlier in the week: Gordon Beattie, Manton Wilson, Jack Boulter, Hodie Adams, Captain Nick Eacher, and Frank Prouse. In his last letter home he assured Mother that everything was going along nicely with him; that he was fine.

How could he now be gone? He had just been fine. He couldn't be dead. We were so close. If he were dead, his soul would be free of his body. Surely, I would feel that. Since God was everywhere, and Jim's soul was surely with God, why could I not feel Jim? Even the place I was most likely to feel him—his own bedroom—felt void of him.

Night after night, before praying for a sign—preferably one that would confirm he was alive—I sat on Jim's bed poring over his drawings, easily identifying the phases of his passions. There was the early Millie period, when her face was just an outline in his sketches; the middle Millie period, showing her hair, then her nose, her mouth, and her eyes; and the later Millie period with full drawings of her, always displaying her joyful, caring manner. There were the automobile pictures: car after car, entire cars and car parts; drawings of just wheels, just fenders; just hoods.

There was one drawing of Paulette, just one. It was unique, I thought, for the presence of colour. It was only as I reached the bottom of the pile that I realized he had used colour in one other drawing. It was a self-portrait of himself in uniform. I put the picture of Paulette on the bottom of the pile and pulled out his self-portrait. I would have it framed and put on the wall in his bedroom. Then I returned to my prayers, seeking a sign.

* * *

It is ironic that with so much death at hand, the business of the local undertakers during the war was so paltry. But with most of the dying occurring oversees, funeral directors had to content themselves with burying women and those men too young or too old to enlist. Without a body to bury, the bereaved family members of a fallen serviceman usually arranged a memorial service at their church together with visitations in their home before or afterward. Given the number of memorial services the Battle of Amiens spawned in Brampton and its environs, efforts were made to have the services occur on different days.

Our family agreed to hold Jim's memorial service twelve days after the telegram was received and to hold our official "at-home" visitations on the two nights before that. It was hoped that the timing would be sufficient for Ina to recover from her near breakdown and for Aunt Charlotte and Uncle William to travel to Brampton from Winnipeg. It also provided ample time for Father to see that Mother, Ina, and I were properly attired for the official mourning functions. Never before had we acquired so much new clothing in such a short period of time. Each of us received three new black dresses—for the first time, all premade. There was no time for Mother to sew us a mourning wardrobe, even if she had the steadiness of hands and clarity of eye sight to do so, which she did not. Nor was there enough time for her to ruin an old pair of shoes. Thus, when Father presented us each with a new pair of black shoes, Mother's collection of footwear rose to an embarrassing number of eleven pairs. She hoped that no one outside her immediate family noticed.

While close friends dropped by our house in the days leading up to the formal at-home visitations, dozens attended on the two evenings we officially received guests. Some stayed for the entire two-hour period, others for just a short time. Some attended on both evenings. One and all provided tender greetings and offered kind words. Many had suffered a similar loss or feared suffering one. Others had suffered different consequences of the war. A few had family members that had been injured; some had family members that were missing. Many had been to the at-homes of the other Peel men who had fallen or were injured in the Battle of Amiens, and they brought condolences from those homes.

Those attending at our home included Jim's friends and classmates, both from Brampton and Toronto, the members of his sports teams, and workers from the Dale Estate. They included nearly everyone who knew Mother, Father, Grandpa, Ina, or me.

Sarah Lawson attended and made a point of speaking to each of us. "It was nice of Sarah to come by," Grandpa said after the first at-home.

"Nice?" Ina repeated. "She was smug and supercilious. She was like a cat with a canary. So glad that it was Jim and not her Eddie that we were all mourning."

"Ina! How can you say such things?" Mother said, clearly shocked. "No one is 'glad' we are mourning Jim. And certainly not Sarah, who Jim would count as one of his best friends."

Anne Gomme was there. She arrived with her brother, Matthew, who had returned from the war, minus one leg, three months earlier. Their brother Jacob was still at the front. I thought of Matthew's skill as a hockey player and skater the year before he joined the expeditionary force. He was mobile with his prosthesis, but I doubted he would ever skate again. Fortunately for Anne, his chest continued to be broad, his arms strong, and his temperament sweet. Crying constantly, she needed a great deal of support while at our house. "I'm sorry," she kept saying to Mother and Father. "I had so hoped he would come back with me. If only he had. I wasn't enough. I wasn't enough. I'm so sorry." Eventually, Grandpa took her into the tower area of the parlour. His condolences with her provided some measure of relief.

All of the local clergy attended—even Reverend McArthur, the new minister of the Presbyterian Church. It had been eleven years since I learned that our family was not allowed to enter the Presbyterian Church. By posing dozens of near futile questions and through numerous prohibited eaves-droppings, I had in the first seven years learned that the edict preventing our entrance was Father's; that the genesis of the edict related to Grandpa; that Grandpa had been one of the builders of the church; that the edict had something to do with Grandpa being "self-made and others destroyed"; and that it was somehow related to a "Scottish fiasco." In the four years since that time, I had learned only two other things: the stone for the church had not been donated to the church by Mr. Gilchrist, the former businessman, politician, and philanthropist, as I had once understood, and the suggestion that he had done so caused great offence to my Mother. I had also come to believe that the stone of the church had been quarried in Caledon near the location where Elsa's grandfather quarried. Mother's reaction to my statement that Grandpa knew Elsa's grandfather, being so similar to her reaction to my statement about Mr. Gilchrist (though thankfully expressed with less violence), made me conclude that there was a connection. But on that night, at that at-home for Jim, I learned one other thing. The reason our family could not enter the church had nothing to do with the current clergy. Reverend Thorneloe seemed to be as well received in our home as all other Brampton clergy.

Of particular interest were three people who were expected to attend the at-home but did not; and two who we would never have expected to attend who did. To our surprise, neither Paulette nor Millie attended the at-home visitations. In fact, neither came to us at any time during our formal period of mourning. The absence of Paulette bothered none of us in the least. "Do you think she even knows?" I asked at the dinner table one night.

"I'm sure she does," Father replied. "Those widow waiters, as we call them, spend every night near the barracks. They are more informed of the status of our men than some members of the general command."

It was the absence of Millie that really concerned us. While she sent a heartfelt note of condolence, she never once called on us. "I'm sure she feels too guilty to show her face here," Ina postulated, "and rightly so. If she had accepted Jim's offer, he might never have enlisted. He could have relied on the married man's exemption. He'd be alive today!" None of us believed that. We knew that Jim would ultimately have responded to the enlistment call. But we all agreed that Millie likely felt guilty. Like Anne Gomme, she might have thought we blamed her for Jim's death. Wanting to disabuse her of any such notion, Grandpa wrote a note in response to hers, specifically inviting her to condole with us.

However, the most conspicuously absent person in the days following Jim's death was not either of these women. It was our cousin John. At that time, he was working with a dentist in Toronto, waiting to return to the dental college in September to complete his degree. Though Aunt Rose and Hannah were with us every night leading to the memorial service, John only came to Brampton the day before, arriving prior to the dinner that would precede the second at-home. That evening, Aunt Rose hosted the family dinner. Aunt Lil was with us, as were Aunt Charlotte and Uncle Bill, who had by then arrived from Winnipeg. As he had every night since Jim's death, while Mother was pouring coffee and tea, Father read us a sample of the condolence letters recently received. There was not enough time to read aloud all the letters that were delivered, so Father selected half a dozen each day that he thought were particularly poignant. That night, I only heard two.

The first was from Mr. Mara, our former mayor and a member of the executive of the 1914 Excelsior Lacrosse Club. It would later be published on the front page of the *Conservator*. Father read it aloud:

> *Dear Major and Mrs. Stephens,*
>
> *This is just a word to say how deeply and how sincerely Jim's fellow members of the lacrosse team that went to Vancouver sympathize with you in your sorrow and bereavement. We knew him as boys know each other. He was only and always good, ever courageous, always chivalrous. His departure causes the first break in the list of those who spent the happy and interesting weeks required to make the trip to the coast. The vacancy created will never be filled, but as we sorrow at the loss of a friend and comrade, we rejoice in the knowledge that one who was so fully enjoyed and deserved our esteem died as he lived—doing his duty. No man can do more.*
>
> *May the kind Providence which blessed you with such a son and the good Spirit which guided his footsteps wherever he went sustain and comfort you and yours in this hour of trial and give you confidence that while today you have bidden him "good night" you will greet him with a "good morning" in the other and happier days, when the sun rises on the golden shores of eternity.*
>
> *Signed on behalf of the Excelsior Lacrosse Club – 1914.*
>
> *The executive, T. Thauburn, A.G. Davis, R. Blain and W.K. Mara*

The second was from Elsa Strauss. The letter was out of the envelope. Father handed it to me and asked that I do the honours. I hesitated. Having sent a letter to her of this nature a year ago, I knew it would be particularly hard to read. I held out the letter and began.

Shelburne

Dearest Jessie,

Yesterday I got a letter from Jane and she told me about Jim. Jessie, you just can't tell how sorry I am. I know what it is, and I can give you my sincerest love and sympathy. But as Wilfred once said before enlisting—he would rather be a dead hero than a living coward. It will soon be a year since our Wilfred was killed, and I can't realize it yet that he isn't living.

Give my best love to your mother and Ina and just lots for yourself, dear. I remain,

Your same old chum,

Elsa Strauss

I had barely said Elsa's name when John stood and asked to be excused. Without waiting for a reply, he left the table, his face red, his head bowed. He was not the first to leave the table in the midst of this mournful exercise. Over the past ten days, there had been several occasions when the emotions of one person or another got the best of him. Since it was my letter that seemed to elicit the reaction, I rose to follow him.

He walked out the front door and then took off at a run. At twenty-one, John was a full-grown man. But he was not a tall man. At just under five and a half feet in height, his legs weren't particularly long. The physical condition he maintained as a member of the Canadian Army Dental Corps was no longer a part of his regimen, and so I was not far behind him when he ended his sprint in the bandstand at Gage Park. We were the only two in the raised structure when I sat down beside him.

He was sitting on the bench, his face in his hands, his elbows on his knees. I sat beside him and rubbed his heaving back. *How strange this grief is*, I thought, *that has the sister comforting the cousin*. It would not always be this way, but at that particular moment I seemed to have more strength than him.

The temperature had cooled considerably since that day that day Ina and I had sat on the verandah watching Mr. Thauburn walk toward us, telegram in hand. Had it only been eleven days? At that moment it felt like months had passed. As John's breathing became normal, I watched the people picnicking on the lawn beyond us. Some children were rolling on the grass. One boy was trying to climb a tree. I looked at the trees in which Frances and I had once seen Millie and Sarah and their friends Clarence and Dutch. How long ago had that been? I looked around the bandstand, trying to picture it festooned in organza and candlelight, Dale American Beauty varietal roses strewn on the blanket while Jim proposed to Millie. Was this where it all started? If Millie had accepted Jim the night of his graduation, would he be dead right now? He would have enlisted, certainly, but would he have found himself in the line of fire on the third day of the Battle of Amiens? Possibly not. But maybe there would have been another bullet, another grenade, another incident—another what? We didn't even know what it was that had taken his life.

Eventually, John removed his hands from his face and sat up. "Did you know Wilfred Strauss too, John?" I asked gently, although I could not see how he would have. "Is that what set you off?"

"No. No, I didn't. That wasn't what set me off. It's a bunch of things, really." A few minutes passed in silence before he resumed. "It's good of you to come down here with me, Jess. But there's nothing you can do to help me. You should go back. You're the one who should be comforted now, not me. I don't deserve any comfort."

I could have left then, but I could tell my cousin was hurt, and at that moment I seemed to have a reservoir of strength. So I stayed with him and persisted. "Is it Jim, then? I know you always looked up to him. Is it because you miss him?"

"I do miss him, Jess. I am very broken-up about Jim. I am exceedingly broken up about Jim. He was such a good man. I admired everything about him. I was proud to have him as my cousin. We had a lot in common."

I waited for him to go on, thinking of what they had in common—aside from their chosen profession and their love of trains. Jim was an avid sportsman. He was a drawer. He had a myriad of friends. He was rugged and outgoing. John was a tinkerer—a builder. He couldn't draw, but he could construct anything required around the house. He was a beautiful pianist. He was shy. His friends were few, but those he had, he held dear. He was gentle and sensitive. I didn't push it.

"We often spoke about our futures," he offered.

"About practicing dentistry together?" I prodded.

He hesitated. "Yes, we did discuss that."

"But there is something else, isn't there?" I asked. "John, why have you just come home now? It's been eleven days since we received the sincerely regret. Why have you only come home now?"

"I have a job, Jess," he said defensively. "There is a great shortage of dentists in Canada now with so many of them overseas. I couldn't just pick up and leave for a week."

"No, of course, you couldn't do that," I said agreeably. "But the trains do run to Brampton at the end of each day, and they do go back again to Toronto the next morning. You could have been here in the evenings."

"Is that what your father said?" he accused. As a matter of fact, it was, but I felt no need to confirm it.

"Well, it's true, isn't it?"

"It's him, Jess. I can't stand the way your father looks at me. And for the record, I'm sorry, but I will not be attending the at-home tonight or the memorial service tomorrow. I don't think I can be in the same room as your father for a while—not even a church sanctuary. Dinner tonight confirmed that."

I decided to tackle one issue at a time. "What do mean, John? What do you mean 'the way Father looks at you'?" Of course, Father had applied a great deal of pressure to John in 1916 to induce him to enlist when Father was trying to help mobilize the 126th Battalion, but that was all solved when John enlisted in 1917.

"Surely you can see it, Jess. He makes little secret of what he thinks of me." I had noticed but felt there was nothing to be gained by confirming that fact either.

"I know he is looking forward to practicing with you one day," I offered.

"He was looking forward to that at one time. That is true. But no longer, Jess. No longer. He won't want me to practise with him in the future. Of that, I am confident. He can't understand why I am here practising his chosen profession and his son is dead in the ground in France. He can't understand it. And I can't either."

"He'll come around, John. Finish your training. Time will pass, and then he will want to take you on."

"You misunderstand me, Jess. I don't care whether I ever practice with your father. I don't care whether I ever practice at all—but because I dislike it so—I probably will. It's the least I can do."

"The least you can do for what?" I asked with some indignation—though no surprise. We all knew that John did not want to go into dentistry. That was another way in which he differed from my brother Jim. "For being alive? John, that's not something you have to punish yourself for."

"No, not because I am alive, but because of why I am alive. I'm a coward, Jess. You read what your friend Elsa said. 'Better a dead hero than a living coward.' I am a living coward. Everyone knows that."

"Who? Who knows that? Why would you say that? You were honourably discharged from the army for a medical condition. You appeared before three medical boards, and this was their pronouncement. They ordered you home to resume your dental studies."

"I appeared before three medical boards. I have a 'roughened mitral area' of my heart leading to 'an irregular heart action and a slightly nervous temperament.' What is that? No one knows. I am little better than the person Vesta Tilley ridiculed for leaving the army with a paper cut." I thought back to the letter Anne sent Ina from the Bull hospital recounting the Vesta Tilley performance of the "Blighty" song.

"Your father did die of a heart attack, John."

"Yes, but he was sixty-eight years old and weighed two hundred and fifty pounds. I am a third his age and half his weight! Maybe I was just too scared, Jessie. Maybe that is why my heart is irregular. Maybe that is why I had a 'slightly nervous temperament.'" Neither of us said anything for a few minutes. We watched a little boy learning to ride a bicycle on the path beyond us. His mother, who had been holding on to the seat of his bicycle, let go.

"The army has made a concerted decision to return doctors and dentists to Canada. You are needed here, and the government agrees."

"That may be, but I did not come home under that program," he said. "And I have to admit to you, I was scared—I mean, I wasn't scared in

England—but I was scared about going to the front."

"Isn't everyone there scared, John? Isn't it frightening at the front?"

"I'm sure it is. I never got there, of course. But I am sure it is. But even so, most people do not develop a heart condition because of it."

"Exactly. Maybe you were born with a weak heart, John. Maybe it had nothing to do with being scared. You enlisted when you were nineteen years of age. You were not conscripted. That's not something a coward does. You went over there as a private and were promoted five weeks later to a sergeant. You weren't cowering in your bed. No one can call you a coward."

"People do," he said softly. "People do. Do you know how many times I get stopped and asked for proof of my discharge? Twice or more every week. Sometimes twice a day. And not just by military recruiters. Average citizens. Teenagers. Older women. Veterans. Everyone feels at liberty to stop me and ask me for it." Earlier that year, after a divisive federal election in which a thousand women in Peel were eligible to vote, the *Military Service Act* was amended to require nearly all able-bodied men between the ages of twenty and forty-five years of age to register for military service. Every man over eighteen years of age was required to carry with him or to have within the building in which he was then situated evidence of his exemption from military service. In the public announcement to exempted men, the minister of justice, Charles J. Doherty, lauded the public for providing the information by which many exemptions, obtained under false pretenses, had been cancelled. He invited further cooperation of that nature.

"I feel sorry for the amputees," he went on. "I feel sorry for those who have lost part of their faces, who are labouring to breathe, who have been blinded or made mute, or made deaf. I do. I thank God every day that I am not one of them. But no one asks them for proof of their exemption. And when I show people my papers, they scoff. And I know what they are thinking. They are thinking that I am a 'Blighty' one, a coward, and I think I am."

"John, you mustn't feel that way. They don't discharge people for being cowards. If they did, they wouldn't be shooting deserters." He did not say anything in reply. We sat in silence for a few minutes. The little boy below fell off his bicycle. His mother was urging him back on its seat.

"Should we go back?" I asked. "They'll be getting ready for the at-home. They won't want us to be late for that."

"I'll walk back with you, Jess, but I am not going to the at-home. I told you that. I'm not going to the memorial service either. My presence will just upset your father further. And that won't be good for any of us."

"John, just ignore Father. He has lost the one person in this world he unreservedly loved and admired. He is broken. He is angry at everything." I thought of the many rants he had uttered against the Canadian Army the week before. "But ignore him. Don't come tonight, if you don't think you can. But come tomorrow. I need you with me. I do."

"Thank you, Jess. That's kind of you. I won't go to the at-home tonight, but I'll think about attending the memorial service. I will." He stood and left. I hoped I was kind. I wanted to be kind. How else could I live with the guilt of pondering myself—even if only momentarily—the very things he accused my father of thinking? Why was he here and alive and Jim there and dead?

The second at-home went much as the first. The kindness of our friends, neighbours, and other acquaintances could not be matched, and yet by the end their heartfelt inquiries regarding the particular circumstances of Jim's demise became too much for Mother. Almost as hard as knowing she had lost her one and only son, her true love, was the lack of knowledge she had about how he had died and where he now lay. Did he die in pain? Did he die instantly? Did he die alone? Was he resting in a turnip field? Was he in a water-filled crater in No-Man's Land? Was he outside a military hospital? Not knowing tormented her. Eventually, she broke down.

"Why do people pose these questions?" Ina asked after the last guest had left our second at-home. "How on earth would we know the answers?" Grandpa explained to Ina that in fact sometimes there were witnesses to these matters, and families had answers to such questions.

Aunt Charlotte, Uncle William, Aunt Lil, Aunt Rose, and Hannah left our house with the last guests at the end of the two-hour gathering. Mother, Ina, and I were carrying cups and glasses into the kitchen, and Grandpa and Father were putting the furniture back to its usual positions when there was a knock at the door. Speculating that a visitor had forgotten something, Mother put down the cups she was carrying and walked into the foyer. A man in a well-worn, old-fashioned brown suit entered. His boots were of a bulky sort—not generally considered compatible with a suit, particularly in August—but they were highly polished. His shirt was clean and pressed; his tie was of an older style and slightly askew. He held his cap in his hand as he hesitantly entered the room. Though I had never formally met him, I knew exactly who he was.

"I beg your pardon, Mrs. Stephens, for arriving so late," he said to Mother before extending the same greeting to Father as he walked cautiously into the parlour. His tall, slim physique was very similar to Father's. He had a full head of grey hair, but where Father's eyes were blue, this man's were green. The two men were clearly of a similar age. "We didn't want to disrupt you earlier."

Disrupt? What an odd thing to say about an at-home. Everyone who attended an at-home was disrupting the family. That was the purpose. That was why they were invited to come. I noticed too his use of the word "we." At that moment he was the only addition to our parlour. Where, I wondered, was his son?

"I'm Kelly, Sam Kelly," he said, extending his hand, "of the Kelly Iron Works."

"Yes. Yes, I know who you are," Father said somewhat curtly. I remembered vividly Father's description on my first day of school, all those years ago, of the Kelly Iron Works Repair Shop and its lot full of broken down, rusting, iron vehicles. "An abomination. A blight on our streets," Father called it. He thought the town council should have closed it. I remembered too what Father had said about his son—that he should be locked up, a sentiment I wholeheartedly shared. If Father had any recollection of that conversation or the many others that followed as I refused to pass the premises of the Kelly Iron Works Repair Shop on my own, he gave no indication. He turned toward Mother, but before he could introduce Mr. Kelly to her, Mr. Kelly left the room.

We exchanged glances of curiosity as Mr. Kelly walked to the front door. But we soon saw that he opened it not with a view to exiting himself but rather to admitting another. Taking him by the arm, Mr. Kelly helped into our home a hunch-backed man with a square, large, flat face on a slightly too-large head. As he hobbled across the front hall into our parlour, his one foot dragging behind him, I stared at my old nemesis.

Instinctively, I reached up and began to smooth my hair. There was not much that could be done. I had no hat to thrust upon it; no elastics or pins with which to twist it up. Most of my hair was in a bow at the back of my head, but that only changed the placement of the ringlets. A mane of curls still fell down my back. I kept my right hand to the back of my head, by habit attempting to conceal as much hair as possible.

"This is my son, Scott," Mr. Kelly said. "I'm afraid he is not able to shake hands."

"That's quite all right, sir," my Father said with an obvious trace of relief. Scott had tears streaming down his face, and his nose was running.

"His left hand is a little firmer than his right. If you would allow him to put it on your shoulder, this would provide him the personal connection that a handshake allows the rest of us," Mr. Kelly continued.

Without waiting for an answer, he gestured at Scott, intending to help him move closer to Father. Scott was still. He looked around the room, taking us all in, but not, I noticed, in the curious way of a stranger. His look was somehow more knowing—familiar. In other circles, it might have been a look that said, "It's been so long since we have spoken." But he had never spoken to us before—the grunts directed at my early schoolgirl self excepted. He did not know us at all.

Scott looked first at Mother. Ina and Grandpa were next. I prepared myself for the wild gesticulation that would accompany his view of me and unconsciously clasped my hair harder. To my surprise, he looked at me just as he looked at the others—with complete silence and a deeply sad countenance.

The time Scott took to gaze at the occupants of the room was sufficient for Father to replace the look of horror on his face with one of mere trepidation. As Scott walked slowly toward Father, I could not tell which of the two displayed the greater amount of unease. It took Scott a few attempts to steady his left hand on Father's right shoulder. Once it found its mark, he kept it there for a few moments, his head bowed, tears falling off his face and bouncing off one of Father's shoes. I silently expressed my gratitude to Father for enduring this form of condolence when I saw him begin limping toward Mother. I cringed at the realization that this ritual was to be repeated with each of us.

As Scott moved from Mother to Grandpa and then from Grandpa to Ina, I realized I would be next. His hand would be on my shoulder just as it had been that night the prior August; the night of Jane's birthday; the night of Eddie's departure from Brampton. The boy I'd run from for years would be standing before me, touching me. I began to quake and then, suddenly, I thought of Jim: Jim leaving the trenches; Jim leading his men over the top; Jim running into a hail of bullets. I laughed aloud. Everyone turned toward me, even Scott, who was momentarily diverted from his trajectory toward Ina. I looked at Scott. I was now as tall as he was, though in no way as broad. He was excitable, clearly—at least he had been—but he was meek too. I could see that now.

Pulling my hands away from my hair, I walked toward Ina. I was standing beside her as his hand was leaving her shoulder. As he placed his left hand on my right shoulder, I repeated the gesture on his.

"Thank you for coming, Scott," I managed, tears trickling down my face too. He grunted in reply before removing his hand and reaching into his pocket. After a few attempts, he extracted two crumpled, folded pieces of paper. With great effort, he provided one to Ina and one to me.

"Scott picked these out especially for the two of you," Mr. Kelly said. "It's hard for him to part with any of these, but he wanted you to each have one. He is exceedingly sorry for your loss. We both are. Very sorry. Your brother was a fine young man. Curious, smart, and imaginative. He had a fine business mind and a sense of decency and respect for others almost unparalleled." With that, they began their slow walk to the door.

"Do you think they came to the wrong at-home?" Ina asked after the Kellys left. "Imaginative? A business mind? Jim was a lot of things, but no one has ever used those words to describe him."

"I'm just thankful they had the decency to come when no one else was here," Father said. "What a commotion he would have caused with a number of ladies present. Should be locked up, I've always said that. And as if we needed to be told the name of his business establishment. It's a travesty in a downtown area to have all those contraptions facing the road."

"It's interesting that you should mention that," Grandpa said. "I noticed when I walked by today a number were gone. He seems to be cleaning up a bit."

"About time. About time. And what in the blazes did he give to you two girls? What is on those pages?" Father asked.

"I have no idea," Ina said. "A bunch of lines and circles. Maybe this is what counts for writing in his mind." She crumbled hers into a ball and put it on the tray to be carried into the kitchen.

I had no idea what was drawn on the page I had been given, but I was pretty sure it had been drawn by Jim. I folded it neatly, smoothing it out as best I could, and then placed it in the large pocket in the skirt of my new mourning dress. I would look at it again later. If I really could not make it out, I could go to the Kelly Iron Works Repair Shop and ask Mr. Kelly about it. That man, clearly the age of my father and without a trace of an Irish accent, was not the handyman of the Governor's story who came to Brampton as an adult in 1873, when my father was a child; his son, likely Jim's age, was not the twin brother of the vile boy born in 1874.

* * *

John did not attend the at-home service that night, but he did attend the memorial service the next day. At my request, he sat at my side. Together we rose when others rose, sat when others sat, cried when Mother cried. Many people spoke at the service. Some were sentimental, some were spiritual. A few were humorous. Every accomplishment of Jim's short life was recalled.

An army man who came from Toronto to attend the service placed a crimson maple leaf on the service roll erected on the back wall of the church. He read from a letter received by Joseph Lawson, Sarah's uncle, written by his son Smirle, who was stationed at No. 4 Canadian General Hospital, Basingstoke, England.

> *He was with us at Salonica as captain in the Dental Corps. A finer type of boy never walked. He was a good straight fellow and could have been with us here today as captain. He said that others older could carry on in his place and that he would go over with the boys. There is no greater spirit of sacrifice.*

He died facing the Germans like a man; that others at home
might live in peace.

After the speeches there were prayers, many prayers—chiefly for Jim's
soul to be welcomed by the Lord, but as others made that simple fervent
request, I silently prayed that the Lord would allow Jim to take a little detour
on that ascent to provide me with the certainty, one way or another, that I
had been seeking for twelve days. With the last prayers said, we rose for the
final hymn, selected by Father as Jim's favourite. Initially, the congregation
sang it quietly, mournfully, almost reluctantly, as they had for the other two
hymns in the service. But by the time we got to the last verse, it changed.
The heads that had previously hung low began to lift; the voices that could
barely utter a greeting upon entering the church found their tenor. As the
congregation lyrically pondered what would be if we walked ten thousand
years, I shut my eyes and lifted my head. Only then did they come into view,
those blue eyes, that fair hair, those chiselled features, his face looking down
at me, Jim's voice raised with mine: "*Bright shining as the sun. We've no*
less days to sing God's praise, than when we've first begun."

I felt a small tug of a ringlet from behind and turned to see who was
responsible. Aunt Lil, Uncle William, and Aunt Charlotte were there, looking
straight ahead, their hands on the back of the pew in front of them. None
of them needed to resort to a hymnal for this anthem. I smoothed my hair
and smiled. At that moment, I knew he was with me, that he was with all
of us in Grace Methodist Church, the church that our grandfather built. It
was only for a moment. It was all I needed.

* * *

Six weeks after Jim's death, we received two letters that answered a number
of Mother's questions. The first was from a Lieutenant F.P. Ryan, an officer
in the platoon to the rear of Jim's at the time he was struck down. From
this we learned that Jim died in a battle fought in the Picardy Region, in the
Department of the Somme, in the Mont Didier Arrondissement, just outside
a village called Hallu. He was struck by bullets to his arms and legs and
was being attended to by two of his own men when Lieutenant Ryan was

advised that Jim was down. Lieutenant Ryan took three of his own men and a stretcher, and, under heavy fire, they lifted Jim and began to move him back from enemy lines. In that process, a shell struck quite close. The explosion wounded two of the three stretcher boys. Jim died immediately from the shock of the attack with no knowledge of what had occurred. Lieutenant Ryan assured us that Jim had not at any time shown any signs of pain.

The second letter was from our own former pastor, Reverend Bruce Hunter, who was by that time a captain serving as the chaplain of the 85th Nova Scotia Highlanders. It was part of his responsibilities to make arrangements for the proper burial of his men. In his amazing account, he told us of the offensive of the Fourth Division—the northern fourth, as he referred to them, for a part of the division had been sent to advance on the south side of the Canadian front. On the third day of the Battle of Amiens, Reverend Hunter's men were positioned on the northern flank, two kilometres west of Hallu. It was Jim's battalion—the 78th—that was to take Hallu. Of Jim's actual battle and demise, Reverend Hunter could not attest. As the padre, it was his responsibility to stay at the regimental aid post of the battalion, well back from the front line of the attack. There he supervised the bringing in of the wounded and oversaw the stretcherbearers—including twelve Germans who were recruited into this work. The night of Sunday, August 11, he led a party of thirty-two men through No Man's Land and with bullets whistling overhead. Amid bright orange flares, they brought in the bodies of our dead. The next morning, he marked out a little cemetery in a field near the aid post to which he was attached. There, they began to bury the men under wooden crosses inscribed with each man's name and regiment.

He returned to the living, or the barely living, in the dressing station, giving them what spiritual comfort he could, and when the Lord determined that no more of this was needed, he oversaw their burial too in the little cemetery he had constructed. It was while he was performing an internment service for one of these men, on August 20, ten days after the attack on Hallu, that he came across a new grave in his little cemetery. On a rudimentary sign were the words "Lieut J.G. Stephens." He was totally stunned, since he had not heard that our Jim had fallen. Nor did he have any idea how Jim's body—an officer of the 78th Battalion—had come to be buried there, among his men of the 85th. Reverend Hunter made some inquiries, and it was confirmed that Jim, like most of the senior officers and many of the lieutenants among the Canadian divisions fighting in the area, had been lost in the drive to take Hallu. No one knew how he came to be buried there.

A PREVIEW OF BOOK THREE:
THE MENDING

Sarah Lawson married Robert Elliott on a warm, sunny day at the end of August 1921. The church ceremony was witnessed by seventy-five people whom the couple would include among their family and close friends, and four times as many they would consider to be mere acquaintances. The large number in the latter category was attributable to the twin facts that everyone in Brampton had the right to attend the public nuptials and that so many had the desire. The union of the almost endlessly patient Sarah Lawson with the only slightly scarred Robert Elliott had, by 1921, taken on an almost fairy-tale quality. Five years had passed since Sarah had last seen Eddie McMurchy. For nearly three years, Sarah and the McMurchys corresponded with Canadian war officials, local, and foreign governments and foreign hospitals and newspapers. By August 1920, Sarah finally acknowledged what nearly everyone else knew: Eddie McMurchy, like Jim and so many other boys from Peel, had made the supreme sacrifice in August 1918. When his plane crashed outside of Amiens, Eddie became one of the thousands of members of the Canadian Expeditionary Force for whom there were no identified remains; no identified graves. Having lived in such a devoted and despondent state for so long, it was right that the affections of this much-loved daughter of the town be transferred to a much-admired son of the town. Brampton turned out in the hundreds to watch the great-great-niece of one of the town's founding fathers join in holy matrimony the great-great-nephew of the other.

There were only two families obviously absent from the ceremony at the Presbyterian Church: the McMurchy family, who, having not yet accepted the death of their heroic son and brother, could not bring themselves to witness the wedding of his life's love to another; and our family. My family was not permitted to enter the Presbyterian Church. No one would tell me the reason why, although I knew it had something to do with my grandfather who was responsible for building much of it; that it had to do with him being "self-made and others destroyed"; and that it involved a "Scottish Fiasco." I had more recently learned that the stone for the church had not been donated to it by our former Member of the Provincial Parliament and that the suggestion that it was so infuriated my mother. Her fury over a suggested acquaintance between my father and the quarry owner grandfather of my friend Elsa led me to believe that he was the supplier of the stone.

Since the churches in our community featured so prominently in our social as well as our religious lives, I had over the years, felt isolated and hurt when I was not able to join friends at concerts, ceremonies, teas or services at the large Presbyterian Church. But on that warm, sunny day in August 1921, when everyone of my acquaintance was at the highly publicized wedding in the big stone edifice, I was not troubled. While the guests gathered in their Sunday best on its wooden pews, I happily sat in my day dress on the swing chaise of our verandah. As my friends watched the bridal party proceed down the aisle, as they witnessed the exchange of vows, as they heard the homily spoken and the anthems sung, I finally learned Grandpa's story. It is a story of gallantry and greed; of enterprise and insolvency; of perception and deception.

AUTHOR'S NOTE

This is a book of fiction inspired by stories relayed to me by my great aunt Jessie Roberts Current over countless holiday dinners commencing when I was a child, coffee shop conversations I enjoyed as a student, and visits we had later in life in her various seniors' and nursing homes. The stories are supplemented with historical facts and strung together by imagination bound only by the realm of the plausible.

Without parsing the entire book to denote which passage falls into which category, let me indicate a few matters that are absolute fact and absolute fiction. Eddie McMurchy, Sarah Lawson, and Michael Lynch are all fictitious characters stated to be nieces and nephews of the town's prominent citizens.

The character of Jane Thompson is inspired by Laeta McKinnon, Jessie's closest lifetime friend, Frances Hudson by Frances Fenton Carroll, another dear life-long friend. Millie Dale is inspired by Jim's true and special friend, Allie Beatty, who was a relation by marriage to the Dale family. All of the McKechnies, Collin Heggie, and many of the other friends of Jessie, Jim, and Ina mentioned in the book were their true and dear friends, but the interactions portrayed within the book are generally of my imagination. In reality, both Laeta McKinnon (Jane Thompson) and Frances Fenton (Hudson) were slightly older than Jessie. Frances's father, W.J. Fenton (Hudson), was the long-time, highly regarded principal of the Brampton High School.

Laeta McKinnon's father, John McKinnon (Thompson), was a senior executive with the Pease foundry. Among other things, the foundry did produce furnaces and during the war, shells. He and his family lived in a large Brampton house, but it was not Haggertlea, which continued to be occupied by members of the Haggert family until 1944. He had in fact three children, Laeta, Douglas, and Jack.

The aunts, uncles, grandparents, and cousins of Jessie are all inspired by her real-life family members: her aunts, Rose Roberts Golding (Darling), Lillian Roberts (Stephens), and Charlotte Roberts Milner (Turner); uncles James Golding (Darling) and William Milner (Turner); grandparents Louisa and Jesse Perry (Brady) and James and Selina Roberts (Stephens); and cousins Jim and Hannah Golding (John and Hannah Darling) and Roy and Bill Milner (Turner).

Jesse Perry (Brady) was a prominent Brampton contractor and mason. His works include the Brampton churches now known as Grace United Church, St. Andrew's Presbyterian Church, and St. Paul's United Church, and the Dominion Building. Jessie was not allowed to enter the Presbyterian Church.

As for the romances: in real life, Jim had a special relationship with Allie (Millie) until sometime before he enlisted. Jim did take up with another woman (who I've named Paulette) just before he embarked for England. The family did not like her. Anne Gomme and her brothers are fictional characters.

In real life, Ina was in love with a boy she was forced to abandon due to his Catholicism. Following the break-up, she did go to Winnipeg, but it was at a different time than presented in the book. The details pertaining to the operations of the Winnipeg Supply and Fuel Company owned by the Robertson family and the activities of the Broadway Church are true, but Ina had no connection with them. Her time at Victoria College at the University of Toronto was as presented.

Jim did graduate from dental college in uniform, along with James William Macdonald, Garnet Stewart Atkinson, and William Gordon MacNevin. I assume that Dean Wilmot spoke at that graduation, but I do not know this to be so. The other speakers are fictitious. The valedictory line: "We have borne the burden and heat of the day—we have weathered the storms of uncertainty and doubt, and withstood many trying ordeals—all to the end that we may be fully prepared for the faithful discharge of our duties in connection with a noble profession," was taken from the University of Toronto's class yearbook, *UofT Nexis*, 1915.

The enlistment and postings of Jim are based on the actual war records of Jim Roberts, although Jim convalesced in the Royal Free Hospital in London, not the Bull Convalescent Hospital for Canadian Officers as portrayed herein. The Bull Convalescent Hospital and other details regarding life in England at that time were as presented. The circumstances of Jim's death are true. His body was found buried in a makeshift cemetery by the family's pastor, Reverend Hunter. It now rests in the Hillside Cemetery outside of Le Quesnel, France. Jim left everything to his mother, except for his camera, which by telegram he bequeathed to Jessie.

The enlistment and postings of Jethro, Roy, Bill, and John are based on the actual war records of the real life characters that inspired them. The training of Canadian pilots out of Hanlan's Point and Long Branch in World War I and the creation of the Nursing Sisters Corps were as described in the book. The first eighteen did leave Brampton in a ceremony as presented— although the number may have been seventeen (accounts differed). It is not clear to me that all eighteen actually enlisted. Jessie and her friends were farmettes, but I do not know what farm they worked on.

While the Straussenhoffer family is entirely fictitious, the life described to them is based on the actual life of the time including the details pertaining to the Ward area of Toronto, homesteading in the west, and the creation of Success, Saskatchewan. The Dale Estate did hire seven Austrian internees in the spring of 1916. The good people of Brampton drove them out of town on their second day there.

The two cantatas said to be produced by Jessie's father at Christmas 1914 and in February 1916 were produced by him. The description of the first accords with newspaper accounts of the time. He did make a spectacle of himself at the second and enlisted immediately afterwards. The Cabal and Jessie's role within it are fictitious, but the content of the advertisements "encouraging" men to enlist are all true.

If Jessie were alive and able to read this book today, she would say that my treatment of her father was a little too harsh and that my treatment of Jessie herself was a great deal too good. As for the generous treatment of her brother, who she adored, she would say, I believe, that it was just right.

People have asked me whether Jessie knew I was writing this book. She did. She knew it was a book about Brampton in its early years and that it would feature her family. I confess I never told her—for fear that her modesty would order me to do otherwise—that she would be made the central character. In the early years of the several I spent on this endeavour, a red-covered journal and a mechanical pencil accompanied me on my weekly visits to her nursing home. She was more lucid then and readily able to elaborate on stories previously and frequently told.

As time went on, the incidents she was able to recall became fewer and fewer. Eventually, she could not recall any incidents that occurred after 1930; then she could not recall those that occurred after 1920; then those that occurred after 1915. When she began to confuse me with her Aunt Rose (my great grandmother), I realized that the exercise that formerly gave us much pleasure was too great an effort for her. I stopped bringing the red-covered journal into her room, but whenever a new nugget was spontaneously divulged during our visits, I would rush to the car to record it. Although Jessie and I stopped working on "the book" together, she never forgot that it was a project of mine.

Jessie died in Mississauga, in Peel County, just south of Brampton, on February 11, 2011. She was 108 years old. She never forgot the lessons of frugality she learned as a child in Brampton. She lived modestly her entire life, saving and conservatively investing. Among her legacies was a $1,000,000 gift to the University of Toronto. The endowment, which the university has named for Jim, Ina, and Jessie Roberts, will support indefinitely the academic pursuit of science by four undergraduate and two graduate students a year. Wherever possible, those undergraduate students will hail from Peel County.

ABOUT LYNNE GOLDING

Lynne Golding was born and raised in Brampton, Ontario. She obtained a bachelor's degree in History and Political Science from Victoria College at the University of Toronto before studying law at Queen's University in Kingston, Ontario. She is a senior partner at the international law firm Fasken Martineau DuMoulin LLP, where she leads their health law practice group. Lynne lives in Brampton. She is a winner of the Ontario Book Publishers Organization 2018 "What's Your Story?" Short Prose and Poetry Competition. This is her second novel. Visit her website at lynnegoldingauthor.com.

BOOK CLUB GUIDE

1. Compare and contrast the feelings of Jessie's family members to the war. How did those feelings change over the course of the war and why did they change?

2. In the second paragraph of Chapter 1, Jessie speaks of the coming war and observes that Canadians did not yet know who they would come to consider "courageous or cowardly; patriotic or traitorous, leaders or followers." With the war complete, how would you classify each of the following: Jim, Bill, Roy, John, Eddie, Anne, and Reverend Hunter?

3. The author describes the period before the war as one of innocence and the period during the war as one of innocence lost. Drawing from *The Innocent* and *The Beleaguered*, what are examples of each?

4. The epigraph to the book is an excerpt from the editorial of the *Conservator* written for Christmas 1914. It was relevant for that time. Is it relevant today?

5. Was the Governor's story, set out in full in *The Innocent* and summarized in *The Beleaguered*, true?

6. How big a role did moralism (the observation of moral laws) play in the lives of Jessie and her family?

7. What are examples within the book of the evolving role of women in society?

8. Friends were a big part of Jessie's youth. Was she a good friend?

9. What are some of the examples of prejudice in the book? It was a time of war, was any of the prejudice justified?

10. Speculation. Why do you think:

    Millie refused Jim's offer of marriage?

    Jim enlisted?

    Jessie and her family cannot enter the Presbyterian Church?

    (The answers will be revealed in Book 3, *The Mending*)

WRITE FOR US

We love discovering new voices and welcome submissions. Please read the following carefully before preparing your work for submission to us. Our publishing house does accept unsolicited manuscripts but we want to receive a proposal first, and if interested we will solicit the manuscript.

We are looking for solid writing—present an idea with originality and we will be very interested in reading your work.

As you can appreciate, we give each proposal careful consideration so it can take up to six weeks for us to respond, depending on the amount of proposals we have received. If it takes longer to hear back, your proposal could still be under consideration and may simply have been given to a second editor for their opinion. We can't publish all books sent to us but each book is given consideration based on its individual merits along with a set of criteria we use when considering proposals for publication.

Thank you for reading *The Beleaguered*

If you enjoyed *The Beleaguered*, check out more literary fiction from Blue Moon Publishers!

Primrose Street by Marina L. Reed

To Love a Stranger by Kris Faatz